THE FAMILY
MORFAWITZ

BOOKS BY DANIEL H. TURTEL

Greetings from Asbury Park
The Family Morfawitz

THE FAMILY MORFAWITZ

DANIEL H. TURTEL

BLACK STONE

PUBLISHING

Printed in the United States of America

First edition: 2023
ISBN 979-8-200-70513-9
Fiction / Sagas

Version 1

CIP data for this book is available
from the Library of Congress

Blackstone Publishing
31 Mistletoe Rd.
Ashland, OR 97520

www.BlackstonePublishing.com

In loving memory of Harry Spiera

BOOK I
CREATION

My soul would sing of metamorphoses.
But since, o gods, you were the source of these
bodies becoming other bodies, breathe
your breath into my book of changes: may
the song I sing be seamless as its way
weaves from the world's beginning to our day . . .

Ovid, *Metamorphoses i*

I

THE FAMILY MORFAWITZ

Hersh has changed our family's origin story into a series of bad jokes, anachronistic jabs so lewd they cannot be told outside the confines of a family home; after all, we are not alien to media scrutiny. Fortunately for him, our weekly Sabbath dinner provides an ample stage for his humor, and his failing memory means these recitals are something of a guarantee.

An element of clockwork is at play as the more closely allied members of our family gather each Friday in one of the ten family floors atop the Tower Morfawitz. Hersh insists that we are crammed, but that is far from the truth. Only when some of the more remote clan join us on High Holidays are we forced to make use of anything but the grand dining rooms themselves. On such occasions, makeshift tables are set up in the entry halls, ostensibly for the children to sit at, but—before the prayers are through—we have inevitably segregated along party lines. Like eats with like. Our walls are thick, and each time the service door swings open, a silence falls on either room.

In any case, Hersh's insistence that some of the apartments are less comfortable than others is absurd, for we occupy the top ten floors, and the apartment layouts—with the exception of Zev and Hadassah's penthouse—are exactly the same.

Zev is sick and ailing upstairs, and Hersh has slowly encroached on the coveted seat at the head of the table, just falling short of sitting in the stately, empty chair. If it were possible to make jokes about Hadassah, somebody might have suggested that Hersh was only trying to put as much distance as possible between himself and her seat at the opposite head. In private, I have often been asked how I can stand to sit so close to her throne and how I keep myself from freezing over. Hersh himself has inquired how it is that I spend so much time with our matriarch, whether I'm planning a coup, ha ha, and wonders that I don't doze off at her constant retelling of our family's recent past.

"I hope," he tells me, "that you're writing it down. She won't be around forever . . ."

But it isn't clear to me that he really believes that, or that anyone really expects the old woman to die. He says such things only in private. Even Hersh has his limits, broad as they are; granted, where these limits might be is not always so clear when his jokes of the Old World begin:

"Once upon a time, your great-grandfather Uri was driving his three daughters home from the market in a wagon, when they were set upon by a group of Cossacks. 'Quickly,' he says to them. 'Hide everything you can. Take these precious jewels and hide them in your knishes, in your schmundies.'" (He has the habit of using multiple Yiddish words as a means of conveying his mastery of the old tongue's vernacular; it does not go unnoticed that his vocabulary is limited to anatomy.) "They do as he says, and the Cossacks come and steal everything but the clothes off the family's backs. Watching his wagons be driven away by his own donkeys is too much for Uri, and he collapses in the dirt. 'Get up, Papa,' say the girls. 'It could be so much worse. We've still got the jewels . . . Come now, what's wrong?' To which Uri replies, 'If only your mother was here, we could have saved the wagon, too!'"

His next routine features once again this infamously large wife of Uri's. Gallina was her name, and she was, by all accounts, a physically tremendous woman. Her girth is the star of a few of his jokes:

"On the night that your ancestors left Russia, the Cossacks come to do their looting and their pillaging. They pull the family out into the yard by the hair on their heads, torch the house, and then take their turns raping the daughters. Finally, the lead pogrommer-in-charge, the big pischer, shoves his own unsullied but very attractive son into the mix and points at Gallina. But the beautiful blonde boy—bless him—refuses. 'But it's a pogrom,' says his father. 'A pogrom is a pogrom.' The boy nods but defends: 'I'm all for the pillaging and looting, Father,' he says. 'I like to burn down a synagogue as good as the next. And the young girls, I understand. Give me one of them. But is it really necessary to have the mothers, too? And in front of their husbands and children?' By this point, the flames of the house have offered up sufficient light to illuminate the youth's superlatively beautiful face, and Gallina stands up and cries out: 'Hey—a pogrom is a pogrom!'"

The jokes go on in this manner, centered around a little village just beyond the border of Poland and in what was then the tsardom of Russia. His geography is correct—as are his names—but his humor, as Hadassah often warns me, has come at the expense of accuracy.

"You want accuracy," she says, "you speak to my brother. If you can get his face free of the Manischewitz . . ."

Actually, his face is buried in port, but speak to her brother I do. Naphtali's memory for events that precede him is flawless; his memory for things he has lived is quite poor. Though he had not yet been born on the night of that great fire, he can tell the story as if he were there at the pogrom, but he will only do so after many glasses. Port is all he drinks, more for the sugar than the alcohol; he is a diabetic and a lush, and both are killing him in tandem. Nevertheless, when the rest of the table has cleared out to hear Hersh try his hands at some new nocturne or other, I sneak Naphtali another glass. Once a week his tongue is loosened, and then history flows from his lips.

* * *

On the evening of the pogrom that drove the Morfawitz clan out of Russia for good, nobody was pulled out of the house, though the rape of the daughters did occur—of the sons, too, with the exception of the youngest, who was a dark and sullen youth called Chaim. Chaim sat

with his mother and, under the vague threat of gunpoint, watched while
the officers went through his siblings; there was never a spoken order to
leave the boy alone, only a tacit agreement between the officers as if they
were stepping around a curse. Chaim's dark, unflinching eyes made them
uncomfortable, and rather than confront this, they allowed themselves
to shy away while at the same time remarking inwardly upon their char-
ity for protecting the innocence of extreme youth. He was nine at the
time, and his eyes only moved away from the barbarity of the officers
to coldly survey his father, Uri, who sat in the corner crying through
closed eyes; they only opened when the captain who was leading the
pogrom—the "big pischer," as Hersh would later distort him—came
into the house and took Gallina by her giant arm.

"Uri!" she cried, more disgusted than afraid.

He finally spoke up. "You can't have her."

"Dear man," said the captain, releasing Gallina and striking Uri
hard across the face. "This cow? I don't want her."

"Oh."

The men looked disappointed, and the captain quickly recovered
his audience.

"Only," he said, "I don't want you to have her either. So I'll make
you a deal. Sound fair?"

"Yes," said Uri. "Wait. What's the deal?"

"Smart man. You there, boy. What's your name?" For he had not
yet had time to develop his company's distaste for the boy.

"Chaim."

"Chaim. You want your mother to live?"

"Yes, sir."

"You want your father to live?"

The boy hesitated. "Yes, sir."

"Good." He handed the boy a pistol. Some of the company looked
anxious for a moment and then regained their calm. The officer smiled
at them and they filled their little glasses with vodka from an open bottle
on the kitchen table and laughed. The officer stomped over to where
Uri sat, now looking at the pistol in his son's hand, now looking at the

officer, the satisfaction at having made a deal entirely gone from his face. It looked as if the man had never smiled.

"I don't want your mother, boy. But I don't want your father to have her either. You understand?"

The boy shook his head and the officer reached down and grabbed Uri by the testicles. Uri stood up from his chair.

"You understand," the officer said again, his voice now loud and violent.

Chaim nodded. He walked forward.

"No," said Uri. "Boy . . ."

But the officer now let go and turned to the boy's mother. He took a knife from his belt and held it to her throat. "Step forward, boy," he said. The boy stepped forward until he was nearly underneath his father's groin. "You save them both or you lose them both. The choice is yours. Not choosing is choosing the latter. There will not be a second chance. I'm going to count down from three. You understand?"

The boy nodded his head. The officer dug the point of his knife into Gallina's skin. It punctured lightly, drew blood. She did not wince, but looked intently at her son. The officer followed her gaze.

"Three," called the officer. The boy shot. Uri's legs shook and his hands flew to his groin. They came away dark and wet. He leaned back against the wall and then slid down it. He collapsed, he lost consciousness. Later, he died. A puddle of blood spread around his fallen body like a dark halo and a tabby cat came from the kitchen and began to lap up the blood. Chaim snapped at the cat and it came to his side. He cradled it with one hand and with the other he held out the gun by the barrel so that the officer could take it by the grip. The officer took it, looking slightly embarrassed; his feeling toward the boy now reflected the attitude of his men. He replaced the knife to its sheath on his belt, wanting to be outside in the fresh evening air. The house now sickened him a little.

"We ought to burn the place down," said another officer, who breathed out hard the taste of vodka. "Wickedness here. That boy's a Jewish devil. Ought to shoot him."

The boy looked at the captain with a blank expression, and the captain could not quite meet his stare.

"No," said the captain. "He held up his end of the bargain. We'll hold up ours."

"But the house," said the drunk officer. "You didn't say nothing about the house."

"Alright," said the captain. "Burn the house."

They burned the house, but not so quickly that the family did not have time to collect what little things they had and pack up their only wagon. One of the yokes was taken by their ox, and the other by their horse. The ox died halfway to the Polish border and the boys took turns pulling the cart in its stead, each doing little more than steering the horse for an hour at a time, while inside the carriage the others slept.

Nobody ever attempted to recover Uri's body. "Out of nothing, into nothing," remarked Gallina once they had safely crossed the border. It was true that Uri had come from nothing, from nowhere. He was a poor but handsome peasant whom Gallina had fallen in love with during her youth and fallen out of love with sharply after. She'd been married before and borne children and was seen as damaged goods. Her father was a generous drunk and Uri conned him into providing a monumental dowry, which was very lucky as Uri and Gallina were nothing if not fecund. Anyway, he could spare the money; Gallina came from a prominent family. Her brother, it is rumored, later renounced his religion and the family name. He was heavily decorated in the war with Japan after nearly freezing to death on a piece of shipwreck flotsam in the Okhotsk Sea. He lost his left hand to frostbite, but used his right, in July of 1918, to execute the Grand Duchess Tatiana.

Not much is known beyond that of Chaim's flight. He never spoke to his children about his life between Russia and Germany, and all that can be said definitively of the next eighteen years of his life is that Poland was crossed. By 1924, Chaim had married and established himself as a middle-class watchmaker in Berlin, and there the memories of his children began to take shape.

There were five of them living under his roof. To his great chagrin, three girls were first: Hannah, Deborah, and Hadassah (in that order). Having so many mouths to feed was a great annoyance to the miserly Chaim, but he desperately wanted male heirs and so he forced himself to keep going. He was luckier next, with Heinrich followed by Naphtali. That, for Chaim, was sufficient, and when his wife bore him another son, they gave the boy away to distant Austrian relations who were having trouble conceiving on their own. He never slept with his wife again.

Chaim's rule over his household was severe. Existence within the collapsed German Empire called for austerity, and such a lifestyle did not disagree with Chaim's natural tendencies. Anyway, none were too worse for the wear when he sent them away to America in 1935 and announced that he himself would not be joining them just yet.

"There is simply too much here for me to do," he told them one night. "I have got to get a fair price for the business. In the meantime, it is no longer safe for you here."

So his wife took the children and went. It is largely assumed by those five children that Chaim was merely making space for himself in which he would be free to pursue an alternate love interest, but nobody knows for certain. In any case, they didn't mind. Throughout their childhoods, his severity had so swallowed them whole that the salt air of the Atlantic tasted to them of freedom; even the smog of New York Harbor held the vague odor of liberty. They dreaded the day their father would turn up on their doorstep, dragging with him the fetters of their European oppression. There was a sense of urgency, then, to each child's need to go out into the world, to make inroads and build foundations that would be capable of withstanding the shadow their father would inevitably cast over the grand cityscape of the New World.

"Naphtali," says Hadassah, bored of Hersh's performance in the next room. "Enough. It does not do well to speak ill of our family."

That's all well and good. Naphtali does not have much more than that to offer. The feared arrival of their father in New York was a day that never came to pass; by the time Chaim decided to join them in America, crossing the border as a Jew was quite impossible. As the war progressed and news of the camps trickled down from nightmare to fact,

the Morfawitz children—for whom the air of fatherless liberty had been
a thing that risked dissipating with every inbound ship on New York
Harbor—finally quit putting down roots and refocused their energies
upward . . .

. . . The Morfawitz children, that is, with the exception of their
youngest brother. You will recall that he had been given away to an
obscure Austrian branch of the family, though nobody else ever seemed
to. Just like his father, this forgotten child had also missed the early
boats out of Europe and was a young boy in Vienna on the day of the
Anschluss, the twelfth of March 1938, when the smiling blonde soldiers
of Germany and Austria danced together as they dismantled the border
posts between what had once been two distinct countries, and Austria
was formally annexed into the Third Reich.

II
ZEV

Hadassah has the habit of repeating herself when speaking from the seated position. It is as if she is stuck in her chair, her beliefs, and her mind all at once. "It does not do well to speak ill of our family," she says again. What she really means is that it does not do well for others to speak ill of her direct ancestors or descendants. She has done enough ill-speaking herself and encourages collective spite against marry-ins and bastards alike, and even the rest of us are not exactly immune. There are, in Hadassah's past, some magnificent cruelties, but they have aged well—like cheese or wine—into something like legend. Naphtali swallows the rebuke with another glass of port, his sister's gray eyes still on him. "Why don't you go into the other room and listen to your nephew play."

Naphtali falls silent. He taps his fingers against the table, and with eyes averted he fills up his glass one more time. Groaning, he rises to join the rest of the family in the parlor.

The subtlety of Hadassah's words is not lost on him, and it is not lost on me; Hersh is his nephew, not hers. She will tolerate his presence, but even after all this time, she will not love Zev's illegitimate children.

With just the two of us now at the table the tension goes out of her. "It does not do well to speak ill of our family," she says again in an echo, hardly more than a whisper.

She looks up from her wrinkled hands. The left one is engaged in polishing the silver candlesticks. A small glass of polish sits before her, looking ominously like water. Silver polish has played an outsized role in Hadassah's life. It is her weapon of choice; she has used it both to poison and to blind. Her use now is more innocent, but she cannot escape looking dangerous with a cup of the clear liquid in her hand. She dabs a napkin into it and rubs three halfhearted circles onto what can only be described as an immaculate surface, and then drops the napkin into the glass and abandons it there.

"Come," she says, "I know it is an inconvenience to walk an old woman home, but do it anyway."

I mumble something about it being an honor and a privilege, and Hadassah smiles as if I am being sweet. We both know I am only doing what is necessary. Many have learned the hard way that it is a wise move to spare no deferential pomp in dealing with Hadassah Morfawitz. She is all the more dangerous when she wants something from you, for it makes her feel weak to not be totally self-sufficient. She wants something from me now.

"And perhaps," she says, coy as a snake, "if Zev is awake, you can stop in and tell him good night."

It is her way of saying what she does not want to say: *How can you tell the story of our tower without speaking of the man who built it? A man who, as it turns out, might be coming up soon to his end . . .*

Hadassah's need to celebrate the family's origins will be her own undoing. More than purely illustrious roots have been buried, roots that might have been better off left undisturbed. For a family so obsessed with vertical positioning, what can be more paramount than the man who sits at its peak, unwilling or unable to descend, even for supper?

The elevator in our building opens directly onto each floor, and going between apartments gives one the feeling of having traveled not in space, but in dimension. The layouts of each apartment are identical, and the changes are merely decorative: the color of the walls, the finish of the floor, the luminosity of bulbs—the artwork, the moldings, the smells. In coming from Hersh's apartment below up to Hadassah and

Zev's, the dark walls are changed for sky blue and eggshell white, the soft herringbone floors for cold gray marble, the incandescence of Edison bulbs for the hospital white of fluorescents. The whole place hums, an abundance of power too brash to be considered in any way chic.

"Well," says Hadassah, "go on in. I know why you've really come."

She gives me a faux-scandalous look; truly, she adores her husband, and the great tragedy of Hadassah's life is that she has not been as sufficient a trophy to him as he has been to her. Or perhaps there were greater tragedies that I know nothing of. In any case, she kisses me good night with a perfunctory cheek against mine, once and then twice, in the European style she has never fully abandoned, and then goes off toward the bedroom.

I find Zev in the living room in his great leather chair, half-reclining, the way one is supposed to sit at Seder. The throne is massive, but even in the shrink of his old age, he fills the thing—an arm on each armrest, the left turned upward to expose the veins of his forearm to the needle of an IV, which stands beside him. The chair is swiveled to face south, and he watches storm clouds gather over the lower half of Manhattan. I never know how present he is, and when I see that his eyes are on mine, there is a feeling that it is he who has snuck up on me and not the other way around.

"Sit," he says. I sit. Over the harbor, lightning flashes. The silhouette of the Statue of Liberty is like the bishop of a chess set, a toy figurine. "Why do you bother an old man?"

"I'm happy to head back down," I tell him. "I'd just as soon not miss dessert . . ."

Zev nods and the ghost of a smile passes over his face. He is different from his wife to win over; where Hadassah wants deference, Zev wants strength. Anyway, we have practiced the opening lines of our little conversations so that now they are like necessary passwords, preambles, or invocations. He is as glad to tell his ugly tale as I am glad to hear it. It is the final means by which he has to be cruel; for me, it is one of my first. "Far," he says, the storm flashing in his cloud-gray eyes, "far across the Atlantic. Where were we?"

"Vienna," I tell him. "A city so cosmopolitan that it put the old New York to shame. If there was anti-Semitism there, you never felt it. It was a subtle thing. You were happy . . ."

* * *

Zev claims he had a happy childhood in Austria. He remembers that Jewish boys were picked on, but was never picked on himself, and so he thought the whole thing was overblown. This speaks less to his optimism than to the fact that he was never haunted by symbolic thinking. If a thing was bad, you felt its badness physically; if a thing did not hurt you, it either was not there or it was not hurtful. His foster family—the Kretinbergs—were honest people, but also rich. As early on as he could understand it, they let him in on the secret that he was not truly their son.

"And why should that matter?" he asked.

"Your blood. Your blood is different."

"What does your blood feel like? I don't feel mine."

"We don't feel ours either."

"Then how do you know that it is different?"

Similarly, when the family discussed the epidemic of rising anti-Semitism, Zev wondered aloud: "Have they hurt any of you? They have not hurt me."

"But they are hurting Jews."

"Then maybe we aren't Jews."

"But we are."

"Who says? If they are hurting Jews but they aren't hurting us, then either they aren't hurting Jews or we aren't. What makes us?"

His foster parents looked sheepishly at one another. "Our blood."

Up until 1938, things had not been bad at all for the wealthy Kretinbergs. They owned a conglomerate of goat farms but lived comfortably in Leopoldstadt, a Jewish quarter of Vienna. Amos Kretinberg was a prominent man but a nonpolitical one, so the civil war of 1934 did little to upset their way of life, and he was just as happy with the Fascist

Party as he was with the Socialist Democratic one. They even employed a young nanny who became Zev Kretinberg's first love.

Magrit Kowalski was beautiful and tall and blonde, the very picture of Germanic racial superiority—ironically, she was actually a Pole. Her Slavic blood diminished her opportunity for employment in an Austria that was increasingly cognizant of racial purity. She could cook and clean and was competent with children, but she was also a sound tutor of Polish and German and mathematics. The Kretinbergs underpaid her, but her Slavic heritage made employment difficult to find among Viennese homes, and nobody else aside from the Jews had any money.

Magrit never complained about her wages. For one thing, the Kretinbergs were kind, and less overtly Jewish than their compatriots, which made employment with them easy; for another, she loved Zev. It was not a romantic love, but it was not exactly a platonic one, either. At the time of the *Anschluss*, he was an old-looking eleven and she was a young-looking sixteen. Though she was brilliant in mathematics, she was also naive. She was very like Zev in believing only in what she could feel or hear or see, but where Zev's perspective was born of cynicism, Magrit's was born of naivety. When the tanks rolled in on the sixteenth of March, she saw it as proof—not of impending doom for the Slavs and the Jews, but of the opposite. For certainly, if such a unified army with its panzer tanks and rifles wanted to do away with the little people of Europe, it would be only too easy; that they hadn't yet done so was proof that they had no such aspirations.

She was fired shortly after, upon Amos Kretinberg's discovery that she'd taken Zev to see the rally. She'd thought nothing of it, she said, and nothing bad had happened.

"Nothing bad!" cried Amos. He'd spent the morning scraping independence fliers off the cobblestones under the oversight of the new Nazi occupiers. His hands were dirtier than they had ever been, his pants torn at the knees. Still, he might have been lenient in his handling of Magrit had not Zev provided evidence of her influence.

"And you!" said Amos, turning to his foster son. "You—who does not believe in their hatred of the Jews, of you, for your blood—yes, your blood! You, what did you feel when you saw their tanks roll into the city you call home? What did you feel upon seeing the red and the white and the twisted black? Did you feel anything? Did you say anything?"

Zev had never heard Amos raise his voice before. The anger confused him. He looked to Magrit, and then back to his foster father. He nodded.

"Yes? Did the block of marble residing under my roof finally find a feeling, find a voice? Tell me now—what did you say when they walked by and your countrymen all raised their hands in salute?"

Zev shrugged and answered honestly: "I said, 'Heil Hitler.'"

So, against the protests of young Zev, Magrit was forced from the house. Zev snuck out that night to go find her, and never made it home. It was a lucky thing, too, for before the sun rose the next morning, the windows of the Kretinberg residence had been smashed through by bricks, and their store had been torched. When Amos left the home to chase down the perpetrators, he was arrested for disturbing the peace. He was thrown against a wall and shot through the back of the head. Zev found his body the next morning and never saw his foster mother again.

He did, however, find Magrit. In contrast to the experience shared by virtually all other inhabitants of that doomed continent, the two of them lived what he termed an "idyllic" life for the remainder of 1938. While the rest of the world was manufacturing steel for guns and railways and submarines and preparing the machinery of war, and while the rest of Zev's life would be spent in apartments and smog-filled cities of brick, glass, and concrete, in 1938 he hid with Magrit in barns and slept against hay bales and frolicked in pastures. When they needed food, he hunted. Though he'd never been trained, he showed a great talent for killing rabbits without rifles, without sound. Everywhere they went, he seduced the local girls. It was both difficult and not. On the one hand, here was a homeless, nearly feral boy and a clear runaway. On the other, god had been disproved by Darwin and then killed by Nietzsche and then dragged through the mud by Hitler, and there was—as Zev put it—"no good reason at all not to fuck who you wanted."

Magrit watched Zev's exploits half-humored and half-jealous. She trained him in the art of love, and eventually, she loved him herself, but only with her body, not her heart. They crossed the eastern border after the bonfires of Kristallnacht. The Czechoslovakian winters were cold and they needed a farmhouse to sleep in, and Magrit bribed an estate owner's son with the only thing she had to offer. She impressed upon him the need for secrecy, called Zev her "jealous brother," said they had been caught in Vienna and were returning to their parents in the Masovian forests around Warsaw. The relation was false, but both the jealousy and the destination were true; Magrit longed for the trees of her home, where the canopies were always bright chartreuse, backlit by the sun above, a place that existed only in peaceful memory and so was untouchable by war.

Zev discovered them at an inopportune time; it was February, and the earth was frozen solid. Still just a boy, he was no match physically for Magrit's lover, and so he said the thing that he knew—from his romps in town—to be the most condemning and offensive thing that could be said about anyone in Eastern Europe.

"Have it your way, then. She's a dirty Jew! They'll hang you as a blood traitor!"

Still stumbling over his half-dropped breeches, the boy fled from the two runaways in his barn and was scared enough to alert the authorities. Zev and Magrit were once again on the run, and the timing was poor; in March of that year, Czechoslovakia was annexed and the two of them were captured as renegade Jews. While Zev's lack of foreskin made it clear he was a Jew, his otherwise Teutonic physique appealed to some sentiment in his overseers, and he found himself in the relatively desirable position of being the youngest kapo at Gusen, where he was tasked with separating the Jews capable of labor from those who were capable only of death. It was an important role at the time because in 1939 they hadn't yet decided on Zyklon B as a more efficient method of murder, and the bullets used in mass exterminations were not cheap; if work could be extracted from a body before wasting the lead, it was Zev's duty to send it for extraction.

One day in June of 1940, the rounds were nearly finished, but the going for Zev had been slow. A train had come in from Berlin, and there had been plenty of sorting to do. And now, toward the end of the day—the same as it always was—came the difficult ones, the ones who had had all day to consider what pleas they might put forth, who had recovered enough from the stench of the cattle cars so as to really want to live, who had made fists all day and rolled up their sleeves so that bulging, prominent veins might make their arms appear capable of work.

Usually, Zev had no problem with these, but the last man of the day gave him pause. Even before he read the man's name, the face alone startled him. It was destitute, yes, but also somehow familiar. The man came close enough for Zev to smell the filth on his body and dropped three thick golden coins on the table. They were soiled from the necessary manner of storage, but they were only on the table for a moment, and then they were in Zev's pocket.

"Name?" said Zev, preparing to send the briber into the group to the right that would go on to work, to live.

"Chaim Morfawitz," said Chaim Morfawitz.

"Family?" said Zev mechanically, before truly hearing the name of his father. It was the next question on the list.

"Gone," said Chaim. "They have gone to America. New York . . ."

But by now Zev had heard the answer and looked his father in the face. Something very close to rage came over him. It was similar to the way he'd felt watching Magrit with her farm-boy lover. He could not place it, exactly, and did not even know how he knew the name Morfawitz, but it was like a flame within him that ignited a fire—not of purpose or kinship, but hatred. He hated to feel connected to something so weak, so helpless—something that could remove from its anus three pieces of gold and offer them up as a plea for its life. Zev wrinkled his nose. He pointed left.

"Kretinberg!" shouted one of the commanding officers. "*Beeilung!*"

Chaim Morfawitz's face had already been screwed up at the injustice of the leftward pointing hand, but now its expression changed to something else. "Kretinberg," he said. "Zev Kretinberg?"

Zev paused for a moment and half-turned to his father. He felt for the gold coins through the linen of his pocket. They were still there. He showed his father his back, and that was the last Zev ever saw of him.

* * *

It is a cruel twist of fate to be destroyed by one's neglected children, but Zev only smiles and says, "Like father, like son."

"Is there justice in that?" I ask the old man.

Zev gives a halfhearted shrug; he has no interest in justice, and besides, he is proud of his wicked deeds. At the very least, this is something like a confession, and while he has not touched a drop of liquor, his attitude is something like drunk on the stormy New York sky. A whole city's worth of light is reflected in his face. It gives his cheeks a rosy, youthful look, and he looks at me as if a great burden has been taken from his shoulders. His age, mixed with his ego, has forced his youth to rise within him. It is probably the first time Zev has told the story; it probably will be the last.

His goal in confessing is not absolution, but something like its opposite; he wants assurance that even after he is dead, he will be capable of causing a stir. Remembrance, too, has some part in it; it would seem unjust to Zev if many of his boldest deeds were to go unrecorded, unknown. To him—who saw firsthand the powers of totalitarian rule, the magnetic pull of unmitigated obedience, who always saw the worst in men and viewed all of humanity as ugly, hairless sheep—it follows that the deeds of which he is most proud are the ones that prove a willingness to depart from cultural norms, to perform taboos, to revel in moral disgust. In his opinion, this distinguishes his person as the rare man among cattle. The notion has not occurred to him that we might be the men, that he might be something else entirely.

He goes on: "So then, America . . ."

So then, America. For that is where Zev's telling of America begins. One moment he is a kapo in Gusen, and the next he is a boarder at the poorhouse in New York. The time between did not exist, for who was Zev to make difficult sea passages and maybe become ill? Who was Zev to wait in long lines and pray for bread? Who was Zev to have no enemy to fight except for boredom and bureaucratic red tape? It wasn't any Zev that Zev wanted to be. And so, either willfully or from the protective force of his subconscious, he has scrubbed it from his memory; to cover the parts of him he is ashamed of, Zev makes the parts he loves wider and more opaque, with enough area to throw a shroud over the truth.

So we come to the first of Zev's exaggerated vices: women, what else? To this boy who had grown beautiful and pubescent in the dull forests of a Europe at war, America of the 1940s was a dreamland. The only thing Zev liked more than beauty was wealth, and there was plenty of overlap to be found in New York City.

It is obvious that the old were once young, but there is something undeniably vulgar about hearing an old man describe a crude exploit as if he were a teenage boy. His first "conquest" in the New World was a young woman from the Welcoming Society of New York. They were tasked with placing newly arrived young orphans into the appropriate poorhouse; Zev was directed to the very best of them, where the wealthy German-Jewish daughters worked and so their fathers made great donations. His second conquest was one such girl, a pretty ladler in the kitchen.

While the sky flashes outside, he brags to me of the exploit: "I pushed her back against the other side of the wall that stored the racks of bread. We shook it so that the loaves trembled and fell from their baskets to the ground like stones. I, who intimately knew hunger, who had so long been deprived of bread, could make a whole wall of it shake with the thrust from my hips . . ."

After a few weeks of strengthening up, he moved on to women outside the system that was in place to feed him. While the other Jewish immigrants went daily to the docks to see if the day's cargo brought another family member or a friend from an old village, Zev had only money and women on his mind; his family, he knew, was already in New York.

III
THE NEW WORLD

Life in the New World cast a reversal of age among the Morfawitz children who had come to New York in 1935. From the womb they came Hannah, Deborah, Hadassah, Heinrich, and Naphtali; they stepped off the boat the other way around. Their mother was the last of all to step foot on the continent. She died shortly thereafter, and poor, simple Hannah, who had undergone her whole childhood in Berlin, whose brain and tongue had formed around the harsh German language, took her place by the fire, knitting and choring and fretting, always the foreigner, never quite the immigrant.

Of only slightly more consequence to the family was Deborah. America agreed with Aunt Deb, but it was the sort of unruly agreement that the world makes with middle children. Deb was young enough that English came naturally, but old enough that she had to study it, work it, make a tool kit out of rhetoric. She marveled at the novelty of English and could never let a turn of phrase or clever homonym go by. Her sole contribution to the Morfawitz legacy was to become pregnant by an anonymous man while working as a soup-kitchen volunteer. Pregnancy out of wedlock was taboo at the time, but Deb refused to be intimidated by the disapproval of the solemn gynecologist; looking down the spread of Deb's open legs during her first appointment, the doctor asked whether she'd had a checkup recently, to which Deb famously replied, "No, just a couple of Romanians."

Hadassah would later chide her older sister for the crude remark. All the chiding in the Morfawitz household fell to Hadassah. She was the one who made the appointments, who kept the house in order, who alone had strong-enough reins to withstand the strong pulls of her siblings. Yes, it was in silver-haired Hadassah that the family found its de facto mother. She pushed them hard toward success and shied away from nothing to achieve it. Hadassah had very strict morals and talked frequently about treating people the right way; only "people," to her, extended merely to the family. The people who peopled the outside streets were something more like dogs. They could be cute or ugly, dangerous or sweet, useful or inane, but their traits were the product of breeding and genetics, and they could be described only by their most pronounced quality. They had little capacity for change. A man can do a stupid thing, and so a stupid action does not necessarily imply a stupid man; a dog who acts stupidly is stupid, and everybody who was not a Morfawitz was a dog to Hadassah. There were consequences to the purity she ascribed to her own blood, the most severe being when she took one look at her firstborn son and, deciding that his deformed ugliness did not recommend him to "people," had him taken from the house.

One must sometimes be forgiving of Hadassah; god only knows the turmoil with which her marriage has plagued her mind—and even she only knows the half of it. As the youngest and the prettiest of the Morfawitz girls, she could have had anyone she desired, and it is not difficult to imagine that her life would have been better off without Zev.

* * *

They met on Rosh Hashanah of 1947 at the Park Avenue Synagogue. The temple did a good deal to sponsor the Lost Sons and Daughters of Israel, where Zev was being given free room and board at the time. Hadassah was not religious, and the family was not rich, but she knew that the congregation was rich, and rich congregations have rich daughters, and rich daughters are designed for bright and beautiful boys.

Such boys were Hadassah's younger brothers, Naphtali and Heinrich Morfawitz. She went about fetching them prize dowries and was half-successful in her pursuit. She secured for each of them an opportunity with the young woman who was unanimously agreed upon as the choicest of the synagogue—a tall, dark daughter of the Kolitzes, a sonless line of the Lithuanian shipping magnates. Amanda was her first name, though nobody ever seemed to remember it, and her prior failed suitors had been Harvard boys at a time when only the richest Jews could overcome the Semitic barriers to Cambridge. Nobody could reasonably suggest their own sons against the opportunities that Amanda Kolitz had rejected.

And yet Hadassah was not reasonable. She saw a line, not of suitors, but of dogs. It didn't occur to her that the Kolitz girl might want nothing to do with some penniless immigrants from Berlin. As usual, Hadassah was right—too right.

Amanda Kolitz's eyes were converted at once to Hadassah's way of seeing the world, and her other suitors ceased to be. The girl fell madly in love with not one, but both of the Morfawitz boys. Her amorous wailing drowned out the loud protestations of her father, and it was decided that the orphaned Morfawitzes would be "observed." And so the family of five parentless immigrants was mysteriously bumped up to second-row seats (hot tickets for the High Holidays) right beside the Kolitz box. And what Gregor Kolitz observed, he admired.

"Those children were brought up the right way," he told his wife. "Their father must have been somebody in Berlin."

"I'm sure you can find out, dear," said his wife, certain there would be no way to do such a thing. "Come to think of it, I've heard the name before. In good circles, too. A little birdie told me that they are Rothschilds by their mother's line."

"The oldest girl told Eve Goldsmith, who told Ted Cohen, that their father was a famous watchmaker. That Einstein himself came to have a watch made at his shop."

"There's a man who knows time."

"Apparently, he sent them away to America just after Nuremberg was passed."

"I'm sure that it cost him an arm and a leg."

"And a life," said Gregor. "Never got out himself. Stayed back to help organize the resistance. To do what he could do."

"A precise man and a hero, both. Good qualities to have. A shame the family is poor."

"Poor, yes," said Gregor. "But only circumstantially poor. Not genetically poor. Genetically, quite rich, if one believes what he hears."

"I'm sure you can find out," she said again, smiling to Amanda, whose eyes had appeared in the crack of the drawing-room door. "And if they really are Rothschilds, well then they might be getting a pretty penny out of the war reparations that everybody is talking about. But why—were you thinking of something?"

And so, with the fabricate dynasty that Hadassah whispered into every corner and the gossiping support of the Kolitz family, an aura grew around the orphaned Morfawitz children until they were esteemed as something akin to royalty in exile. Suspicions of ancestral wealth were mixed with certainties of descendant wealth once it became generally known that one of the Morfawitz boys would eventually become heir to the Kolitz fortune.

The only question remained: which one? Both were tall men and excessively handsome—but that is where their similarities ended. "Those Morfawitz genes are short," went a favorite phrase of the Park Avenue congregation, "but they are good."

By the time Naphtali was sixteen, he looked like a full-grown man. He had boyish blonde curls but the chest of the Farnese Hercules. In April of 1944, he claimed to the recruiting officers that his birth certificate had been forged by his mother upon immigration, and he enlisted in the naval forces. Naphtali was still a cadet when the D-Day invasion occurred, and his year in conflict included a train to California, where he boarded a cruiser and sailed for Japan. They were halfway between Hawaii and Manila in August of 1945 when the Fat Man was dropped on Nagasaki. The ships made a spectacular one-eighty and were the first to return home.

Though he never did so much as open fire on an enemy combatant, Naphtali was quickly considered to be a hero, and by the time Hadassah was making inroads into the Park Avenue Synagogue, it was common knowledge that he had both stormed the beach at Normandy on the sixth of June and, seven days later, invaded Saipan; for bravery, it was whispered, he'd been offered the Navy Cross, which he rejected on the basis of a pacifist ideology. This was at odds with the general brutality with which he boxed, which he did very well and very often. Team sports did not agree with Naphtali; it was not that he was selfish, but rather the opposite—he could not stand the thought that a mistake of his had let down others. He was hard on himself, and it endeared him well to everyone else. Boys his own age, boys younger, and boys older all adored him. Fathers recruited him for their Sunday baseball leagues without knowing if he played. He had intelligence enough, but very rarely had to use it. He became violent when he drank, and afterward, he would nearly drown himself in remorse. His eyes were always changing color from happy blue to wrathful green.

Heinrich, on the other hand, never lifted a finger he didn't have to. He was dark and brooding; of the Morfawitz children, he most resembled Chaim. He was just shy of being wiry, yet he was strong and gave the impression that his thinness followed the overworking engine of his mind. For long stretches of time, he would sit still as if his thoughts had gone off somewhere and left a shell behind. He might forget to eat, to drink, and whenever such a state of catatonia overtook him, he would blend into the room like furniture. He wore thick but simple spectacles—perfect circles, thin wire frames—that magnified his pale gray irises. If he was taciturn and distant, it was disinterest, not shyness, that made him so. Once his interest was held, though, he thought of little else. After August of 1945, it was difficult to pull Heinrich's nose from a physics textbook, and at seventeen he enrolled to study in the relevant department at Columbia. Hadassah had a singularly difficult time controlling the elder of her younger brothers. The only way she could get him to sit in temple was to replace the cover of Heisenberg's *Nuclear Physics* with that of the *Standard Mevorah Siddur*, which was in use by the Park Avenue congregation at the time. A result of the swap was that Heinrich quickly gained a reputation for being deeply religious. He did not notice Amanda until Hadassah asked him what he thought about her as a marriage prospect.

This did not stop Amanda from noticing him; but of course, she noticed Naphtali, too. And so ensued a tug-of-war, where poor Amanda Kolitz was pulled alternately toward the negative charge of Heinrich and the strong positive one of Naphtali. Women—including Amanda's mother—tended to favor Heinrich. Men favored Naphtali. The children favored Naphtali and the elders favored Heinrich. A balance of indecision was achieved, and it might have gone on indefinitely had that fateful Rosh Hashanah not occurred when Amanda Kolitz's eyes were—for a moment—spared the back-and-forth from Naphtali to Heinrich and raised to a third possibility.

In fairness to Amanda Kolitz, the attention of the entire congregation was momentarily suspended when Zev Kretinberg was invited up onto the bimah. He represented the Lost Sons and Daughters of Israel and thanked the congregation for its support of recent immigrants and victims of the European war, a group that included himself. With an accent that nobody could place, a build like Naphtali, the penetrating gray eyes of Heinrich, and a magnificent story of escape from war-torn Europe, he was a worthy subject for admiration and awe. He was not like the filthy Eastern European refugees who smelled of ghetto and boiled cabbage, who wore white stockings and wool coats in September. Here was not a Jew to accept as one does cancer, but to aspire to and emulate. All the more so because he'd proven himself by taking control of the Lost Sons' finances and rebuilding large parts of the derelict poorhouse, ingratiating himself with the correct people without overt flattery or any flattery at all. Yes, Amanda Kolitz saw him, but so did her parents, so did the rabbi and the cantor, so did the Morfawitz family.

So did Hadassah.

She—to whom the entire world outside her family seemed to be of another species entirely, who had never truly seen a man that was not one of her younger brothers, who was still a virgin because she'd never taken any man into consideration—felt suddenly the rush of pubescent libido rising in her like the long, single sounding of the holiday shofar. She was warm and then very cold. Her legs trembled, she crossed her arms over her chest. She felt her pulse to make sure that nothing had gone wrong in her heart.

* * *

The Morfawitz family had already been invited to break the next week's fast at the Kolitz household. A quarter of the congregation was invited, but there were invitations and then there were *invitations*. The first floor of the penthouse was for unassigned seats, and then there was also a dining room set for twenty, where both Zev Kretinberg and the Morfawitz family had been invited to dine with their hosts.

Ellen Kolitz, after much prodding by Amanda, had agreed to seat her next to Zev; somehow, though, she wound up very far away, seated squarely between Heinrich and Naphtali. Gregor Kolitz would remember that the change had been of his design.

"Weren't you just saying," said Hadassah quietly to him, as they all sat down to eat, "that it's about time she decided?" She was seated to the left of Gregor Kolitz's place at the head of the table. On her own left was Zev Kretinberg.

"Yes," said Gregor Kolitz, believing it himself. "Yes, I was."

Hadassah smiled at her hosts and then quickly looked away. In their money, Hadassah took great interest, but in their persons, she saw them as they were to her: of little consequence. They would be dead within the year. He by poison; she by suicide.

Now, Hadassah was normally a beautiful girl, but tonight she looked exquisite. Her dress was blue and green, with black spots like a peacock's eyes. Amanda Kolitz, on the far side of the table, glared—first in jealousy at Hadassah's sitting next to Zev, then in jealousy at Hadassah's beauty, then in awe at Hadassah's beauty, and finally, in relief that she was seated so far away from Zev Kretinberg that she could cite distance as an excuse for why he paid her no attention.

Zev was asked many questions before he was allowed to settle into his corner of the table. They wanted to know where he'd lived before the war, which camp he'd been in, how he'd gotten out, when he'd arrived at Ellis Island, what was his feeling upon seeing Lady Liberty for the first time. Finally, when the preliminaries were done, Gregor Kolitz leaned over his plate and considered Zev closely, looking back and forth between him and Hadassah.

"You look like one of them," he said.

"One of who?"

"Of these golden Morfawitz children." He surveyed Hadassah's face, her open neck, her chest, and then looked up to the other side of the table. Zev followed his glance until his eyes fell on Amanda Kolitz, who quickly dropped her own. She was sandwiched between Naphtali and Heinrich. "My daughter must decide between those two. And she must do it quickly. Well—what do you think? Who would you choose for your own daughter?"

"I haven't any daughter," said Zev.

"Even so."

"That's ridiculous," said Hadassah. "He doesn't know my brothers."

"Nor do I know you," said Zev. He looked at her directly for the first time, and she looked back at him. "Are they your brothers?"

Zev turned to survey the far side of the table.

"That's it," said Gregor. "Which one, which one."

Naphtali watched Amanda, Heinrich watched Zev. In his magnified eyes, there was something like a smile.

"The better-looking one," said Zev. "No glasses."

"Oh," said Ellen Kolitz, who was on Gregor's other side. "But how can you say Naphtali is better looking of the two? Heinrich has his charms."

"Naphtali," said Zev, trying the name out on his tongue, as if hearing it for the first time. "Heinrich." He looked up at Ellen Kolitz. "I'm sure that Heinrich has his charms as well. But marriage is a union. The two must fit."

Beneath the table, Hadassah felt his strong hand just above her knee.

"And if it was my own daughter," continued Zev, "who knows? But your daughter has an honest face, a face that will take offense at not being trusted. Heinrich looks . . . what is the word? Suspicious. Yes, suspicious. Naphtali seems like the more trusting of the two."

"Naphtali would surprise you," said Hadassah. The Kolitzes looked entertained as if they had stumbled onto a rehearsal set. Hadassah did not notice them. She spoke only to Zev. "He isn't as simple as that girl makes him seem."

"I've heard that love will do that to a man," said Gregor.

"To a woman, too," said Zev.

Hadassah took her knife beneath the table and pricked Zev in the finger. He smiled at her and removed his hand from her knee. Gregor and Ellen Kolitz considered the matter closed, and Heinrich seemed to understand this from across the table. He offered Zev and Hadassah a knowing, conclusive smile, and they went back to their soups.

"How did I do?" said Zev quietly. Neither turned toward the other.

"You tell me," she said. "You've sized them up from half a room away. Size me up, why don't you. I'm right here." Zev did not say anything, and Hadassah went on. "I know your tricks," she said. "When we first arrived here, I used my accent also—to say things that it otherwise would not be appropriate to say. To trick them into thinking that the inflection is the strange part, not the content. I'll warn you now because you seem to be an ambitious man. You will not interfere with my family's affairs again. Do you understand?"

Zev raised a spoonful of soup to his lips and blew steam from its surface. When he spoke again, his voice was clean of accent. "And when did you come to America?"

"In 1935," she said. "Before it all really got going. My father found us passage on a liner." As if reading the hull from a harbor she said, "The USS *Libertaria*."

"He must have been an influential man," said Zev. "A watchmaker, I hear."

"So you do know who we are, then?"

"One hears things," said Zev. "Tell me, where are the others?"

"The others?"

"They say you have two older sisters."

"Are you so eager to meet them?"

"Oh, yes," said Zev. "Us orphans have got to stick together. Like family."

"We've got a family already," Hadassah said to him. "I suggest you find your own."

They did not speak again for the remainder of the dinner. Dessert was served buffet style and there was much drinking and merriment. News somehow spread through the crowd that Amanda's selection process was finished and that she would be engaged to Naphtali Morfawitz once the holidays were over. Hadassah was in the thick of it, kissing Kolitz women on this cheek and then that, preparing to be welcomed into their family. She kept a smile plastered on her lips, but it never reached her eyes; they were flat and catlike as they traveled through the crowd of women, scanning the apartment, searching fruitlessly for Zev.

He stood on the balcony, looking out over the city below, the red river of brake lights, the dark rectangle of Central Park like a hole cut out of night. The glass of scotch in his hand smelled rich, and he thought of money and of gold and then of his father. Far below, some unplanned procession of cars drove over the same loosely covered manhole, setting steel against steel like a pulse, counting arrhythmic heartbeats into the moving imperfections of night and of darkness.

"I suppose that I have you to thank," said a voice behind him.

"For what?" Zev began to say, but he turned and found himself face-to-face with Heinrich. "It's you."

"It's me," said Heinrich, holding out his slender hand. "Heinrich Morfawitz."

"Zev Kretinberg."

"Well, why I thank you, Zev Kretinberg, is for getting me out of that marriage, and away from those terrible, charitable people."

Zev looked out at the skyline. "From what I understand," he said, "all that I have gotten you out of is an inheritance to the most valuable real estate in the world."

"The most valuable real estate in the world," said Heinrich, "is the narrow intersection where being a moral authority meets being a cunt. These people talk endlessly of causes, of Israel, of a land of our own, and of the necessity of doing something. But all the something ever amounts to is talk. All the 'causes' only ever amount to topics of conversation suitable for dinner. They believe in God when it means a fashionable seat at temple and a penthouse party to follow. Well, Zev Kretinberg, what about you? Did the war give you cause? Did it give you God?"

"Did it give those things to you?"

"Cause?" said Heinrich. "God? Please. The only thing the war gave away was that, in any case, Herr Hitler was right about life being merely a land grab between people. He was right about there being no God, and nothing exactly swooped in from on high for counterpoint. He was right, only he was wrong in one serious way: he thought that it was about the nation or race and not the individual. Divisions larger than the self and smaller than the planet are arbitrary."

"He was wrong in a worse way than that," said Zev. "He lost."

Heinrich smiled. "Is losing being wrong?"

"Yes," said Zev. "The worst and most severe form of it."

"Well, at least there's a consistency there," said Heinrich. He rubbed his fingers together as if testing the fabric of space. He turned his back to the balcony and looked over the crowd inside. "It gives you a leg up on these people."

"And what makes you any better than them?" asked Zev.

"Nothing," said Heinrich. He had a strange and high-pitched laugh. "Nothing at all. Only, I don't believe that I'm a saint."

Zev turned away from the window and inspected Heinrich's face. "And yet," he said, "you don't consider yourself to be quite the devils that they are."

"Oh, I'll stop you there," said Heinrich. "I never said that they were devils, only that they were mean."

"What is the devil if not mean?"

"But of course, he's not," said Heinrich. Once again there was the laugh. "The devil is not mean—he is not even particularly strong. The devil is not the unyielding oppressor. He is the charming timid, the cunning weak. He is the ex-slave who convinces you that suffering is noble."

"This coming from the man who is trying to convince me that he is relieved that his stronger, bigger brother has just been chosen over himself for marriage."

Heinrich turned to Zev with a sudden quickness, a flash of anger. "Don't be so sure, Zev Kretinberg, that we have the same definition of strength." He spoke quietly now, and his words hung in the air. "Kretinberg," he said, mulling it over. "Kretinberg. The name sounds familiar."

"Does it?" said Zev, turning back toward the city.

Heinrich leaned against the banister beside his younger brother. "An Austrian branch?"

"Branch of what."

"What indeed. How old are you, Zev Kretinberg? Would seventeen be awfully short?"

"My papers make me twenty."

"Do they? The same age as my sister."

"Is that right. Which one? I hear the Morfawitz clan is numerous."

"More so than some imagine," said Heinrich. The glass of his spectacles shone with the lights of the city below, and it looked for a moment as if he had two white disks in place of eyes. "In any case, we're down two girls tonight."

"Are they sick?"

"Each in her own way. And on Yom Kippur, of all nights. The evening of repentance."

"And does your family have much to repent for?"

"Some, more so than others," said Heinrich. "But really, this question is better asked of you."

"I don't follow."

"I think you do," said Heinrich. He moved very close to Zev so that their shoulders touched and there was no space left between their bodies. "The question that has dominated this world for thousands of years is whether it is right for a son to repent for the sins of his father. It is asked of every prophet, every god. So I'll tell you once, Zev Kretinberg, that I don't care what you want with my family. With our family. I don't care if it is revenge for our father shipping you away, or if it is a need for affection that you somehow feel cheated of. Neither of those seems to me to be entirely correct, and to be frank: I do not care. What I desire, little brother, is distance and solitude and a life to myself. My dear sister Hadassah, with time on her hands, would never let that happen. And so that will be your job. You have fixed for me the problem of this betrothal, and for that I am grateful. For that, I will leave you here to your devices. But do not make the mistake of believing we are even; you have fixed for me a minor inconvenience. I, on the other hand, could destroy you now. One day I might just call on you to repay the favor. And you won't forget, will you, Zev Kretinberg?"

Heinrich began to move away, but he was quickly pulled in by a strong hand on his forearm. It held him and would not let go. When Zev spoke, his lips were very nearly in Heinrich's ear. "I don't know about any of that," he said, but before he could say any more, Hadassah came out onto the balcony.

"Heinrich," she said, "if we don't leave now, we'll be trapped here all night. Your presence will be awkward, considering."

"Yes," said Heinrich. He straightened his jacket. "I'll go, I'll go. I was just getting acquainted with our new friend Zev Kretinberg."

"Is Zev Kretinberg our friend?" she said, looking at Zev.

"Oh, I think he will be. The walk home is long and dark, and I'm going downtown. Zev, you wouldn't mind walking my sister home, now would you?"

The five Morfawitz children lived close enough to the river that they could smell it in the morning and just above One-Hundredth Street so that Hadassah could claim—with only a slight stretching of the truth—that it was not East Harlem where they lived but the Upper East Side. She and Zev walked home along the river, with the twinkling yellow lights of Queens reflected in the water and the constant hum of cars on the FDR Drive below them. It was a dark night and a dangerous walk home, but Hadassah knew that she should not be afraid. They did not speak much, which was rare for both of them; Zev was used to charming young women with his tongue, and Hadassah was used to the nervous blabber of young men who were confident enough to approach but had then been leveled by her eyes. She appreciated Zev's silence. The whole night seemed to bend around them. She had planned to lose him before they crossed over into Harlem, but she took comfort in the fact that he, too, had been poor, had been homeless, had been orphaned and still was. They shared the oppression they'd faced in Europe and the poverty they faced now in the New World. But both were alight with a burning need to escape circumstance and a cold certainty that they would.

"It seems you've done a great deal of work securing marriage for your brothers," said Zev. "What about yourself? There are many men in the congregation who could make you a rich woman."

Hadassah stopped and turned to face Zev, and the quitting of her heels against the pavement made silence scream against the dark. "Is it those men who you're thinking of when you ask me that question?"

"It is not."

"Then don't pretend," she said. "I would rather you not talk than pretend."

"I was thinking of me. Do you prefer that?"

"I do."

Hadassah turned and kept walking. When Zev caught up to her side, the sudden seriousness had left the conversation, but neither forgot it had been there only moments before.

"Only, I like the name Morfawitz," said Hadassah. "I'm not so keen to lose it."

"So I'll take it. Zev Morfawitz. Has a ring, does it not?"

"Were we discussing rings already?"

Zev laughed, but Hadassah's voice became serious again. "Do you truly care nothing for your family, for your name?"

"Remember that my name does not come with a family. And what's in a name on its own? Kretinberg? Far too Jewish. I've heard a man does better with a goyish name in New York City. Morfawitz, at least, could be a Pole."

"If you're trying to cover up Jewry," said Hadassah, "best dispense with the first name as well. Zev is a dead giveaway."

"How's Jack, then."

"Better."

"Jack Morfawitz. You can be Jill."

Hadassah did not answer. The backs of their hands touched, and then she thrust hers into her pocket. They walked together to the sound of one another's footsteps, which had fallen into stride, and now they stood before the little tenement where the Morfawitzes lived. Hadassah's jaw twitched as she surveyed the building; her circumstance outraged her. Long curtains of opaque plastic streamed down across the facade, for the landlords had fumigated for cockroaches earlier that week and hadn't yet bothered to take the plastic curtains down.

"Well," said Hadassah quietly. "We've been exterminated."

"It appears to be the case."

Wind like a breath gently filled the narrow street. It lifted the plastic drapes and scattered the toxic smell of fumigate poison into the dark and the night. As the breeze died down, there was the smell again of evening air. A rat lay on the ground, belly up, an inadvertent victim of the poison. Its front paws paddled gently as if running in a dream.

"Would you like to be exterminated, too?" said Hadassah. She looked at Zev and in her eyes there was something severe.

"I shouldn't mind so much. As long as it's comfortable," he said. He looked down at the rat's white belly. "Like drifting off to sleep."

"You'll be comfortable," she said. "And even possibly you'll sleep."

But as they approached the door, she turned around and her face was half sorrow, half mirth. All of it was cruel, the face of an athlete who has mastered her sport. "I forgot," she said. "Not tonight. My sister isn't well."

"You don't seem to me like the type who forgets."

"No?" she asked. "That's sweet."

For all his composure, Zev could not bear something being taken away once he considered it won. And yet he knew that the battle was lost.

"What's the matter with her?" he asked.

"This is the matter. What you're trying to do."

"She's pregnant?"

"She got into trouble, and now she's learning the hard way why it's best to do what I'm doing."

"And what is it you're doing?"

"Saying good night to you, Zev Kretinberg." She did not smile but leaned forward and kissed him on the cheek. "Jack Morfawitz. Whoever you are, good night."

IV
YIDDISH CURSES

Naphtali and Amanda were married the following February, and Zev and Hadassah followed in October. Zev stayed true to his word and took the name Morfawitz as his own. "If you are founding a family dynasty," said Hadassah, "best practice is to have a single brand." Zev also made good on his intention to use the name Jack for all things business in order to make his religion less overt, but it never caught on at home.

Gregor Kolitz who had always longed for a son to succeed him in business, now found himself with two. He took Naphtali and Zev into his business and became very quickly like a father to the fatherless young men; at any rate, he thought so. He projected onto them the affection he'd reserved for sons and remarked that he'd never known a happier time.

"I feel," he told his wife, "as if I've lived in a great empty house my entire life, and only now is it beginning to be filled."

Filled indeed. Within a month of his marriage to Amanda, Naphtali had moved into the Kolitzes' Upper East Side penthouse while he looked for an apartment to buy.

"You never want to rent, my boy," Gregor told him. "You keep an eye on the market, and when you see a deal, you pounce. Now, you and Amanda are only starting out, so it's alright to look for something small.

But before long you'll have children—eh, eh, you'll have children before long, yes?—and then you'll want something larger. There are transactional costs that make many purchases unwise. Best to settle somewhere and stay. Within reason. Two bedrooms, at least. Three would be better, to prepare for other children."

"Then five would really be best," said Naphtali. His voice was so genial that it was impossible not to believe him. "After all, I've also got sisters to look after. You'll remember Hannah, though nobody else ever seems to. And then there is Deb and her newborn."

"That's right," said Gregor. It was the only scandal that the Morfawitz family had against it, and it embarrassed him a little. "And still no sign of the father? Just . . . run off?"

"It's difficult to say," said Naphtali. "I don't think Deb has looked very hard to find him. It's possible even that he doesn't know. She's like that sometimes."

"But the baby's alright? What's his name again?"

"Hers. Penelope."

"Penelope. Funny name for a Jew."

"It was Zev who suggested it. There was a child on his boat to America named Penelope. He says he became attached to the name."

"He doesn't seem like the type to get attached."

"Well," said Naphtali, "attached or not, he's been very good to that child."

"Yes," said Gregor with a smile. "You could've done worse for your in-laws. At any rate, there's family that you won't have to worry about providing a roof for. From everything I hear, the young man is rising fast. As are you, my boy. As are you."

"Well, even with Hadassah and Zev going off to live on their own, I can hardly afford many bedrooms on my salary. I'm sure you'd like to get me out of your hair."

As a consequence of the conversation, Naphtali was given a raise. In the spirit of fairness, Zev was given one, too. To take the burden off Naphtali and Amanda, Zev and Hadassah purchased the apartment that the family had been, until then, renting out. They were approved by the co-op board, who thought they had taken great advantage of the young couple because the paperwork did not allow for another sale without board approval. Gregor Kolitz was only let in on the details after the transaction was closed; Zev had wanted to surprise his new mentor with the gravitas of ownership. He was dismayed at what Zev had signed on to, but finally conceded that property was property, and what Zev had really better do is purchase insurance.

"A wealthy man moves down to Florida," a favorite joke of Gregor's began. "And his real-estate agent tells him that he'd better get three types of insurance: fire, theft, and hurricane. 'I understand the fire and the theft,' says the man, 'but how do you make a hurricane?'"

As it turned out, fire was the only type of insurance that Zev and Hadassah would need, and it did not take them very long to cash in on it. The fire burned through the building like the tinderbox it was, killing three and injuring nine. Despite the late hour, the Morfawitzes had been out—in a very public place, and with very many eyes on them— and so were spared both injury and suspicion.

"If it hadn't been for your advice about the insurance," Zev said to Gregor, in reporting the calamity, "we would be done for. Just absolutely done for."

In his magnanimity, Gregor invited them to stay at the Kolitz household. And so it came to be that they were all housed under a single roof on the Upper East Side. The timing was lucky, too, for soon thereafter, Gregor Kolitz—whose health, until then, had been perfect—grew terribly ill.

"I'm so fortunate to have a daughter that takes such good care of me," he croaked one evening, not to or of Amanda, but of Hadassah— to her, too. His sight was failing, but he knew who she was. On the last night of his life, he attempted to change his will so that Zev and Hadassah, as a union, would be considered another child. Hadassah refused vehemently, and in the end, she got her way—all in the presence of Ellen Kolitz, who grew more disgusted as she watched; ambition for money was something she understood, something she'd already accused the Morfawitz children of in her heart. But the fact that Hadassah's actions denied the charge made Ellen feel unjustified in her hate, which made her all the more hateful.

She interrupted Shiva to go into a rage, kicked out all the clan Morfawitz—including Amanda—in their funeral clothes, then invited them all back inside, upon which Hadassah, in full view of the room, and with an expression of utmost solemnity and sorrow, whispered something kind and daughterly into her ear. That is what the mourners thought, anyway—Ellen Kolitz did not think so. She went out, wailing, and turned back only to scream something toward Hadassah, toward the clan of Morfawitz children who stood with all the dark dignity of the Burghers of Calais; against that gray wall she hurled her best Yiddish curse: "*Er hot khsunh gehat mit der tokhter fun dem mlakh fun toyt, aun zi zol hobn shteyner aun nisht kinder.*" He has married the daughter of the angel of death, and she should give birth to stones and not children!

This was something of a shock to the Morfawitz children, not for the content, but the language; they had no idea that Ellen Kolitz could speak Yiddish. They spoke it themselves, quite frequently, and had believed it was a sort of secret communication for themselves to use among these wealthy American Jews, none of whom would have had any reason to keep alive the poor tongue of the shtetl. In fact, they were right; none of the congregation spoke a lick of Yiddish—including Ellen Kolitz, who had learned the curse from her mother but could otherwise not even say *gut nakht*. When Hannah—silent, goodly Hannah, who hardly ever spoke a word—whispered back into the dense silence, "*Heng dikh oyf a tsiker-shtrikl vestu hobn a zisn toyt,*" Hadassah reared on her older sister, and none of the children spoke for the rest of the night. This was perceived as a dutiful silence, born of concern for the dismayed Ellen Kolitz. The other mourners were also under the impression that the quiet girl had said something very sweet, ending with "and have a peaceful night." But Hadassah seemed very afraid, and even Zev was frightened into silence.

It was only later, after the policemen had come and gone, and after Ellen Kolitz's body had been fished out of the East River, that he allowed himself to laugh. The sun was just rising as they finally got out of their funeral clothes and into bed.

"Oh, sweet enough, indeed," he said to Hadassah as he unzipped her dress from behind.

What Hannah had said was, "Hang yourself with a sugar rope and you'll have a sweet death."

Hadassah turned around sharply to rebuke her husband, but she found herself kissing him instead. "We'll have to be careful, though."

"Oh, we'll be careful. So careful."

"Be serious."

"I am being serious."

He unhooked the clasp of her bra and buried his face in her chest while, over his head, she speculated aloud to the walls: "I wonder if she understood us all this time. Imagine that—the old witch spoke Yiddish."

"Let's see if she really was a witch," whispered Zev. "Let's see if you give birth to stones . . ."

He pulled her down into the bed. Gregor and Ellen's bed, as it happened, where they were discovered the very next morning by none other than Amanda. Too shy to wake them herself, she complained to Naphtali, who sat stoically through the grievance.

"Well," he said, once she'd exhausted her speech. "It is not as if your parents were going to use it."

* * *

But one should not come away with the impression that Zev always got his way, or that Hadassah was impervious to curses. It would be two years before she gave birth, but Ellen Kolitz's last words stuck with her, and when Hadassah finally looked upon her firstborn son's deformity, she thought of the curse and trembled. She got the thing out of the house, and it was such a hideous creature that nobody tried to convince her otherwise.

Meanwhile, Zev and Naphtali made fast work of commandeering the Kolitz dynasty. Naphtali was left to manage the core shipping business, while Zev extended his fingers into whatever fertile soil he could find, an opportunism not limited to business. And while perceived

failure in childbearing had hardened Hadassah, success was beginning
to soften Zev.

As far as he was concerned, he was simply having very bad luck finding his now pregnant mistress an apartment. There was a good deal for a
duplex on West Fifty-Third, but—despite a strong connection through
the temple and an interview that could not have gone better—the co-op
board ultimately rejected his purchase. Same thing for a single bedroom
on Seventy-Second Street and then again for a penthouse in Harlem.
Well, this was 1949 and the world was more puritanical than it is today.
But the rental market was no kinder to Zev and his mistress, Leah. Just
when something seemed to be closing, it inevitably fell through. The only
reasonable explanation was Hadassah's pulling strings behind the curtain,
yet she never said a word to his face, and Zev was left to wonder whether
his wife's heart and disposition could really hold such different truths.

Fortunately for the family's prospects, Hadassah's jealousy contained
a preternatural savvy for real-estate investment. Pushed off the island of
Manhattan by Hadassah's wrath, Zev found an apartment for Leah in the
run-down manufacturing district of Brooklyn, just across the Williamsburg Bridge. Fueled by a vicious post-war sentiment toward the Germans
who dominated the neighborhood, Williamsburg was in steep decline.
The landlord who sold Zev the apartment practically begged him to take
another, and Zev contracted instead to purchase the entire building—
which consisted of three residences above a Bavarian beer hall on the
ground floor—all for the price of the land. Directly across Driggs Avenue
was another residential building that was vacant out of counter-German
protest, and across Broadway was a defunct metal-pressing plant with a
crumbling cast-iron facade, broken windows, and an Italian street gang
called *I Pitoni* that camped out on the second floor.

Zev purchased all three properties just in time to catch the flood
of Holocaust survivors who had finally managed to break through the
bureaucratic sludge of American immigration. The black-hat Hasidim
came in droves across the bridge. They came on foot, and where they
could find Jewish-owned lodging, they took it. The few Germans who
had remained in the area were desperate for a bridge of their own, a

metaphorical connection that would allow them to capitalize on the influx of would-be tenants. What they needed was a Jew whose mind was not so clouded with retribution as to be blinded to opportunity; what they needed was Zev. Before long, he owned a sizable chunk of South Williamsburg, centered on the intersection of Broadway and Driggs. Even the buildings that he did not own outright were publicly attributed to him so as not to put off the Polish Hasids with the knowledge that a portion of their rent was finding its way into German pockets. Zev had no compunction with deceiving his own; he was growing quite rich.

V
BAUMANN'S BEER HALL

Leah gave birth to her twins on the Fourth of July, 1950. Asher and Abby grew up quick and strong, held in awe by the immigrants who saw them as a sort of ideal for what European Jewry could evolve toward, given enough time on American soil.

Abby did not appreciate the deference paid to her by neighborhood boys. It first provoked in her loneliness, then hatred, then the view of men as being overall pathetic. As soon as she could, she left Williamsburg and found no reason to return for a very long time.

Asher, on the other hand, enjoyed his lordly life. At ten, he was drinking Köstritzer at Baumann's Beer Hall and eating pork knuckle sandwiches whenever he pleased. When he got into a neighborhood brawl, the other child usually curled up and took his beating. Asher had disciples and admirers, but no one that he could call friend. He took good care of his mother and could not begrudge Zev the lack of attention paid to her; he agreed that she was nothing but a burden. Also, she had lost what little wits she'd had. Her routine did not lend itself to intellectual growth. She knitted all day, spoke with her cats, and avoided Abby's room to keep up the pretense that her daughter might still be there.

For a boy so spoiled by the affections of his community, Asher curiously expected little from his father. In his mind, the world had a natural order that was strangely geographic: the admiration of Brooklynites converged on him like sunlight through a magnifying glass, as if his seat at the base of the bridge had made him the gatekeeper to high-towered Manhattan; he, in turn, worshipped his father, whose ambitions were already altering the skyline of New York.

What Asher learned, he learned by himself, and nothing was more sacrosanct to him than self-reliance. He was not charitable, so he did not expect others to be. If he wanted his father's affection, he was going to have to be of some use. He grew from a spoiled princeling into a diligent feudal lord. The streets around Zev's properties were kept clean, the buildings themselves were in flawless repair. Rat colonies and street gangs were stomped out alike, and even the lowest of criminals knew to let that little part of Brooklyn be.

By the time he turned eighteen, Asher was more or less running the Brooklyn operations, and he was running them well. Properties that had always lost money were beginning to turn a profit. They were mortgaged and new properties were bought. A line of credit was extended to the entrepreneurial Hasids that no goyish banks would lend money to, and interest from these investments brought in more money than all the properties combined. Baumann's Beer Hall, where a twelve-year-old Asher had gotten drunk on dark ale, was now a thriving steak house. Traders from Wall Street took limousines across at lunchtime, ate porterhouse steaks, and drank big-pour highballs and dirty martinis. Something about crossing the river made people feel as if they were on vacation, and Asher learned to exploit this. The place became quite famous.

So it came to pass that when Hadassah and Zev asked their second-born son, Adam, where he wanted to go for his Bar Mitzvah dinner, with the whole of Manhattan's fine dining laid like a doormat before him, he answered, "Baumann's Beer Hall."

They came in at prime time on a Saturday night and were made to wait thirty minutes before being brought to a table. It had not occurred to them that reservations were required in Brooklyn. The place was filled to the brim, and they were forced to wait at the long oaken bar, where a gruff bartender mixed Zev and Hadassah a Manhattan each before they ordered—"Because, you know, youse look like you come from Manhattan"—and poured a Shirley Temple for Adam, with a cherry and a dash of rum to top it.

Zev had not visited Brooklyn for several years by that point; Asher ran it all so well that there wasn't any need. Asher, upon seeing his father standing there, thought that Zev had wanted to surprise him, to check in; in reality, Zev had simply forgotten all about the place. *Baumann's, Baumann's*—it rang a vague bell in his memory, but his experience of the dusty, run-down establishment he'd purchased twenty years ago at auction and that of the bustling hot spot where his legitimate son had requested to be taken were so disparate, so severed, that the connection hadn't been made. It was made now, and Zev laughed. He was impressed with Asher and called for him to join them at the table.

"I hardly think," Hadassah said, "that he's an appropriate acquaintance for Adam."

"Nonsense. Adam, boy, don't you want to meet the man who owns this place?"

"You own this place," said Hadassah. But the fight had gone out of her. She was not the sort of woman to waste her energy and she saw that this battle was lost. Besides, she remembered that sow, Leah—plain in the face but round where it mattered—and was ready to take some pleasure in what sort of son that thing could have reared in Brooklyn, of all places. But now that she saw Asher, a change came over Hadassah. Here was another—well, another *person*—not a dog, not a cow. She felt the way she'd felt upon seeing Zev for the first time, and her mind raced with possibilities and uses for the boy; for if there was anything that Hadassah demanded more than the fealty of her husband, it was the exaggerated success of her family. The former, she knew, was a lost cause.

"It's awfully hot in here," she said, unbuttoning the top of her blouse. She leaned over the table, artfully offering a view of her chest, which was—at thirty-eight—still firm and desirable. She wanted to test Asher's weaknesses and was glad to see that his eyes remained on hers, but she took note of how he winced when the restaurant was critiqued. "Now why don't you tell us," she said, sitting back. "How's your mother?"

"The old bat," he said.

Hadassah smiled and thought: *smart boy*. And aloud: "It isn't nice to speak about one's mother that way. Adam wouldn't speak about his mother that way. Isn't that right, Adam?"

"I want that," said the boy, eyes trained on a fudge sundae being brought to a nearby table.

"Dom," snapped Asher. "Fudge sundae for the boy."

"I'll make it right away, sir."

"No—that one. The other table can wait."

"Right you are." He dropped the dish down before Adam.

"Smart boy," said Hadassah. "You were telling us about your mother."

"She doesn't leave the apartment."

"Such a shame. And for such a pretty girl. She was a pretty girl, wasn't she, Zev."

"She wasn't so pretty," he muttered into his glass.

"And your sister? What sort of girl is she? Much help?"

"No help at all," Asher said, and Hadassah took note of his bitterness. "She's a college girl. Boards at Barnard. The train would take just an hour. Four hundred dollars a year to board there and it saves just an hour a day."

"Two hours, surely," said Hadassah. "She's got to come back, after all." She stirred her drink but didn't drink it. "Our niece, Penelope, is also at Barnard. I wonder if they know one another."

Zev took a large drink and lost interest in the conversation. His eyes scanned the room: the beige plaster walls with timber posts running through them like the outside of a Bavarian market; the dark oak panels with streaks from a sponge, evidence of nightly cleaning; the decorative row of large ceramic beer steins. He thought of Austria, of youth. Beside him, Adam slurped at a melted spoonful of ice cream, and Zev curled his lip, disgusted, a reaction that did not escape Hadassah. She briskly changed her tone.

"I'd like to meet your mother," she said to Asher, for while she quite liked the boy, there was still the matter of proving to Zev that her own stock was better—none of this sneering at her son. So what if Adam enjoyed his sweets? He was of Morfawitz blood and deserved every good thing he got. "You said she didn't get out much. Well, it's a boy's duty to take out his mother when she gets lonely. I'm sure she's quite lonely. Why don't you bring her down."

There was no hint of an upward inflection, no dressing up the demand as a question. Asher wondered what he'd done wrong. He looked to his father as if he might step in to reverse the demand, but Zev was not paying attention. Asher cleared his throat and went wordlessly to fetch his mother. Ten minutes later they came back to the table; Asher had fixed up his hair and Leah had thrown a black coat over her nightdress. The skin hung off her once youthful face. She looked, moon-eyed, at Zev, and then at Hadassah, and finally down at the table.

"Asher tells me that your daughter is at Barnard," said Hadassah loudly as if speaking to a child or an immigrant. "You must be very proud."

Leah bit her lip and nodded. She wrung her hands beneath the table.

"*Anything to eat, Mom?*" said Hadassah, nudging Asher.

He looked around to see if any of the waiters were watching before repeating in a low voice hardly more than a whisper: "Anything to eat, Mom?"

"I . . . I already ate," she said. She looked up for a friendly face and her eyes finally rested on Adam. She smiled at him. "Is . . . is this your son? Such a . . . such a beautiful boy. Isn't the ice cream wonderful, young man? I always think that the ice cream here is wonderful . . ."

Adam said nothing but kept on eating the sundae. Hadassah took the spoon from his fingers and placed it in the bowl, then slid the dish across the table so that it sat before Leah, who looked down at it terrified as if the thing were a coiled snake.

"We wouldn't want you to go back to bed hungry," said Hadassah. "Not after we woke you up to join us."

"I wasn't asleep," said Leah, but she seemed uncertain. She looked down at her wristwatch as if to confirm that it was not yet her bedtime.

"Don't be polite, dear," said Hadassah. She reached across and pushed the sundae closer to Leah. "Eat."

Asher looked between his mother and Hadassah and said nothing. Leah raised the spoon to her mouth and took a bite of the now liquid sundae.

"Well," said Hadassah, standing. "It's getting to be that time."

"Stay for a drink," said Asher. "We'll have one at the bar. I'll put Mom to bed."

"Nonsense, dear. You sit with your mother while she eats. But we ought to see more of you. Come visit us sometime in the city. Wouldn't that be nice, Zev?"

"Very nice."

"How about Shabbos next Friday. He ought to meet the family. Wouldn't that be nice?"

"Very nice."

Hadassah looked at Asher, saw the eagerness in his face, and wanted to break it.

"And his sister ought to come, too. She can take the car down from Morningside with Penny. That's that, and I won't hear another excuse."

"That's that," said Asher, and out of habit: "Your dinner, of course, is on the house."

Leah smiled up at her son's magnanimity and Hadassah took note of this comfort.

"My husband," she said, to no one, to everyone, "is the house. Don't forget it."

"No," said Asher, and he saw them to the door.

VI
ASHER

Asher was sure to arrive early for Shabbos. Nobody had taught him that extreme earliness was just as unwelcome as its opposite. Nobody had taught him many things. He was a masterful host but had never truly been a guest, and Baumann's, though popular, was not exactly a five-star restaurant. Certainly, Asher had never attended a religious function before in his life.

He brought an expensive triple-crème, which he'd specially ordered as a gift, but—being dairy—it could not be served on the same evening as a meal involving meat, which the Morfawitz household invariably had on Friday evenings. Asher knew quite a bit about meat, but the wrapped tenderloin that he'd brought as a gift was from the hindquarters of the animal, and so was not even allowed in the apartment on the basis of its being *traif.* And so, after being relieved of his two gifts by the servant and traded for a gin martini, he sat in the sitting room of the mansion crossing his legs one way and then the other, drinking his gin far too quickly. He was unused to silence. When he finally heard voices coming to join him, he stood upright, very stiff, twice switched the hand that was holding his drink, before simply throwing it back and setting the empty glass down on the table.

Abby was the first to enter the room, and she looked vaguely annoyed. Penny had decided not to come after all but had sent a sort of ambassador in her place, who was easily the most beautiful woman Asher had ever seen. She wore her hair long and straight and tucked into the gold temples of her lilac-tinted glasses, like the photographs Asher had seen of Gloria Steinem. She did not remove the glasses indoors. Her blue jeans and white blouse were a far cry from the opulence of the sitting room, but rather than seeming inappropriately casual, she instead made Asher feel suddenly ridiculous in his suit.

"My brother," said Abby. "Daphne."

She smiled at him without quite extending her hand, and Asher was hard-pressed to move his limbs at all but was saved from the faux pas of lovestruck paralysis, for just then Hadassah and Zev entered from the far side of the room.

"Asher, dear," she said, kissing him on both cheeks. She saw his martini on the table and quickly put a coaster beneath it. "Well, let's all sit."

Asher found his place card down by the head of the table, between Daphne on one side and Naphtali on the other. Naphtali seemed to know all about him; everybody seemed to know all about him. Nobody seemed to remember that the Kolitzes had lived there once. Memories of that family had been erased from the walls; every portrait, every photograph was of one or another of the Morfawitz clan. Even Amanda Kolitz, at the far end of the table, seemed hardly to exist.

Naphtali started right off with politics. What, he ostensibly wanted to know, was Asher's opinion on Vietnam. Immediately he launched into his own account of the war. "If you want to know all about it. I was shipped out for the Japanese theater in the winter of that final year . . ." He'd told the story so many times that it came off his tongue like the practiced fiction that it was, and the rest of the table did not bother to listen. Asher might have been enthralled with Naphtali's tales of war had Daphne not settled down beside him. Her soft milk-white skin brushed against his forearm. His polished shoes touched the canvas of her sneakers, and he opened his mouth to introduce himself, but just then Naphtali leaned forward over the corner of the table so that his face was just before Asher's.

"Have you ever been to war?" he asked him.

Asher was conscious of the sweet perfume of Daphne to his left and the hungry, bellicose breath of his uncle to his right. He managed to shake his head and Naphtali retreated, clearly disappointed.

"Oh, thank god," said Daphne, with a hand above her heart. "I don't go in for that sort of thing. War, I mean. I don't go in for war. We don't. None of us do. I'm sure your sister's told you all about it, hasn't she? She's just joined but I'm sure she has. Hasn't she? Good. I always like somebody to know a thing before I tell them about it. I don't like spilling the beans, I mean. They can get very touchy about what I say. What *we* say, I mean. Especially to boys." She looked up and added for the benefit of Naphtali, "Or men." But he was not paying attention.

"So then," she continued, her voice like a runaway train, "you work in the business, like all the rest of them?"

"Of who?"

"Of the Morfawitzes, of course. They all work in the business. You are one of them, aren't you? Penny said you were. She said that they all work in the business. She won't, of course. What with inequality and the homeless being more important than building fancy new houses, and with saving the planet more important than murdering cows. We got all mixed up with the environmentalists when we started, just to have the numbers up. Now we're up, and they're not pulling their own weight, if you ask me. Or if you ask us, rather. Really, Penny is the one you'd want to ask. But of course, you know all about Penny."

"No," said Asher. "I don't."

"That's right," said Daphne. She raised a hand to her mouth. "I've been awfully stupid. Penny *did* tell me all about it. Well, Annie is already—"

"Abby."

"Abby is already signed up for our committee. It's important that we have a few like her, who can speak about having been raised by"—she dropped her voice to a whisper—"single mothers. We think it's awful how little support she was given from the start. Penny and I do, at least, but I'm sure Abby feels the same."

Asher had never considered himself to have been raised by a single mother; by his estimation, it was he who had done the raising. He picked up his fork.

"Oh," she said. "But of course, you don't like to talk about it. How would I like it if a perfect stranger started asking me all sorts of questions about my family? And of course, it's very inappropriate to talk about your mother, us being where we are. No, we'd better not."

She'd been whispering the entire time but when Asher looked up, he saw Hadassah watching from the far end of the table. It was a reptilian glare, like that of an adder about to strike out with her fangs, not because she hates you, but because you have trod near her nest.

When it came time for the guests to leave, a chorus of "same time next week" was extended to all, but when Zev made the mistake of saying it to Daphne, Hadassah was quick to correct him. "He means, dear," she said, with a voice that had taken on the false sweetness of a maraschino cherry, "that it was nice to have met you."

It was clear to everyone that the vitriol was meant for Daphne, but Zev was not everyone. He did not like to be overruled. Suddenly, he looked around at the opulence of his holding box and felt himself to be a sort of caged animal. On the stone wall above the table was a Kolitz heirloom, a timeworn tapestry of hunting scenes, and his eyes were drawn to the dogs, to the brown-spotted white bodies of the German short-haired pointers whose weaving wool was not even dyed and appeared pallid yellow, the color of a low moon seen through the smog-filled air of Brooklyn. He felt in his bones his tameness, his domesticity, and suddenly longed to walk through the wilds, through the night and the darkness, to watch the breath escape his lips in wisps of smoke and rise into evening air unwarmed by central heat or even fire.

"I'll drive you home," he said suddenly to Asher. Everybody stopped their goodbyes and stared; favors were uncommon for Zev. A tension seemed to emanate from Hadassah as if she were a maelstrom pulling at the fabric of space. To escape the mounting pressure, the guests quickly made their murmured goodbyes. Abby and Daphne went through the front door and everyone else went to their rooms. Only Asher, Zev, and Hadassah remained.

"I'm sure he wants to be free of us," she said. "He'll take a car."

"I'll drive you home," Zev said again, not daring to look at his wife. His cheeks were flushed with wine. Hadassah said nothing to her husband but beckoned for Asher instead. He looked between his two hosts and Hadassah took note that he did not answer her call until Zev gave him a nod of the head. Things might have gone differently if he'd gone straightaway.

"Asher, dear," Hadassah said to him quietly as Zev went to fetch his keys. "I want you to remember something. You are, no doubt, a very smart boy who has had to deal with his fair share of problems. But while my husband may like you as a plaything and while my brother may like you as a new audience, know that neither will respect you if you stay here forever. They'll put you to work and they'll make you a rich boy, but you'll always be a boy. And the longer you stay the harder it will be to leave. Roots are like that. Well, good night."

As soon as her footsteps had died away, Zev returned. Asher had the impression that he'd been waiting for Hadassah to leave, that he was a little afraid of his wife.

Zev drove with the windows open so as to have no need or opportunity to speak. That was fine by Asher. Speeding down the FDR Drive with the cool air of early spring roaring all around him, he felt no desire to talk. None at all. There was tension in his heart. Brooklyn now was the thing across the water, the vast darkness with small squares of yellow light. For so long it had been the reverse, with Manhattan as his destination, that he now felt he was looking out from the inside of a mirror. It was a mirror in which he'd seen the version of himself that he wanted to be; he had stepped through the plane of glass and now he was his own dreamlike reflection, looking out at himself as he was.

They flew across the bridge and Asher saw the light of his own bedroom window go by, saw the silhouette of Leah standing in hers. They drove past without stopping.

"I know a place," said Zev. "I'll teach you a thing about women."

The air crackled with his excitement: not purely sexual excitement—though that was there, too—but the excitement of a child who is going to break the rules. Asher thought of saying no, but he knew he could not. He cherished the chance to know his father better; he did not know that Zev's sole notions of fatherhood had come from war-torn Europe, where officers would take their doomed young cadets to the windowless hovel where a ruined town's young women had avoided one form of destruction and been saved for another.

They parked outside a red-shingled house beside a narrow alley. Deep in its darkness a yellow light buzzed above the door and threw the father's and son's shadows out behind them as they approached, long at first but then shorter and shorter, until there was nothing behind them but a puddle of dark. "Patrick," said the woman who answered the door. Zev nodded but looked beyond her, eager eyes scanning the dimly lit room. "Who's your friend?"

"My son," said Zev, patting Asher on the back. Asher looked down at the welcome mat and thought that for the thinness of the woman's face, her feet were surprisingly fat. They poured over her black slippers and she had hardly any ankles. "My son. Also Patrick."

"Patrick," said the woman, looking him up and down. "Katelyn. How old are you, Patrick? Do you take whiskey neat or with breast milk?"

"He's old enough."

"Neat, then."

"We aren't here to drink whiskey."

"But you'll have a drink anyway. Because you are here. At my house."

Zev stared at her with blankness in his eyes and Asher felt that the world risked splitting apart if his father's path were not followed. But the blankness passed and Zev nodded.

"Good. You go on in and my girls will be in with it soon. Both of you go on in."

They sat on a rough horsehair couch. The cushions were deep and seemed to pull them toward the ground with uncommon force. They sat, saying nothing. Asher counted seconds by heartbeats, and the seconds moved fast. Then they heard the girls coming.

Both the girls were called Shannon, and both men were introduced as Patrick. There was no question as to which girl was meant for each.

Zev's was the better looking of the two, but Asher didn't mind. His Shannon brought him whiskey.

"Mam said to bring it with milk," she said. Her voice was strangely delicate, and she gave the impression that she could endure great physical pain but might shatter if she were spoken to harshly. "But I didn't put none in. I'm glad I didn't. You don't look so young as Mam says."

"Is she your . . ."

"Mother? No. Ha ha. You hear that, he asked if you were my mother."

"Sweet thing."

"My mother. Well, I bet you aren't so sweet as you look. He really your father then?" Asher nodded. "Then certainly not so sweet as you look."

"Is your name really Shannon?" he said.

She smiled at him. "No."

Asher finished his whiskey and she led him upstairs, and when it was over, she led him back down again and then went off to sleep. It had not taken long. He sank back into the horsehair couch and went to sleep himself, dreamt of her milk-white skin, the constellations of pink freckles, her body moving slowly, almost in stop-motion, with her heavy breasts hanging off her ribs and her eyes alight with pleasure that he knew was insincere. But he felt the sincerity of her wanting him to believe it, and that was better for him, in a way; her lying had been kind.

It was past midnight when he awoke to Zev gently slapping his face. His father's hands were damp and smelled of soap; his hair was wet and combed. They did not speak until the car pulled up in front of the apartment building on Broadway, in the shadow of the Williamsburg Bridge, the abandoned savings bank blotting out a dome-shaped section of the stars. Asher remembered vaguely that it was Zev who owned the buildings.

"Here's what you'll do," said Zev. "That girl from dinner. You'll call her tomorrow. You treat her no differently than you treated Shannon."

"Shannon," said Asher. "Do you know her real name?"

"It's Shannon. If she tells you it's Shannon, it's Shannon. Don't go inventing reasons to feel badly for somebody else. If you think something is wrong, then it is weak of you to do it; true freedom is refusing to believe that anything is wrong."

"Yes, sir," said Asher. He felt a strange surge of happiness. It was the liberation of the fathered son, who can transmute his sins to virtues by the magic of his father's law.

Asher slept, and in the morning he took the train to visit Daphne. He tried to treat her the same, but he could not; he knew her name, for one. For another, half the time she spoke he was struggling to understand just what she meant; she spoke in quotations and statistics, in obscure facts and other people's arguments. Asher wondered if she knew what she was saying half the time. They walked through Central Park for three hours, and he felt that he learned a great deal about the works of Henry David Thoreau and the sexism implied by the phallic shapes of Manhattan's towers as they rose above the Great Lawn's southern canopy of trees and the difference between the Mandarin duck and the mallard, but he learned nothing about Daphne, and finally, he dropped her back at her dormitory. He watched her go and thought of Shannon, who at least was honest in the way she moved across his body.

For three months this life carried on. He counted time by Sabbaths. By the thirteenth one, he felt truly a part of the family and mouthed along when blessings were spoken, but an undeniable change had gone through him. He wanted desperately to see Manhattan as his home and Brooklyn as a place only fit for slumming; to see Zev and Hadassah as his parents and Leah as a sad stand-in or surrogate mother who had given him nothing but a rental in her womb; to see Daphne as the ideal of a what a real woman was like and Shannon as nothing but a cheap and easy pleasure, like a dive bar or a ten-cent slice. He knew the arguments for a better life, but in his heart he could find no conviction.

He began to worry, too, that his roots were extending too far into the concrete soil. He had never noticed the enlistment posters before, but he noticed them now—they were everywhere. They asked, like his uncle, if he was prepared to serve his country. They asked if he was a man, if he had ever gone to war. And every Friday night as Hadassah kissed him on either cheek, she reminded him that to his father, he would always be a boy.

* * *

Mid-July. He lay one evening in Shannon's arms on a wafer-thin mattress
that had been pulled out onto the fire escape. An impoverished heat
plagued the third-floor apartment. The walls insulated to keep in sound
had kept in heat as well. By comparison, the summer night was cool,
and by the moonlight he counted freckles on Shannon's pale arms. He
looked between the girl and the moon but thought instead of Daphne.
He wondered what she felt like, or if she were real at all; had she been
so inoculated to the animal pleasures of touch and comfort, smell and
sex, and so seduced by the fictions of virtue and right, of wrong and
restriction, that she'd ceased to be real? Shannon and her calloused white
palms, sticky with sweat and with grime—did these exist because he
could touch them? In which world were the greater pleasures—in which
the more severe pains?

He lifted Shannon's arm and slipped out from underneath it. They
had closed the window and the window was locked. Wind blew through
the alley below and Shannon stirred.

"Are you going?" she mumbled without opening her eyes.

"I was trying the window. Zev might be waiting."

"Patrick," she said. "You're all Patrick."

"Patrick might be waiting."

"I've got to tell Patrick something. You Patrick. I've got to tell Patrick
something."

"Tell me then. I wouldn't want to keep him waiting."

"I'll tell Patrick," she said. "I'll tell . . ."

She turned over in her sleep, showed her back to the moon so that
the white skin curled tight around her spine and outlined the back of
her ribs. Asher pulled the blanket over her and climbed down the fire
escape, gently lowering the fire ladder at the bottom and then pushing it back up once his feet had touched the ground. He walked north,
out of Bay Ridge and along the promenade of Brooklyn Heights. The
light of the moon was interrupted by the shadows of towers across the
water, its white reflection cast in the rippled surface of the crawling East

River like the spine of some great being lying facedown with its head or its feet in the west. Like Shannon, or whatever her name was. The walk home was quiet—silent, even—and he could not tell if his heart had slowed to match the pace of his feet or if he'd slowed in his steps to match the cadence of his heart. When he came to his house he wanted to drink or to speak, but the beer hall was closed, and besides, there had been nobody there whom Asher could really speak with for a very long time. His mother was asleep, and there was no one to talk to. It seemed to him that the whole of planet earth was unconscious, but he lay awake all night.

When he went to see Daphne in the morning, she was sleeping, too. He had passed by the gate that was meant to keep boys out of Barnard and went straight to her dormitory. He knocked twice, and she, thinking it was a friend at the door, answered in her nightclothes.

"Oh," she said when she saw him, shrinking back into the room.

"I want to come in," he said. In his insomniac daze, he grabbed at her wrist.

"Oh," she said again, squirming free.

"I want to touch you. Don't you want to touch me?"

"Oh, I . . . wait outside and I'll put some clothes on. No really, you must. I'll only be a minute."

He waited half an hour before the door opened again. Out stepped Daphne, looking as clean and perfected as a Victorian painting. "Now," she said, in a similarly antiseptic voice. "That's much better, isn't it? To meet like real people, not go barging into one another's rooms. And me in nothing but night things."

"I liked you in night things."

"And with nothing on my face! Well, let's go."

They went. They walked through the park as they always did, and she told him once more about how much wrongness was in the world and Asher heard in his mind the words of his father and with each thing Daphne condemned he saw a cuff snap shut around her.

"And so you see," she said, "even if I *wanted* to. Which I'm *not* saying I do, but *even if* I did, I couldn't. It wouldn't be right. Oh, sure, it would be fun. But anybody can have fun, so if you want to really count you can't let that entice you. Well, not everybody . . . I mean, there are so many people who can't, isn't that right? Isn't it right that it's wrong for two people to be so happy just because they want to be? Why, we'd be no better than Dante's incontinent souls, like Francesca and Paolo, reading about Lancelot and not getting very far. Well, *I* don't want to be blown about like that by my desires for all eternity. Do you?"

Asher stopped walking and stared at her. "Do you even believe in God?"

"God? God no. But you can *not* believe in God and still realize that you'd like your own two feet on the ground, can't you? Oh, there isn't any use in my trying to tell you."

She took him by the hand and led him several minutes on a path he'd never noticed. There were many paths he had never noticed. Now he began to. The wind was strong at their backs and the going was easy. They walked until they stood before a tree surrounded by shrubs.

Daphne approached the tree like an oracle approaching an altar: reverent, yes, but also a little terrified of the things that she might learn. Her outstretched fingers trembled as they made contact with the bark. Behind her, Asher drew closer until he saw what grooves her fingers danced in: what their curve was, what their shape. Carved deep into the wood was a sentence. It read:

> Next time you want to hear me speak
> You'll have to snap a branch off first.

Daphne's fingers lingered on the *b* and then she flattened her palm against the wood and looked up. It all seemed very practiced. Asher followed her gaze up the cow-spotted bark of the great London plane to where the first limb stuck out not ten feet from the ground.

"Look closely," she said. He looked closely. "There's a ring there that is not even a year old, burned into the bark by a rope pulled tight against it. Her name was Erica."

Asher found the pale ring. "Someone hung herself here?"

"Yes," said Daphne. "Or, no. Not quite. She tried to."

"Unsuccessfully."

"Yes. Well, you don't have to look so disgusted by it. I mean, she tried her best."

He was quiet for a moment. "You said 'was.'"

"Was?"

"You said, 'Her name was Erica.' But her name *is* Erica. She's alive."

"Why are you so focused on alive or dead? How can you be so myopic? Don't you understand the point?"

"No."

"The point is that somebody tried to kill herself here to escape the cruel reality of late twentieth-century America. The point is that the grave injustices served up here and there by the world are so great that normal people—people like you and me—are so disheartened that they want out, that they'd rather kill themselves than live in such a world."

"She didn't kill herself," he said. His fingers were balled into fists and he pressed his knuckles into the bark. "You mean that you enjoyed her little act."

"I mean," said Daphne, "that how can anybody be selfish enough to think about flirtatious love, about casual sex, when such suffering exists in the world?"

The fight went out of Asher's shoulders and he stood there and began to laugh. The day was beautiful and the sun on his shoulders felt warm.

"You mean," he said, "how can anybody live while others are dead."

"That's what I mean," she said, and then covered her mouth with her hand. She leaned back against the tree, felt against the bare skin of her shoulder the carved quotes of environmentalist groups and women's liberation groups and the martyrdom awe of a suicide tree. A part of her longed to be held and kissed, but she could not separate the things she felt from the things she was being told to feel. She insisted that her skin had been cruelly carved into with the knives of society's ailments and woes, but to Asher, her skin only looked lovely and youthful, pink in the warm morning sun.

Her voice was another matter. She rambled on now, but he did not know what she was saying and he did not think that she knew either. He became suddenly aware that although she was speaking, the words didn't have any meaning to anyone, but especially not to him, especially not to her. They were only noise, breath twisted into sounds and phonics. Between their bodies played a different conversation and to try to put it into words would have cheapened it and so he left it there, silent as a shadow. He turned around and walked away, walked out of the park, down Fifth Avenue, down Madison, down past the glowing lights in all the windows. He did not stop walking until he found himself on the apex of the Williamsburg Bridge, and suddenly he looked up and turned around with the feeling of having just woken up and not knowing where he was. He looked back to the city and decided the buildings were like Daphne's words, holographic and meaningless, placeholders, cosmetic solutions dabbed over raw rock and earth. How hard must the rock at the tip of Manhattan be, he thought, to have withstood such powers of erosion as the Hudson and the East Rivers? The heat overwhelmed him. He sat down with his back to the river and his face to the river, too, and to the twin bridges to the south and then the silhouette of Lady Liberty like a woman's shadow at night, and he wept. He went back home and kissed his mother on the cheek.

She was weeping, too. "Bubbala . . ." she said. She pointed to the living room. Sitting there was Shannon. His Shannon. The part of his life in which she existed was so far removed from his mother's living room that he could not exactly see her. He once again had the feeling of having just woken up without knowing where he was. He squinted at her.

"It's Shannon," she said.

"I know." And then: "What's your real name?"

She stared at him for a moment without answering. "Cleo," she said. "It's short for Cliodhna. Awful name. It means 'banshee queen' in Old Gaelic. Or at least it was the name of a banshee queen. I was never certain which."

"It's not an awful name."

"It's awful," she said. "Banshee queen."

"Mother," said Asher. "Go into the other room and shut the door."

"Oh, she already knows all about it," said Cleo.

"About what?"

"What do you think, about what?" She put a hand to her belly. "I tried to tell you last night but then you ran away."

"You were asleep."

"You snuck down the fire escape like a rat."

"Cleo," he said, sitting down beside the window. "I like that name. It's your real one, isn't it?"

"Yes," she said. "Is Asher Morfawitz yours?"

Asher turned around and looked at his mother. "She knew it was Morfawitz . . . she was worried about money . . . I told her she shouldn't be worried about money. My son's a . . . a rich, rich boy . . ."

"Don't blame her," said Cleo. "It's you who said the name Zev. You don't hear the name Zev very often. I found his picture in the paper."

Asher looked out the window, back toward Manhattan at the glittering towers glowing orange in the sun.

"You shouldn't be worried about money."

"I don't want him to grow up without a father."

"Go home, Cleo," he said. "I need to sleep. I'll come and see you in the morning. We'll work out what to do when I come see you in the morning."

"Early," she said, attempting to be stern but now unable to hide her excitement. "You make sure he's up early," she said to Leah, with whom she was now trying to ingratiate herself as a daughter, already preparing for a life of familial relations. Leah nodded and finally went into her room and closed the door.

After a sleepless night and many miles on foot, Asher sank into the chair by the window, watching the sunset deepening by its orange to red to purple reflections in the windows of towers across the glittering river. He saw two lives spread out before him: one born of morality and one born of desire. Shades of gray did not sit well with him, and in his mind he wondered what would be the difference between Daphne's rejection of his physical touch on the basis of some arbitrary code of ethics and his own acceptance of a worse life only to satisfy some anachronistic ideas about the role a father ought to play. He thought of going to his father for advice, but he remembered Hadassah's words: "*He will always see you as a boy.*" The credo pulled at his heart as if a hook were caught there, and looking at the reflected fire across the river, the burning river itself, the lost and empty space above it, he decided he would incinerate this moral mind of his, he would drown it, he would lose it.

By the time Leah rose in the morning, her son was gone; he had not gone to begin a life of paternal duty in Bay Ridge with a pregnant Irish whore, but to begin his ethical purge. For burning, there would be napalm; for drowning, swamp; for losing himself, a jungle on the far side of the world. He packed a light bag and walked to the enlistment station on Avenue I, and five weeks later he was there.

VII
HERSH

With her husband's illegitimate and fast-rising progeny out of the way, one might think that Hadassah was finally given over to some hard-earned rest; at the very least, she herself might have reasonably expected that Zev's weekly escapades in Brooklyn would stop or slow down. But Zev had an excuse waiting in hand.

"That's a strong business he's built there," Zev told her. "It makes money. With the boy gone, somebody has got to run the business."

This was a half truth somewhat typical of Zev; for while it was true that the business did, in fact, need somebody to run it, it was also true that somebody had already stepped into this function. This somebody had been previously unknown to Asher, except as a small matter of payroll, and entirely unknown to Zev, who hadn't stepped foot within the restaurant since his dinner there with his wife and his son until he went there the day Asher failed to show up for their appointment.

* * *

And now it is finally time to introduce Hersh, the worst of the lot, by my estimation, though he seems to be most people's favorite.

After he'd gone on to do the many, many things that he would do, people would commonly ask what Hersh had been like as a child. Always they got the same answer from anybody who knew him: he was a sneak, always sneaking, always doing sneaky things. Slyness came naturally to him. He had an aversion to walking down the middle of a room and always knew where to step so that his footsteps wouldn't squeak. Hersh told lies, not for gain, but only to see what sort of things might be believed. In a pinch, he could outrun the fastest cop. The only person he feared in the whole world was his father, and this was because the old man was immune to his charms.

Another child of Zev's countless, careless escapades, Hersh was born to a widower in Jersey City. Despite a comfortable home life, Hersh grew up tough—he sought out toughness. He eschewed the local Yeshiva boys outside of school and was decidedly the only Jew in the neighborhood gang known as the Cambridge Aces. By the time he was fifteen, he could recite the Talmud straight through by heart and also hot-wire a car. He left Jersey City as soon as he could and—deciding that one river was not enough distance—crossed the East River as well into Brooklyn. His father's identity was never kept from Hersh, and he studied the man from afar like a poem, watched him and rewatched him, tried out his phrases and made sure he had a feel for his cadence. Hersh understood that the man was probably immune to flattery and had never seen him smile except in the presence of a beautiful woman. Also, Hersh was wisely apprehensive as to how Hadassah might react to his existence, though he probably was not apprehensive enough. He watched quietly as his half brother Asher was admitted into the Morfawitzes' inner circle, and he made his own quiet advances into the vacuum that Asher was leaving behind in Brooklyn.

Hersh started working at Baumann's Beer Hall in December of 1968. He began as a dishwasher and barback, but quickly made his way into the desirable position of a waiter. Here is how it happened: On Christmas night, he was bringing a tray of used mugs from the bar to the kitchen when a waiter named Igor lightly poked him in the gut and called him *detka*. "Better fatten up, *detka*," is what he said. "Those scrawny arms won't last a week." He poked young Hersh again.

Later that night, when Hersh was coming back out of the kitchen with a tray of clean mugs, he supposedly tripped on the leg of someone's chair, toppled forward, and hurled the tray across the room, striking Igor clean in the chest and face. Once he had cleaned up the mess, Hersh was told by the manager that he was fired. Hersh begged and pleaded and spoke about how badly he needed the money, and finally pointed out that it was early in the evening on what was bound to be the busiest night of the year, and the manager was now a waiter short. "Let me work for tips tonight in Igor's place," he pleaded. "And at least I'll have a little cash to get me through the holidays."

The manager begrudgingly agreed. He was surprised as everybody else when, as they pooled their tips at the end of the night, Hersh had collected three times as much as the next best waiter. What's more, he insisted that a third of his share go to Igor, a third to the manager for allowing Hersh to work, and a third to remain in the pot for everybody else to divide. He himself would take nothing, if only they'd let him keep his job. Everybody agreed that Hersh should be elevated to the position of waiter, at least to fill in for Igor during the holiday rush, which became a permanent position when, two days later, Igor died of unknown causes in his home.

Hersh went on to have a spectacular but short-lived career as a waiter at Baumann's Beer Hall. Patrons either loved or hated him for his surly manners and tart tongue. That New Year's Eve, the wife of Brooklyn's Concrete King warned the manager—who relayed the warning to Hersh—that expensive champagne ought to be served in flutes without the slightest smudge. Hersh returned several minutes later asking, "Alright, which one of you ordered the clean glass?"

So complaints poured in but they were balanced by the tips. It was not long before many of Hersh's customers became regulars. On three consecutive nights, multiple groups of his favorites showed up, and—as he couldn't be on all their tables at once—he spent the three nights schmoozing at tables that weren't his and letting his own charges go unserved. "Hershey," the manager said on the third night as they pooled tips at the end of the shift, "if you're going to do all the talking and none of the serving, maybe we ought to switch jobs." He laughed but laughed alone; Hersh pulled out four hundred-dollar bills—one from each table that wasn't his—and dropped them into the till.

"Maybe he ought to," said the cashier, breaking down the large bills into something more distributable. The waiters took a vote, and that's exactly what they did.

This was around the time that Asher was beginning to abandon his responsibilities at the business in order to spend more time with the Morfawitz family in Manhattan, where they had expanded from shipping into real estate, consumer goods, and public relations. The restaurant business now seemed lowly to Asher, and he left its operation largely to the manager. So the role that Hersh stepped into, which had once been bound in its powers to the hiring and firing of waiters, now became limitless. By the time Zev walked into the place after Asher had failed to show up to their appointment, Hersh had effectively usurped control of his older half brother's steak house.

* * *

When Zev arrived at Baumann's Beer Hall, it was early in the morning and the place had yet to open. He hadn't stepped foot in his restaurant for over a year, and it occurred to him now that he didn't have a working key. He had to ring the bell several times before the night porter answered the door. The porter didn't know who he was. The waiter who was polishing the long mahogany bar didn't know who he was. The barback who was filling up expensive and half-empty bottles of scotch whiskey with a cheap house blend didn't know who he was. They accepted in a reluctant sort of way that he really did own the place, and yet they wouldn't let him back into the kitchen.

"We really ought to wait for Hersh," was all anybody said.

"Where's Asher," said Zev. "I want to see Asher."

"Asher," said the barback. He squeezed a cork back into a slender green bottleneck. "Haven't seen Asher in months."

"In months? But he lives just upstairs."

"You ought to talk to Hersh."

The barback had poured the cheap whiskey up above the brim of the bottle and now went off to wash his hands, and perhaps to fetch this Hersh.

Zev did not hear his son approaching and was surprised to feel a hand against his shoulder. Then he looked into Hersh's face and was surprised to see his own—younger, thinner, but certainly his own—staring back at him. The resemblance was so uncanny that even Zev, who was notoriously slow to recognize the fruit of his sins, could not deny that the man before him shared his blood. He could even guess at the boy's mother.

"It's Miriam, then," were the first words he said to his son. Hersh, who was so used to playing off his counterparts' adherence to social norms, was caught speechless for the first time in his life. He nodded and his face turned red. Even the barback was embarrassed for his silence and went back to diligently polishing the already immaculate bottles.

"Well, then," said Zev. "I suppose you know who I am. I'm looking for Asher. Does he know?"

Hersh shook his head.

"Where is he?"

"Asher isn't home?"

"Listen, boy," said Zev. "I know your mother didn't mind the lies I told her so maybe she didn't mind yours either. I do."

"He's gone," said Hersh quickly. "Left yesterday morning. Packed a bag and walked to the Union Jack. He'll be halfway to Vietnam by now."

If this bothered Zev, it was not out of any paternal affection he had for Asher. Rather, he'd spent so much of his life running away from war and he was shocked that a sensible boy like Asher would go chasing after it. He thought his progeny cleverer than that. To a man like Zev, for whom wealth and power were paramount, and who had achieved both of those things, it was impossible to comprehend the subtle depressions and dissatisfactions that plagued young Asher's mind. In some ways, Asher had been much happier before being introduced into the world of his father and the lavish absurdities that Manhattan had to offer. Once upon a time, he'd felt that by running a small restaurant on the bad side of town he'd been doing fairly well for himself; now he understood the vastness of space and opportunity, and the panic he felt was something like the opposite of vertigo. But Zev understood none of that and could not think what on earth would have made the young man choose a war on the other side of the world over an apprenticeship aboard the fast-rising engine of the family Morfawitz.

"What the hell is in Vietnam anyway?" he wondered aloud.

Hersh then saw through the window that his secret weapon for trapping his father was arriving just in time. Two knocks came from the door, and Hersh moved to open it. Zev grabbed him by the arm, and Hersh was surprised at how much raw strength was in his father's hands. "Hold it," said Zev. "How do you know he really went?"

"I had somebody follow him," said Hersh, his sly confidence returning.

Zev nodded his head as if this was no great surprise. "And did you have somebody follow the rest of our family? Did you have somebody follow me?"

"No," said Hersh. "I followed you myself."

The knock came once more from the door.

"I really ought to get that."

Zev was frustrated. This boy, who was clearly his son, did not seem to understand the state of things, or who could and could not be followed, or who owned the place, or who—ultimately—was keeping everyone employed. He opened his mouth to voice these grievances, and to make a general declaration as to who, in fact, wore the pants at Baumann's Beer Hall, but then the door opened and his tongue went slack. For while it was evident that Hersh did not understand a great many things, it was also evident that he did understand some other things very well.

Her name was Iona. She was a foreign exchange student from Sweden whose studies hadn't quite panned out. She had no interest whatsoever in the restaurant industry, but Hersh had promised her better pay and fewer hours than anybody else could, and the fact was that Iona was a rather lazy girl. She was also not immune to the charms of men, although Hersh was careful that she would have no cause to think of him as someone of interest, and also to make sure the waiters knew to keep their distance. He was counting on Iona to entice Zev into spending more time at the restaurant and to take notice of who was running the place. Also, he'd planned it very well and made certain that she was receptive to sneaking in a good word or two on his behalf.

Hersh hadn't exactly known when Zev would be coming around, only that Zev's free time was during this block in the morning, and so had ordered Iona to come there daily under the guise that she was there for an interview. Really, she'd already been hired, but Hersh understood that if he could appeal to both Zev's love of women and his love of power, then he could expect to see quite a lot of his father. When Iona came in and handed in her résumé to Hersh, he barely even looked it over before putting it down on the bar.

"Thanks," he told her. "But we aren't hiring."

"Please," she said. "I'll do any kind of work. You'll see in my experience section that I've been a hostess for three years now at The Palm, which I would travel to from my studies at Columbia, which you'll see in my education section. But now I've graduated and am looking for more than part-time work and also to move out of the city. That's my address there in the header."

None of this was true. She'd been studying at Brooklyn College, not Columbia, and had never stepped foot in The Palm. Also, she was living in Queens. The story was a fabrication they'd rehearsed beforehand, and Hersh realized now that it was somewhat wasted labor because it would not have mattered if she could only speak her native tongue or even barked at every customer; Zev was smitten.

"That's very impressive," said Hersh, turning back to the bar. "But we aren't hiring."

Now Zev, as if he'd been privy to their rehearsals of the scene, did exactly the thing he was meant to do.

"Not hiring? You're forgetting that I just told you to get rid of today's maître d'."

"Mark's been with us sixteen years, sir."

"Sixteen years is a long time to be in one place."

"Oh, I couldn't," said Iona. "I couldn't take somebody else's job."

Hersh winced at the clumsiness of her lie and the clear, rehearsed falsity of her dialogue. But again, he had underestimated how little Zev cared for the lack of moral character that a lie implied about the liar.

"Young woman," he said. "You can and you will. We do not have a hiring sign outside, which means that any shift we have available will have belonged to someone else. Now, this is America. You want a job here, you go and get it by being the best at it. When one takes into account that the human mind and body both erode with age, tenure and capitalism are at odds with one another."

"Well," answered Iona, willing herself to blush. "My mind and body are not so old just yet."

"We'll see," said Zev, not exactly leaving to speculation which aspect of Iona he was more interested in testing. "Now, let's go up to the office and have a proper interview."

He turned to Hersh to ask him for the key to the office, but Hersh was gone. He had left the key on the bar, with a large maroon tag on it that said OFFICE. He was waiting in the bar when Zev and Iona returned. The interview had been a glowing success. Not only was Zev able to solve the problem of Iona's unemployment, but he was also able to solve the problem of her wanting to move out of the city, for there was a soon-to-be-vacant apartment on the third floor above the restaurant, and Iona could rent it out for a portion of her wage. Her rent would be low and her wages would be high. She smiled as she left to go pack up her apartment in Queens, and Zev went up to the third floor to tell the tenants who lived there of their impending eviction.

VIII
HADASSAH'S ATTEMPT AT SECURITY

It worked. In almost no time at all, Zev was coming to the restaurant nightly, Iona was dropping jaws at the cash register, and the line to sit was longer than ever before. Hersh, familiar with the precepts of associative psychology, had Iona whisper his praises to Zev at exactly the right times. Father and son became close—much closer than Zev had been with Asher; for while Asher had been loyal and honest, Hersh became indispensable. He was willing to do anything to please his father—anything at all—and Zev appreciated that the legal and moral considerations and other pesky hang-ups that hampered the rest of the world were not limiting factors for his son. Hersh was glad to find a mentor who would push him to the limits of what he was able to do. He had sized up his father appropriately and felt that the favor had been returned in kind.

But they'd both forgotten about Hadassah.

For she was keenly aware of the subtle differences in her husband's attitude when he was simply finding some physical release outside of their marital bed and when he was truly involved with someone else. The first she tolerated; the second she did not. So when Iona had been working at Baumann's for a little over three weeks, Hadassah followed Zev into Brooklyn one night unannounced. She was in the door only a few minutes after him, but Zev and Iona were already gone.

"Where's my husband?" she asked Hersh at the front.

"Oh," he said. "It must be Mrs. Morfawitz. I'll go and get him right away. He's meeting now with the stewards."

Hersh was off in a flash and managed to find Zev and Iona just in the nick of time. They were pressed up against the locked and refrigerated dry-aging box in the basement, where the hindquarters were hung up to age.

"Quick," said Hersh, taking a key from his pocket, "there isn't much time."

Indeed, there was not; Hadassah didn't move with Hersh's stealth, and they heard her footsteps on the stairs. The refrigerator door closed just as Hadassah rounded the corner, with Iona firmly inside.

"Ah," said Zev with his back to the metal door. "My beautiful wife. What a lovely surprise."

"Cut the schmaltz, Zev," she said curtly. "Where is she?"

"Where is who?"

"Whoever you're shtupping down here. This has gone on long enough."

"But nothing's going on!"

"So what are you doing down here? Let me into that room."

"Getting into that room," said Hersh, inserting himself for the first time, "is exactly what he's doing down here. You see, that's where we keep all the beef. But the product is expensive—there's something north of a hundred thousand in inventory even now. So it's kept under lock and key. Asher had one key; I have the other. Or had, more like it. It's broken off now, see?"

He held up the broken stub of a key. Hadassah watched him for some time, her eyes thin and mistrusting. Then she looked at the keyhole and saw the other half stuck firmly inside. She pressed her face up to the little window but saw nothing except rows of hanging carcasses in the dim red light. She looked at the thermostat on the wall beside the door, turned the dial to make it colder, and then climbed the stairs, leaving Zev and Hersh in the basement.

"Quick," said Zev once he was sure his wife had gone. "She'll freeze to death in there."

"She won't," Hersh told him. "It's only set at thirty-four."

"Well, she won't be comfortable."

"No," Hersh agreed. "But Sweden is a cold country, and that really was the only key."

So as soon as service ended for the evening, they began to dismantle the door. It took all night and by the time they rescued Iona in the morning, she was nearly hypothermic.

"You didn't tell me you were married," she said, shivering and delirious as Zev carried her up to her room. "I would never be with a married man . . ."

"Iona," he said sternly. "Remember what I said to you about capitalism and decline when you insisted that you wouldn't take another man's job. I wear a wedding band on this finger. This is America, and one takes what he wants or else he gets nothing."

She looked down at her own bloodless white fingers. "Talk about a body in decline," she said. Her English was getting quite good.

Zev left her to sleep and went back down to the restaurant, where Hersh had coffee ready for both of them. Zev noticed that Hersh did not look tired. Something about the young man suggested he was used to getting by on very little sleep.

Zev rested the mug down on the long mahogany bar and they sat there in silence for some time. Then, Hersh's lips curled up at the corner and he started to laugh. Zev considered the evening and he, too, began to laugh. He'd just decided that he liked this son a bit more than the other when a pounding at the door interrupted the sense of gaiety that had crept into the place on the early rays of sun.

"We're closed," called Hersh through the door. "Come back at a quarter to noon."

The pounding came again and Hersh opened the door. A man stood there in a gray jumpsuit with a pair of sewn eyes as a logo on the breast patch.

"Whatever you're selling," said Hersh, "we aren't buying. Come back at a quarter to noon."

But the gray-suited man was already holding out a receipt. "You've already bought," he said. His accent was deep and Russian. "The order came in last night. Emergency rush. So here I am. Emergency rush."

"I'm telling you we don't want it."

"I'm telling you it's already paid for," said the man, shoving the receipt into Hersh's hand. "We install today."

"What is it?" asked Zev. The man had gone out to his truck, which was parked outside, with the same logo on its door. He unloaded some equipment and was carrying it back inside.

"It looks," said Hersh with a sigh, "as if your wife has purchased security cameras for the whole premises. The apartments as well. Don't you worry. Go home and get some rest. Hersh will take care of this. You'll see what sort of things your Hersh will do for his father."

Zev went home and the security man began his installation of fifty cameras on the premises. Hadassah had made sure the priority was speed and not aesthetic; here and there hung wires loose and unhidden, but despite Hersh's vocalized dismay and hostile oversight, the installer kept up his proud work like a juggernaut.

He worked tirelessly all day and was finishing up his work as the sun was going down. He had worked from the bottom up, installing cameras in every hallway, in every dining room, over every door, and now they had come to the roof. With the sun going down red-orange behind the dark steel skeleton of the Williamsburg Bridge, Hersh watched the sweat pouring from the smooth baldness of the installer's oversized head. The many beads caught the dying sunlight and glowed so that the installer had the appearance of wearing a jeweled crown, and from Hersh's tired perspective, he looked something like a peacock with its tail feathers erect, one hundred eyes afire in the waning orange light.

Hersh sat down on the parapet and began to hum. A musical mood was evoked. He got no more than thirty seconds in before the installer interrupted him.

"Quiet," he said. "Need concentrate. If you want to help, be ready to hand me camera. Need concentrate."

Indeed, Hersh noticed that the man's position was precarious at best.

He was balancing deftly on the thin edge of the parapet as he fastened a bracket to the tall post of the chimney.

"Very well," Hersh said to him. "You know you aren't very pleasant. Are you married?"

"No."

"No, I didn't think you would be," said Hersh to the man's broad back. "The reason I didn't think you would be is that you remind me very much of a friend of mine back in Jersey City. He looked like you, he acted like you. His voice even sounded like yours. He was always falling in love, but whenever he tried to verbalize his feelings, his words came out sloppy, just trembling with nerves. So he got his head into a bad way and began to imagine things. This one girl, a Stephanie, would not give him the time of day. He chased her day in and day out, until finally she was really afraid of him. Well, he didn't see it that way; he simply thought she enjoyed teasing him a little too much. So one night in the summer—a hot night like this one—he sees her walking alone down by the Hudson Waterfront and he follows her there. After a while, she catches on to his being behind her, and she breaks into a run. Our head case of a fellow thinks she is continuing the game and begins to trot himself. Desperate, she runs down a narrow little path which leads onto the banks of the river—not a pretty place, littered with glass bottles and wrappers and used condoms and syringes. Well, he thinks that she is simply luring him away somewhere with a little more privacy. But now, with nowhere else to go, she wails out and attacks him and even sprays mace in his eyes. Our fellow goes absolutely berserk, and without his vision he begins to imagine a thing or two. At least that's what the court documents later said. For they found him wading in the river, entirely without sight, singing madly and clutching a piece of flotsam plywood in either hand, thinking he had a firm grasp of her wrists. He swears to this day that he doesn't know what happened to her. 'There and then gone,' he says, as if she disappeared. They never found her body. But stranger things have occurred on the Hudson, the river that flows and flows, from the high white cliffs of the Englewood Heights to the Palisades far, far below . . ."

His voice had taken on the singsong quality of a lullaby, and his words had fallen into verse. The installer's eyelids were drooping, and he swayed in his balance on the parapet.

"Here," said Hersh. "Catch." He yelled the last word and the installer's eyes sprang open just in time to see the camera—a pricey little piece of equipment—go soaring over his head. In the abrupt shock of his coming-to, he forgot where he was standing, leaned too far over as he reached for his camera, and fell from the roof with a yell. His body fell four stories and then splattered in a mess on the sidewalk. He had managed to catch the camera midflight; it came crashing down and broke beside his body. Later on, when the ambulance came to take him away, little bits of glass from the shattered lens were mixed in with the blood that had dried black in the street, glittering dark as obsidian shards in the moonlight.

So that was the end of video surveillance at Baumann's.

IX
WITHOUT FATHERS

No foul play was ever proved or even suspected by anyone except for Hadassah. Zev calmed her down and made things right between her and Hersh, but the truth is that he was a little afraid of his son. Afraid, but also happy, for in Hersh he'd finally found a true protégé, and he now had high hopes for the boy. The restaurant suffered slight reputational damage, but it had always enjoyed a sort of notoriety for being popular with the mob, and the ultimate effect was that the place's macabre appeal was enhanced. Hersh was famed as the distraught evening manager who'd watched a man fall to his death and could do nothing to save the poor fellow.

Hadassah wasn't so easily appeased as was the public. The incident inspired her to draw a line in the sand, which had the vague shape of the East River. Hersh had proven himself quite capable of handling any situation, she reasoned, and there was no use in Zev going over to Brooklyn. Zev, for his part, was growing tired of Iona and didn't put up much resistance.

But as it turned out, the damage was already done; precisely nine months after the bloody incident at Baumann's, Iona gave birth to a boy. He was not the world's brightest boy, but he was a remarkably talented athlete. By the time he was eleven, he was the youngest player on his middle school varsity team, where his only real competition was an Irish boy one year older named Patrick Byrne, whose mother's first name was Cleo, which was short for Cliodhna, which meant, in Old Gaelic, "banshee queen."

Something distinguished the boys from their peers, and they became fast friends. They were having a sleepover at Patrick's home one evening, and Cliodhna could hear their whispers through the walls once the lights had been turned out.

"I have a secret," Iona's son said to Patrick. "I know who my father is. My real father. My mother told me it's one of those rich Jews in Manhattan. Who are the richest Jews you know of in Manhattan?"

"The Morfawitz family," said Patrick. The family by then was quite famous.

"That's right. My mother told me that my real father is Zev Morfawitz himself. I'm going to find him one day and he's going to make me rich."

"Well," said Patrick, in jealousy turning his back, "then that also makes you a Jew."

Not long after—in the spirit of competition—Patrick Byrne was compelled to ask his mother about the identity of his father. He had just turned thirteen, and she figured that the timing was appropriate, given his heritage.

"Sit down beside me," said Cleo, "and I will tell you about your father. His name was Asher Morfawitz. And I haven't seen him in many, many years . . ."

Nobody had seen Asher in many, many years. Nobody had heard from him either. He had stayed in Vietnam after the war, where he drank and then drugged himself nearly to death. Zev Morfawitz had all but forgotten his son when Patrick Byrne came and knocked on the door of his mansion. Patrick had never seen somebody so strong or so rich as his grandfather, but he stood there proudly with the dirt of poverty still on his cheeks, and he demanded Zev take him to Ho Chi Minh City, and Zev was so tickled by the little Irish boy that he quickly agreed.

BOOK II
SONS

The palace of the Sun towered up with raised columns,
Bright with glittering gold, and gleaming bronze
Like fire. Shining ivory crowned the roofs . . .

Ovid, *Metamorphoses ii*

I
ON THE RIVER

The home of Gabriel de Leroux sat on two hundred hectares of land some three hundred kilometers southwest of Da Nang, Vietnam. His grandfather had first come to French Indochina in 1887 and was largely responsible for pushing the border west into the heart of the Southeast Asian peninsula. His reward was a grand estate centered on a large hill, atop which sat a Second Empire–style house with a copper mansard roof. The roof had long ago turned green. Many windows looked down on the sides of the steep slope. In the early days of the estate, the hill had been terraced for farming rice. Where the hill leveled out, the flat green quickly gave way to a great rubber plantation comprising some forty thousand trees. The air was thick and always humid; heat rose constantly from the earth, and the surrounding mountains seemed always to pull along on the horizon toward the house as if the world were converging on his hilltop.

By way of explaining this phenomenon, Leroux believed that the little hill where his family home was perched was transforming into a mountain, pulling all the surrounding earth inward to this epicenter. According to Leroux, his Laotian wife's body was the object of contention in a struggle between earth and sky. Because her native religion had never allowed her to become baptized, he reasoned that the devil considered her unclean soul to be his property, while God believed it to be of an indisputably celestial substance. As a result, the earth would not release her soul but could also not stop it from rising. Leroux believed that the mountain would continue to grow until her body had breached the gates of heaven and that, until it did, all the far corners of the earth would converge upon the position of her grave, the way a napkin's corners will come together if it is pinched at the center and lifted. Leroux would feel along the exterior walls of the house, where he found violent erosion of the mortar and stress fractures in the brick and stone. Unwilling to attribute any fault to the original mason—an earlier Leroux—he took the dilapidated state of his ancestral home as evidence confirming his theory of the moving earth. He was confined to a wheelchair and had not been to the basement in years, but he believed the foundation of his home was in ruins, that the whole thing was likely to collapse. He believed that the wine cellar had been crushed by the movements of his capricious earth, that the bottles of wine had shattered and bled his generation-old vintages into the hills and the streams that ran beneath them. Every morning, he paid a servant boy to collect a pail of water from the streams flowing at the foot of his hills so that he could taste the water daily; the wine, he reasoned, would begin to appear there, and Leroux believed he could taste it. The old man suffered from giardia and could not keep an ounce of fat on his bones.

Leroux's eyes barely worked, and cataracts flashed whenever he moved them in the light. They had adopted a nearly white shade of blue. A leather pocket full of toothpicks hung from one arm of his wheelchair, and the discarded ones were scattered about the house; by the way they glistened with still-wet saliva, it was possible to tell how recently he'd been in a room and to trace his wheelchair's path through the mansion. And so his servant boy, Bao, had no trouble finding the old man to let him know the trouble down at Loi Vao Nam was over. Better still, a paddy race was about to begin.

* * *

Zev and Patrick hired a repurposed tree-crusher to take them through the last leg of the jungle. The path was clear without any trees, so much of the vehicle's weighty accoutrements were unnecessary, but no other vehicles were available. Leroux's house was on the Laotian side of the border, but nothing indicated their crossing aside from a bamboo gate with a troupe of lar gibbons scattered about. The gibbons howled and waved their white hands when the truck slowly rumbled by, but there were no other guards to speak of. The canopy was dense and gave the impression that the sky was either cloud-covered or else that it was night, and they were both a little surprised when the dense and wild jungle gave way to neat rows of rubber trees with enough space between them for daylight to pour through. Around each trunk was tied a little bowl for collecting the valuable white sap.

At this threshold between jungle and farm, they met their first group of guards, though they did not belong to the broken armies of either Vietnam or Laos. They were Montagnards who were vaguely allegiant to Leroux because long before the war had begun, he'd run the plantation in as kind a way as possible; he'd provided high wages and good food and dry shelter and was neither strict nor very productive. They cared for him now as one does a grandfather who is slouching toward dementia, and his location on the border had allowed the estate to go more or less overlooked during the war. The workers on the grounds were in different factions, but many of them had returned from war exhausted by the idea of further escalation, so they allowed Leroux to remain nominally in charge, although his words did not mean very much to anyone.

So Zev and Patrick were brought not to the mansion, but to a small hut at the base of the hill with bamboo walls and a tin roof. It had rained very recently but the hut inside was dry and a little fire was going in a central iron stove.

"Sit," said a little man, whose name was Trong Tri. He was not so intelligent, but he was the only one of the small tribe who spoke English fluently, and so during the war he'd been well-positioned to take power. Now they regarded him as a leader, and he was just smart enough not to push the boundaries of despotism. His English was no longer of much use to anyone, but he provoked no disturbance in the order. He felt the precariousness of his position and was cautious with his words. "Why do you come here? Is there talk again of war?"

"No," said Zev. "We've come to find my son."

"Your son?" said Trong Tri. He began to laugh. "What would the son of a man like you be doing in a place like this?"

"I could not agree more," said Zev. He was losing patience quickly. "But the fact remains that he is here."

"And you," said Trong Tri, speaking to Patrick. "Have you also come to find your son?" He let out a high-pitched laugh that was silenced immediately by the young boy's fist against the table.

"It's my father," said Patrick. "Now bring him here or else . . ."

The smile disappeared from Trong Tri's face. He looked at his own forearms and then surveyed Patrick and noticed that he and the boy were roughly the same size. And the older man was a giant compared to either of them. Despite the fire and the sickening heat, Trong Tri began to feel a chill, and he touched his fingers to the drawer where his revolver was kept. Zev removed a pistol from his belt and held it pointed at the little man's head.

"I warned young Patrick here not to make empty threats. Well, here's a loaded one. Keep your hands above the desk. Patrick, show him the picture of your father."

Trong Tri's hands were steady as he folded them on the desk. He'd been accustomed in the war to being on the wrong end of a gun, and the familiar situation made him somehow comfortable. Then Patrick slid the photograph across the table and a wide smile broke across Trong's face and his demeanor changed completely.

"Ah!" he said, elated. "Mr. Asher." He was so happy the situation had not further devolved that he momentarily forgot himself and spoke in rapid Vietnamese. He called outside the window and Zev clicked back the hammer of his gun. Trong Tri quickly raised his hands before him and switched back to English. "Sorry," he said. In the now relaxed atmosphere, his English regressed into a sort of pidgin. "So sorry. You mean Mr. Asher. I should have know. Mr. Asher very popular here. Everybody know Mr. Asher."

"What did you call out the window?"

"I tell them, 'Go to fetch Mr. Asher.'"

Trong Tri stood and went to the far end of the room and Zev kept the gun trained on him, but there was less tension in the room now as if the fabric of space had been let go. Trong Tri pried the lid off a closed wooden casket. It had been a coffin once but now was filled with straw. Trong Tri removed a bottle and held it out to Zev. Suspended in the yellow liquid that filled its round body were a scorpion and a snake. Bits of detritus floated in the murky yellow water. Trong Tri put three glasses on the table and filled them up. Patrick looked at Zev, who shrugged and watched Trong Tri. Trong Tri drank and then rushed out. Zev and Patrick watched him go, and then clinked their glasses and drank. They winced at the taste but smiled once it had gone. The mood in the hut had changed.

"I do hope you aren't drinking cobra wine," said a voice in the open door. Zev turned around but Patrick did not; he had never met his father and was afraid to face him now. "It's lighter fluid, more or less. If you're desperate for a drink I've got whiskey."

Zev looked at his son. It was impossible to tell whether his hair had grayed or if it was simply dirty. A full beard covered his neck. His body was slim but strong, and the only parts unchanged were his eyes, which gleamed pale blue, colored points in an otherwise sepia figure.

"You look good," said Zev.

"I look good?"

"There's something to see, anyway. That's what's important."

"Important . . ." echoed Asher. The old unpracticed language was clumsy on his tongue. "Why have you come? Were you so bored in New York?"

"Why bored?" said Zev. "Why not sentimental?"

"Because it does not take thirteen years to become sentimental." They stared at each other for some time. "Well," he said finally. "You're here. You might as well sit down."

The outside heat seemed to press in on them from all directions. While Zev and Patrick sat, Asher walked over to a little window, flung open the shutter, reached out, and made a smacking motion downward with his hand. From the inside, the target was invisible, but a young boy leapt up from underneath the sill and Asher said something to him that neither Zev nor Patrick could understand. The boy ran off.

"Can't see what the use is in his spying," said Asher. "Speaks no English."

"Well," said Zev. "It's sometimes fun to hear what one is not supposed to. Even if it goes misunderstood."

"There's a difference," said Asher carefully, reacquainting his tongue with English. "Between misunderstanding and not understanding."

"That's true," said Zev. "This is your son. You'll remember his mother. Shannon was her name."

Patrick opened his mouth to speak but Asher got there first. "Cliodhna was her name," he said. He had not taken his eyes from Patrick's face since the boy had turned around.

"Cleo," said the boy, "is her name."

"Is her name," said Asher. "She's well?"

The boy shrugged. There was a great silence in the room and then the tension left, like sweat being wrung from a towel.

"I'd apologize about the heat," said Asher, "but really there isn't a good time to come."

In Zev's mind the old boredom began to churn. Pleasantries, he felt, were the conversational equivalent of rats. They produced in him a gustatory disgust as if one had run across his feet. Pleasantries had evolved to such sophistication that even in a humid jungle on a wild continent, three generations of fathers who were strangers to their sons and sons who were enigmas to their fathers could sit in a hut that none of them owned, sipping the rotting remains of scorpions and cobras, and open their mouths to speak about the weather. About humidity. As if it mattered at all whether they were in the sea or the Antarctic or on the gaseous plains of Jupiter.

"Why are you here?" Zev asked Asher suddenly. "Why did you remain? Things were just getting comfortable for you, weren't they?"

"Comfortable?" said Asher, sinking into Trong Tri's chair on the far side of the desk. A boy came in with a jug of water and six warm cans of beer. He set them on the desk and went out. "No, comfortable is not how I would describe it."

Asher did not say anything for a long time. He lifted a beer and then put it down again.

"From as early on as I remember," he said, "everything to me seemed significant, too significant. There was an awful weight to everything. I did not think about it much before I met you —really met you, you understand—because I wanted to be significant and so I accepted and chased those things. The tasks I completed were the tasks of a young man longing for acceptance and standing. They were not merely jobs, but labors, and so significance was alright."

Zev stood and took a beer from the desk and opened it and drank. He had the feeling he was hearing words that had been practiced and rehearsed many times over. It sounded as if Asher had only had the Bible to read these long thirteen years and had slipped into ancient vernacular.

Asher continued: "But how unrelenting that weight becomes once it touches you! Nothing, nothing can you do without the drag of your little action provoking a ripple and a tide. I tried—oh, I tried! I could never just fuck a girl; we were always making love. Just once, I wanted to have mean eyes that showed lust and only lust and a cruel body that carried out such callous demands, that would desire and then expend itself of that desire and be empty, truly empty!"

Asher stopped speaking and they saw that he was breathing hard. He reached forward again and took the beer can from the table and opened it but he did not drink.

"And so I came here. There is something pleasant about people who look nothing like you. It is easier to treat them like animals. And so I did. At first it was only the locals, but then it was the other soldiers, too. I realized that nobody looks like me. And what I discovered was that whereas in New York I could not look across a room without my glance meaning twenty things to thirty people, here I could drive a military transport off a bridge and kill every person aboard and it would not matter one bit. I could stand twenty-five blindfolded natives shoulder to shoulder and mow them down and it would not matter one bit. I could lay waste with napalm to a jungle that was ancient before Christ was born and it would not matter one bit. Do you understand? None of it mattered one bit."

He took a sip from his beer and looked up at the ceiling, where the rhythmic, clumsy beating of a beetle's crashing again, again against the lightbulb seemed to capture the very soul of the dripping air. When Asher spoke again his voice was soft.

"There is a great river which flows from these mountains down to the sea. One night we slept on a raised embankment. Like Joseph, I dreamt that I was the sun, but I had no brothers, no stars or moon around me. My light was burning dim and I was falling from the sky. The darkness of night was crumbling all around, shaking its dark dust at me like something physical, suffocating, pulling at my brightness. And suddenly I awoke and there was soil all around me. The embankment had collapsed, and we were swept into the river. As far as I know, I was the only survivor of the company. It did not matter. They would have died sooner or later anyway. Probably sooner. And as I floated down the river, I suddenly felt happy. For the first time in a long, long time I felt happy and I felt free. Nothing could touch me. I could scream, I could piss, I could shit—none of it mattered. My lungs and my bladder and my gut—everything inside me and around—we were all going the same way, the same direction, and it did not matter how we got there. The river would not mind."

Asher smiled into the ceiling. "And when finally I emerged from the river," he said, "it did not matter who I was. When I was in America, there was always a past to contend with. If I was in New York, then I was the tough boy from Brooklyn. In Brooklyn, I was something of a king. In the Irish quarter I was a lover and a customer and in Morningside Heights I was an intruder, a vagrant, a breaker of the peace. Here I could be anything. Nobody knew my name. I could have walked down from heaven or up from hell for all they were concerned with my past."

Zev had never been one for talking much, and the years had not made him loquacious; certainly, he'd never been one for listening. He tried for a moment to steer the conversation, to talk about things that fathers and sons talk about, but none of them had any idea what such things were. Zev had been away from his son for so long that he could fool himself for a moment into believing it was time, and not sheer unfamiliarity, that made them strange to one another. But it had been a long day and his patience had worn thin. He'd agreed to come out of some romantic notion about the jungles of Asia, the mystique of steaming weather, ocean-like monsoons, lithe, exotic women. Now he saw there was only bad heat and depression, bad work and worse morale. He felt fooled by his own optimism.

"I'm going out," he said. "A father ought to spend some time getting to know his son."

"Is that so?" Asher raised his eyebrows and even Patrick could not keep from smiling.

"Well, anyway," said Zev. "I'm going out."

"Be careful," said Asher. "There's a tiger about."

"I've got a gun," said Zev. He patted it.

"So have most of the men," said Asher. "They're on edge. They're more dangerous than the tiger."

"Do I look like a tiger? What do you think, Patrick?" He screwed up his face in a snarl.

"No," said Patrick, who wanted to be alone with his father.

Zev went out. Part of him hoped to find the tiger. That, at least, would be exciting, but he had gone no more than five minutes along the rubber-tree paths when he found himself in a cluster of huts. Faces appeared in the glassless windows and then they were all around him. The women and children wanted to touch him, to feel hair that was not black, skin that was not their own shade; they hadn't been in the war and the only white man they knew aside from Leroux was Asher Morfawitz. The men were less enamored, but friendly once they saw he had their women's favor. Also, Trong Tri was with them and spoke to Zev in English, slyly at first, but then openly, and finally even with warmth. So Zev stayed with them a while and learned about how Asher had come to live with the Montagnards on Leroux's decrepit estate.

* * *

Private Asher Morfawitz had been rescued from the Viet Cong while being transferred from one POW camp to another. A South Vietnamese task force had raided the transport line and killed many Northerners on purpose and some American captives by mistake. They sent flares to a nearby reconnaissance team so the saved Americans could be airlifted out of the jungle; this was very near the end of the war. The South Vietnamese team never saw combat again. They went back to their home at Leroux's, and only when they arrived did they find that two Americans had hidden themselves away during the airlift. One of them was dead and the other one was very nearly there; he had an infected wound from a deadfall and had gone four days without his fix of heroin.

Asher Morfawitz had been cared for at Leroux's. Medics had tended to his wounds and provided him with antibiotics. They tied him to a bed to stifle the palsies of opium withdrawal, familiar to them by now but so violent that he seemed to be possessed by evil spirits; such things were not unheard of in the jungle, and there were plenty of ghosts now to go around. They were not taking any chances. So when he woke up on the seventh day, his wound was painful but healed and he was covered in sweat and tied to the bed and had no memory of where he was. A daring escape was staged. He bit through his cloth restraints and used the zipper of his pants to saw away the rusted iron of his jail cell. He was in the basement of the mansion and he climbed out onto the earth through a window. "*Bỏ trốn! Bỏ trốn!*" called the servant boy; Asher had the misfortune to have crawled out from the cellar during Leroux's daily inspection of the mansion's crumbling foundation. Leroux did not see the young private escaping—remember, he saw nothing—but the boy ran over, expecting Asher to be in far worse shape than he really was. The recovery had been astounding, something like miraculous. Asher drove his fist once into the servant's face and the boy screamed an alarm as he saw the fist coming and then collapsed as soon as contact was made. Asher took off like a madman but found his runway short; he looked down on the steep terrace and the rice paddies and the clean rows of rubber trees with despair.

Asher was spurred into action by a group of men whom he assumed to be prison guards but really were only in the habit of raiding the mansion's wine cellar whenever Leroux was out on his morning inspections. Asher ran the other way and leapt down onto the first terrace. The water was nearly a foot deep and broke his fall, but it made the going very slow. From the parapet of the second terrace, he spotted a rice cart below him on the third; it was pulled by a team of two water buffalo that looked as if they hadn't broken a trot in ages, but Asher wrestled a reed lash from one of the women working the paddy and began to whip the ancient beasts. Slowly but surely, they broke into a light jog. At the first sounds of gunfire, they began to trot. At the volley that followed, they galloped as if their lives depended on it. Perhaps they did.

Asher rode the chariot in this manner all the way down the terraced hill. Once the confusion regarding the identity of the charioteer had passed, the shooting stopped. They watched with amazement, enraptured, overjoyed. It had been a bleak decade for the lot of them, filled with amputated limbs and infections and napalm; Asher Morfawitz astride a water buffalo chariot was the most magnificent thing they had seen in a long time. They cheered him from the hilltop as he slid down the final embankment and out toward the neat columns of rubber trees. Also, they had each taken their turn caring for the dying American and they felt for him something like love.

The ex-soldiers on the ground, though, could not see his face through the layers of fresh mud, and they stood in his way. Only one of them was armed and Asher charged straight at him. With the sun behind him and the twin buffalo as a shield, Asher might have trampled the little man, but at the last moment the gun fired and the buffalo staggered in fear and fell down. Asher flew into the mud. He rose quickly and ran straight for the man with the gun, who by now could see it was their American patient and lowered the gun just as Asher's body slammed into his. Very quickly, Asher flipped his body around so that he held his opponent in a chokehold, stole the man's bowie knife from his belt, and held it pointed to his neck.

"Stay back," he said, for all the others were gathering quickly. Asher looked desperately around and saw that his buffalo had been hit by a bullet and was bleeding through a hole in its neck. Darkness spread out around its throat where the blood and the mud became one. The huge blackness of its eyes pulsed with fear. "I'll kill him," he said. "Stay back or I'll kill him."

But they could not understand and so kept moving forward. Their shadows began to touch him, and Asher began to cry. He let go of the knife and the man was slow in rolling off. Everybody kneeled beside the broken American in the mud and finally he recognized their faces.

"I'm sorry," he said. "I'm so sorry. I never learned to tell you all apart."

When they finally found Trong Tri, who alone among them spoke English, he explained to Asher that they could arrange to take him back to the American base. Asher refused. "I'm not going back," he told them. "I'm never going back."

"I talk with some like you during war," said Trong Tri. "Also they say no to go back. They go back. A week, a month. They go back. Just like you. Be okay."

* * *

As Trong Tri relayed the tale, Zev became very excited. Novelty was dear to him and he'd never seen water buffalo in any capacity, and certainly not in the function of charioteers.

"We must arrange a race!" he cried. "A race, you understand?"

"A race! A race!" the Montagnards took up the cry at once. "A race! A race!"

They carried torches with them, for it was dark now and also they were drunk. The plantation came alive in the firelight. The neat rows of trees cast out shadows like flames, evenly spread then oddly, bending, stretching, syncing, and splitting with bodies, melting into the darkness behind and being reborn against the flame-lit earth ahead.

"Asher!" cried Zev, as they came upon the hut. "Asher! We're going to have a race!"

He pounded on the door once, twice, three times and then realized the door was not locked. He went in and as many of the crowd as could follow him did so.

"You two seem to be getting along," said Zev. Asher and Patrick were seated across from one another, eating plain white rice and splitting a bar of rationed chocolate that Asher had kept these thirteen years for a special occasion. It was badly spoiled and neither looked to be enjoying the stuff. But they were determined to eat their celebration, no matter how bitter and rotten it truly was. Each was smiling. A bottle of whiskey had been brought and emptied and a bottle of snake wine was nearly through as well; no longer assisted in its buoyancy by the yellow wine, the cobra's dead body folded in on itself and the bottle looked somehow even less sanitary than it had when the thing had been full. Zev sneered.

"Here while you've been babbling off to one another we've invented a new national sport. Trong says it's going to replace soccer."

"You don't even know what country we're in," said Asher.

"You . . ." began Zev, but then he had to admit that he didn't. And besides, Asher hadn't said it harshly but coyly, lovingly even—as one says a thing to a half-demented father. They watched one another, and each had enough alcohol warmth in his heart so as to confuse it for something like affection.

"Dad was telling me all about the war," said Patrick, caught up also in the sentiment. "And he was telling me about Brooklyn. And about Baumann's. Can we go to Baumann's when we're back?" He turned to Zev. "Dad's coming back."

Zev surveyed his son. He saw in his eyes a pleading for help and a willingness to lie, a desire to swap out the necessity of an honest present with the ease of an agreeable one.

"And we're going to have the famous steak at Baumann's," said Patrick, flushed and happy with the drink. He didn't realize that he'd tread on something dangerous—a competition between father and father. A maudlin competition, but a competition nonetheless, and so a thing that Zev could not refuse.

"A steak at Baumann's, are you?" said Zev.

"Yes," said Patrick. "Anything I want."

"Yes," said Asher. "Anything you want."

"Make him swear it," said Zev. "Your father left home without a word to his family and never returned. Do you trust the word of a man like that?"

"That's alright," said Asher. "I swear it."

"Those are only words," said Zev. "You've got to swear it on something you mind."

"I'll swear it to God."

"You don't mind God."

"I don't mind anything," said Asher. He finished his snake wine and winced.

"You minded that river," said Zev, who was feeling the strange liquor beginning to work. "How about that? Swear on that holy river of yours, whatever stream of piss carried you here. And if you break that vow, may everything you do be significant."

The room was very quiet. Trong Tri and all the Montagnards understood that something of gravitas had been voiced, even though they did not understand exactly what it was. They felt it. Patrick felt it, too. He did not understand either—not because of any barrier of language but because he lacked the experience. He was still at a time in his life when he longed to have purpose. He stared at his father, worried that Zev's curse in case of a broken promise was actually a reward, an incentive to break it.

"I don't know the name of that river," said Asher.

"I hardly think that matters," said Zev.

"Alright."

"Alright?"

"Alright." Asher nodded and a cruel smile came over Zev's face.

"Now, Patrick," he said. "Be very careful. You'll want to think on your request for some time. You only get one. You can ask your father to come home tomorrow, but what good is that really? He could come right on back to the jungle. Also, there are ways around it; after all, if you ask to share a porterhouse at Baumann's, then he's got to come home to share it, doesn't he? Can't share a steak from across two oceans, eh?

You've got to think, boy, really think. And for the sake of our mournful family, do make it something that brings your old man home to stay."

Patrick turned from Zev and watched his own father's face. He did not want to be cruel, or trick his father into anything, and his grandfather's malicious intent disgusted him a little. He'd never known before that the middle-aged and elderly come in the same sort of varieties as the young; some are kind, some are wicked, and years do not converge the psyches so much as pull them apart.

Zev saw he had lost his grandson's favor and so turned back to the matter at hand.

"Anyway," he said. "As I was saying, we've invented a new national sport. Actually, you've invented it, Asher. We're organizing a paddy race for the morning and we've decided that it's got to be you. You're going to race those buffalo like you did when you escaped. Trong says it was the most glorious thing any man has ever seen and we're all dying to watch you do it again. Only it's got to have a little competition in it. You've got to pick your match."

Asher watched his father, and a curl came to his lip. "Alright," he said. "It's you. I pick you."

"Me?" boomed Zev, poorly disguising his glee. He did not care for the novelty of the sport half so much as he needed the deification that the Montagnards had bestowed on his son. The boy had been there thirteen years, after all, and had accomplished nothing save that one magnificent morning of failed exodus, and it had seared him as a god in their minds. "Excellent, excellent. I accept your challenge."

The men cheered, the women cheered, the children cheered, too. The only person who did not cheer was Patrick. "No," he said, quietly at first and then repeated it with sufficient volume so as to be heard above the excitement. "No!"

The room quieted and watched him.

"What do you mean, 'no,'" said Zev.

"I mean no. I want to race him."

"Out of the question," said Asher. "I nearly killed myself that morning. It's far too dangerous."

Even Zev was inclined to agree, albeit along a different line of logic. "No can do, sonny," he said. "I'm going to wipe the mountain with your father's sad face! Now—who wants bets? Who wants action?"

The din started up again but was drowned out by Patrick once more.

"No," he said. He did not shout; his voice was dense. It had taken on more weight without needing more volume. "You told me anything I want. You promised on the river."

"I didn't even know what river it was," Asher said in meek protest.

"That doesn't matter," said Patrick, for he had inherited not only his male line's phenotype but also their obstinacy and rage. "You promised and now you've got to. I want to race you tomorrow and you've got to."

Asher took three long breaths while looking at his son. Neither blinked. All the cheer had left the room. "Very well," he said. "We race in the morning."

"And if I win . . ." began Patrick.

"Nothing if you win," said Asher, his sober voice hardly more than a whisper. "If you win, nothing. If you lose, also nothing. If you insist on racing, then my promise is paid."

Patrick pushed his tongue to the roof of his lip and his eyes narrowed. He looked as if he might rescind but then only nodded his head. *Fool*, Zev seemed to say with his face. With his mouth he said nothing. He turned and went out of the hut.

II
RACING CHARIOTS

In the morning they were all set to go. Deprived of his role as competitor, Zev took it upon himself to conduct the whole thing, and he mustered all the organizational pomp and circumstance of a polo match. Proper benches and chairs were brought out from the mansion onto the lawn so they could look down upon the race. Only, Zev then realized that the slope was too steep for anyone who was not seated precisely on the edge, and since he was determined now to make the organization of the spectacle more important than the success of either participant, that wouldn't do at all. And so, the chairs and benches were brought all the way down the hill from the mansion onto the short lawn in front of the rubber trees.

"It will be just like you saw him the first time, Fong," he said to Trong Tri. "From just the same place."

The chariots would begin at the top of the slope and go across each terrace, looping around the mountain seven times before ending in front of the spectators on the little lawn, where a finish-line ribbon of delicate rice paper had been carefully arranged between two bamboo poles.

As for the chariots themselves, they were little more than planks of beechwood harnessed to the water buffalo. There was no need for wheels; the buffalo would pull the chariots through rice paddies so that the riders were doing something akin to water skiing.

Asher's and Patrick's buffalo stood haunch to haunch at the starting line, and their masters mounted their respective chariots. As far as the animals were concerned, it was another day of work.

"It's not too late not to go," said Asher. He hadn't slept all night, had planned a soliloquy to persuade his son to decline the race, but the words went all to pieces. The thing had stopped being a game. The old, familiar feeling of significance had begun to plague him with the rising of the sun. It warmed his hands through the makeshift leather reins, rose into his feet by way of the beechwood platform and the tepid paddy water beneath.

"Yes, it is," said Patrick, looking nervously down over the edge of his chariot, over the first terrace, over the cascading pools of shallow brown water that reflected the gray morning sky. "If you can do it, I can do it. We're the same. I have your blood and we're the same."

"Will you allow me to give you a word of advice?" He took his son's stoic silence as a yes. "Keep a bend in your knees, but don't crouch. Place your left foot in front of your right. Press your right foot down hard to slow a little, but remember that it won't do much. Be easy with the reins. Don't try to overpower the buffalo—it can't be done. Think of yourself as a gentle guide. They want to succced as much as you do. Possibly more. They know the paddies well—trust them. The rein is a better tool than the whip. They understand all about being steered and controlled, but not pain. The paddies are soft. If all else fails, jump. There is no shame in jumping."

Patrick did not turn to his father and Asher was uncertain if the boy had even heard him. A sliver of sun poured in through a gap in the fog and burned pink on Patrick's face. His eyes glittered gold as they trained down the mountain to where Zev was readying himself to call the race to a start.

Zev reached into his jacket pocket and pulled out his pistol.

"On your marks!" he called.

Trong Tri was upon him. "No, sir, no! The buffalo very scared of the gun. Rear up, like. Throw rider." He made a sound like a whinny-ing horse.

"Can you hear me?" he shouted up the mountain. Asher nodded; Patrick's whole universe had stopped letting in sound. "When I drop this white flag, you begin! Three, two, one—begin!"

He dropped the white flag, which was really a piece of rice paper. Other pieces of rice paper had been folded and stuffed into the Montagnards' shirts as makeshift collars because Zev wanted the feeling of grandeur. All in all, more rice paper was wasted that day than had been used in the entire year before.

Off they went. Whatever civility had presided over the competitors' warm-up conversation was entirely gone now. It was less like a race against one another and more like a run against themselves, against time. On the first stretch, Asher held the lead, but even though Patrick was so close on his tail that his buffalo could have bit off a splinter of wood from Asher's chariot, it was not immediately clear that Patrick was even aware of his competitor's presence. So totally were the two focused on the shining runway of paddy that this negation of all else seemed to emanate from them in great waves and fall from on high with each slosh of splashed water so that those watching from the ground forgot themselves entirely. When Patrick's buffalo pair skidded off to one side, making the chariot lean like a promontory over the terraced slope, it was as if space itself were holding its breath; when they pulled him back onto the track, it was like oxygen had been allowed on earth once again. When Asher lost his footing as his duo fell gracelessly from one pool to another, it was as if each spectator's stomach had dropped in their gut, and they swallowed hard, together.

You will remember that the hill was terraced with concentric paddies that formed a staircase of descent, such that the riders, going around from terrace to terrace, were hidden from the spectators' view for half of the ordeal. After the first visible stretch, Asher had held a strong lead, and he'd maintained it well into the third; but as they rounded the third corner, Patrick took the inside tract, and nobody was surprised to see him emerge in a great splashing lead as the fourth stretch of the visible contest began. Each time the race curled around behind the mountain, the spectators seemed to become aware of their own existence; each time the two came roaring back into view, it was as if time itself had stopped, and the thing progressed as if in slow motion.

The cavalcade came into its penultimate visible stretch and they were close enough to the ground now that the spectators could appreciate the expressions on their faces. There was no congeniality between them anymore. In fact, neither seemed to understand that the other existed; it was as if the spirit of competition had lodged itself as insecurity in each mind, and the foe had become self-worth. The spectators surrounding Zev were transfixed, drunk with the same concentration each racer had adopted. Even now, as the race took its sixth and final turn, disappearing for the final time from the spectators' view, nobody spoke, as if they'd been transported to the far side of the moon, as if that were where all the interesting parts of life might now play out.

As they heard the chariots galloping into the final tier of visible paddy, a great scream broke the spell. It was not the sort of scream invoked by elevated competition; it was horror, and it came from the back of the spectators' ring. For out through the high stalks of grass that separated the hill from the rubber trees, the tigress had come stalking. The great orange-black beast did not care for the race and she could not be ignored. The Montagnards made a half circle around her, each backing up when she turned in their direction. They rattled whatever metal they had to make noise, brandished and beat bamboo sticks, screamed, sang, stomped, clapped, cried. The tigress moved side to side, her green-yellow eyes scanning the mass of villagers for a chink in the collective armor but finding none. She seemed to be on the verge of turning back into the jungle.

But now Zev pushed his way through to the front of the crescent of villagers that contained the tigress. He was neither scared nor enthralled; he was angry that his show had been interrupted at the very climax of suspense.

The tiger looked at him as he stepped forward through the ranks. "Shoo," he said. "Go on!"

The tiger turned once and then again, stalking with her eyes trained on Zev, her great shoulder blades rising and falling, setting waves into the striped fur of her back. Suddenly she stilled and seemed ready to pounce. Zev, more from impatience than fear, raised his pistol and, without a moment of hesitation, opened fire.

Noise erupted on the thick jungle air. The first shot melted into the second and then into the third, echoing like rolling thunder. The villagers ducked and screamed, held their hands above their heads. Nearby canopies exploded as frightened birds took flight. All three shots had missed the tigress, but she bounded off into the jungle, camouflaging with the shadow and sunlight that fell splintered through the rubber canopy. Zev dropped the pistol to his side.

"Quiet down," he roared, for the villagers were still shrieking. But slowly, as the roll of gunfire was absorbed into the humid air, the shrieks took on a different sort of terror—not the terror of immediate physical threat, but that of true horror, wailing sentimental woe. For at the sound of Zev's gunfire, the buffalo had reared. Asher, somewhat inoculated to the natural panic toward gunfire, had kept a cool head, had leapt from his beechwood plank just as the buffalo reared and bucked, and he landed safely on the cushion of paddy water just as his animals calmed and then stopped without a rider. Their heads were now stooped to the paddy, drinking.

Patrick, on the other hand, had never heard a gun fired before. He and his buffalo had opposite reactions: they reared while he ducked, they pulled up their great horned heads while he threw down his small soft body, his fists still gripping the reins. Unwilling to let go, he then rose as the leather grew taut, as the tension pulled him to his feet. He lost his balance, slipped from his platform, all the while remembering that the reins were his only hope. He released the whip and the cart released him, and his flying body was projected through the air, off one terrace and over the next, providing just enough pull that the buffalo followed, and the three animals came crashing down into the water together.

There was the crunch of bone and the slap of flesh on warm water and flesh on hot flesh. One buffalo rolled through the slight mud wall that kept the terrace intact and then spilled onto the dry ground below. A torrent of brown water and mud immediately followed as the paddy emptied itself through the breach. Next to flow through was the second buffalo, with a broken bone protruding through the flesh and muscle of its thigh. Attached to the maimed buffalo's mouth was a taut leather strap, and on the other end of the strap was Patrick's lifeless hand. Next came the beechwood chariot, reduced now to splinters and twigs.

All this refuse spilled out like water from a dam and spread slowly toward the spectators. They made a half circle around the growing pool as they had around the tigress. All was silent. There were no birds even to sing, and the only sound was the light running of water as the paddy drained through its breach.

From the terrace above, Asher rose slowly. His body, his face were covered in mud, and the whites of his eyes shone like twin stars. The villagers turned their heads down in shame, stuck their chins to their chests, and though the puddle had now spread out and covered their feet, they knelt in the mud and wept. Only Zev remained on his feet, his pistol loose in his hand and his eyes on the broken form of his grandson.

III
MARILYN KOWALSKI

They did not stay much longer than that. Asher couldn't remain where people were intimate with his tragedy, where they treated him like the mourning father he was meant to be. A chopper was arranged. It carried them out from the jungle, and all the Montagnards stood with their black hair whipping about in the helicopter wind, watching sadly as Asher and Zev departed. They flew to Da Nang and then to Ho Chi Minh City, where they boarded a plane back to New York.

Patrick's coffin lay in the cargo hold below. Asher had insisted on taking the thing back himself, but now that he was in the air, he missed the jungle. The stewardesses made him nervous, as did all the suits and the ties, the cold air streaming through the vents. After drowning his flight nerves in liquor, he dreamt in Laotian the whole flight back, and when he awoke he thought that either he was still dreaming or that something was terribly wrong. They were above New Jersey, and all around them bombs were exploding, bursting in the air. Only, the other fliers all seemed comfortable—excited, even. All down the plane, passengers were pushed away from the aisles, toward the windows; they pressed their foreheads up against the glass, watching, and it took Asher a moment to understand that there weren't any bombs, only fireworks. It was the Fourth of July, and also his birthday. From one side of the plane were the firework displays of the Jersey Shore; from the other came those of Long Island, Connecticut, and beyond.

Asher did not wait for Zev at the gate. He took no note of the crowd except for its loudness, of the windows except for their brightness. He went straight back to Brooklyn, hid his face as he walked past the entrance to Baumann's and up the stairs to his mother's apartment. He stood in the doorway and rapped his knuckles on the door. When Leah saw him, she hesitated, but only for a moment. Then she embraced him and led him inside without a word, sat him down at the kitchen table of his childhood, and put chicken stock on the stove.

Asher sat for a prayer vigil with Cliodhna, but they did not say a word to one another. She would hardly look in his direction. The funeral mass was the first time Asher had set foot inside a Catholic church, and he sat in the back row and didn't speak a word there either. As the mass filed out, the family lined up to accept condolences, but Asher remained seated and nobody spoke to him. Since he'd stepped foot in America, the only word he'd spoken was to the customs agent who'd asked if he'd been abroad for business or pleasure. "Pleasure," he'd finally said, for he hadn't been there on business.

Now he sat in an empty church, sunlight falling red-purple-blue through the stained-glass windows. The last of the mourners had gone and Asher had decided not to follow them to the grave. To mourn the death of an unknown son, he determined, was only self-important. Nobody wanted him there and he didn't want to be there either. He closed his eyes and felt the yellow warmth of the sun as it fell through the stained-glass halo of some apostle or other. He didn't know their names.

Something about his son's funeral broke the spell of sadness that had come over Asher. His explicit cause for leaving had been given form. It had lived, had died. It had been buried, had been mourned, and now Asher could begin to reinstate himself within the world.

And how changed was that world from how he'd left it!

Asher's grievance against his father—that Zev had come along to Asia to collect his son after thirteen years merely out of boredom—was both perceptive and naive; for while it was true that Zev had been bored, it was naive to think it would have taken him thirteen years to become so. No, much of the thirteen years had been packed with indefensible events, all undertaken with one goal in mind: to keep at bay Zev's boredom. It was only when more than a decade of extravagant drama had petered out and seemed to finally be settling did Zev decide that Asher was worthy of rescue.

* * *

First, there had been the meteoric rise of Hersh within the company ranks, which had commenced with the catastrophic death of Hadassah's security-camera installer. Hersh had been only seventeen at the time, yet he slouched toward misconduct like a man twice his age. Following this fiasco, a series of lawsuits had sprung up around the Williamsburg property portfolio of the Morfawitz family company. That was to be expected, what with a working man dying and all. And yet, the lawsuits pertained to more than just one man falling off one roof. There were violations filed with the Department of Buildings on the catty-cornered property as well, and then on the apartment building down the street. Facades were found to be in disrepair, boundaries were found to be crossed, maximum building heights were found to be exceeded, provisions that protected rent-stabilized or rent-controlled tenants were found to have been violated.

"We must find where these are coming from," said Hadassah to Zev one evening. All Morfawitzes involved in the family business were in attendance, but it was only the two of them who spoke. "We are being attacked. Do you hear me? Our family is being attacked."

She spoke harshly, but the incident drew her and Zev closer as the shared threat by a mutual enemy commonly will. Also, she felt truly sorry for Zev; you will remember that he could not read in English, so his attorneys were required by law to read him in its entirety each suit that was brought forth against the company. He suffered from what the doctors described as vascular headaches and migraines, and EEG scans showed severe abnormalities. When he was not in the office, he stayed in bed with the lights turned out and a cool compress over his eyes. The family now had surrounded the bed with chairs, for under his instruction they were never to have a meeting without him. He had never been sick before in his life.

"Who would do such a thing?" he moaned. "What have we done to deserve enemies?"

Mild laughter rippled through the room, beginning with Hersh and spreading to all the other seats. At Adam's booming laughter, Zev cried out for silence, then moaned at the pain that such exertion had inspired.

"You have plenty of enemies," said Naphtali.

"*We* have plenty of enemies," said Hadassah. She looked around the room, daring anyone to challenge her. "That's no matter. But *we* have to find out who this one is. It's going to kill my husband."

For all of his faults, Hadassah still loved Zev. Perhaps it was not a romantic sort of love, but an inevitable love of necessity and truth, the way that gravity loves mass.

"Things have been quiet for me, Mrs. Morfawitz," said Hersh. He stepped forward out of the shadow. "Why not let me do some digging."

Hadassah regarded the bastard son coldly. He'd been banned from the corporate offices since the security camera debacle and had been trying to wheedle his way back into the family's good graces ever since. Hadassah was intent not to allow this to pass. She looked to Adam, to see if maybe the solitary, unassailably legitimate heir would step in and offer his services. He would not. Nobody would.

"Fine," she said.

"I'll need access to the office. My files, the lawsuits . . ."

"Fine."

"*His* files . . ."

"Don't push it, Hersh."

"Well, Mrs. Morfawitz. It isn't *me* being sued. What good are *my* files going to do?"

"Fine. But if you haven't got him in a month's time, you're out for good."

"Him?" asked Hersh. "Are we certain it's a him?"

"One month," said Hadassah. "Are we clear?"

"Crystal."

Hersh walked out, whistling a tune.

It did not take him very long to find out who was the perpetrator of the legal crusade against Morfawitz & Co. Probably he knew it already.

One Marilyn Kowalski had graduated from Harvard Law School in 1967 at the top of her class. Don't think from her pedigree that she'd lived a privileged life; born as a Catholic in Poland during the war, she'd spent her first four years in dark forests, making hardly any noise. She'd never known her father, and her mother cared for both Marilyn and her twin sister with only the communal help of a rebellious band of Jews and Romani who lived out the war in the vast Masovian forests.

As the war progressed, the group became well-armed enough to occasionally ambush a small Wehrmacht division or raid a supplies brigade. Food wasn't plentiful, but they were also far from starving. Still, only Marilyn grew, while her sister remained stunted and thin. Actually, there was nothing wrong with her sister; the problem was Marilyn. Her mother fed them only at night, taking turns breastfeeding between the two whenever they stopped for short rests, and very early on, Marilyn learned how to trick their mother into feeding her twice and her sister not at all. This happened to such an astonishing extent that Marilyn grew up quickly, while her sister stayed a half-developed thing, splotchy in the face and colicky besides.

By the time the girls were four, so exaggerated was the span of their developments that Marilyn was often left to look over her sister. Such was the case one night when the little rebel band had stalked what they believed to be a Nazi medical contingency into an advantageous spot and realized, far too late, that they had mistaken grenadier transports for ambulances and were woefully mismatched. They lost many men in the hasty retreat, but there was enough distance between them and their pursuers that by the time the Germans had arrived at the campsite, everything had been disassembled and the band was fairly well hidden and dispersed throughout the wood. All they had to do was to remain silent, and then Marilyn's stunted twin began to whine.

Searchlights came closer and closer and Marilyn did the only thing there was to do before the sound reached their pursuers; she placed her hand over her twin sister's mouth to keep her quiet. It was largely a successful hushing. The Nazi Party went by them unaware. But when Marilyn took her hand away, the poor young thing had suffocated.

Marilyn understood that it was not only her hushing hand that had killed but the unrelenting nature of her greed. She understood this bad impulse toward selfishness within her bones, and so she worked all the time against it. Also, she developed a love for underformed and sickly things, tried to find in them the light that she had snuffed out in her sister; she was kind, especially to those in need of kindness, and came to see deformity in a subject as being a manifestation of the external world's neglect rather than a scarcity of value from within. Similarly, she saw her own strength and wisdom and intelligence not necessarily as things that were natural to her soul, but as things she had sucked from the outside world with too much avarice; she felt, in some way, that she owed something back to the world as penance for her sister. She made decisions sometimes that seemed to clash with her interests and was careful to avoid the heights that she deserved.

For instance: instead of taking the position she had been offered as Supreme Court clerk to William Joseph Brennan Jr., she decided instead—to the chagrin of her professors and mentors, many of whom considered her to be the most capable student they had ever known—to pursue a career at the Real Estate Board of New York. Her professors, themselves champions of law, could have understood if she went in for the attractive salary of a corporate law firm or the moral weight of a DA. But real estate? For Marilyn Kowalski?

But it seemed she knew what she was doing. Marilyn had an exceptional capacity for rising through the ranks and also for discovering and exploiting weak points in the law. She had a quick and clever mind that was less interested in wittiness than it was in completeness and consistency. She lacked the theatrical flair some of her prosecutorial counterparts possessed but could smell out logical flaws like a truffle pig. Also, she was interested in welfare—not the sort of lofty political welfare that her professors suggested she be involved with—but the tangible sort. During a day-trip interview at a Madison Avenue firm, she'd walked by a cordoned-off street where a woman had been struck by falling bricks from an ill-maintained facade. Marilyn knew an opportunity when she saw one, and here was a path both to money and to good. She realized that a change in the city's housing code of 1968 demanded better facade maintenance but that it was going unheeded because the only thing landlords could think of were the new air rights transfer provision and the market that ignited around it. Marilyn filed civil suits against some of the largest family-owned real-estate holding companies and was willing to settle for large sums of cash as well as for agreements to comply with new safety laws. Most of these families had played the game of making each building a separate entity for liability purposes, which meant that suits could be filed against each individual property and blanket releases were impossible.

The tactic worked marvelously well. Zev's vascular ailment was shared by more or less all of his corporate counterparts (though, being able to read the suits themselves, perhaps to a lesser extent). But nobody found out who was the unifying force behind the various suits as quickly as did Hersh.

As a rule, Hersh avoided smugness; he reasoned that people had enough to dislike about him without his wearing an expression that invited further hostility. This reasoning was sound. And yet, even he could not keep a certain amount of self-satisfaction from appearing in his smile when he marched Marilyn Kowalski into the Morfawitz home the very next day. Without a word, Hadassah brought them up to Zev's room, where Zev's attorneys were beside the bed, reading the day's lawsuit.

"In furtherance of this, and these demands . . ." they were saying.

Marilyn cut them off: "You are hereby ordered to appear before . . ."

As Zev listened to the voice, his moaning died down and then stopped entirely. He sat up slightly in the dark room with the cold, wet compress still over his eyes.

"Magrit?" he said. "That voice. That's Magrit's voice."

Thinking that he'd heard the voice of his long-gone nanny from Vienna, with whom he'd spent the early war in the European forest, Zev removed the compress from his face. His eyes, too impatient to adjust, flitted from figure to figure until at last they came upon Marilyn's silhouette in the open door, framed as it was by the hallway's yellow light.

"It is Magrit!" he said. "Magrit!"

"Well," said Hadassah. "That's it. He's gone mad. This bitch has made my husband mad."

Zev paid his wife no mind but stumbled over to where Marilyn stood, undaunted by the half-naked Zev's hard-stomping approach, which didn't stop until they stood face-to-face on the precipice of the hallway and the bedroom, on the border of darkness and light. His fingers touched the wall beside her body and slid down until they found the light switch. He hesitated and then flipped it, and the room exploded in light. Everybody shielded their eyes. But Zev—despite his migraine, his restless nights—stood tall and with eyes wide open.

"It is Magrit," he said. "It's Magrit born anew."

"Not so new," said Hersh, for he was annoyed at the shift in attention. He had been unable to get Zev from bed, and he didn't like that Marilyn could do it so simply. Also, he was only comfortable when he was in the know, and he knew nothing whatsoever about this Magrit, if she even existed. Plus, he had some vague and lingering concerns about the mental health of his father and mentor. "She's pushing thirty."

Hadassah gave Hersh the first kind look she'd ever given him, but Marilyn didn't seem to mind the jab. She looked at Hersh with raised eyebrows, and he took an involuntary step backward. He hadn't been so pierced by a stare since his first face-to-face meeting with Zev at Baumann's. He suddenly understood: Marilyn Kowalski had the same eyes as Zev, the same unflinching stare.

"Magrit," said Marilyn, turning her attention toward Zev and considerably softening her countenance. "Magrit was my mother's name."

"Yes, yes. It's like I said. Magrit Kowalski born anew. You look just like her. Born anew, I say."

This time, nobody challenged his assertion, and evidently Zev's headache was gone.

"Now tell me," he said, "what's become of your mother? I haven't seen her since the war."

"She died," said Marilyn. "Before we ever stepped foot in America. Just as we were coming into New York Harbor."

"Well," said Zev, intent on making his reunion with the ghost of his childhood crush a happy one, "there is no room on this earth for two Magrit Kowalskis."

"My name isn't Magrit," she said. "It's Marilyn."

"Marilyn Kowalski. I am Zev."

He stuck out his hand just as Marilyn raised hers to her mouth, which—in her first involuntary motion in a long time—had fallen open.

"No," she said. "Zev? My mother's Zevala?"

"Oh, yes," said Zev, nodding as he beamed into the blissful past. "Your mother would have called me Zevala."

"You're . . . well, on all company forms you're Jack. Jack Morfawitz. But if you're Zev . . . if you're my mother's Zevala . . . then . . ."

"Oh, dear god," said Hadassah. She brought her hand to her cheek.

* * *

Dear god, indeed! At any rate, Zev's days of headaches were done with. Marilyn quickly joined the company ranks and proved herself to have the best mind for strategy among those in the family business. Even when she spoke in platitudes, her wisdom was practicable, digestible. She infused a certain righteousness in the business which, though perhaps long overdue, wasn't welcomed by all. Hersh in particular did not like her.

"Your problem," he said at her very first Shabbos, "is that you've got a stick way up your ass."

"Yes," she said. "It's called a spine."

"Listen. You're far too smart to be so moral. Why don't you just tell us what it is you really want."

"Oh, but I disagree. One must be able to conceive of wickedness before one's failure to commit it can be said to be on a moral basis. You have to be very smart to be very moral. Only a very big cup can be very empty."

"Whatever that means," said Hersh, draining his wine.

Marilyn never backed down or gave an inch that she had claimed. She was, in some ways, a counterbalance to Hersh's recklessness, and probably saved the Morfawitz companies a fortune in legal expenses, direct and indirect both.

IV
A SCANDALOUS WEDDING

By the time Asher came back from Vietnam, there was no question as to Marilyn's value to the family. She had earned her place at all tables.

And what a table theirs had grown to be! Around it now sat Zev, with Hersh and then Abby on his right and Marilyn on his left and Hadassah directly across; Asher, whose seat had remained empty while he fought and then wallowed in the swamps of Vietnam, but had now been reclaimed; Naphtali, whose hair had whitened completely, whose youthful musculature had softened into a formidable girth, whose skin was nearly brown from spending his days in the Sagaponack sun; Deborah, who had aged gracefully and taken up charitable work as the head of New York's food bank and was a published green-movement poet; her daughter, Penny, who did not do much of anything at all but was astoundingly pretty; Adam, who had grown from a spoiled, sparring youth into a downright bellicose young man, who was impulsive and ill-tempered and not at all well-liked, and probably would have been tossed out if not for his being doted on by Hadassah as the sole non-deformed and legitimate progeny of her union with Zev . . .

Also, there was the legitimate yet ugly progeny of this same union who had been thrown aside at birth, along with his bride, who many disparagers have publicly dubbed "the mail-order Morfawitz." His name was Hezekial; hers was Ahava. In the interest of letting good names remain good, it has to be said that it was not Hezekial who ordered her in the first place. In fact, he had very little to do with it at all.

* * *

Adam Morfawitz had gotten himself kidnapped while studying abroad in Rome. Other students who were present at the event fell just short of laying the blame squarely on Adam's behavior, but the implication was clear: the boy was an absolute ass. He began by insisting that the bartender's name was Luigi, spitting out the homemade limoncello, and ordering a shot of Jack Daniels for everybody at the bar who could sing "The Star-Spangled Banner." Then he made a grab for the owner's daughter's breast and challenged the girl's two brothers to a fight, which he handily won. Despite his atrocious manner, he'd inherited his father's physique and probably was, as he put it to the bar, "a better brawler than any Jew since the Maccabees." He had hands like a cat and a jaw like the Rock of Gibraltar.

Adam then threw a wad of lire on the table and said that it was for anybody who would spar, then sank into sad reverie about his rich father who loved his bastards more than his true-born son. All the while he hadn't stopped his drinking. His fellow students had left, rightfully uneasy about the anti-American sentiment inspired in the café's local patrons by Adam Morfawitz's behavior.

According to all patrons and the owners, Adam left the bar, but he never made it home. Where exactly he was abducted was a matter of serious international investigation. Upon his recovery, the question of where the kidnapping had occurred was put to Adam, who could not give any answer; he'd blacked out by that time. In any case, he could not have been very difficult to abduct.

When Adam woke up, it was twilight, and he was locked in a stone room in a medieval complex that dated to the beginnings of the Roman Renaissance. It consisted of two bulky towers and a portcullis that had perhaps once hosted a drawbridge, but this had been reduced by half a millennium to an iron gate with a single door. The towers were less than one hundred feet apart, separated by a barbican wall roofed over with crumbling terra-cotta. The slide, fall, and shatter of a roof tile roused Adam from his sleep and brought him to the window, which was barred with an iron cross so rusty it came away with one great heave from the herculean boy. He was preparing to squeeze himself through the small opening when a rat ran across his foot and darted toward the door. It was so dark in the little room that he could not see where a rat might have come through, but Adam reasoned that it must have come from somewhere, and that where there were small holes, there were bound to be large holes, too. In a rare moment of humility probably inspired by the conditions of his awakening, Adam lacked the temerity needed to jump through a small window onto a roof of unknown strength, some unknown fall into the dark distance below.

He was quickly rewarded for his caution. Before the rat made it out of the room, a cat emerged at the window ledge—only its yellow eyes shining—and leapt upon the rodent. In the softening darkness, Adam's vision returned. He saw the cat's eyes shining up like twin sickly moons, the dying rat's tail whipping harmlessly across its face. The cat's shape and color began to take form in the graying dawn sky. It was a small and spotted tabby, and two stories in Adam's memory collided and persuaded him that he should trust the little beast: the first was *Alice in Wonderland*, which he'd skimmed for illustrations but never actually read; the second was the story of his grandfather Chaim the watchmaker, who'd apparently kept a tabby with him always since he was a little boy.

The tabby leapt back up into the window and then out of it, and Adam followed. With a mystic cat as a guide, his confidence returned. Perched on the stone sill, he looked down at the sea of red-orange terra-cotta below him and laughed. The roof was not very far below him but it was not directly below. Had he jumped earlier, he would have fallen to his death onto the stone bailey. Now he maneuvered within the small sill and leapt after the cat, easily landing on the roof, but cutting his leg against what remained of the rusted iron crossbar. He gasped from the impact and from the cut and began to slide down the slope of the roof but caught himself. He heard the sound of the tiles breaking below, and then the purring of the tabby.

Adam followed the tabby along the narrow spine of the ridge that connected the two towers. With a hunch in his back like a comic-book thief, he crept soundlessly behind the cat. As he reached the window on the far side, a dim orange light went on inside it. Adam dropped down so that his body was against the warm tile, but the cat only looked back, impatient. Slowly, but without much caution, Adam rose to his feet and stepped forward until he was just outside the lit window.

Several things were different about this side of the tower. There were actual windows, with double-thick panes. Also, they had no restraints. There were electric lights inside, like the one that Adam was looking in on. The room was finished, with insulated walls, a rug, and a dormitory-style bed. Adam thought for a minute that he was back at the college, in some unknown section of the campus, but reasoned correctly that a fortress of this magnitude would've been a difficult structure to miss.

With his face nearly at the window, Adam saw motion inside. A girl was rising from the bed. The light was the lamp on her dresser, and it was reflected in a worn but body-length mirror that stood leaning against one wall. The mirror image of light was softer, less taxing on the eyes than the light itself. Adam watched it, watched the girl approach her own image and—for the first time in his life—Adam's heart swelled with love.

She was beautiful like nothing he'd ever seen. An old-world beauty who seemed to possess the timelessness of a sepia print or daguerreo-type without sacrificing her real-world fullness. She watched her body in the mirror, turned to watch her profile, and in her face there was the sorrow of somebody starkly aware of her own mortality, of the cruel-ties that time would ravage on her youth. Without shedding a tear, she seemed to weep for herself, and on the far side of the glass window, with his heart pounding in his chest, Adam wept for her, too.

He did not weep for long. The tabby cat pawed against the window, and the sound broke the spell of his love and of her narcissism simultaneously. Adam spat out, "Traitor!" and lay once more against the tiles, a little to the left of the ridge. Unstartled, the girl inside said, "*Salut*, Bule," walked calmly to the window, and turned a latch. She pushed the window open, and he could see his reflection in its clean surface. With the image of the girl's beauty fresh in his mind, his own reflection appalled him, and he held his face low to the tiles, willing her not to see him, wanting to die rather than be discovered.

But the tabby betrayed him once again. As the girl went to take it in her arms, it turned back and nodded its slender head in Adam's direction. The girl made out his sprawled form on the rooftop. She watched him with a frozen face that could not be called unsmiling. Adam stuttered something unintelligible and pointed across the red-orange sea of rooftop tiles to the crumbling stone of his own tower cell, where the single dark window stared back.

The girl spoke to Adam in a tongue he did not understand and with a voice like the slither of retreating waves against sand. What she said was this: "You are hardly the first boy to be spying on me." With the cat cradled in her arm, she turned back into the room, leaving the window wide open. Adam accepted what he took to be an invitation and climbed in through the window, pulling it shut behind him.

* * *

The tower that Adam had been taken to was in the Commune of Calcata, an hour north of Rome along the Treja River valley. The fortress had been condemned by the government but had been in use ever since by smugglers, kidnappers, and various other breeds of criminals for the useful old towers and relatively secure holding cells. The imperfection of confinement was acceptable to the users of the cells because there wasn't anywhere for an escapee to go; the fortress-town itself was perched atop crumbling volcanic cliffs, and the descent was precarious to those who knew the way down and all but sure death to those who did not.

The towers that concerned Adam and the girl, whose name was Anastasia, were held by two opposing groups. Those who had taken Adam were mere criminals, kidnappers who held rich boys for ransom. Being somewhat overeager and inexperienced, they were not even particularly good at their jobs. For instance, regarding Adam Morfawitz, they had done next to no reconnaissance. All they knew before kidnapping him was that he'd pissed off some locals by bragging about a rich father, among other things. They assumed the best path forward was to get in touch with the boy's rich father by way of a ransom note. The note was written meticulously by a contact in New York and delivered through the Morfawitzes' mail slot. It made the contrived threats of severed body parts to follow, et cetera, et cetera. Needless to say, Zev could not read a word of it, for it had been delivered to the home and not the office. Loath as he was to bring light to his flaws, instead of requesting a translation from his wife, Zev threw the letter in the fire. Next, they called him, but they called him collect, and Zev hung up on the operator. "Me," he bellowed. "Me, to pay to talk to them! You call, you pay!" Finally, they called him from a private landline. "Well, fine," he said, upon hearing their demand. "Cut off the little bastard's finger. What does he need with ten of them anyway."

They got in touch with Hadassah instead, and things seemed to be going in a better direction. She, at least, demanded to speak with her son before going any further. Alas, when they went to fetch the boy, he was gone.

The far tower—where Adam Morfawitz had escaped to—was occupied by a nobler sort of criminal. They were smugglers and human traffickers, true, but their main business was sneaking those who could pay out of Soviet states. Passports were difficult to forge and even more difficult to come by, and most of their business had turned into selling wealthy daughters to foreign suitors with a dowry so that the marriage might open the gates of citizenship. They took a percentage of the dowry, but it was, all in all, a good deal for everyone, and they were not so unreasonable in their belief that they were doing benevolent work. They even provided, as part of their standard agreement to the parents who were sending off their daughters to freedom, that the daughters would have full discretion over whether or not they accepted any marriage proposal.

Most of the girls were eager to leave the high Commune of Calcata and took the first good thing that came their way. When it came to rare American suitors, rejections were simply unheard of.

But this was not the case with Anastasia. She'd been raised in Bucharest by a grandmother who'd fled Russia as a girl. In her spoiled youth, Anastasia had been promised wealthy British suitors with ancestral estates in Cumberland and Kangra plantations in the foothills of India. Anastasia was a harsh critic of faces and a harsher one of bodies. She demanded to see photographs of both before entertaining any offer. For any other girl, this demand would have eliminated all prospects to begin with, as few men at the time were willing to send a photograph of themselves unclothed; however, as Anastasia was willing to reciprocate the physical candor for any suitor whose body she approved, the photographs flowed in, one after the other. And to every single one she shook her head so that by now the proprietors of the tower's little business were desperate to get the girl off their hands. Also, their files were overflowing with photographs of half-naked men.

When Adam Morfawitz came down upon them, a wooden plank held before him like a sword, Anastasia behind him like a damsel being rescued, they almost let the pair go, but a vague sense of duty kept them honest. The two proprietors—man and wife—trained their guns on Adam, and he could see that they meant business. He pulled up short and made his surface area wide before Anastasia.

"I'm leaving," he said. "I'm taking her with me. I'll have your heads for this outrage."

The man with the gun pursed his lips. "American?" he said.

"Yes. American. And my father is Zev Morfawitz. You're going to wish that you were never born."

"Morfawitz?" said the wife. She transferred the gun to her left hand and with her right hand picked up a pen. *Morfawitz*, she scratched on a pad. She kept the gun pointed but now looked the boy up and down. She muttered something to her husband and then switched back to English. "Jews? And where from in America?"

"From New York City. My father is the biggest developer in

Manhattan and he will have your heads. My uncles are the wealthiest men in Long Island and New Jersey. They will also have your heads. Count on it."

"Easy, boy," said the husband. "We haven't got enough heads to go around." He turned and spoke now to Anastasia in quick Romanian, asking her opinion. She responded that she'd seen quite enough, and she was satisfied. She'd heard enough, too, for while English was foreign to her, America and New York were familiar words. The husband and wife conferred in a language that was neither English nor Romanian, and all seemed to be going well until there was a pounding at the door; Adam's captors had followed their once captive's escape route and had come to reclaim their prize.

A phone was brought in and Hadassah was finally able to speak to her son. She confirmed he was alive, he was safe, his fingers were intact. She spoke with the smugglers but refused on principle to speak with her child's kidnappers, and so the smuggling husband and wife found themselves in a position of some power. They discovered that the Morfawitz family was rich—richer than they could possibly have hoped for—but also that they were averse to marrying off their golden boy under such coercive circumstances.

"It's alright, Mother," said Adam into the phone, for the smugglers held one receiver and Adam held the other. Anastasia stayed beside him. "I'll marry her. I didn't want to marry one of those girls from the synagogue anyway."

"Oh, you didn't, did you?" said Hadassah. Four thousand miles of hot copper wire did nothing to thaw her icy voice. "And all my hard work was for nothing, was it?"

"You've never seen anything like her," said Adam. "Dear god, Mother, she's a goddess. The most beautiful woman I've ever seen."

"Ah! Listen to the boy. And is your mother not a woman, Adam? So go on. Tell me about this goddess of yours. And I might remind you of the first three commandments. Ah—it's a Saturday, no less. One through four. Wait, wait. Make that the whole first tablet."

Adam did not understand the bulk of his mother's words, so he ignored them as was his habit. Instead, he launched into a lengthy tirade about the beauty of Anastasia that made all present who spoke English blush. He was too uneducated to understand triteness. Flowers and sunsets and spring days and doves were all mentioned. It was Hadassah who cut off her son.

"Yes, yes," she said. "But her name, what's the girl's name?"

Rambling as he was, Adam understood that the inquiry was after not her name, but her religion. He hesitated, and then positively stalled. Judaism and passion burned together in his mind. Finally, with his face burning red, he managed to speak.

"Ahava," he said. "Her name is Ahava."

"Oh, oh," said his mother. "Ahava. Well, she just must be a Jew then, mustn't she."

"I hadn't thought of it, Mother."

"No?"

"No. But now that you mention it, yes. I believe she is."

"Isn't that lovely. Now give me back to her guardian and I'll have it all settled."

"Thank you, mother. Thank you."

"Anything at all for my family," she said.

While Hadassah Morfawitz and Anastasia's smugglers worked out the details, Adam sat with Anastasia's hand in his own, speaking to her of New York in a tongue she could not comprehend. He didn't bother to listen as the plans were fleshed out: the couple would be allowed to remain in Italy on a preemptive honeymoon of sorts, as long as the funds were wired from New York to the kidnappers; the smugglers could not simply give the dowry to the kidnappers because they were under contractual obligation to Anastasia's parents to pay the full dowry forward to her betrothed's parents only; once the negotiated ransom was received, it would be split equally between the smugglers and the kidnappers. All in all, Adam's kidnappers wound up with less than they would have liked but were in no true position to bargain and they knew it; Anastasia's guardians received half the ransom fee, in addition to finally being able to realize the percentage of Anastasia's dowry that was theirs to keep, and getting the difficult girl off their hands to boot; the Morfawitz family, though, were the true financial winners as the prospect of a marriage dowry was all but gone in the United States, and the dowry earned far exceeded the meager ransom they had agreed to pay, but the ransomers—being unable to understand the bulk of the negotiations—did not understand this.

"Your family has done splendidly through all this," said Anastasia's foster father to Adam. "And what a bride to earn!"

The details had been finalized and the honeymoon had come to an end. Adam still loved his bride-to-be dearly, yet he'd now had time to consider his mother and worry.

"Yes," said Adam. "Mother won't be happy though. I'm surprised she came around so quickly after working so hard to find suitable girls at the synagogue. Oh, I suppose it doesn't really matter. Probably she understands that not one of them compares to Anastasia."

"Ahava," corrected the girl's foster father. "You must remember now that her name is Ahava. It was a condition of your mother's that her son's bride should be Jewish."

"Yes," said Adam. "Of course."

He gestured to the little boat they were boarding. It would take them from Ostia to Naples, from Naples to Sousse, to Malta to Bodrum and finally to the Port of Haifa. Ahava would gain citizenship in the Jewish state as a Soviet refugee, and from there would be like laundered money, suitable for transfer to the United States under the auspices of marriage.

"Do I need to sign anything?" he asked, as the foster father handed over the papers.

"Nothing," he said. He turned to Ahava and switched languages. "You, on the other hand, must sign here for remittance to your parents. That you consent to marry the son of Zev and Hadassah Morfawitz."

"Gladly," she said, scribbled her name, and planted a kiss on Adam's cheek.

Four months had elapsed between when Adam was kidnapped and when he arrived back in New York with Ahava. They had been in Italy, in Tunisia, in Malta, in Turkey, in Israel, and now they were finally home.

Ahava pressed her pretty face to the airplane window as America came into view. She'd been practicing her English and had grown truly affectionate toward Adam.

"I thought," she said, "that first thing to see is the Statue for Liberty. But this I cannot see."

"No," he said. "It's on the water. We can go to it if you like. After the wedding tomorrow."

"Tomorrow," she said, snuggling up to his shoulder. "Tomorrow I am finally married."

They went through customs without any trouble, and as they stepped into arrivals, Adam held her hand tight.

"Mother will love you," he said. "There she is."

Hadassah greeted them. She hugged Adam close to her chest and held her eyes closed in relief for his safety. Opening them, she saw that their hands were still linked. She tapped Ahava's wrist twice with two fingers.

"Ah-ah," she said. "A Jewish girl is not supposed to touch a man before her wedding. You know this, of course."

"Of course," said Ahava. "It is very pleasant to meet you."

The two women stood facing one another. They were the same height, but Hadassah wore heels. What she lacked in Ahava's beauty and youth, she made up for in middle-aged elegance and fine clothing. She held Ahava's wrists softly in her hands and inspected the girl up close.

"Such a lovely creature," she said quietly, her voice filled with gentle and genuine admiration. "Such beauty cannot go to waste."

She took Ahava's jaw in her hand and turned the girl's face side to side.

"Yes," she said. "Exquisite."

"Thank you, Mrs. Morfawitz."

Hadassah dropped her hands and allowed a great smile to spread across her face.

"Come now," she said. "You must call me mother. Well, there is plenty to do before tomorrow. Let us go."

Two men in dark suits came and collected the luggage. Positioning herself between her son and her daughter-in-law-to-be, Hadassah led the way outside, where two separate cars were awaiting them. Hadassah opened the rear door of the first car, and Adam went in. When Ahava tried to follow behind him, Hadassah steered her firmly into the second car's open door.

"Remember dear," she said, getting in. "Not a touch until the wedding. But I'm riding with you, now. A mother ought to get to know her daughter."

Hadassah and Ahava's car went to the Plaza Hotel, where a bridal suite had been rented and the Morfawitz women were waiting.

"This is your new auntie Deborah, and her daughter, Penny. You and Penny must be the same age and I'm sure you will get along famously. Your sister Abby has strange ideas about men in general and marriage specifically and won't be attending, but she's really a darling and you'll come to love her as well. Aunt Hannah is ill, has been for twenty years. But this is your sister Marilyn, who I think you'll come to know best of all."

All the others smiled politely when they were introduced and were quick to turn their eyes away. But Marilyn looked at Ahava with sorrow etched across her face. When she spoke, her voice was soft. "You are marrying a good man tomorrow," she said. "For all his flaws, he is a good man. He is strong, he is wise, he is useful. And you are pretty enough for two."

"Thank you," said Ahava. She was confused, but she kissed Marilyn on the cheek. "We will be best of friends. I know it."

Marilyn nodded and then turned to Hadassah. "You're a beastly woman," she said, and went out.

"Now, now," said Hadassah. "The bride ought to get some rest. Tomorrow is a big day."

* * *

All of New York City knows what happened next. The wedding was held at Park Avenue Synagogue, and beneath the colored sunlight that fell through the stained-glass windows, Ahava approached the bimah. She was led by Naphtali, who stood in as the girl's father. He gave her away to the son of Zev and Hadassah Morfawitz.

Only not to the son that Ahava had intended.

She was so distracted by the awe that her beauty inspired in the crowded room that she did not realize the cruel trick that had been played on her until she was standing there beneath the chuppah, gazing down into the mismatched eyes of her ugly betrothed.

"Where is Adam?" she said, thinking that perhaps the unfortunate creature before her was the rabbi, for she had never met a truly holy Jew before, and her Eastern European prejudices had given her the impression that they might look something like this. "Where is my husband?"

"This is to be your husband," said Naphtali. He released her arm crudely and descended the bimah.

"But . . ." said Ahava, doubting her mastery of language, wanting the problem to be one of comprehension and not one of truth. "But I am to be married to Adam Morfawitz. To the son of Zev and Hadassah Morfawitz."

"I am the son of Zev and Hadassah Morfawitz," said her unfortunate husband-to-be. "You are to be married to me."

Ahava turned and looked around the room. The sunlight was now red, now purple, and she could not make out a face. Breath left her lungs in short, sharp gasps that pushed the sun-colored dust through light beams in the space. It occurred to her that she knew only a single person on the continent, on the landmasses of both North and South America, and that he was not to be her husband. He was not even in the room. Her dress felt too tight. Tears came to her eyes and she did not bother to brush them away, perhaps because they offered the advantage of blurring the image of her husband before her and of the multicolored synagogue all around. Her senses folded in, surveyed the rising heat inside her body, the pinks of her shut eyes, the crescendo of her pulse. Her heartbeat skipped from an andante to allegro all at once . . .

I should know; I was there—was with her on the stage, my eyes more or less level with the veins jumping in her neck. And just like my bride, I went somewhere else, too, as I watched the frilled white fabric twitch again, again against the fairness of her skin, like the second hand on a dying clock whose time cannot progress . . .

There was one such clock above the wall in the home where I grew up, and while I knew that I was aging, time often seemed a frozen thing. Also, the boiler was old and despite the incessant rattling of the pipes that played in concert with the clock, the radiators never seemed to achieve a drop of steam. So there was a literal aspect to the freezing as well, but mostly it was figurative—for me more so than for most—as the home was not "my home" but "a home" for young orphans, and they did everything they could to push children out from underneath their roof. Adoption was the goal, and it was frequently accomplished. I have no real complaints: we were well-educated and well-fed, and received haircuts at regular intervals and always on picture days when a photographer was hired to make a catalog of the home's children for interested parents to look at. Most of the children were chosen fairly quickly, and the record stay—aside from mine—was thirty-seven months. I stayed for twenty years; they stopped taking my picture.

By the end I was considered more an employee of the home than a prospect for escaping it. And a good employee I made, too. My first labor was to clear the home of pigeons, which I did using wire traps that sprung when they landed on the rafters. With only subtle tweaking and by working in the walls, I evicted rats as well. Wires are wires, and it was not so difficult afterward to set up the rooms to be listened in on from afar; you see, they kept no physical records, but the director had been there thirty-six years and must have known who had dropped me on his door.

Indeed, he did, which raised the natural question: why? While my ephemeral housemates came from either tragedy or poverty or both, it seemed that my family was well, they were intact, and they were rich. Perhaps they had something against children? Couldn't be, though, since they had them. Some terrible mistake? More information was needed, and in short, I spied—and yes, on my own family. One set of old walls is remarkably like another, and it was not long before I posed as a ConEd repairman and tapped the great mansion myself.

It was in this way that I learned of Adam's kidnapping, and also how I devised an immediate solution to the family's predicament. Hadassah had resigned to marrying off her golden boy, but the words in the contract only stipulated that the groom had to be her son. And— *voila!*—I chose this moment to appear and let my mother figure out what use my lineage would now be. One could tell, even from afar, that it was the sort of thing she'd like.

As a matter of timing, it was fortunate as well, for the orphanage was giving me the boot. I had stopped being a serious candidate for adoption at twelve, and though they'd kept me on as an employee for the better part of a decade, a remodel of the director's office had exposed to him my wires and became the pretense on which they closed the door on me for good.

But even as one shuts, another opens, and I was eager to begin a new life outside those dismal halls. I was most curious to meet my brother Adam—curious to see how Morfawitz blood could manifest to be the one thing that gave him value, while in my veins it amounted to a bundle to discard. Also, there were imperfect parallels between my childhood and what I learned of Ahava's through their phone conversations, and I thought our shared circumstance might give us a common cause, so I left that frozen clock behind and escaped its fruitless ticking . . .

So that was what I thought about as the rabbi belted out the Hebrew details of our union. What I said was just a whisper: "I do not envy you now, and I do not expect you to love me, though in time you may come to. I am good and I am strong and I will make a good companion."

My words had been carefully chosen, obsessed over, and repeatedly practiced, but I could see right away that they did not matter. My bride let out a small audible cry that was absorbed and muted by the thick curtain of the arch and the carpet of the bimah and the sheer volume of space beneath the high-beamed roof. As the ceremony progressed, from prayer to procession to dance, she was swept up by those most powerful currents that exist on the island of Manhattan: good etiquette and resistance to faux pas. She felt these things and did what was asked of her, did what she must do to please the blue-and-yellow faces of the strangers in the crowd. While their eyes were watching her, she was powerless to move except as demanded of her by the tide of expectation. Her beauty, which had for so long trained every eye in every room upon her figure, now made certain that everybody watched the bride, increased the power with which she was pushed through the force fields of horas, of lifted chairs, of wedding cake, of tuxedos and dresses, of silk yarmulkes and patent-leather shoes, of diamond pendants and silver watches, of the gold ring upon her finger.

As soon as the party got underway, as the eyes left Ahava and split their attention, the spell was temporarily broken. Ahava fled from the hall.

Watching her go from the family table, I buried my face in my wine-glass. It was the first time I'd ever been drunk and also the closest I'd ever sat to my mother. She said nothing to me throughout the ordeal. Even as she watched my new bride slip out, she turned in her chair to face Zev.

"A real Jew," she told him, "always reads a contract before she signs it."

Zev only shrugged and then finished his wine.

* * *

I am aware that the episode reflects some discredit on me, but I am used to discredit, reflected or otherwise. Mirrors have never been friends. For one who looks as I look, if there is anything worse than growing up in a home full of motherless boys, it is growing up in a home full of motherless boys and having a talent for surveillance that allows you to hear what is said behind (and sometimes about) your back, which is apparently lopsided due to a slight misalignment of the shoulders. They called me "limp leg" or "not so easy Hezey" or "zigzag Zeke" (for the gait which my mismatched legs allow me to progress at) or, worst of all, "Hezey half-mast Morfawitz" (justification for which evades me).

Yet I received the unintended benefit of becoming inoculated early on to odium, and so I am comfortable enough in my ways to speak of myself quite clearly. The only thing I hold real regrets about is my marriage of coercion to an unwilling bride, but—as is made note of above—there was an aspect of necessity, both for my bride and for me. Besides, it is not as if Hadassah was ultimately successful in depriving my wife of Adam, if that is even what she wanted to do; I admit that no matter how many eyes and ears I have, the inner workings of her brain and her heart are mechanisms which both still escape me.

What is very clear is what she intends for me now: to shine a light on the rise of our notorious clan. Her impression is that I am honored by the task of making her a golden throne of history to sit on. It is, perhaps, inconceivable to Hadassah that what I illuminate might have been kinder to leave in the dark, but it is not inconceivable to me; the fester in here is intolerable, and we could all do with a little airing out.

Anyway, it is not as if I am tarnishing an immaculate image; just after my scandalous wedding, even as the engine of Morfawitz success continued to increase its horrible speed, cracks began to appear in our once pretty facade. The train, already moving quite fast, gained impossible speed with Asher's return to New York. For Asher, like all the men in our family, is wholly unsalvageable and a force of destruction. If I am to retain credibility, however, I must be sure to include episodes not only that admonish those to whom my spite is owed, but also to those (rare few) whom I genuinely admire, and finally, alas, to myself. So, without bias or grudge, I slink happily back to the places I belong—in the shadows, in the wires, in the walls. Faithfully I record what I have heard.

And to my mother I relay the advice given to me on a picture day of my youth when I was naive enough to believe that I still yet might find adoption; after deploying a comb in heavy combat with the tangle of my hair, I sat up as straight as my crooked spine would allow and implored the photographer to do my picture justice.

To which the old man said, not incorrectly: "You don't need justice, you need mercy!"

V
THE SERVANTS SPEAK

When Asher left for Vietnam, the Morfawitzes were a family on the rise; when he returned, they were bona fide celebrities. Their magnificent wealth, their otherworldly beauty, their immigrant mysteriousness, their scandalous weddings, their ominous workplace accidents . . . all spun a cloud of power around the Morfawitz household, and they were easily the most talked-about family in New York.

After the initial culture shock of returning to a developed city and the routine of a weekly Sabbath meal, Asher found himself looking forward to a quiet, undisturbed life. Of all the things he'd missed out on while abroad, he felt the lack of family and love most keenly. But in his family there were many new and unfamiliar faces, and the old ones were distant. Their knowledge about his past, about the sorrow that had made him a soldier and a nomad, chained him to a demeanor he wanted only to leave behind.

For the family's part, they found him intolerable.

"Scandal—I'm all right with scandal," said Hersh to Zev one day shortly after Asher's return. He closed the door to Zev's corner office and sat down on the white leather sofa. "Give me all the scandal in the world. But this moping about? How can we let him keep moping about?"

"Hello, Hersh," said Hadassah. He hadn't seen her sitting in the high-backed chair on the client side of Zev's desk. Hersh looked as if he might rise, but then thought better of it and committed to his easy pose.

"Hadassah," he said.

"As it so happens," said Hadassah, "I agree with you. This moping about will not do."

"What we need," said Zev, "is to find him a girl."

"Well," said Hadassah. "It's always worked for you."

"Darling—"

"Don't darling me. Well? Hersh—anybody come to mind?"

"I hadn't thought of a girl," said Hersh. A sly smile came across his face. He'd never had to share the spotlight with any other male bastards, and he didn't like the thought of starting now.

"Liar," said Hadassah. "You listen to me. I put up with you because you do your job well and you amuse me and you get my husband out of the trouble that you get him into. One bastard boy is enough. Now, you find him a girl that'll keep him out of trouble, and that's that. You understand?"

"Now that you mention it, there is one . . ."

"Hershel," she said, trying to adopt her husband's tone, the only one that ever seemed to make Hersh afraid. "If there is a scandal, I will throw both you and that other bastard to the dogs. Do you understand me?"

"Scandal?" said Hersh. "Who wants scandal? Why the hell would I ever want a scandal."

"You make me sick," she said, rising.

"Good to see you, Mum."

He lay back casually on the sofa with his feet dangling over the armrest. Hadassah rose and walked from the room.

"Well," said Zev, once his wife was safely out of earshot. "Is there a girl?"

"There's always a girl," said Hersh.

* * *

Carrie Politz was a stunning young woman, and it was no surprise that Asher fell head over heels in love with her. Just about everybody else had. She was a tabloid queen who could make or break a restaurant by a repeat appearance or a sour expression on her face. Women asked for her autograph and men asked for her number, and Carrie was loath to grant either wish. She exclusively dated movie stars, novelists, and tycoons, and none of them truly exclusively. No, it was no surprise that Asher fell hard; even he agreed the real surprise was that Carrie had any interest in him. But then again, he'd been gone a long time and did not understand the immensity of the Morfawitzes' newfound celebrity. Nor did he understand the scrutiny with which his affairs were bound to be analyzed by the general public.

Carrie, on the other hand, understood these things completely.

So, for that matter, did Hersh.

In the short term, the plan worked. Asher became cheerful and bright, retook his place at the family table, and became a man of utility around the office and the businesses, which now included arms for the core businesses of shipping and real-estate development, but also for each of the offshoots. There was restaurant management for the original location of Baumann's as well as a Long Island outpost that had opened in 1970; consumer products production and distribution for Baumann's branded sauce, spinach, and bacon; nine butcher shops and groceries placed in Morfawitz-owned residential buildings across the city; a public-relations office that specialized in restaurant and real-estate industries and that had ties to all the major newspapers and magazines. Inevitably, this meant Asher was encroaching on territory that had fallen under Hersh's rule, but if Hersh minded at all, he hid it very well. His attitude to his half brother was in turn loving and generous, helpful as a benevolent mentor can be. Nobody would have believed it was Asher who had been responsible for the initial success of Baumann's. He probably no longer believed it himself. But neither did he care; he was helplessly in love.

Hadassah was surprised at how generous Hersh was being with his power, for not only had he encouraged Asher to step up as head of acquisitions and new developments in Manhattan, but he had somewhat exiled himself to the shipping branch of operations, normally handled by Naphtali, and traveled frequently between New York and the Mediterranean.

"You're up to something," Hadassah said to him one day. "I don't know what it is, but I don't like it."

"Goldfish," said Hersh, "only grow to be the size of whatever jar you keep them in. I only want to give my dear brother some room to grow."

"Half brother," she said.

"Family is family. I quite consider you to be my own mother."

"I'd prefer it if you didn't."

"Well, I do," said Hersh. "And Asher might, too, if we give him some time to really get into the groove of things. His girlfriend certainly seems to be quite taken with our people."

"Yes," said Hadassah. "Quite."

That much was true. Carrie's fascination with the family was rubbing off on Asher, and it was at this point that he began to formulate plans for a Morfawitz Tower on Central Park South, with the top floors reserved for family residences. The whole thing was near to being a projection of Carrie's estimation of the family. Everything Asher showed her had to be doubled. If he showed her the same window twice, it was doubled in size once again. When Asher divulged that he'd gotten a deal on marble countertops from Calacatta, the Azul mine in question was no longer good enough, for good mines did not give discounts. No effort or expense was spared on architecture, engineering, or the bribery of officials to pass the plans through quickly. The public-relations branch of the family was put to work covering up the forced eviction of a city block's worth of slums.

* * *

The groundbreaking ceremony was a black-tie event and, as Carrie Politz put it to the paper, "the veritable talk of the town." That was before all the drama.

Carrie was Asher's date, and Asher himself was to be both the master of ceremonies and the grand honoree. No more than a minute into the speech, however, he was interrupted by a crowd of protestors who had pushed their way into the event with cardboard signs held high above them. They made easy progress through the crowd because they were filthy and nobody wanted to mar their best black tie so early in the night. Marching upon the dais, the protestors said some nasty things about the Morfawitz clan particularly and then the Jews generally, in broad but vicious terms.

Asher's speech had been boring and nobody thought too badly about either the interruption or the anti-Semitism it espoused. It all seemed peaceful enough.

Then somebody brandished a gun.

"It's him," cried the gunman, pointing the dark barrel at Asher. "There's the kike responsible!"

As he pulled the trigger, the family witnessed a rare moment of selfless heroism from a most unexpected place: Hersh dove in front of his half brother and took the bullet in his upper right shoulder.

Miraculously, the papers all caught the act, so by the time Hersh woke up in the hospital, a candlelight vigil was gathered in the street below the window of his room at Mount Sinai's ICU. Hersh graced the crowd with the shadow of his hand against the glass—a great cheer went up below—and then walked out of his room in nothing but his backless gown and joined the family in the waiting room.

A sigh of relief went through the place. "Hersh—Hershel—Hershey!" they all cried together. Hadassah was the only one who didn't rise.

"Now, now," Hersh said, clearing a ring of space for himself. "We're a family. We've got to do whatever we can for one another, and I haven't an ounce of regret. Only this damn arm! Well, it's going to keep me from my work in the Mediterranean. I don't suppose anybody else will want to do such lowbrow stuff, but it's a shame. It was going to make the family a damn lot of money."

"I'll do it," said Asher. His face was solemn and pale. "Whatever it is, I'll do it. I owe you my life."

"Not at all, not at all," said Hersh, pointing to his bandages. "Maybe your shoulder, ha ha, but not your life. You wouldn't want the job, Ash. I tell you, it's beneath you."

"If it's good enough for you, it's good enough for me," said Asher in the most valorous voice he could muster. And then he said again: "I owe you my life."

Hersh looked at his half brother for a long while. "Well," he said finally. "If you're sure."

And he avoided Hadassah's hot glare.

* * *

Asher began spending long stretches of time outside of New York. All the family members were assigned chauffeur-bodyguards; Asher's was named Corvin, and when Asher was out of town, his man did not have much to do.

"Keep a close eye on Carrie," Asher told him every time he left the country. "Make sure my sweetheart is safe and take her wherever she wants to go. And make sure she keeps good company. I won't have her getting lonely without me."

Corvin did his duty well, in that he kept her out of harm's way and also kept a very close eye on her. He wanted desperately to rise in the company ranks and saw Asher as his ticket to doing so. He was a hard worker who never complained and rarely slept—which was lucky, as Carrie was a creature of the night. She came and went at odd hours, and always Corvin was there to take her where she wanted to go—whether that was to Broadway or dinner or even to a gentleman's house.

"Come, come, Corv," she would say to him before slipping out the town car door into some apartment or other. "He said he didn't want me to be lonely, didn't he . . ."

It went on like that for some time, and Carrie's wantonness grew more conspicuous the longer Asher was gone. Corvin's sense of duty weighed on him, and he became in the habit of spilling his troubles to a Morfawitz maid called Rita.

"I've got to tell him," Corvin said to her one evening. He sat down in the staff kitchen, where Rita was busy drying dishes. "She's just a hussy. Getting worse and worse, and I've got to tell him. He's going to find out eventually and it's got to be me who tells him, otherwise it's my ass. No, no, not going to lose my shirt over her. At first it wasn't so bad. What do I know whose house she's going to at night? Maybe she's got a sister. Maybe they're having a dinner party. Maybe she's taking care of her pa. It's not my business and I'm sure I don't care. Well, that's one thing. And Mr. Asher told me—he *told* me—make sure she doesn't get lonely. He did say that. Well, lonely and *lonely* are two different things, and that girl isn't either one. That's for sure."

"So what's changed?"

"What's changed? I'll tell you what's changed. I used to drop her off, just her, and I picked her up, just her. So that was just me doing my job. But then I start to see things. Maybe a man meets her at the door. Maybe he walks her to the car. Maybe he kisses her goodbye as she gets into the back seat. Well, I keep my eyes to myself. So if it's just a quick kiss maybe I don't need to see that, and so I don't. Maybe I blinked. Only the blinks get longer and longer and then she gets even worse. Just yesterday, she needed a ride to the Met. *That's great*, I said to myself. *Nice clean fun, Carrie's going to watch the opera.* And she even was dressing so modestly—a nice big dress. Not like those skimpy things she used to wear. So I think—*okay, the girl is getting some sense. Asher was alright about her after all.* Only, when she gets in the car, she says to me that we've got to make a stop. Well, that's what I'm here for, I told her, to make stops. So we make a stop and where do you think we stop at? One of those apartments where she always spends the night. 'This isn't the Met,' I told her. She just laughed, 'No, no. Definitely not the Met. We're just picking up a friend, Corvie, that's all. You don't mind.' Corvie. Nobody has ever called me Corvie in my life. So this man gets into the car—good-looking fellow if I say so myself. *Okay, Corvin*, I think. *Now, you just drive these nice people to the opera. Maybe it's her brother. You don't know.* Well, let me tell you. That wasn't any brother of hers. The things they were doing in my back seat . . . never seen that before in my life. So I just drive and drive. And when I get to the Met, you know what she goes ahead and does?"

"What?"

"She says, 'Keep on driving, Corvie. Who likes the opera after all?' You know who likes the opera? I like the opera! And I'm going to save up and buy myself some tickets and put on my best Sunday suit and go see it one day. And you know how I'm going to afford those tickets? By keeping my goddamn job. That's right. By telling Mr. Morfawitz about all this wicked stuff that's been going on in my back seat, and then by keeping my goddamn job."

Rita set the dishes aside and came to sit beside Corvin. She put her hands over his own and felt his heart racing in his pulse.

"In my own back seat!" he said. "I've been scrubbing that thing all morning. He gets home today and he's going to have to sit right in that seat where she did all that . . . whatever it was she was doing. Asher's been gone four months and has to come home to sit in that filth. Oh, I cleaned it as best I can but there are some things that soap and water won't get rid of."

Corvin fingered the crease of his chauffeur's hat and his hands were trembling with rage.

"Well," he said. "I got to go. He'll be landing soon."

"Wait," said Rita. "Sit down. Please sit down."

"I'll be late."

"There are worse things than being late," she said. "And you've plenty of time to get there. Now, please sit."

Corvin sat slowly and removed his hat and laid it on the table between them.

"Listen," said Rita. "I wasn't always such a lowly dishwasher here. When I started off with the Morfawitz family, I thought there were big things coming for me just the same way you think there are big things coming for you. Marilyn herself had taken me under her wing, and I was something like her assistant. Where she went, I went. Whatever she needed, it was me who got it."

Corvin looked around the kitchen at Rita's current circumstances. "What happened?" he asked her.

"What happened . . ." said Rita. Her eyes wandered off into the past. "This is right around the time of that craziness when that boy

got himself locked up in Italy and then Mr. Zigzag showed up. And
that Hezekial was a strange boy if I've ever seen a strange boy and I tell
you, I've seen some strange boys. He looks strange enough, sure, but
that's not what I mean. It's his eyes, it's always in his eyes. This sort
of strangeness. One's bigger than the other and they just look at you
funny, sneaky-like. I always caught him staring at me and then as soon
as I look at him, he acts like he's been caught committing some crime.
He looked at me sometimes, sure . . . but mostly he looked at Marilyn.
How he did follow that woman around, sometimes with his body but
always with his eyes. If a man was looking after me that way, I'd tell him
to take a damn picture."

They were interrupted then by Tehrani, who was Hadassah's private
driver. He came into the staff kitchen, took a jar of pickled herring from
the refrigerator, looked between the two of them sitting there, and then
went out. The room was very quiet. Corvin checked his wristwatch, but
Rita laid her hand upon his arm to stay his itch, all the while watching
the now-empty doorway as if to ascertain that they'd been left alone.
When Rita spoke again, her voice was hardly more than a whisper.

"Well," she said. "He *did* take a damn picture. I don't know how,
I don't know where, but he managed to get himself a photograph of
Marilyn in nothing but her drawers . . . He's always been sneaky and
maybe he went ahead and hid a camera in her closet, but oh, this was
something evil. I don't know how he got it and I don't care. But that
woman is modest as a nun—never even had a boyfriend that I know of
or any men around. And somehow that ugly man goes and gets himself a
picture like that . . . Well, that's not even the half of it. Nobody would've
known about that picture if that was all there was . . ."

Rita's eyes came back into focus, her attention returned to the little
kitchen where they sat. She looked at Corvin now and there was compassion in her face as if they shared a shameful history between them.

"Now here's the part I can't understand," she said. "There must be
some goodness in that man's soul because he goes ahead and confesses it
to her. I delivered the note to her myself. Now, I was supposed to deliver
all sorts of notes to her and she *asked* me to read them before so that

I could tell her which ones were important and which she could toss. This one was important. He confessed to her and poured his heart out. I nearly cried just reading it. He says that he was hopelessly in love—not just with her, but with everybody. That all he wanted was to be loved back, but that it was so hard for him on account of being so ugly. He said that in the orphanage where he grew up, none of the others even looked at him, and they winced when they looked up and saw his face. So he buried himself in mechanical things, in little machines that didn't care what he looked like. He said that sometimes he asked the machines for help with getting to know somebody, some real person, with blood and veins and hearts instead of copper wires and electric currents and a mainframe. He tinkered, he spied, but it was never with a meanness, only because he wanted to see what people were really like with one another. What they were like when they were by themselves. What they were like when they were with someone it didn't disgust them just to look at . . .

"Well, that letter was really something. Three pages long. And then folded up inside those pages was the photograph that he'd snuck by some contraption or other, with an apology written across the back. I looked at that photograph—I admit it. It was strange how well he captured her. It looked like a professional photographer had done it—I can't imagine how it happened without anybody being there to press the button, but he drew out the diagram of wires and gadgets and timers for her because he thought that she would appreciate knowing how he got around a closed door."

"And?" said Corvin.

Rita was quiet for a moment before she answered as if she needed to figure the thing out in her mind before divulging the rest.

"Here's the really strange part," she said. "Ms. Marilyn goes ahead and sends him back a note. She gave it to him herself, so I never did read that one. But I can imagine what it said. I think she liked him, admired him, maybe even loved him in a way. Not his body, but his brain. I think she wanted him to love himself in the same way she loved him. But that wasn't all. No, no. *That. Was. Not. All.* I couldn't believe what else was in that note. You're not going to believe it either." Rita lowered her voice and leaned in close to Corvin. "She gave him back the picture. Written below his apology were the words: '*never again!*'"

Corvin looked nervously at his watch one more time.

"How'd you know that?" he said. "If you never read the letter, how'd you know that?"

Here, Rita's kind and neutral face gave way to something scandalous. She could not keep a titillating twinkle from her eyes.

"One day sometime later," she said, "Marilyn walks into Hezekial's room. You know it used to be an office before they brought him back into the family, and she made an honest mistake walking in there. And my, oh my, what a mistake it turned out to be! For that boy's legs don't work very well, but his hand was working just fine. You understand me? Just fine. And what do you think Mr. Hezekial was looking at while his hand was working just fine? That picture of Ms. Kowalski in her drawers! Can you imagine the scandal? And make matters worse, she timed the entrance just perfectly. You understand? Or maybe seeing her in the flesh after looking at her picture was too much for him. Well, I don't need to tell you what happened. I'll only say that that picture was ruined for good. *Ruined*. Even if she didn't storm over and tear the thing up, that picture was *ruined*. You understand?"

"Oh, I understand alright," said Corvin. The scandal had cut through his worry, and his lips curled in a little smile. "But Rita, Rita. How do you *know*? How do you know any of this if you weren't there?"

Corvin's mirth seemed to remind Rita of the impropriety of her own delight at the scandal. Her eyes lost focus again, dove back into the wreckage of her past.

"I'll tell you how I know," she said. "Because Marilyn ripped up that ruined picture and wrapped it in tissue and threw it away. She brought the trash to the trash chute herself—a very strange thing for her to do. That was always something I did for her, take out the trash. Well, I admit I got a little curious. If something was wrong with my boss, I wanted to know what it was. Maybe she was pregnant or something. That would change things, wouldn't it? I've got a right to know if things where I work are going to change . . . Was it snooping? Maybe yes, maybe no.

But sometimes if things are going to change, then a person has got a right to snoop . . ."

She'd raised her voice inadvertently and now she calmed herself again.

"So, I go down to the trash room where the lowly maids work, and what do you think I see? Those three sisters are having a hoot. You know the three that used to work here—pretty girls, all of them. And they found the torn-up picture, with all the pieces stuck together. *Stuck. Together.*

"Corvin, there are three times in my life I've been really in a rage and twice I've been really afraid. I felt each of those things that day. First, I was angry. So angry at those three brats laughing at Marilyn, that I did the only decent thing to do—ran up and told her right away what had happened. I didn't even think about it, just ran up and told her. I didn't expect any reward, it was just the right thing to do. *I'd* want to know. Wouldn't you? Well, do you think Marilyn gave me any reward? Do you think she appreciated my telling her the truth?"

Rita stood up in a rage and gestured to her maid's outfit. "This is what she did!" she cried. "Demoted me, threw me out! She said that if I wanted to spend so much time around trash, I could make it my full-time employment! Oh, I cried and cried. I dreamed that she'd come back later and tell me she was only embarrassed, but she never did that. And here I am today. Trash, nothing but trash, and meanwhile those three girls got to keep on going with their jobs as if they hadn't done anything wrong."

Silence rang in the staff quarters, emphasized by the patter of footsteps from above. Corvin rubbed his hands together.

"Maybe," he said. "Maybe she just didn't like you to begin with. Maybe she was looking for a reason to get rid of you. Nobody ever got fired for telling the truth. That was right what you did. She didn't fire you for that. I refuse to believe that she fired you for that."

There were tears in Rita's eyes and she leaned her cheek against her fist.

"I'm begging you, Corvin, for your own sake, don't go."

Corvin looked at Rita's pain, and then he looked down at his watch.

"Mr. Morfawitz isn't like that," he said, rising to his feet. "Asher is a good man."

"Oh, Corvin. You fool. Don't you see? It's got nothing to do with being good. Marilyn is a good woman. It's got nothing to do with being good. These big people believe that they know everything that goes on with us little people. It does not fit with their ideas about the world that we could be a source of anything but cheap labor or cheap pleasure, that we could ever be a source of true harm or true surprise. There is nothing more threatening to somebody like that than to let them into the great secret that they refuse to see: that little people are people, too. And when you whisper that to them, they won't thank you for the lesson. They'll be courteous to you as a man is to a dog, but once you stand on two feet and say, 'Here—I have human eyes, human ears, a human brain—so what stops me from being human?' then you are no longer protected by the fence that keeps the dog outside the house. And without that fence there to protect you, you'll see what they're really like. They're cruel, they're mean, they'll rip your life to pieces. Even the best of them."

"Asher isn't like that," Corvin said again as he left.

"Asher isn't like that," he repeated to himself over and over again on the ride to JFK. "Asher isn't like that." And by the time he arrived at the airport, he so believed the claim that before he'd even taken Asher's bags, he removed his hat from his head and held it over his heart as if preparing for an oath. He looked Asher Morfawitz full in the face.

"Mr. Morfawitz," he said. Asher smiled to see his chauffeur and slapped him on the back, and then made for the rear door but Corvin moved to block his way. A subtle change came over Asher's face, and Corvin looked down at his feet while he spoke. "Sir. You've been good to me and I want only the best things for you. When you tell me to watch over Ms. Politz, I watch over her. You told me to keep her safe and I kept her safe. But I know who I work for and I've got to keep you safe, too. And as a man I know that being safe means also having a safe heart. Well, sir, it pains me to tell you that your heart isn't safe. That you trusted it to the wrong woman. She's no good. None at all!

She's been sneaking around behind your back and I've watched her commit the most heinous sins a girl can dream up. Just last night, Mr. Morfawitz, just last night, she had me pick her up and her gentleman both, and they just had me drive them around. There wasn't nothing I could do. Nothing I could do but come and tell you first thing. I said, I said—'Now, Ms. Politz, Mr. Morfawitz takes such good care of you. Don't you want to come and pick him up from the airport with me? Or shouldn't you be waiting at his home when he arrives, after such a long trip?' She only laughs at me. 'Corvie,' she calls me. 'Not at all. I want you to tell Ash that I'm not around tonight but that I'll be by at some point tomorrow. You know how much I love him. Well, since he'll be so tired tonight I want you then to leave him home and come pick me up. I've got tickets to the Met.' Well, sir, I know what tickets to the Met means! Last night they had tickets to the Met! Well, unless *Aida* was playing in the back seat of my car then they didn't go watch any opera. You understand what I'm saying? In the back seat of this car. I've been scrubbing all day but there are some things that don't come out with soap and water. Sit up front with me, sir. Just this once. I couldn't stand the thought of you sitting in that filth back there. Go on and say something Mr. Morfawitz. Please go on and say something."

Corvin finally looked Asher in the eyes and saw his own image reflected there. Those cold blue eyes were working hard around the edges, the focus growing deep as night itself and then shallow as a sidewalk puddle. Rita's words came back to him quietly, like a bubbling spring, but the spring was fed by the great silence between them and now it rushed and now it roared; he could see the trodden dog fence he'd laid low and he understood now how big his employer really was. There was nothing grateful in Asher's eyes, nothing kind in Asher's voice, nothing generous in Asher's hand that balled into a fist and then came crashing into Corvin's nose. He fell back against the car.

"Sir," he said, raising his hands before him. "Please, sir. I only wanted to help."

"Oh, you've helped!" said Asher. "Driving Carrie around from this bed to that—did you get a cut of the action they paid for their whore or were you only the idiot chauffeur? Did you get a cut of her pussy or did you only sit up there watching like a sheep while they defiled my car?"

"Sir . . ."

"Stop whining! Get up, you sorry pimp. Give me your hat. Give me your jacket. Where did she say to pick her up from?"

"Sir . . ."

"I said give me your clothes! Up, up. Return your uniform! You don't work for me anymore! And if I ever see you again, so help me god, I'll kill you!"

And with that, Asher sped off in his car, leaving Corvin without hat, jacket, or ride, crumpled on the arrivals sidewalk in the international terminal at John F. Kennedy Airport.

VI

HORSE COUNTRY

The sun was low in the sky when Asher pulled up outside the address Corvin had given him. It was a brownstone on Horatio with a bright blue door, and Carrie was waiting on the stoop with a man.

"Hi, Corvie," she said without looking in his direction. She got into the back with her lover. Asher said nothing and kept the hat low over his eyes.

He began to drive, slowly at first. But as he watched them in the rearview mirror through the darkly tinted glass, his heart raced and he drove faster, then faster, faster, through the crisscrossed streets of West Village until he spilled off Barrow and onto the West Side Highway.

"The Met is north, you know, Corvie . . ." said Carrie in the back. Asher did not hear her. Corvin certainly did not. "Well, I suppose it doesn't matter . . . how quickly you learned! But do slow down . . . we're going a bit fast . . ."

At eighty-five miles per hour, Asher swerved and skidded, screeched and accelerated, weaved through the fabric of cars and of night. The red traffic lights he ran sent fallen rays down through the windshield, and through the tint of the separating glass, Carrie could see her driver bathed in a dark and hellish glow.

"Corvie," she said. She tapped the window with her palm and

then slapped it again and again. "Corvin. Open this window at once. Corvin . . ."

But even as the window slid down, even before Asher turned to face her, she knew it was not Corvin who was driving.

"Oh, Ash," she said. The breath left her. With his face plunged into shadow beneath the chauffeur's visor, she could see only a red silhouette of the man she'd once loved and the shine of wetness on his face. Carrie saw at once that there was nothing to be said. She leaned back into the soft leather of the seat, fingered the seat belt, which was unbuckled by her side, and then folded her hands in her lap.

"Now, look here, man," started her lover. He slapped the divider glass as it slid up to split the space in two. He hit it once, twice, and then Asher turned violently to face him and even though the tinted plane that separated them was now completely up, was nearly opaque, he could see enough of Asher to be truly afraid. Afraid not only of physical harm but of total destruction. Such was Asher's fury. And then, as if born of descending divinity or rising evil, a growing light behind the seething silhouette made the shadow more complete by surrounding it with brightness.

This light was neither divine nor evil. It had no particular sentiment. It was not even metaphorical. It was the double headlights of an eighteen-wheeler, and it drove head-on into the side of Asher's car.

* * *

When he awoke at New York Presbyterian, Asher was expressionless as they told him what had happened. The vehicle had been thrown off the road, across the little park, and into the Hudson River. Carrie's lover died instantly. His head had split against the plexiglass divider. Carrie lost consciousness that she would never regain, but she did not die. Despite the doctor's protests, Asher removed the IVs from his arm and wandered out into the hall. "Carrie!" he called, "Carrie!" so that even the five on-duty nurses could not restrain him, and he was only quelled when they agreed to show him to her room.

"Only, don't expect her to look anything like the Ms. Politz you know," said the doctor as he opened the door. "It's remarkable that she's alive. We need to be grateful that she's even alive."

It was remarkable, thought Asher as he walked into the room. What was left of her skin was black and purple, and the gauze bandages that wrapped her head were stained yellow and red and brown.

"Will she make a recovery?" he asked, and the question felt foolish as it passed through his lips.

"No," said the doctor. "Dear god, no. I dare say she'll never wake up. If it wasn't for the baby, there would have been no use in saving her."

"The what?" said Asher, the color going from his face.

"The baby," said the doctor. He continued speaking but the world became muted for Asher as he approached the mummified body he'd once loved. His eyes traveled down along the layers of bandages, of cast, of tubes going in and going out. He could make out her breasts, larger than they had once been, and then the swollen mound of her belly.

"I've been gone for four months," he said to the doctor. "How can this be?"

"Oh, she's more than six along," said the doctor. "And I'll have to recommend that we take it as early as can be. Her body isn't long for this world, but with a little luck we can make a safe delivery."

Asher did not leave Carrie's side for the eight weeks that followed. He accepted no visitors, read no books or magazines, ate only bread, drank only water, sat in a state of silent penance and meditation. They cut the baby out of Carrie's womb at thirty-three weeks and did not bother to sew her up before cremating what remained.

He named the boy Abner after Carrie's late father, and took it home, not to his apartment in New York, but to his mother on the Brooklyn side of the Williamsburg Bridge.

His mother was still alive—she was not even particularly old—and yet she refused to care for the child.

"But I am unfit," cried Asher. "You see what happens to the things I love. You know what happens to my children."

Leah held her son's face in her hands and brought her lips against his forehead. She kissed his tear-stained cheeks and whispered, "And you know what happens to mine." She brushed her wrinkled hand along the infant's head. "Do with Abner what a wiser mother would have done with you. Take him to my family. They will care for him as a young boy should be cared for. Take him out of this gray box. Take yourself out, if you can."

So Asher took his motherless son up the Hudson River Valley, past Peekskill and Poughkeepsie, past Albany and Troy. The child slept the whole ride up to Saratoga, horse country halfway to the Canadian border, where Leah's family was from.

Of the contact, Asher was unsure of the relation; he knew only that the man must be rather old and that a childhood riding accident had left him paralyzed below the waist.

Asher found the sound of nearby water pleasing, and the bucolic scene emitted warmth and a nostalgia that he'd never known. He drove down a long dirt driveway that was lined by a wooden fence, odd trees, and grazing horses, and pulled up to a small white farmhouse beside a brown-red barn. An old man and his daughter had come out onto the porch to greet them. Or rather, the old man had come out when he heard the car approaching, but the daughter sat perfectly still on a swing to one side of the porch. On a more ostentatious house she might have looked like a gargoyle or a lion statuette. There was a table set before her, and a deck of yellow cards upon it. Asher remembered his lonely years of playing solitaire in his mother's cramped apartment, and he smiled at the girl. She did not smile back.

Asher stopped on the second step, so as not to be taller than the old man in his wheelchair. He passed the sleeping child to his new guardian.

"No need to stand below me, sonny," said the old man. "I've been in this thing a good long while and I'll be in it a good while longer. It hasn't made me an incompetent parent, has it now, Olivia?"

"No, Papa," said the girl, still absorbed with her own game.

"Well, see? Now, that's it. That's it. And you, let's get a look at you." The baby's wrap fell down and the old man turned the naked thing in his surprisingly strong hands, inspecting every inch of him.

"Of course," said Asher, "I'll pay any expenses. Just tell me what you'll need."

"What I'll need," he said, still not looking up from the baby, "is for you to be off right away. Any father who thinks that expenses will cover what devotion cannot is a fool and a poison to his boy. The one wise thing you've done is to bring the boy to me. Now you've brought him—and be off."

With that, the old man turned in his chair with Abner in his lap and went into the house. Asher took one step in pursuit, but then the door slammed shut and there was the sound of a bolt sliding into place. Asher stood there for a moment, face-to-face with the house.

The girl looked up from her game of cards for a moment, and they caught one another's eye. The girl smiled as if they shared some small benign secret between them, and then shrugged and returned to her game. It was a final gesture, somehow definite. Asher went back to his car and turned the keys in the ignition. The motor rumbled to life and drowned out all thought.

VII
HERSH RESPONDS TO BRIBERY

Things were hardly ever quiet with those early Morfawitzes, but now they were particularly loud. In the eight weeks since Asher's accident, there was much cleanup to do and reputational damage to prevent; after all, two people had been killed.

Hersh, however, had bigger worries. Hadassah hadn't forgotten who it was that had introduced Asher and Carrie in the first place, and she blamed Hersh for the entire debacle.

Only, things hadn't turned out as Hersh had expected them to. He'd fallen victim to that Morfawitz weakness that the lowly maid Rita had so precisely diagnosed: the failure to appreciate the ability of nonfamily members to deviate from their prescribed courses. And so he had arranged with his close friend Carrie Politz that there would be great money and fame in it for her if she could successfully seduce Asher Morfawitz and then drag him into the ranks of tabloid royalty, from which height it would be impossible to hold a normal job. Also, he had predicted that if Asher's photograph became a frequent one in the paper, Hadassah herself would have him pushed out. While she tolerated useful bastards, she did not tolerate public ones who might draw undue attention to her husband's infidelity. Hersh himself was quite adept at staying in the shadows. But he'd miscalculated—miscalculated badly.

Not only did he see too late that Carrie Politz had an ego and libido of her own, but he'd failed to consider that a lowly chauffeur might be driven to action by honest virtue.

As his current plan to appropriate Asher's birthright had fallen through, Hersh instead decided to be brazen about his thievery. During Asher's eight weeks of vigil by Carrie's side, his office was left open, his documents unguarded. Hersh figured he could easily slip inside, forge the signature on several deeds pertaining to Baumann's Beer Hall and related companies—the one part of the business in which Asher, and not he, was the heir presumptive and minority owner behind Zev. Later on, he might suggest that Asher had sold him the shares and that perhaps his half brother's memory had been addled by the tragic accident.

Only, the crude plan went bad just as soon as it commenced; as he stole into Asher's documents one morning before sunrise, he was intruded upon by Boris, the lead foreman for Morfawitz Tower, whose foundations had finally been dug. Asher was in charge of the project and kept the official architectural and structural plans in his office. Every morning Boris came to take them to the job, and every afternoon he brought them back. And so the foreman caught Hersh red-handed.

"Alright," said Hersh, preferring to have the thing out in the open. "What do you want?"

"Me? I'm just a worker, Mr. Morfawitz. It doesn't matter to me who sits in what chair here. It doesn't matter to me who owns what. Does a check from Hershel Morfawitz look any different than a check from Asher Morfawitz?"

"Yes," said Hersh. "I suspect that they would have different signatures."

"Or maybe not," said Boris, grinning. Hersh rose coldly and the smile fled from the foreman's face. "I only mean, Mr. Morfawitz, that it doesn't matter one bit who pays me, just as long as I get paid."

"But of course, you'll get paid," said Hersh, reaching into his pocket. "And you'll continue to be paid."

"That isn't what I meant, Mr. Morfawitz. I meant to be paid for my work."

With money in his hand, Hersh felt stronger, more secure.

"But, Boris," he said, holding out the bills, "you are being paid for your work. What else would you be paid for? Certainly not to see things."

"No, sir," said Boris. He slipped the bills into his pocket with too much confidence for Hersh's liking. "I don't see anything, sir. We just started pouring the concrete yesterday, and some of it must have splattered in my eye. Who can see with an eye full of concrete?"

"Two eyes, I hope."

"Oh, two. Two, for sure."

"Good," said Hersh. "Well, be more careful in the future. Construction sites are dangerous places."

So Boris went out with Hersh's money.

Hersh had been fighting a shadow war against Asher for so long that he'd forgotten what true confrontation felt like. Now he felt it again, and in the quick beating of his heart and the thoughts running through his head, his old cunning quickly returned.

Poor Boris, on the other hand, was further blinded; not by the fictional concrete, as he'd suggested, but by the confidence that cold cash lends when it is stuck in a gambler's hand. All day, he was bursting with the secret, with the little victory he'd won against his boss. As he skimmed the last section of concrete underpinning, making the surface level as a plane, he saw in his mind a big flat yard with a pool and a tennis court and the greenest grass that money could buy.

"We're going home, boss," said the last of his crew behind him. "That's as level as it's going to get."

"It's got to be perfect," said Boris, thinking of his life. "You all go on. I've got to wait here for the night watch."

It was evening by the time the night watch came around.

"Bad traffic, Don?" said Boris, still bent over on his knees, skimming the edges of the concrete pool. "Oh, don't answer that. It's alright. In fact, it's better than all right. Things are going to change for me now. I stumbled on a bit of gold today and my life feels changed already . . ."

But what Boris felt then was not the foretold change coming to fruition; it was a kick in the ass that sent him flying forward. He landed headfirst in the pool of wet concrete. Sputtering, flailing, sinking, and with a face full of stone, he turned to face the night watch but saw nothing.

Hersh looked down on the drowning man, and when Boris's blind fingers came groping for the dry edge, Hersh brought his foot down on them and ground them under his heel. Wherever Boris sought safety, he was pushed back into the quicksand of cement. It dragged him down and seeped all the moisture from his skin. He gave one last cry for help; the concrete filled his open mouth and sealed his lungs.

VIII
HERSH IS EXILED

When the poor foreman's body was discovered the next morning, newspapers abounded with the ghoulish photograph of the fossilized man. It was the next episode in a string of grisly high drama that had plagued the Morfawitz household since Hersh's arrival more than thirteen years ago, and it was, for Hadassah, the last straw.

"*Fercockt*," is how she put it as she stormed into the family office and threw the *New York Post* at Hersh's head.

"What is that," said Hersh. "Yiddish? Who understands Yiddish anymore?" He gave a cough that sounded suspiciously like *alte makhsheyfe*.

Hadassah rounded on him and for the first time in his life, Hersh was afraid physically of someone besides Zev.

"Alright, alright. Let me see what it is," he said, opening up the weaponized *Post*. "But, Hadassah, this is horrible. So horrible . . ."

"You know," said Hadassah, "I think that you would derive great pleasure if I were to stand here and tell you that I would see you destroyed if it took every last ounce of me. The truth is, I don't give a rat's ass about you. So here's what's what. You can stop reading the damn *Post*. You did a good-enough job covering up whatever it was that you did. They've got nothing on you. For now. But I know it was you, Hershel. I know, and I'll be damned if I'm going to let you bring shame to this family. Now, I don't know what sort of reporters are there now, or what sort of police will eventually get on it, but you're going to leave before they do, and you are not going to come back."

"Hadassah, Hadassah. You aren't thinking straight. What could I possibly have to do with such ugliness? And if I did—*hypothetically* if I did—then the worst thing we could possibly do is to run. Like you said, they haven't got anything on us. Which is the only way it could be, as I didn't do a thing."

"*We*," said Hadassah. "*We* is an interesting word. When you say 'the worst thing *we* could do,' it implies that there is a best thing *we* could do, which generally implies that we have similar interests and goals. Well, my little *gonif*, it could not be farther from the truth. What is best for *you* might be to stick around so if this whole thing festers it'll stink us all up rather than just you; what is best for *me* is if you run off now, so that if anyone with half a brain gets on this case, then when they come asking after you, *I* can tell them: 'How should I know what happened to Hersh? What is my husband's bastard son to me? Oh, he fled? Well, that's just like him—to do a bad thing and then to run away from it. Very much like his father in that respect, Detective.'"

Hersh crossed his legs and leaned back in his leather chair and put his feet up on the desk.

"But Hadassah," he said, "if it is, as you say, that *I* and *we* are separate, then what on earth could entice me into going for your sake?"

"I thought of that, too," said Hadassah, opening her purse.

"A bribe?" said Hersh aloud. "I've had enough of those for a time. I thought better of you, Hadassah. Really, I did."

But his voice trailed off. Hadassah had removed a small silver revolver from her bag and was pointing the gun at Hersh's head.

"You don't respect subtlety, Hersh, which is why you're afraid of your father. Two can play that game."

She stood calmly with the LadySmith in her outstretched hand. Hersh had frozen with his eyes on the short barrel's black pupil, but now he looked up at Hadassah and smiled.

"*Schmegegge*," he said, the mirth heavy in his voice. "*Schmegegge*, you old witch. The thing is probably not even loaded. Somebody so afraid of *collective* scandal because of the tangential *personal* shame it brings is not going to shoot her husband's son. They'll say you were the jealous cuckquean. I can see the headlines now."

Hersh spread his arms wide before him as Hadassah pulled back the hammer with her thumb.

"No," she said. "What I'll say to them is that I started carrying protection because I feared for my own safety. Who wouldn't, with all that's been going on? And when I confronted you about it, you tried to shoot me, and so I defended myself."

Hersh laughed. "But Hadassah, I haven't even got a gun."

"Oh, no?" she said, stepping forward. "You think you're the only one who knows how to get into an office that isn't yours? Why don't you take a look in your upper right-hand drawer."

Hersh removed his feet from the desk and returned to a formal sitting position. He froze with his hand on the drawer. "You're serious?" he said. Hadassah stood there, still as stone, the pistol steady in her hand. Hersh opened the drawer. "You realize that you're arming somebody with a perfectly sound excuse to shoot you in self-defense?"

"The only defense that matters to you, Hersh, is my husband's misguided affection. But remember that you are his plaything—nothing more—just like your mother was his whore. Even you are smart enough to know that if you ever pointed that thing at me, you'd be done for."

"So why don't you just tell him that I did?"

"One liar in a marriage is quite enough."

"Here comes the other liar now."

Hadassah did not turn her back to Hersh, but soon enough she heard Zev's footsteps.

"What's going on here," he said. Then he saw the gun and fell quiet.

"He's your little monster," said Hadassah, her eyes never leaving Hersh. "You deal with him. Get him out of the country. Do it today. I don't care where you leave him. You both know what happens if I see him again."

She dropped the gun by her side and turned to go.

"Don't worry, Zev," said Hersh. "That thing isn't even loaded."

Hadassah turned and shot at the chandelier, and the ceiling exploded in dust. Hersh ducked in terror; Zev winced but then smiled at his wife; Hadassah gave each of them a quick, stern glance and then replaced the LadySmith to her purse.

* * *

They took off for Athens that same night, having decided that the Mediterranean shipping affairs would suffer greatly in Hersh's complete absence and that it would be safe for him to maintain some quiet involvement from across the Atlantic. Hadassah demanded that Zev bring Hersh to Greece, where he would strip him of his passport before returning solo to New York City.

"There and back," Hadassah told him. Zev had called her from the pay phone at LaGuardia. "Only because he'd give anybody but you the slip. If there is so much as a lick of trouble, you'll find nothing but locked doors at home, and a file for divorce."

"Hadassah," he began.

"Don't Hadassah me. If you don't do what I ask there won't be anyone here to Hadassah."

She hung up. She'd seen the proud gleam in her husband's eyes that morning when she'd brandished the pistol at Hersh, and she knew that she had him. She was right, too, only she overestimated the staying power of her hold. Zev, after all, was capricious in all he did—raging in his tempers, ecstatic in his passions, whimsical as a Himalayan storm. As he stared at the receiver, the monotone buzz of a dead copper line filled his heart with a longing to be back in his wife's loving arms and good graces.

But the flight to Greece was a long one.

Hersh made it his mission to point out every beautiful woman they saw. "Hadassah's got the lock on you now, bub," he'd say. "How are you ever going to sneak off without old Hersh there to corral the heifers? Take a look while you can, a good long look while you can . . ."

Hersh was terribly afraid of being caught somewhere without the ability to leave, and even he had limitations. As the hour of Zev's departure grew near, he became panicky to the point of downright petulance.

"There's nothing to Greek girls," he cried as they walked the streets of Athens. "You'll come to visit your son and be stuck chasing gorgons. Leave me somewhere better, for my sake and for yours. Have a heart."

"You know I won't be visiting, Hersh."

"Then let's make the last dance a good one. I can arrange it all quickly. There's nothing in the whole world like the Greek Islands. What do you think makes me spend so much time in the Mediterranean?"

"The islands aren't going anywhere."

"No, but neither are you. You think Hadassah is going to let you come visit the one country where she knows this little *gonif* stays?"

Zev turned and grabbed Hersh by the collar. "Hadassah does not *let* me do anything. I do as I please. Do you understand?"

"Oh, sure. Sure. So then what would you like to do?"

In the end, they went. "Take a snooze and we'll be in Rhodes before you know it," said Hersh. "A fitting place for an American colossus to awake."

Hersh had the captain go forty-five knots, the luxury yacht's maximum speed. They made their way to Rhodes and then past it, down through the Karpathou Strait and out of the Aegean Sea. The barbiturates Hersh had put in Zev's drink kept him sleeping through the day and the night, by which time they had completed the crossing.

Hersh knew how somebody without a passport could go about getting one. He had been the one to launder Ahava's citizenship by way of naturalization in Israel, and his contacts in Tel Aviv were alive and well. Yes, if he could get into Israel, he could get out of Israel, even with a different name. It would not be safe to return to the States for some time, but he would be free to roam in exile.

Zev awoke to loud music and bright sunlight. There was a pounding in his head that was not helped by the rocking of the boat. Steadying himself with one hand against the sleek wall, Zev found his way to the bathroom, relieved his bladder, and then climbed up to the deck, allowing his eyes to adjust and unblur.

It was a scene he found appealing: five small boats surrounded their own large one, and many half-naked women were lounging about, drinking abundant champagne. Off in the distance was a white city with a magnificent tan beach.

"Hersh," he grumbled, trying to induce anger that wasn't there. He found his son lounging beside some brown women, who could not have been twenty-five. "This isn't an island."

"It's an island of liberal democracy amid an ocean of oppressive regimes," said Hersh. "If that's what you mean."

Zev took one great step forward and Hersh quickly leapt to his feet and raised defensive hands before him.

"No, that isn't what you meant. Well, no. It isn't an island. Here is the Promised Land, Zev. Seventy-five years ago, this place was nothing but sand dunes."

"Your passport," said Zev, roughly patting down his pockets. "You've stolen back your passport."

"No, no. I'm not a thief, you know. Check your own pockets first— it's right there."

One of the girls reached up and touched Zev's arm. "Won't you have a champagne, Mr. Morfawitz?"

Hersh smiled. "Yes, Mr. Morfawitz, won't you have a champagne? These brave young ladies are serving in the Israel Defense Forces. Soldiers, every one of them. Won't you drink to their courage-at-arms?"

Zev looked down at the girl and then touched his pocket where the passport was.

"I'm going to lock this away."

"Change into a swimsuit while you're at it. You won't catch a tan in New York."

Zev locked the passport in a safe in the cabin and lay spread-eagle on the bed. Now that he understood what beauty and sound were outside of this room, out there in the sunlight, the shade and the silence seemed oppressive. New York, after all, was a long way away, and how long were the chains that he wore? What was he so afraid of? He, whose last maritime adventure had been crossing the Atlantic as a wartime refugee; he, who had escaped the gas chambers at Gusen? What had he to fear from a small wife, one sea and one ocean away?

When Zev returned to the deck, the women gave a great cheer. He had on pink trunks, a white Havana shirt, and a straw-brimmed hat, all of which had been hung for him by Hersh. A glass of champagne was quickly put into his hand. His cabin wonderings had left him feeling youthful and dangerous, the hot sun and lullaby rocking of the boat left him warm and sentimental in a way that he hadn't been since before the war.

So, he thought to himself as he looked out at Tel Aviv, the barbiturates still swimming in his mind, *this is the Promised Land.*

When he had found the boat out of Europe as a boy, there had been a choice: Israel or America. Many had chosen the former, and he thought all of them insane. Now he looked at the white city and memories of his youth flooded Zev's mind, and his memory flashed with each sunbeam off the surface of the sea. They converged like rays of light through a magnifying glass, threatening to thaw the frozen shell that a feral youth and a vicious employment and a cold Atlantic crossing had left him with. He felt the one spiritual tingle of his entire adult life.

"Here," said Hersh, handing his father a pair of Windsor sunglasses. "Don't stare too long, it's like the sun. Glass in Tel Aviv and then white stone in Jaffa. If there's one thing consistent about the Jews is that we make ourselves difficult to look at."

Zev smiled, and though the dark lenses hid his eyes, Hersh could tell that the smile had reached his crow's feet, too, and Hersh was suddenly nervous, for Zev was acting very strange.

"Your uncle Heinrich once said that if there was one thing to note about Jews it was that we were like oil; we rise to the top and don't mix well with water. He said that we've never been seafaring people—that even when confronted with the necessity of crossing bodies of water, we have always favored miracles to wind."

Hersh looked at Zev curiously; there was an unmistakable paternal tone to Zev's voice, and Hersh worried at the dose of barbiturates he'd given his father.

"I haven't spent much time with Heinrich . . ." said Hersh. "I didn't think you had either."

"Oh, I haven't. But I will. You will, too, I suppose."

"What do you mean by that?"

"Oh, I don't know."

"You're acting awfully strange," said Hersh. He put his hands on his hips. "And what do you mean calling him my uncle? Are you feeling alright?"

Zev found his son's face in the darkly tinted world, considered sharing with this boy his confidence, his terrible secrets. Just then, the young soldier approached them and put her hand on Zev's arm.

"You look just like John Lennon in those," she said.

"That's right," said Hersh. "He sings like John, too."

Zev looked at Hersh and smiled, but it was a thin smile now, and it didn't wrinkle the skin around his eyes. He threw back the glass of champagne in one go and handed the empty glass to Hersh.

"I know you drugged me," he said. "You'll never do it again."

"No, sir," said Hersh, more comfortable with the explicit threat than the strange pathos of a moment before. "Never."

* * *

Some hours later, Zev awoke in the dark cabin of the yacht. All was quiet except for the hum of the engine, and Zev knew that the boats had all gone. It was night, late night, and what light came through the round porthole windows was that of the stars and the moon. Zev checked in the safe to make sure that Hersh's passport was still there; it was. But he knew his son was gone. He climbed onto the main deck and asked the captain how long they'd been at sea. Eleven hours was the answer. They had eleven more to go.

Wake fanned out behind the boat like the forked tongue of a serpent, white against the midnight surface of the sea. A curtain of stars above them like holes punched into the fabric of night. The moon was low and huge on the horizon, its craters and round edges sharp against the sky. No, he hadn't been drugged again, he'd simply needed sleep. How long had he been moving in a state of exhaustion? Had his life become an engine burning more fuel than it made up for in output of force? What had that sunshine sentimentality been all about? Was he trying to tell himself something? He looked up at the sky and could not help but notice constellations. Heat rose from his body to his face and he blinked once and then again.

"Oh, what the fuck?" said a little voice behind him. Zev turned around and saw the little soldier's frame, nothing but a naked silhouette down the stairwell where she blended into all the other shadow. "What the fuck, where did everyone go?" She began to curse in rapid Hebrew.

She climbed up to join Zev on the deck, but still in the low light he could not make out her face. He turned back to the sky and saw only dots now, nothing cohesive, nothing grand. He dropped his eyes and looked down at the black surface of the water, the random motion of unbroken waves, their crests glowing white and then fading. He turned around and looked at the soldier and began to laugh. The warm wind of night was howling, a harsh song sung by the black ocean.

"Oh, this isn't funny," she said. "What the fuck, what the fuck." She called to the captain: "Turn back! You've got to turn back!"

But her voice was drowned in the midnight wind, and the captain did not turn. Zev stepped toward her and put his arms around her body. The wind whipped around them now, treated them as one; but Zev felt the ethereal membrane between them, keeping them apart, keeping him apart from the world just as the stars were kept apart from one another, just as they did not form constellations except in desperate minds. The night was sharp; his eyes adjusted. The girl called again to the captain, but the captain could not hear. When Zev answered her, his words were not for the captain or the girl, but for his ears alone, for the benefit of no one—for the benefit of night.

"No, no," he said. "Press on."

BOOK III:
HOMECOMING

. . . her father bade
her brother Cadmus search through all the world,
until he found his sister, and proclaimed
him doomed to exile if he found her not;—
thus was he good and wicked in one deed.
When he had vainly wandered over the earth
(for who can fathom the deceits of Jove?)
Cadmus, the son of King Agenor, shunned
his country and his father's mighty wrath . . .

Ovid, *Metamorphoses iii*

1
ANOTHER FAMILY OF INTEREST

It was not just any young soldier that Zev brought with him back to Greece. Erzsebet's family is worth taking note of.

Her grandfather, Mikel Cohn, had been born in 1880 to a wealthy German Jewish family on the Lower East Side. They became significantly wealthier in June of 1904 when the *General Slocum* caught fire and sank in Manhattan's East River. It was a steamboat filled with the congregants of St. Mark's, an Evangelical Lutheran Church in what was then Little Germany. The church had chartered the run to transport over a thousand of its women and children to a picnic somewhere up the Long Island Sound. It does not matter where; they never made it. Their wool dresses were heavy and, when soaked with water, drowned them. Others were burned, others were crushed by falling timber—there are countless ways to die in a shipwreck, and not many survived.

Mikel Cohn purchased half of the East Village not even a full year after the *Slocum* went down. Nearly every apartment building had lost some tenants to the steamboat, and nobody wanted to stick around in a place so densely populated by ghosts. Mikel used his significant influence to acquire the property. This influence was born from his being not only a German Jew with money but also the ranking equivalent of a brigadier general in the Jewish American Mafia.

Kosher Nostra, they called it in the papers, but really it was no laughing matter. They were just as brutal as their Italian or Irish counterparts, and sometimes exaggeratedly more so because of the hurdle to being taken seriously that they had to overcome. All of Kosher Nostra favored Germany in the First World War, for the ones who came from Ukraine or Poland still had memories of pogroms and for the Jews of old Europe, the national borders were not of such importance.

Cohn, patriot of the *vaterland* that he was, dreamt up a scheme whereby he shipped in old packhorses from the West to his upstate farm, where his children would lacquer the gray and dying things in black shoe polish and ride them down to the show stable in the East Village. Then he sold them off to the American army as warhorses. Anyone who knew anything about warhorses by that time was already engaged in the European theater, and besides, the animals passed the makeshift test for being war-broken with flying colors: they were so deaf that they would not react to gunfire.

Anyway, it was a good fraud and would've gone unpunished but for one Sergeant Brinkley, whose leg was crushed beneath a horse of Mikel's at Cambrai. Downed by artillery fire, horse and rider were so far advanced within the trenches that they couldn't be reached for two whole days, and so they lay there in the mud, the horse dying slowly and not without fight, screaming and thrashing its legs in the air, shifting its great weight atop the sergeant, grinding together the crushed bones of the poor man's shattered leg. That the horse bled so much saved the sergeant, and in the court documents he claimed to have sustained his life by drinking from a trickle of blood that slid down the horse's back. Also, a violent rainstorm came and combined with the gunpowder on the air to dissolve the shoe polish that had made the horse look young, while the sergeant, his leg going gangrenous, his lungs filling with blood and with rain and with shoe polish, had no choice but to watch as his warhorse—as if ambushed by Father Time himself—withered and died atop him.

The sergeant got it into his mind that the real culprit was neither the Germans nor their *Maschinegewehrs*, but rather the man who had sold the bad horses. After an amputation that took his leg below the hip, Brinkley enjoyed a miraculous recovery, and in the curing heat of fever, he incubated his gripe into a simple plan. He spent the next eleven years of his life finding Mikel Cohn and, when he finally did in September of 1929, shook his hand and then shot him square between the eyes. The mob lawyer who was to execute the estate decided that he could make a quick buck in the stock market before passing on the fortune to Mikel's wife and two young boys. On October 29 of that year—Black Tuesday—he lost it all and hung himself from the rafters of his East Village apartment.

Mikel's wife had always been afraid of her husband's profession, but Mikel and the money had protected her; now she was nearly penniless, too. She spent all that she had left and took the younger of her boys to settle on a kibbutz in Palestine. The firstborn son was old enough to stay, which was lucky because she could not afford the sea passage for two. The son she brought with her had four children by three wives over the course of many years, so that the eldest son was thirty when the youngest girl was born. Her name was Erzsebet; his was Caleb.

* * *

Caleb Cohn might have been a strange man no matter how he was raised, but he was also raised quite strangely. His father had a tongue like silk and his mother was the very epitome of a wandering Jew. A Romani who had come down from the Caucasus Mountains on bare feet, she led a donkey through Azerbaijani and Armenian and Persian lands, through British-controlled Mesopotamia and into Transjordan, out of Transjordan and into the deserts of Palestine. She claimed to have eaten only manna on the way and said that it tasted of liver. The kibbutz where she gave birth to Caleb was filled with the most practical, most atheistic Zionists that Europe had produced, and yet everyone believed she was a witch. On Caleb's thirteenth birthday, she disappeared. Nobody had seen her pack her bags and she had no possessions to speak of. All she left to Caleb was a taste for the macabre and the leather reins with which she'd led her donkey down from the Caspian Sea. The donkey itself had died.

His father, Adar, gained a soft power from both his family's mafi-oso past and his wife's mystical reputation. After she disappeared, he claimed to consort with her ghost. He turned the kibbutz into some-thing of a feudal kingdom, and Caleb grew up something like a prince. So when, after Erzsebet's disappearance aboard Zev Morfawitz's yacht, Adar sent his three remaining children off in different directions to find her, they had no choice but to go. Adar banned them from returning unsuccessfully, and the threat of exile was not without teeth. Caleb and his siblings up and left.

Caleb went west with nothing but his mother's harness. He wore it as a belt. He followed the direction in which Zev's yacht had gone, and sailed within miles of the port where Zev had dropped her off in Crete. But Caleb knew only that the yacht had been leased to a Morfawitz from New York, and he went past that island, and then went past some more. He went past Malta, past Sicily, past Sardinia and then the Baleares. He sailed through the Strait of Gibraltar and up the coast to Lisbon. Adar had never let him leave Israel, and now he had forced him away. The old man was a grouch and a tyrant, and Caleb knew he would never return. Upon seeing the Atlantic spread out before him, he felt that he should cross it, and he willed his sister's path across the ocean so that he'd have a cause to go.

Caleb's life was dominated by such feelings, and he acted on them all. He felt the presence of his destiny as he slipped between the islands, and in some ways, it eclipsed the concern he had for his sister. In his cabin, he hung the leather reins from the shower rod, made a noose of one end, and slipped his head inside. He pulled down until the blood drained from his brain and he saw spots and then darkness, and in the dream that followed he was escaping from the clutches of a great blue dragon that both rose from the Mediterranean and was one with it; his running turned into a walk, and far ahead of him was his mother leading or being led by her little donkey, a bell around its neck keeping time; suddenly, she was atop the donkey without ever having mounted it, and then the duo stopped and the mule turned back and smiled with its great flat teeth, and Caleb saw that on its forehead there were horns.

When they made landfall at Lisbon, Caleb wandered the docks with the empty reins in his hands, feeling for changes in temperature. The clouds parted and the leather felt warm, and he looked up, staring into the sun, and when he looked down again and his vision had cleared of black sunspots, he was staring at an advertisement for a bullfight scheduled for that evening. On the poster was a woman atop a horse, her thick black hair swept sideways by motion so that splinters of darkness radiated from her like a crown of shadow, and directly before her was a bull with two great horns; its body and the horse's formed one line, and it seemed to Caleb that he was back inside his dream. He could not understand the poster, but he ran his fingers along the words: *Venha ver Harmonia, a cavaleira mundialmente famosa!*

If there were either a necessity or an opportunity for purchasing tickets, Caleb did not see it. Outside the stadium, he was swept up by a dancing crowd with red bandannas, and the human tide carried him into the arena, pressed him up against the barrier that separated the spectators from the bullring, where the blonde dirt looked almost like sand. The bull came in first, waved its horned head side to side, and then stopped short once it heard the roar of the crowd, scanned the sea of human faces with its black eyes. A film of sweat made its black fur shine.

"You do not look like you belong in this section!" shouted a man beside Caleb.

"Why not?"

"Local section. You are not local. American?"

"Not American."

"All Americans want to come to see bullfight."

"Not American."

"Since Hemingway, all Americans want to come to see bullfight. They go to Seville, to Pamplona. But after Franco, they do not like the bulls so much. So now Americans come here. They see us no different."

"What?" said Caleb, shouting now to be heard above the crowd.

"We are all Spain to Americans," the man shouted back.

"Not American."

"All Spain. All Europe is Spain to Americans. Except for certain parts of France. And Germany. Of course, there is Germany. But Portugal is cheapest. That is why Americans come now. Yes?"

"Not American."

"But here she comes, she comes. Harmonia! *Harmonia!*"

His voice shifted seamlessly from loud conversation to roar, and it was echoed all around by similar men, similar mouths. Caleb felt the leather of his belt and his fingers came away warm. He turned his face up and smiled at the sun and then felt the breeze of motion as the *cavaleira* flew by on her horse, a trail of dust kicked up behind her and the smell of stale earth and sawdust settled on the dancing crowd. The glitter of her sequined costume cut a shining arc through the brown-red cloud, the silver tips of her *bandarilhas* flashed deadly in the sunlight. She seemed to be an extension of the horse between her legs, and the horse an extension of her mind. It sidestepped the bull with a dance, a movement that Caleb had never known horses to be capable of performing. And each time the two great animals came close to one another, the horned one came away with a long spear stuck into the muscle of its back.

Once Harmonia had done her work and left, a chill spread through Caleb's fingers. He pushed away from the barrier, toward the exit.

"Ha!" cried his neighbor. "Some Americans are like this. They want to see blood, they want to see blood, but then as soon as they see blood they feel sick. They run home. They go away from Portugal, from Spain. They go away from all their Spains."

But Caleb left the stadium and did not turn back. He did not see the *forcados* come out, and by the time the matador was performing his caped dance, Caleb was already out of the arena. He wandered for some time and then found a dark hotel café on a side street in the shadow of the stadium. The food was oversalted, and the drink overwatered, but Caleb was beyond tasting. He saw only the trace of the *cavaleira*'s glow, whether from sequin or from spear, like a signature drawn with flame against darkness. The flame flickered and rose, and Caleb felt warm in his bones. He looked down into his ale and saw strange markings in the froth.

"Whatever you are looking for, it isn't in there," said a person beside him. The voice was deep, nearly like a man's but he could tell it belonged to a woman. He looked up and saw her. The *cavaleira*. Her face he could not recognize, but he remembered her hair, the plain firmness of her body.

"It's you," he said.

"You could say that to anybody."

"I saw you on the horse," he said. He did not know any of the technical terms for a bullfight. "Your English is very good."

"And your Portuguese is quite good," she said. "You must have heard me talking with Miguel."

She looked away from him and toward the bartender, and it was only then that Caleb noticed she was no longer in costume.

"My Portuguese is very bad," Caleb said. "Nonexistent. And besides, I thought we were in Spain."

She looked him fully in the face, seemed to teeter on the brink of rage, and then burst out laughing. From behind the bar, Miguel laughed, too, and said something in rapid Portuguese.

"You know why he laughs?" said Harmonia. "You understand what he says?"

Caleb shook his head.

"He laughs because in all the years that I have come to this place, nobody has ever recognized me. They see only the costume and the horse. They do not see me. If I am not wearing the costume, if I am not atop the horse, then they do not see me. And now, on the last time that I am to come here, somebody recognizes me. And an American, at that."

"I'm not American," he said.

"That's too bad."

"Why is that too bad?"

She grinned at him. "I could use a guide."

He looked at her, and she at him, and between their eyes passed something.

"That's why your English is so good," he said. He looked back into his drink. "You are going to America. Why?"

"Why? Because there is no opportunity here. Every year there are less in the arenas. The people do not like it. They take their ideas from Spain and what Spain does not like, soon Portugal does not like. It used to be that all of the *cavaleiros* were from the old families, from the ancient aristocracy. When I was able to join I thought, 'Look now, Harmonia. Look what you've broken into! You'll be rich soon! As long as you keep stabbing bulls and dancing with your horse, you're bound to be rich soon!' Well, I was a fool. They were all leaving it, that is all. Now they go to be educated in America and come back to open banks. There is no room left for bullfighting in Portugal."

"Is there room for it in America?"

She smiled and turned her drink in her hand. "No," she said quietly. "But my only skill is horses. To breed them, to ride them, to show them. And America is the best market for horses. They pay thirty times over for Lusitanos such as mine. In Portugal you say, 'Here is the best Lusitano in Portugal, the best for fighting bulls.' And they tell you: 'Yes, but who fights bulls?' In America you say: 'Here is the best Lusitano in Portugal. The best for fighting bulls.' And they bid up your animal as if it were the death mask of Manuel the First. That it is another country's best means something to them there."

They sat quietly for some time, and then she asked, "What is your excuse?"

"My excuse?"

"For good English. Mine is a future in America. What's your excuse?"

Caleb smiled at his golden reflection in the beer. "A past in America," he said.

"So you did come from there."

"No," he said. "My family. My blood."

He pointed to his arm, to his veins.

"You should come with me then," she said. She finished her drink. "It is good to chase one's blood."

"Yes," he said. "Blood is everything."

Harmonia nodded and stood, kissed Miguel once on either cheek, and said her goodbyes. She looked around the empty bar, at the streaks of dust that held the late-day sunlight. She began to go out and then turned back to Caleb.

"We leave tomorrow with thirty horses," she said. "There is always room for one who knows how to handle horses. Do you?"

"I have never touched a horse in my life," said Caleb.

"That's alright," she said. "As long as there are horses in your blood."

Caleb smiled as he touched his fingers to the leather reins of his belt. A cargo ship was an antique way to cross the Atlantic, but it had its advantages. For one, there was room for thirty horses. For another, the captain was able to marry Caleb and Harmonia on board.

II
THE RAGE OF HADASSAH

Caleb and Harmonia settled in the horse country of the Upper Hudson Valley, where they sold half of her stock and used the proceeds to purchase a barn where they could breed and train the other half. Caleb got along well with the horses, and he could do the work of several men in the stables because he never grew tired or bored. The love of Harmonia and the smells of the Hudson Valley infected him with a sort of profound contentment; and he, during those long summer months, thick with heat and pollen, felt that he was dreaming. And then one night he woke up.

While the sweetness of the land and the fresh marital bliss were both novel, there was still the matter of Caleb's missing sister. They had never been close—he was of a different mother and many years her senior— but as Harmonia attributed his success with the horses to the presence of horses in his blood, he began to wonder if that blood was now galloping through the veins of others. Thoughts of her existence fell from his subconscious mind like spring melt and then coalesced into a large pool that, as autumn came, froze over, and in its increased volume pushed against his waking soul, distracted him so that his thoughts were bloated and slow.

"What's wrong with you," said Harmonia one day. "You aren't acting like yourself."

He had never told her of his sister. Now he did. He told her of his father and of the ship that had taken his sister away. He told her of his witch mother and her donkey and the leather reins that sometimes acted as his guide. He looked down at his hands and then finally hooked two fingers through his belt and looked up at Harmonia.

"I think I need to go to New York today," he said. "There's something that I think I must do."

"Think?" she said to him. It was the first harsh tone she'd ever used with her husband. "What is all this 'think'? You have a sister who has gone missing. I don't know this sister and so I don't care for her. But if you should go, then go. If you should stay, then stay. Stop hiding behind that belt of yours and pretending that the mysterious nature of your impulses is an excuse for what you do with them. It's not where impulse comes from that makes a man a man. It's what you do with them. Don't blame that leather strap of yours. Don't even touch it. In fact, give it to me."

"I don't have another belt," said Caleb.

"Well, you're going to New York," she said. "You might as well do some shopping."

Caleb slipped the belt off his waist and left it on the table. He took the car and went. It was not even a three-hour drive, and he arrived on the Upper West Side of Manhattan before noon. He'd lived his whole life in a place where everybody knew everybody else, and though the city was larger than anything he'd ever seen, the logical connection between size and familiarity was obscured by sheer habit, so he did what he would have done to find somebody on a neighboring kibbutz: he asked where the Morfawitz family lived.

"Oh, sure," was the answer he received. "But that's on the other side of the park. And if you want my opinion, the Vanderbilt Mansion is the better of the two. It's only three blocks up."

* * *

Adam Morfawitz knocked on the open door of his mother's study and she did not look up from her work.

"There's a man at the door who wants to see you," he said.

"Tell him to go away."

"He says you know him."

"I don't," she said. "Who is he?"

"He won't say."

Hadassah laid the pen down on the desk and finally looked up at her son. He was a beautiful boy, she thought. He was a beautiful boy who did not know what was good for him. Certainly, he seemed intent not to marry, though she'd lined up the prettiest girls at the synagogue for him to take his pick. She had been sensitive—oh, had she been sensitive!— to the variable tastes of men, had even tried to think like her husband. For her son she'd collected black-haired girls and blondes, girls as tall and skinny as lampposts and ones with such bosoms and tuchuses that you could fry a latke over. But he had never known what was good for him and he had never been a clever boy.

"Well," said Adam, unable to hold his mother's piercing gaze. "Should I tell him that you're coming?"

"No," said Hadassah. "You stay here. I want to talk to you."

"But he's waiting at the door."

"I'll go down. It'll only be a minute. You wait."

She closed her checkbook and left her glasses on the table. Hadassah Morfawitz never went barefoot, even at home, and Adam listened to the sharp click of her heels against the hardwood floors of the hallway and then the marble of the stairs. He hadn't been in his mother's study for some time, and he thought how strange it was to have a place in one's own home that one is unfamiliar with. He went to the bookshelf, half-removed several volumes of a leatherbound *World Encyclopedia*, and then pushed them back into their place as if he were testing for levers to some secret passage.

Finally, he came to the window, which was slightly open despite the autumn chill. He'd never realized that the window of his mother's second-floor study sat just above the entry to their home, but he realized it now; every word said on top of the stoop could be heard with astounding clarity. Adam stood and listened to the conversation as it unfolded downstairs.

A man was speaking, and his voice made Adam nervous—not because the voice itself was nervous, but because it was calm. It was far too calm a voice for someone speaking with Hadassah Morfawitz. It was steady, nearly autonomic, and it refused to be trampled over by the brute force of Hadassah's ire.

". . . she was taken, you see. There was a boat that took her. A boat that had been chartered in Greece."

"Well, that's very sad," said Hadassah Morfawitz. "There's plenty of synagogues around if you should feel the need to pray."

"I'm not looking for a synagogue," Caleb Cohn began.

"There are many churches, too," she said, meaning it to be an insult. "Goodbye now."

There was the sound of the door groaning shut, and Adam waited for the thud of its close. It never came. Instead, there was the slap of a hand against the heavy wood.

"The boat," said Caleb, in his hypnotizing voice, "was chartered to Zev Morfawitz. Now, I know as well as anyone that a name can be widespread, that those who own a common name might not have any formal relations. And it may well be the case that you are the Morfawitz of a beautiful residence while he is a Morfawitz of a Mediterranean yacht. But coincidences are funny things, and I thought that it would be best to simply ask."

"Zev Morfawitz is my husband," said Hadassah. "He's never been on a Mediterranean yacht in his life. And without any offense meant, Mr. Cohn, you seem middle-aged enough to me. Any sister of yours would be far too old to hold my husband's interest."

"But, you see—"

"I see nothing, Mr. Cohn, save an unwelcome visitor who has been far too long on my stoop. I won't pretend to know what sort of advantage you hope to draw from interfering with my family's affairs, but I can promise you that none of it will serve you well. My advice to you, Mr. Cohn, is to forget the Morfawitz name and leave this island far behind you."

The door slammed and the great bolt slid into place. It seemed to

Adam that both his mother and Caleb remained put for the same amount
of time, each watching the closed door from opposite sides and then
each turning, simultaneously, and moving away from it. He heard the
sound of Caleb's footsteps going down the street outside and the click
of Hadassah's heels against the stone stairs within.

When she came into the room, Adam was trying to pull the
window shut.

"Leave it," she said.

"I just thought you might be cold."

Hadassah leveled her son with a glance and then took her seat behind
the desk. She looked at the chair across from her, and Adam obediently
sat down with his hands folded on the desk before him.

"Well," she said finally. "It appears that you are not the only one
in this house who is hell-bent on dragging our good name through the
mud. Haven't you men any pride in your family name? Well? No, don't
speak. If there's one saving grace that your poor mother clings to, it's that
you seem to be intent on not producing any grandchildren, and so even
if you do drag our name through the mud, it won't be a very long line!"

"But the one time I show interest, you—"

Hadassah slapped her open palm down on the table and Adam fell
quiet. "I do not want to hear your excuses," she said.

Hadassah's hand slid along the wood, her gold wedding band hissing
as it left a trail of ruin in the polished desktop's stain. With her hands
off the table, she leaned back in her chair and looked out the window.
In Adam's eyes, she seemed to deflate, to sink into the heavy crimson
leather of her seat. Her fingers, curling on the smooth wooden arms of
the chair, were spindly, beginning to wrinkle. For the first time in his life,
he had the thought: *my mother is growing old*. A feeling of love swelled
in his chest. Despite her cruelties, she was his mother, and whatever
heartbreak she'd laid on him, she had borne tenfold herself.

"I don't think it's fair," he said suddenly, without precedent. "The
way that Father runs around."

"Nothing is fair," she said, her eyes still out the window and the
pale sunlight glowing cold on her face, showing deep creases of shadow

in the lines around her lips. "Nothing in this whole world is fair. But why should it be? Fairness is a made-up word. Make up a word. Say something—the first sound that comes into that little head of yours."

"Pulsh-dana," said Adam after a moment's hesitation.

A rare smile barely curled the corner of Hadassah's lips as she repeated the word. "Pulsh-dana. Things might as well be pulsh-dana as fair. Neither word has any meaning." The smile left her mouth as quickly as it had come, and now her face was stern as she looked away from the window and toward her son. "And don't let me ever hear you talk badly about your father again. Don't you, at the very least, respect your poor parents?"

"I respect you," said Adam dutifully.

"Well, let me tell you about your respect, my lovely little *nishgut-nik*. Respect is like love. It's only worth the lover. You can buy love for a nickel if you know where to go. And if you don't, just ask that shikse tramp of yours who married your brother without a moment's protest. Better yet, ask your father."

The mention of Ahava brought fire into Adam's blood. "I thought we weren't to speak badly of father," he said.

"I said that *you* weren't to speak badly of your father," said Hadassah. She stood up. "I can do whatever I damn well please."

Hadassah's heart pounded with fury and with shame. She could stand anything in the world but pity, anything at all. Her son's words had cut through the only heart that her being possessed: pride. Pride not in herself, but in her family. Pride in her ability to keep it together, to keep it strong, to keep it climbing toward success. An unfaithful husband to her was less meaningful than a son who pitied her for an inability to hold her husband's interest.

She saw now that she'd fooled herself into taking a back seat to her husband's affairs for too long. She had disguised her complacency as stoic rationality; as long as her husband expended no effort on his extramarital children, what did she care where he stuck his thing? And wasn't it true that she'd either put his bastards to work or out the door? Wasn't it true that Asher was a broken man, who worked tirelessly at enriching the Morfawitzes? Wasn't it true that Hersh had helped Zev build up an empire, and had nothing to show for himself? Wasn't it true that she—Hadassah—held the pen that moved the tidal flow of money from the vast Morfawitz coffers, endlessly enriched by the labors of her husband's bastard children?

But now she saw that it was only justification so that she could avoid the battle. She looked at her reflection in the polished silver on her desk and saw not silver-haired Hadassah, but doddering Neville Chamberlain, wide-jowled Daladier, eager to ink the Munich appeasement, while her husband, like Hitler, stomped his boots on the cold Czech ground, trampled the sanctity of marriage. She decided now: no more. Her husband had war tales of fleeing north to Poland? *Let him try*, she thought. *Let him try*. If Zev insisted on weaponizing his children, she would weaponize her own.

Hadassah considered her son—not his face, but his shoulders. His arms, the bulk of his presence. The strength in his veins. She saw what an athlete had been born of her womb, and she suddenly felt something like pride. When she spoke, her voice was sweet, and Adam slouched toward it like a butterfly to honey.

"Adam," she said, her voice thick and solemn, "make yourself useful and follow that man. He is trying to ruin our family. It is one thing for us to speak of your father in here, amongst ourselves, among family"—she lingered over the word, let it settle in the room—"but quite another for a stranger to come and voice accusations. You heard what he accused your father of?"

Adam looked guiltily toward the open window.

"It's alright," she said. "It's good that you know."

"What did he want?"

"What most people want," she said. "Money. And so, what will you do?"

Adam's tongue caught in his throat. He had rarely been asked a question by his mother that wasn't rhetorical.

"I'll—" he stammered. "I'll go find him and—and I'll. When I find him, I'll—"

"Do nothing, my little *hitsiger*," she said. She laid her hands on Adam's shoulders. "When you find him, you'll do nothing. You'll follow. You'll watch. And then you'll report back to me. It's time you learned that there are other people capable of the dirty work you tend to. Now," she said, going back to her seat on the far side of the desk, "go and get that man's license plate. And Adam?"

"Yes, Mother?"

"Do bring a pen. You've got a memory like a sieve."

Adam—his body trembling with the excitement of utility—nodded and ran out. He followed Caleb through the park, ducking conspicuously behind bushes and trees, his large frame bobbing and weaving through the space behind Caleb like a buoy towed in the wake of a boat.

Two times Caleb turned around at the feeling of eyes on his back; out of instinct, he touched his fingers to his waist but there wasn't any belt there so he kept walking. When he came out of the park, he went straight into a men's store, and Adam—neglecting to recognize the transparency of glass—came straight up to the glass storefront window and peered in. He brought his hand above his eyes to stop the bad glare of the sun, made a pocket of shadow between the window and his face, and when his vision had adjusted, he was staring straight into Caleb Cohn's wide eyes. He ducked around the corner and hugged the wall so that only one of his eyes was exposed to watch the store's entrance. He counted fast seconds by the pounding rhythm of his heart against the smooth stone of the facade.

Caleb came out some minutes later, a new belt around his waist. He looked each way and then walked quickly to his car. Adam followed him into a small alley where the car was parked. Caleb opened the driver-side door. As soon as Adam saw the license plate, he turned around and began to run home, but then stopped himself; he'd forgotten to remember the numbers. He turned back to the alley, where the car had not yet moved. Its engine was running, and a pale line of smoke rose from the exhaust. Adam moved closer to read the plate again. He checked his pocket for a pen but hadn't brought one, and so he stood there, staring at the license plate, reciting the characters in his head and then aloud. He looked so addled so as to be beyond suspicion.

Through the rearview mirror, Caleb seemed to think so, too. He got out of the car but left the front door open, the engine running.

"Can I help you?" he said.

Adam stood there, half-paralyzed. He wasn't afraid, only in his mind the instinct to be violent was fighting hard against the task of remembering the plate. Caleb approached him cautiously, approached him the way one approaches a shark beached on the sand as if trying to hypnotize the great beast with a calmness of gait as if it were possible to lull away its predatory instincts.

It didn't work. Adam balled his fists and struck Caleb once on each side of the head. "That's for my father," he shouted, and then ran off, reciting the plate number out loud all the way across the park. Caleb sat with his back against the car, breathing slowly in and out until the spots cleared from his vision, and then got into his car and drove off home.

III
HARMONIA

The next morning, the first frost of the year spread ice crystals along the glass of Caleb and Harmonia's bedroom window. The window was half-open. The cold front had taken the valley by surprise, and outside the cocoon of their sheets, the room was freezing. Caleb made to rise before the sun as he did every morning, but Harmonia put her naked arms around his naked body. Always she was tender in the morning.

"Stay," she said. Her words were clouds on the frozen morning air that had invaded their bedroom. "Your face is all swollen. And besides, you're so warm. Stay."

She tucked her head beneath the sheets and, with her fingers in Caleb's hair, tried to restrain her husband.

"The barn is open."

"Stay," she said again, still half-asleep, but she knew that he must leave her and released her fingers from his hair.

Caleb rose and shut the window.

"Leave it open," she said softly. "If you've got to freeze then I'll freeze, too."

"You don't mean it," said Caleb. She didn't. He kissed the comforter where he thought her head might be and went out from the room.

His bootsteps crunched against the frozen blades of grass, and the oval of ground that was lit up by his lantern was white as snow. Caleb had never seen snow before, and he'd never seen his breath against the air. The crisp silhouette of trees taking form against the predawn sky was pleasant, and he tried to commit everything to memory. The dark was perfect, too perfect, for the light above the barn door—slightly open— had gone out, and he was guided only by the dark shape that the barn structure cast against the indigo sky.

In the barn the familiar smells of horse manure and hay were diminished by the cold, but they were there. Another smell was there, too, but Caleb thought that perhaps it was the frost, that maybe there was an odor to coldness. He pulled the barn door shut behind him and then suddenly knew someone else was in the barn.

"Who's there?" he asked the darkness, but it gave him no reply. He turned off the light of his lantern, and it extinguished with a click. They stood there, the two of them, listening for one another's breath. Caleb's pounding heart seemed to overwhelm the delicate silence, and so instead he swung out with the heavy lantern in a wide and violent arc. It swished through the air and exploded against the barn door. He had missed the intruder but apparently scared him, for following the sound of shattering glass came the thunderclap fire of a gun.

Caleb threw himself to the ground. He'd heard gunfire plenty enough in the Defense Forces, and for a moment he envisioned himself back in Israel as if his father's hook and reel had dragged him back across the sea. The ground was cold, but against his skin it felt like scorching sand.

By the time the memory subsided, the intruder had slipped through the barn door and was running away, back toward a car that was parked on the street. Caleb tried to follow but by the time he was halfway to the street, the car was driving away.

Caleb walked back toward the barn. There was the thumping of something heavy beating again and again against wood, and he understood what had happened before he could open the door. He opened it anyway. The bullet had hit one of the horses in the neck, and it lay on its side in the stall, its hoof kicking at air, at nothing, at death itself, but kept missing its mark and striking against the wooden post instead. It made a drum of the barn, and the sun seemed to rise faster as if encouraged by the percussion.

Caleb stood there and listened for a long time and then became aware that Harmonia was approaching.

"What's happened," she said. "I thought I heard . . ."

But then the trick she'd thought had been played on her ears stopped being a trick at all. Her face went white as she looked into the barn. The drumming slowed and then stopped. The horse died.

By the time the sun was overhead, they had wrapped the dead horse in a polyester tarp and half-dug a hole that could fit it. They made coffee in the kitchen and sat together at the table, and then Caleb turned to look out through the west-facing window above the sink. He stood and walked over to the sink, turning the water on hot and running his hands beneath the faucet. Quickly, it began to steam and still he let his hands remain. Harmonia came very close to telling him to be careful, but she knew her husband well and this behavior was not unusual. She said nothing, only watched him as he watched the world.

He watched through a film of steam and his breath made little pockets of clear air when he exhaled hard and pushed the steam to either side. It was just the opposite of how his breath had behaved that morning, making white clouds on the clear sharpness of the morning air. In the twin clouds of vapor, he saw two paths spread out before him.

To the left there was the hazy word *remain*. The sun lifted and fell from the curve of the *r* and with it rose Caleb, into morning air that might be so hot to draw sweat from his body or so frozen that it had painted frost on the window like graffiti while they slept; from the belly of the *n* dropped children, five of them, four shining girls and a boy. In this cloud were happiness, simplicity, a New-World Eden bounded by stone walls and birch fences, leaves that oranged in autumn, and the smell of horses.

In the cloud on the right there were no words, only a crimson film. There were five children, too, but they were consumed in yellow fire, poison, ice. A great snake coiled around him, around him and his wife and his children, and squeezed them all to death.

Caleb held his breath and the clouds of happiness and despair met and merged, fell into one another, and behind the white veil was the frozen ground outside. He turned back toward Harmonia and saw that in her face there was an unfulfilled vendetta, that she wanted him to go find some vessel for her rage, that she willed it to be his rage, too.

The faucet still ran hot, the steam was one pillar behind his back. To remain would be to keep his wife but lose her; to go would be to risk them both, to shed this skin of humble country life and let fly their reptilian flags. But that skin, too, would shed, and what—if anything— would be left of them when it did?

He walked slowly toward his wife, aware of every step, and bent down to kiss her on the forehead.

"Where are you going?" she said.

"Where else?"

"You don't have to go. Just stay. The thing is done."

"Nothing is done," he said. "They killed your horse."

"They killed my horse."

"They took my sister."

"That, too."

They were quiet for some time. The water was still running and now Harmonia rose and shut the faucet, and the silence left behind by the lack of running water was unbearable. "Don't go," she said.

Caleb smiled at his wife. "You don't mean it," he said. She didn't. "But aren't we happy here?" he said. "Do we want to throw it all away? And for what."

"You know," she said, as if his lips had allowed her own to break the spell of silence, "my father used to say: *nenhum homem pode dizer-se feliz enquanto não chegar o seu fim*. He got it from some book, I don't know what. You understand? When we first moved here, I found a serpent in the garden."

"This far north?" said Caleb.

"Everywhere," said Harmonia. "Everywhere there are serpents. This one had a mouse inside its belly. It looked like a carnival balloon."

Caleb was still enchanted by his wife's accent, and it took him some time to really hear her when she spoke. "And?"

"And I cut off its head. There it was in the garden, in the half sleep of digestion, and I thought it was just a branch at first. Then I really saw it and I jumped. Then it jumped. Then I chased it with the shears and snapped its tail off. And then it moved slower and I went and cut off its head, just above where the mound of the mouse was. I kicked a little hole in the soil with my shoe and kicked it in and then covered it up again. But as soon as I turned away from it, I wondered if I'd maybe cut through the mouse's tail as well."

"I don't think it would've mattered if you'd cut through the mouse's tail."

"No," she said. "I was only curious. I'd had a mouse once, you see."

"And you never had a snake?"

"I never had a snake."

They were quiet for some time. Harmonia looked out the window.

"So had you cut the mouse or not?" Caleb finally said.

"Not," she said, smiling at her own faulty language. "No. I don't know. I couldn't see where I'd buried it. I'd walked all over that garden and all my footsteps looked the same."

"Well?"

"Well," said Harmonia, "until I jumped, that snake was having a good time."

"Until you jumped you were having a good time, too."

"That's true," she said. "But I'm still having a good time."

"So we're agreed then," said Caleb. "That we're really happy here."

"Oh, yes. But don't forget about the cobra. The snake. The snake was also happy." Harmonia was quiet for a while and she lit a cigarette. "Don't forget about the snake," she said again. "We can't just lay here waiting for another one to jump us."

"Well, it didn't seem so bad for him until the end."

Harmonia looked at Caleb as if he were a child who had spoken out of turn. "I hardly think that's any consolation," she said. "You know, I had a friend once who fought seventy-nine bulls and killed all seventy-nine of them. He was served the best wine and best cigars and ate with the most important men in Portugal and Spain. And he was torn open by a bull because he went to bed too late one night, from drinking too much of that good wine. And what do you think he said when he was dying? Do you think he said, 'Well, at least I had a belly full of wine last night.' No. He only said, 'It hurts, it hurts, it hurts.' And then he died. The belly full of wine didn't do him any good, and anyway his stomach had all spilled out."

"So what do you suggest I do?" said Caleb.

"We."

"Yes. We. What do you suggest we do?"

Harmonia finished her cigarette and rubbed it out against the table and then swept the ashes into her hand. She went to the window behind the sink, opened it, and dumped the ashes out.

"When I met you and agreed to take you with me to America," she said, "you told me that your blood was here. Is that true?"

"So that's why you agreed to take me with you," said Caleb.

Harmonia ignored the remark. "Is it true," she said again.

"Yes."

"Well, then I think it's time you go and find it."

IV
BARNABAS COHN

Caleb had no family left to find in the mafioso sense. Kosher Nostra had long ago dried up; there was more money to be made on the island of Manhattan than there was in downtrodden outer boroughs where the Mafia still held sway. And besides, for any Jew with half a brain, there was more money to be made in legitimate professions than in the low-level crime that the families still kept up.

But in the literal sense of family, Caleb's roots had not run dry; and that is how he and Harmonia came to find Barnabas Cohn.

When Caleb's father had been taken to Israel as a child, his older brother, Eli, had been left with what small business the family still controlled. This had been reduced to the stables on St. Mark's Place, where all the bad business with the horses had been conducted, as well as a butcher shop next door. During the worst years of the depression, he'd been forced to sell the stables, but the profit from that sale had allowed him to hang on to the shop.

Barnabas Cohn was Eli's first and only son, and his father impressed upon him two rules: everything they had was always for sale, and there was nothing they didn't have. "In the business of dead meat," he was fond of saying, "one protein is really like the next."

After the depression, customers were used to bad meat, and it wasn't so uncommon to swap in local-caught pigeons for more traditional birds. In order to avoid suspicion, Barnabas's father sold live animals, too, and always kept a chicken or two in the back to prove his honest wares to better customers. He charged extra in such instances to cover his loss of the genuine product and chalked up the heightened price to the cost of burlap sacks, for whenever he sold a live animal, he tied it up and the customer would take it home to slaughter.

As would become his habit, Barnabas took the rule one giant step too far. On the very first day that he was left to mind the shop alone, an older Irish gentleman came in, leaning on his cane, and asked for a live rabbit. With his father's law in mind, Barnabas ran out the back door, took an alley cat by the scruff of its neck, and threw it into a thick burlap sack. With the thing still clawing against the rough fabric, Barnabas tied a double knot with two lengths of rope, charged for the sack and double for the rope, and sent the old man on his way.

Later that day, when Barnabas's father had returned to the shop, Barnabas walked in from a cigarette break in the alley, only to find the old man holding out an empty sack to his father.

"That was the fastest rabbit I ever saw," he was saying to Eli Cohn. "I done opened the bag and he jumped right out and run away. Never saw a rabbit so fast . . ."

Eli looked at Barnabas from across the store. His eyes meant to convey anger, but Barnabas felt only pride. He was beaming. He'd turned an alley cat into a rabbit and the trick would never be discovered. It might as well have really been a rabbit.

"So I wonder," the old man said, uneasy at the tension in the room whose origin he couldn't discern. "I only wonder if I could get another rabbit. Missus expects a stew, you understand."

"Right away," said Barnabas, moving back toward the alley.

"No," said Eli, blocking the door. "We're out of rabbit." And then, for good measure: "That was our last one."

For while he might dabble in the business of moral lessons, he was not at all in the business of refunds.

These rules translated metaphysically in Barnabas's young mind into a sense that all that mattered was the present and that it could be molded however one wished. He grew up heavily mistrusting the future and deeply discounting the past. All that mattered to Barnabas was to continue to charge after a desire that was always in flux.

Which is not to say that he was shallow, or even that he was not very smart. He was brilliant, in fact, only he had no regard for reality. Despite being last in his high school grade in terms of attendance, he was first in the class on every standardized test.

"It's a shame," said his principal upon graduation. "A boy like you could've gone to Army." He was a military man himself and found no higher institution than the academy at West Point. And since nothing rubbed Barnabas quite so badly as the concept of shame, he shrugged his shoulders and he went. Don't think I mean he was accepted; far from it. He didn't even apply. But he didn't see how that mattered, and it didn't stop him from going. Later on, he pulled the same stunt with MIT and then Harvard. While hanging around at this latter university, Barnabas fell in with Timothy Leary and managed to involve himself in the up-and-coming psychologist's experiments. As a consequence, during his several years at Cambridge, Barnabas Cohn had done far more psychedelics than the human brain was meant to cope with, if it was meant to cope with any at all. And when, in the years after he left, the scientific bases of the experiments were thought to be debunked, Barnabas did nothing whatsoever to lessen his consumption.

* * *

So this was what remained of Caleb Cohn's long-lost family. In many ways, these two cousins reflected one another. Caleb, for whom the real world projected onto the workings of his mind so that he believed ripples of sunlight were harbingers of fate, was the opposite of Barnabas, whose mind projected its designs outward so that the sparks raging across his neural synapses formed purple streaks of color through the air as real to him as wind or solar flares. They were like two sides of a door that connected the real and imagined worlds.

Now they stood on opposite sides of a very real door: it was the door to Barnabas's apartment on St. Mark's Place, above the old butcher shop. The butcher shop itself had been converted into a bar with five stories of tenements above. Barnabas owned it all and lived in the penthouse.

Caleb and Harmonia stood at the door, knocking fruitlessly for some time. Caleb held his ear to the door and listened for movement inside. Then they knocked again. They waited, listening. They had just decided to head back down the stairs and turned around to do so, but then found themselves face-to-face with a little man who seemed to think nothing of their listening at the door. He only stood there politely, as if waiting in line.

"There's no use in knocking," he said. "You just have to go in. The man never answers his door." As if to demonstrate his point, he took two great steps forward, turned the doorknob, and entered. "Never locks it either."

He spoke with definite adoration, with love. Harmonia thought that maybe the two were lovers. She asked.

"Oh, no," he said, beckoning them to follow him into the apartment. "Barnabas isn't gay. You thought so because of the gay bar? Yes, many people do. But no. If you want to know the truth, he doesn't care one way or the other about the bar. It used to be a sports bar, but there were so many fights. Every night, fights. So he tried to make it a singles bar and still there were plenty of fights. So he says to me, 'How about a gay bar? Gays don't fight.' So I ask him, don't you know about Stonewall?' 'Yes,' he says, 'but that was against cops. We won't have any cops.' So I ask him how he knows he won't have any cops, and next thing I know he puts a sign in the window: Gay Bar. No Cops."

Indeed, the sign was still in the window; Caleb and Harmonia had spotted it there. Someone had written in the word "real" between "No" and "Cops," apparently to make allowances for costumes.

"But the sign isn't the reason that cops stay away," the man continued. He went through the house, opening cabinets here and there, peeking his head inside, and then closing them again. "Really, his family is tight with the cops. They're old Mafia, the Cohns are. Say, what'd you say your names were? Mine's Aiden."

They introduced themselves as Cohns, and a wide smile spread across Aiden's face.

"Ah," said Aiden. "So that's what you're doing here. I see."

The Cohns' mere relation to Barnabas seemed to make them like royalty in his mind. He ushered them toward a circle of low sofas bathed in white sunshine beneath a giant skylight. The floor was dark wood, but a giant tartan rug spread out in a great imperfect square beneath the whole space, stopping just before the living room turned into an open kitchen. The rug itself was stitched with multicolored threads but lacked a discernible pattern. In the center of the sofas was a collection of wooden statuettes—some ankle-high, some like true Goliaths—which had clearly been carved in place; wood shavings were pooled in great puddles on the rug, and the whole place smelled strongly of varnish. In addition to the statuettes, there were low tables and stools, indistinguishable from one another and distinct from the statuettes only in that their top surfaces were somewhat flat; the legs or stumps were still quite intricate. Atop each of these flat surfaces—as well as several places on the floor—stood glasses of wine, some full, some half-full, some empty with only a dark film of grape sugar and sediment to coat their bottoms. Some glasses had multiple stripes of different opacities of purple, like rock layers in a canyon wall, as if somebody had taken such a long pause from drinking that some of the wine had evaporated during the hiatus. The odors, the vapors, and the wine all reflected the sunlight and gave the whole space a vinaceous glow. A remarkable amount of glass was being used, and all around them sunlight broke on the prisms into little rainbows and flew off in strange directions.

Aiden brushed the wood shavings off the couch and beckoned for them to sit. They looked at one another and shrugged, for although the place was a pigsty, its excess had an unmistakable opulence. Clearly, the man had money.

Things that they had noticed about the building began to come together, suggested slight attempts to maintain order, with more money than effort behind them. The staircase was soft because of multiple layers of carpeting stapled down as if it were preferable to lay new carpet than clean the existing; the sidewalk in front of the building was crumbling from too much salt used carelessly in winter; the outside walls had been painted many times over rather than washed even once.

Harmonia, more direct than her husband, struggled to make herself stern, for her voice had to fight with all the aromatic air.

"How did you come to know Barnabas?" she said. "What is the nature of your relationship?"

"Ah," said Aiden, kneeling and looking under the couch as if he might find Barnabas hiding down there. He'd been asked the question before, for his relationship to Barnabas was unclear. Ostensibly, they were partners, but Aiden gave off a deferential feeling for his friend, one that bordered on worship. He rose again and smiled down at Harmonia and Caleb. "I will tell you."

He then relayed to these two new Cohns the story of how he and Barnabas had met. Aiden had been in his plebe year at West Point (for his parents had refused to send him to any college where they'd need to pay tuition) when Barnabas had arrived one day at the gate. He'd taken a taxi from New York City and it was unclear what on earth had brought him north up the river valley. He'd been dropped off at the admissions office, where he saw the river through the great windows. He could not peel his eyes away and could think of nothing but going for a swim. He signed in, but then stole away down the great stone steps toward the river. He undressed on the banks and stepped into the cool flowing water. He dove down and swam for as long as he could before coming up for air, and upon breaching was immediately run over by the crew team, whose quad scull crashed into his face.

When Barnabas came to, he was lying supine in the boathouse, coughing up water. The coxswain was kneeling over him and had just administered CPR. The rest of the crew were standing all around them, and no sooner had Barnabas opened his eyes than they began to be unkind. Mostly they referenced his nakedness and slightness and the diminutive size of his penis. They twisted their towels into rat tails and snapped them at both Barnabas and the coxswain, who had apparently cast his lot in with the drowning young nudist by administering CPR.

What happened next is a confidential matter of military personnel documentation. The admissions secretary, wondering where the student went, tracked his progress down the stone steps and found his clothes on the riverbank. Thinking he'd drowned, he ran over to the boathouse to find a suitable search vessel to take out into the river but instead found a strange scene in the crew team's locker room. Everybody was without clothing, and the masculine military spirit had been completely and decisively abandoned. All of them were summarily expelled, except for Barnabas, who had never been admitted to begin with.

Barnabas gained nothing academically from the day he spent at West Point, but he gained a close friend in the coxswain who had administered the CPR.

"That was me," said Aiden. "We've been together ever since. In Cambridge, in the Pines, and back here in the good old Village."

Harmonia looked at Aiden skeptically. All she could think to say was: "You rowed crew?" For the boy was very slight.

"Yes," said Aiden. "Or no. I didn't row. I was only the coxswain."

Harmonia had stretched the boundaries of her athletic vocabulary and looked at him blankly.

"They sit at the front and are only useful if they weigh very little." He clapped his hands together. "I was always very little."

Aiden had lifted one corner of the rug and then set it down again, and now he sauntered back toward the kitchen, opening every shelf he passed and then closing it again. Finally, he gave a great shout for joy. He had found Barnabas, crouched in the plumbing cabinet underneath the sink.

"Out," said a voice. Despite its clear indignation, it was ethereal and light, something like a song. "Out, out, out."

"But Barny," Aiden said, "what are you doing in there?"

"It's the darkest place in the house . . ."

"But why, Barny, why?"

"Because no light gets in . . ."

"I mean why do you want to be in the dark?"

"You're the one who's asking how to make it dark, not me . . . I'm just saying, you turn off the light . . ."

Harmonia half-rose to see the cupboard doors shut, Barnabas still inside.

"Won't he come out?" she said.

"Oh, no, Mrs. Cohn. There's no question of that. Not when he's in a state like this. No one's home, you know."

"No one's home . . ." she said. She looked around at the vast apartment, at the many wine glasses, and the sheer scale of untidiness made it difficult to attribute to one person. "Is it only Barnabas who lives here?"

"That's right," said Aiden. "Just Barny and his girl."

"The man who lives here is married?" said Harmonia, not bothering to disguise her incredulity. Caleb could feel the harshness in his wife's voice; she was not impressed with his people. She was not impressed with his blood. She looked around the room with a vague disgust drawn on her face and he suddenly felt that his veins were filled with dreck.

"Oh, no, Mrs. Cohn," said Aiden. Evidently, he liked to feel the surname in his mouth. "I mean his daughter."

"You're joking," she said, her boot accidentally prodding a wine glass. "This man has a daughter?"

"Two, actually. One of them is a bit of a brat though. Doesn't see so much of her father. The other is"—he waved one hand around in a vague elliptical pattern—"about."

"She's here?"

"Unless she's at work," said Aiden. He looked at his watch. "No, she ought to be here. Only, she won't come out until she's interested. That's her way, you know. I daresay she learned it from her father . . . though she isn't quite as bad. I swear, sometimes it isn't easy to say who is the child and who the parent."

"No kidding," said Harmonia.

"Anyway," said Aiden. "What was it you wanted to discuss? You're welcome to wait, of course, but it could be a very long time . . ."

She looked to Caleb and he looked at her. Their hands joined together. They both felt the same sensation and were hesitant to give voice to this thing that haunted them; it would somehow serve to make the trouble real. Finally, it was Harmonia who spoke.

"My husband came to New York to find his sister," she said. "She was kidnapped on a yacht from her native land of Israel. My husband traced the boat's owner to Manhattan and . . . well, when he went to confront them, it didn't go so well. It's the Morfawitz family. They're apparently well-known. They had somebody follow us back to the barn."

"They killed one of her horses," said Caleb.

"They killed one of my horses."

"I see," said Aiden.

"And they beat up my husband," said Harmonia.

"I see," Aiden said again. He pondered. He opened his mouth to speak again, but just then a door flew open from the hallway behind the kitchen, and in walked a young woman of remarkable beauty. She had long yellow hair and a figure that was mostly visible through her very large but gossamer shirt. The shirt was all she wore, and it did not leave much to the imagination.

"Ah," said Aiden. "But here's Seraphina now. We were just talking about you."

Seraphina came up and sat on Aiden's lap and kissed him on the lips. She came over and did the same to Caleb, who—though stunned—did not seem as if he disliked the experience.

"That's enough of that," said Harmonia, rising. She had come to America but in her moral heart the rigidity of Portuguese Catholicism reigned.

"Oh, there's nothing to worry about there," said Aiden, laughing. "Your husband is not the right age for our Seraphina . . ."

Harmonia looked Seraphina up and down. It was true that she was young. Certainly not thirty. "You talk about such things with your father just there in the kitchen?"

"Oh, Barny is not the type of father to mind that," said Aiden.

"No kidding," said Harmonia. It had become her favorite English idiom.

Seraphina had now walked up to Harmonia and kissed her also on the mouth. Harmonia's face burned and she sat down again beside Caleb. All the while, Aiden kept on talking.

"Who better to talk of these things with than a father?" Seraphina said suddenly. Her voice was sharp and clever. "It is only if you expect the Oedipal, the Lottian drama, that you should inhibit speech and so hope to inhibit action. But really, besides Dad, every man on earth is prejudiced. And Aiden here, of course."

"Don't be so sure!" said Aiden. "But it's just like I told you, she's never interested in anything until she is, and then you can't pull her away. Didn't I tell you that she'd stay in her room until she heard something that interested her? Well? So now she's come out. Seraphina, this is Caleb and Harmonia."

Harmonia was looking at her strangely. "So what did you hear us talking about that interested you so?" she asked.

Seraphina did not look away from Harmonia, but she sat next to Aiden and leaned her head against his shoulder.

"Oh yes," said Aiden. "What were we talking about? Let's see. Ah, you were saying that you were having some trouble with the Morfawitz family."

Aiden looked at Caleb's face, which was still black and blue.

"On the positive side," he said, "they are not very difficult to find. If I had to guess, the one who beat you up was Adam Morfawitz. A dummy but an absolute brute . . ."

He kept talking and Caleb listened with great interest. Harmonia, on the other hand, stopped listening. She was watching Seraphina closely. The girl had a maniacal look in her eye and held her hand over her mouth to keep from laughing. In the span of a few seconds, her demeanor had changed, and now she seemed severe and full of woe.

"Do you know Adam Morfawitz?" Harmonia suddenly asked her. The conversation between the two men stopped at once. Both of them looked at Seraphina.

"Oh no," she said. She began to giggle and held her hand up to her mouth. "No, I don't know Adam Morfawitz. I've never seen Adam Morfawitz in my life." Suddenly the laughter left her and now her eyes were once again sad. "I'll never be introduced to Adam Morfawitz in my life."

"Did you expect to be introduced to Adam?" said Harmonia.

The pulse again—joy and then woe.

"Oh no. Who expects anything nowadays? How should a girl expect to meet—well, it's only proper that . . ." Suddenly, she flipped her wrist as if she had a watch there, which she didn't. And anyway, her eyes remained fixed on Harmonia. "I ought to get to work," she said.

"To work!" said Aiden. "It is a lovely place where she works. A beautiful bridal studio. She models the dresses in the window. Don't you see it? Who wouldn't want to look like Seraphina on their wedding day? Well, it isn't only the brides-to-be who see her in the window . . . oh no, no, no . . . and Fifth Avenue is not such a bad place to be seen . . ."

"We'll drive you," said Harmonia. She stood up.

"Oh, that's alright," said Seraphina. "I don't mind the subway."

"Dressed like that? I wouldn't hear of it."

"Go on with them, go on," said Aiden. "These people are your cousins, after all . . . And maybe put some pants on . . . You won't be warm in that . . ."

"No kidding," said Harmonia. They all went out together.

* * *

They drove the short trip in near silence. Seraphina sat in the back, not saying much of anything at all, but when they arrived at the bridal shop where Seraphina worked, she leaned forward over the center console and kissed Caleb and then Harmonia on the cheek. "Uncle," she said. "Aunt!" And then she got out and shut the door.

"Well," said Harmonia into the silence. "I trust you understand what's going on."

"No," said Caleb. "I haven't any idea."

"That girl is involved with Adam Morfawitz. You saw how she came out once we started talking about him? She practically—how do you say it—drooled. Yes, drooled when we said his name."

"But that's ridiculous," said Caleb. "She's just a young girl and the Morfawitz family is very rich and powerful. It's enough. And anyway, so what if she is? Is that all?"

"No," said Harmonia. "Here's something else: we're being followed."

"Followed?" Caleb turned around and looked through the back windshield. "Followed by what? Followed by whom?"

"That blue car behind us. It's been around us since we parked at your cousin's house."

She was so distraught by his relations that she did not like to voice their names.

"Nobody is following us," said Caleb. "That's just a common kind of car."

"You watch," she said. "As soon as you pull away from this place, that car is going to pull away as well."

With his eyes fixed on the rearview mirror, Caleb took his car out of park and began to go. The whole world seemed to hold its breath as they moved away from the curb and rejoined the flow of traffic. But the blue car behind them only pulled up slightly, so that it was parked directly outside the bridal shop, and then it remained where it was.

"You see?" said Caleb. "Alright?"

Harmonia cursed in Portuguese and tapped her nails against the window.

* * *

An aside: it is difficult to convey how menacing the tapping of Harmonia's fingers is—less like a motion of impatience than that of a zipper closing shut on the world. It is a tic she picked up in her bullfighting days, with her grip on the hilt of her sword. *Tap, tap, tap, tap*: the way a long jumper apparently traces out the exact places where his feet will leap from. Having never been one for jumping, long or not, I wouldn't know.

However, I frequently experienced this idiosyncrasy of Harmonia's while interviewing her, Caleb, and Barnabas, to whom I am indebted for a great deal of information, and who were to remain, for some time after this episode, more like a cohesive family than any other blood relations I have mentioned. According to Caleb, it was a gesture reserved for bulls and Morfawitzes, and it was best to allow silence to rein after Harmonia closed shut the world with the drop of her fingers.

What she was closing shut now was herself from this world, for the Cohns were to disappear twice: temporarily, now, and then later on, forever. It would seem an injustice not to come out and say that this is not due to their lack of importance; I can think of no higher praise than to be excluded, by choice, from my family's affairs.

V
SERAPHINA

But actually, Harmonia's instincts were mostly correct, both on account of the car and the girl. The car had been following them. Inside was the man Hadassah had paid to track their plates back to the barn, the man whose stray bullets had killed one of Harmonia's horses.

Only, it wasn't Caleb and Harmonia, but their passenger, that the man in the car was following. For here, Harmonia had been right but wrong again; Seraphina was involved with a man of the Morfawitz family—only, it wasn't Adam, but Zev. In Harmonia's mind, people lived in generations, and it was unfathomable that a man of Zev's age would have anything to do with a mere child like Seraphina.

However, the transgression was not unfathomable to Hadassah, who knew all about her husband's predilections and made it a point to know all about his affairs so that his indiscretions would remain discreet. This was especially true if they were being conducted on the island of Manhattan, for she wisely did not trust her husband's level of caution, and while her heart was sufficiently calloused to overlook Zev's infidelities, her gargantuan pride would not allow for a scandal to go public.

The news that Zev's pretty, young mistress who pranced in the window at the bridal shop was somehow associated with Caleb Cohn, who had accused her husband of kidnapping aboard a Mediterranean yacht, boiled in Hadassah's mind. She had thought nothing of their same last names, as Cohn was a common distortion for Ellis Island to have made of the priest class, Cohen, and there were plenty of Cohns running about. But now her warning signals were firing, and Hadassah decided it was time for something to be done.

And here is where Hadassah and Zev were something truly monstrous. For we cede a certain forgiveness to the tidal wave that knows not what havoc it wreaks; but should it freeze its fleeing victims by the mechanism of a face drawn in foam upon its surface—should it be not only unyielding but seeking in its prey—this then we can call wicked. For tigers can be vicious and snakes can be sly and hawks show no remorse for the young mice they tear apart, but only humans can be really bad. And for how frequently Zev and Hadassah liked to deify their own attributes, the fact is they were human. They were human; they were bad.

* * *

Less than a week after Caleb and Harmonia first met Seraphina, Zev walked into Tyra's Bridal Shoppe where the young woman was employed. Perhaps it will be unsurprising to learn that Zev—to whom no higher pleasures existed than women and the breaking of taboos—very much enjoyed making love to Seraphina while she modeled her white bridal dresses. The store was conveniently located on his short walking commute between office and home, and he was by far its most frequent visitor, though he had—at this point—not been in for several months.

His visits had been going on for some time and had only to do with himself. He was completely ignorant as to the existence of Caleb Cohn, and the only thing he knew about St. Mark's Place was that it was where Seraphina called home. As a general rule, he never visited her there. They only knew one another carnally, and only within the confines of the shop, and only when she was wearing a white wedding dress that Zev could desecrate. Zev thought her name was Sarah; she thought he called her the nickname affectionately. It did not occur to Zev that she could possibly know anything about him.

"Oh, hello, Mr. Morfawitz," she greeted him at the door, giggling in her pseudopsychotic way. "We haven't seen you in a while. I have some new ones that I think you might like to see if you'd follow me along to the back. Isn't the wedding next month?"

The other shopgirls rolled their eyes, but then they looked away. Zev Morfawitz was good for the purchase of one wedding dress a month, and they had been feeling his absence financially, for he tipped them fantastically well. Besides, they enjoyed the scandal, and it gave them a reason other than sheer jealousy to look down on the beautiful model who always danced with such grace in the window.

As soon as they were alone, Zev began. He made a mess of her hair with his eager fingers as he pulled her head back to expose her neck. He brought his mouth down to her pulsing vein with such force that Seraphina could not help but gasp. His hands fought against the complexity of the lace frills of the dress until they found her legs hidden in their folds, and then he pushed his hands up along her thighs with all the unrelenting, impersonal force of a tide and buried his face in her chest.

"I want to talk," she said over the crop of his now-graying hair. "You never want to talk."

Zev mumbled something into her chest, and she sighed.

"My father used to warn me about men like you," she said. "Always want to take, take, take, but never give a thing but this."

Zev stopped for just long enough to pull his head back and consider Seraphina's face. There was no sympathy in him, no compassion; his impression of Seraphina started and ended in the bridal shop, and he regarded her as little more than an animate mannequin. He was honestly surprised to learn that the girl had a father.

Seraphina took his stony expression badly, and she wrapped her legs around his body and pulled him closer.

"Oh, don't stop," she said. "I always talk too much. That's my problem, I talk too much."

"Yes," said Zev.

After several more pulses of silence, she spoke again.

"I had a visitor today, you know."

"Did you?"

"A woman who works in a very special kind of store around here . . . not respectable, like this one."

"Is that so?"

"She said she knows your wife."

"Is that so?"

"She said that . . . she said that you do something awfully special when you go to bed with Mrs. Morfawitz. That Mrs. Morfawitz, that she . . . well, oh, that she quite likes it. She said that she made a special purchase recently, and that well . . . No, no—don't stop, baby. Don't stop. Don't be angry. I'm not angry. I only, well . . . I'm only curious."

Zev hated to hear the word *baby* in such context, but otherwise found nothing objectionable in Seraphina's talk; certainly, he found nothing sacrilegious in his lover's mention of Hadassah. Impiety was beyond him. What had stopped him was what had made Seraphina speak in the first place: curiosity and pride. Had he been doing something remarkable with Hadassah so that she was spreading the news of his prowess to her friends? What was this thing she had purchased? Was it for use by him or was it possible that Hadassah might be seeing somebody else? Zev had considered that their bedroom relationship since marriage had been one of perfunctory duties and long dry spells with occasional spikes of passion. But had Hadassah seen it differently? After all, he thought, for all of Hadassah's sophistication and complexity, she was rather inexperienced in the bedroom. His wife had a sort of grace that kept her from being too eroticized. She was possessed of both physical and emotional frigidities. He wondered now whether any other man might have ever mustered the courage to undress her. This all raced through his mind while his body mechanically performed the functions asked of it by his warm-blooded, mannequin bride.

"Baby," said Seraphina. "Baby, you're not here, I can tell when you're not here, I can."

"Where else should I be?"

"Oh, don't get angry. Please don't get angry."

"I'm not angry."

"I only . . . Well, you keep telling me that you're going to take me somewhere nice, or to see your home . . ."

"I never told you that."

"Sure you did. Well, anyway I *want* to go. It isn't fair to only meet me here. It isn't fair. I feel like nothing but a doll."

"Yes," said Zev, about her being nothing but a doll.

"Oh, baby. Thank you. And maybe . . . well, maybe we could try that thing. The lady from the store . . . well, I don't think it's bad, but . . . she said, she said that they get a bad reputation but really it shows that you love somebody. That you're comfortable with them and are a little bit vulnerable. You're a little bit vulnerable with me, aren't you? Well, why can't we try it. You do it with your wife all the time is what that woman said. So why can't we try it. If you really like me then why can't we?"

"Try what?" said Zev. He was not curious now, only automatic. His sexual life was now full of routines, and all of them bored him. He closed his eyes, trying to shut out the sound of her voice, and determined never to see Seraphina again.

But just then, she whispered something into his ear. It broke through the surface of his routine like a breaching whale.

"Hm," he muttered now, his low voice competing for sound with his excited, heavy heart. "All that in a tub? What's that . . . keeps it in her top drawer? Hadassah?" And then, being as unwilling as ever to admit inexperience in carnal pleasures, he said, "Yes, of course in the tub. Don't be stupid."

He had no idea what Seraphina was talking about, no idea who the woman from the scandalous store might be, but that did not stop him from being excited at the prospect of this mysterious fantasy.

The thought so consumed his mind on the walk home, that he nearly asked Hadassah about the equipment in question but realized finally that it might be difficult to explain to her where he'd gotten the idea. He resolved instead to check on it himself the next time she was out. In a stroke of good fortune for Zev, this turned out to be that very night.

"Heinrich is asking to see me," said Hadassah. "He's never asked to see me in his life. There must be something wrong."

"What time will you be back?"

"I'm not going to take a car all the way down to New Jersey and then back in a night."

"You're staying with Heinrich? But you've never spent a night away from home."

She looked up from the small overnight bag that she was packing and stared directly into her husband's face. "Would you prefer for me to stay here?"

Zev thought for a moment. "No," he said. "He's your brother, after all."

"Well," she said, turning her face back to look inside the bag, "the maids are gone as well, so you'll be all alone for the night. What will you do for dinner?"

"I'll find something to eat."

"I'm sure you will."

He watched from the window as her town car pulled away from the mansion, and then opened her top drawer and found exactly the device Seraphina had described. It seemed better suited to solo use, but not of the type that Zev might get any pleasure out of. Still, it was a curious thing, and the blandness of his sex life compelled him to see what pleasures it could offer. So later that night, once he'd phoned Hadassah at Heinrich's landline in Atlantic Highlands and confirmed that she was at least two hours away, he went ahead and phoned Seraphina and she was there by ten o'clock. By midnight, she was dead.

* * *

The device in question was one gigantic battery, the sort of thing better suited for a car, but neither Zev nor Seraphina knew that it carried any charge. So it was with naive optimism that they attempted to lower the device into a place where electrically charged devices ought not to go: the bathtub. Zev got a minor shock; Seraphina, on the other hand, absorbed the majority of charge and died right there in the water.

Zev was not half so nervous about the police as he was that Hadassah would see a police report that had any degree of accuracy, so he rolled the body in a carpet and brought it back to Seraphina's apartment in the East Village. He'd never been there before but found her address on her license. It was after three in the morning when he arrived and there was no one on the street, yet he parked eleven blocks away and hauled the rug and the body all that distance on foot. The building was a walk-up and Seraphina lived on the penthouse floor. There were no keys in her purse but the apartment door was unlocked. Zev opened it and went quietly in. He unrolled the rug in the kitchen and watched her lifeless body for some time before lifting it and placing it inside the tub. For good measure and to make it seem plausible that the scene had really happened there, he recreated the accident in Seraphina's bathroom. He filled the tub with warm water and dropped a radio inside. The room flashed only slightly, but otherwise, nothing much happened and the radio shorted and then everything was still. Smoke rising from the surface of the water was the only movement in the place, and there was nothing at all to make a sound. It seemed ridiculous that such a little thing could kill a woman who had taken twenty-nine years of life to grow. Ridiculous and almost funny.

Zev looked down at her pink and naked body. For the first time in a while, he thought about the bodies at Gusen and how little they had seemed to him, how thin and easily penetrable the membrane separating life from death. Here was not a woman, only soil in waiting. Some remnant soap on the bottom of the tub had been excited by the water and the heat to form suds on the surface, and they gathered around her head and breasts and knees and toes—whatever of her body had risen above the surface.

Zev went to the sink and splashed water on his face. He looked in the mirror and realized that his face was growing old. Deep lines ran like jet streams across his forehead, cut vertically down to break his brow, like nails shot downward into a coffin. He looked at his hands and scrubbed them clean in the hot water. The steam rising from the basin obscured his reflection and he appreciated the kindness that the fog did for his wrinkles. He breathed shapes into the steam. He looked at the reflection of Seraphina's body in the tub, curiously aware that he was watching not a body but only the culmination of its light against the mirror. He looked back to his own reflection and tried to feel the same dispassion, the same remove, but could not; he was something different.

But now Zev got his second shock of the night, and the more severe of the two. He felt something brush against his leg and then embrace it. He looked down below the sink and saw that the vanity cabinet was open. Two arms, covered with red freckles and orange-brown hair, emerged from the dark storage cupboard to hug Zev's right leg. Zev's lip curled in disgust and he took two steps back from the phantom arms that emerged from the cabinet's underbelly. But the arms held on tight to his leg, and in his retreat, Zev pulled out a set of shoulders and a head, a torso—a fully grown, fully naked male body from the space below the sink. It was as if the vanity had given birth and Zev had acted in the role of a midwife. A face looked up at him now—a tan face dotted with red freckles and topped with a balding crop of orange hair.

"Father?" said the man. He was almost as old as Zev himself—far too old to be acting in such a way. His eyes fluttered as if in ecstasy and he seemed to have a difficult time focusing.

"Let go," said Zev.

"Father?"

"You parasite, I said let go!"

Zev lifted his other foot and drove his heel into the parasite's red face. Still, the man held on and so Zev kicked again, again, until finally he heard the strange nose crunch beneath his heel. Blood sputtered from both nostrils and the man fell back, unconscious.

Zev hovered above the body, saw that it was still breathing. He wondered: Was this Seraphina's husband? She'd never mentioned one, but that was not altogether unexpected, considering. But no, thought Zev, this man was too old to be her husband. Although he had to admit that attraction to older men would not have been out of character for the young, dead Seraphina. Was he a brother? A friend?

In any case, the man was clearly alive and also clearly addled. When he came to, he would have to contend with a dead wife, or friend, or daughter. Zev thought there was little chance of the clearly insane man doing this competently, but he was not going to stick around to find out.

VI
THE OPINION OF TEHRANI

Dusk the following day, and Zev was nervous. It was a feeling he hadn't had since the war, and he felt himself wondering whether he should have called the police about Seraphina's death right away. "After all," he said to himself, "the thing was obviously accidental."

Still, he could not help but mentally retrace his footsteps, think about each place where his fingerprints might be. That man who had been hiding beneath the bathroom vanity was clearly insane, but he was not blind. His eyes had been glazed over, yes, but they might not have been entirely useless.

From deep wells of self-preservation came two sentiments that were alien to Zev: he regretted his evening with Seraphina, and he missed his bastard son. Hersh, who was at home in the shadows, would have known what to do with the scandal. These unfamiliar feelings rushed Zev and made him nearly sick. He had no apprehension at being responsible for a death, only alarm at this novel notion of regret and at the possibility that—if things went poorly—some lowly police officer might be in a position to tell Zev what to do.

Zev picked up the phone in his study without knowing who he meant to call—Hersh, Hadassah, the police?—and put it down again. He went from the study to the dining room and sat in Hersh's chair.

He stood and walked to the phone and held it to his ear. He listened to the dial tone for some unknowable time and then replaced the receiver. He called for a glass of brandy and then remembered that the help had gone. Why had the help gone? He got a glass of brandy himself. Why had the help gone? There was no reason for the help to have gone.

What could Hadassah know? What could Hadassah *not* know? He hadn't been exactly careful. And yet, hadn't they always had a sort of understanding? She must have known about the girl. But did she know where she worked? How could she know about the girl and *not* know where she worked? She pranced around in the storefront window, for god's sake. And if she knew about the girl and knew where she worked, was it really possible that she would not have done anything? The bridal shop was only a few blocks away from their home. Could she have been expected to sit there and do nothing? And what would she have done? He knew his wife well enough to know that she would have acted indirectly, in a manner as untraceable as wind. Wasn't that how she'd driven Asher's mother from the island of Manhattan, how she'd driven Asher to Vietnam, how she'd driven the Kolitz woman to suicide? Hadn't she done it all wordlessly, so that there was not even a wisp of a ghost on which to lay the blame?

He poured himself another glass of brandy and threw it quickly down his throat. Perhaps, he thought, there was a simpler question, a question that was easier to answer: why had the help gone? The help had never gone before, and he'd been so eager for the realization of his fantasy that he hadn't stopped to consider why they'd gone now, and why they'd gone on the same night as Hadassah. He felt a straining in his neck and drummed his fingers against the table. In his mind he saw a mousetrap springing shut, its hammer swinging around in a high arc and down onto a block of wood like a guillotine. Only, at the moment of contact, in the place of the mouse was a mannequin bride. Where a cube of baiting cheese ought to go was a great empty house without servants.

Zev was on his seventh glass of brandy when he heard the front door open. Hadassah came in and closed the door and stood in the foyer for some time. Zev could not see his wife but he could hear her, or rather,

not hear her in her stillness. Here was a woman who made her presence
known by whatever means were at her disposal, whether they be sound
or vacuum. Then there was the sound of her footsteps, her heels against
the hardwood floor. He'd never considered how much he could recognize her rhythm, but he considered it now as he waited.

As if she'd known where he was, she walked straight to the dining
room where Zev was sitting. It was a funny place for her to come.

"Funny place for you to come," he said.

She stood on the threshold of the room and seemed to take up all
of the doorway. She was tall and austere.

"Where else should I go?" she said.

"Take off your heels. You'll bang your head against the ceiling."

"Are you drunk?"

"Why shouldn't I be."

"You're drunk."

"Yes."

A rare smile curled the corners of Hadassah's mouth. She stepped out
of her heels but did not seem to shrink in size. Zev was disappointed.
She walked—soundlessly, now—to her chair at the opposite head of
the great table and ran her fingers along the back of it. All the while she
watched her husband, and he turned his brandy in its glass.

"Come sit beside me," he said.

She pulled out her chair and sat down and crossed her legs.

"I said come sit beside me," he said.

"I heard you."

"So why do you sit over there?"

"This is my seat," she said innocently. "Where else should I sit but
my seat."

"When a man tells his wife to sit beside him—"

"Are we going to talk about what a man and wife should do?"

She put her elbows on the table and Zev took another sip of brandy.
"So that's what this is all about."

"Hm?"

"Have a drink," said Zev.

"I never drink."

"Neither do I."

"Then who," said Hadassah, "is that sitting in your chair?"

Zev looked down into his glass as if intending to study his reflection.

"Have a drink," he said again.

"Bring me one."

Zev stared at his wife over the long mahogany tabletop. He called for a drink and then remembered that the help had gone.

"Why did you send them away?" he said. "Where did they go?"

Hadassah raised her eyebrows and her eyes themselves were flat. There was a sound at the door.

"But here's Tehrani now with my bags," she said, and called out for her porter. He appeared in the doorway, a small brown man. There was something funny about his face, thought Zev. Too much work. It looked patched together by surgery. It did not look only clean-shaven—it looked as if it were incapable of growing hair. The skin hung loosely under his chin, but his cheeks were firm and his forehead showed no wrinkles.

"Yes, Mrs. Morfawitz," he said. His voice was like a child's, but he strained to make it baritone.

"Get us a drink—" Zev began to say, but Hadassah interrupted.

"Take my bags up and then come down, won't you."

"Yes, Mrs. Morfawitz." He went away.

"He could have gotten you a drink first," said Zev.

"I never drink."

"Neither do I."

"That again?" said Hadassah. "I'll tell you what. If you'll get me a drink, I'll have one. Then we can both be trying something new."

Zev looked at his wife for a long while and then let out a sharp, booming laugh. Laughter came from his lips unnaturally, and it put Hadassah on edge. Her sister Deborah had put it best: "Each time he laughs, I think of Poe's Raven speaking. Words don't belong inside a bird's beak, and a laugh does not belong inside our Zev." That was how Hadassah felt now.

Zev finished his glass of brandy and then left to get the bottle and another glass. When he returned, he sat down beside Hadassah. He set the bottle down on the table between them and put an empty glass down before her.

"What if I wanted ice," she said. He looked up at her and she smiled. "When you walked in just now, you did not even look at your seat. You just came and sat in this one."

"This one is beside you," he said, pouring her glass full of brandy.

"That's sweet."

"I didn't mean it sweetly."

"I know. You meant it practically, as a matter of fact. 'This one is beside you.' So it is."

"So?"

"So, it's a thing that I've always liked about you, Zev." She took a sip of her brandy. "Had you said it sweetly I would not have trusted you."

Zev raised his glass to his lips but froze before drinking. "And you trust me now?"

Hadassah put her glass down and crossed her arms over her chest. She leaned back in her chair and stared at her husband. "Most people are attached to the seats they sit in," she said. "You aren't most people. You come into a room and it doesn't matter where you were sitting before. What matters is where you want to sit now. What does it mean for me to trust you? I know you. That is enough. I trust that when you come into a room you are going to sit where you please, whether or not it is where you were sitting before, whether or not anybody else is sitting there now. That isn't most people's idea of trust."

"You don't often think about most peoples' ideas."

"That's true," she said. She took another drink. "Anyway, it's mine. Call it trusting or knowing. I trust myself to know how you are going to behave. I trust you to behave that way."

Zev was drunker now than he'd been in a very long time. It made him say exactly the things he wanted to.

"Are we talking about being faithful?" he said.

Hadassah looked at him and her shallow smile curled into something like a snarl. It was one thing for him to do the things he did, but another thing entirely to voice those deeds inside her home. She drank before answering her husband.

"Faithful," she said. Her voice was like a whisper and it smelled now of drink. Spirits filled the space between them. "Faithful? It ought to be faith-worthy. Who is full of faith? I am empty of it. I am far from full of faith. Far. And yet I have not so much as looked at another man."

"That's because you don't see them as men next to me," said Zev. Hadassah wanted to deny it but could not. "It doesn't take you any self-restraint."

"Do you strain to use so much of that yourself?"

He looked up at her. "The only people capable of being very good are the ones who think of being very bad and then don't do it. What was it that Marilyn once said? Only a very large cup can be very full."

"It was the other way around," said Hadassah. She turned the glass in her hand. "It takes a very large cup to be empty."

"It amounts to the same."

"A thimble can be full."

"It amounts to the same," Zev said again. "So there, maybe I'm better than you after all. You never think about it, to begin with. What sort of restraint does it take to not do a thing you don't think of?"

Hadassah drained her cup of brandy and leaned forward into the thick cloud of spirits between them, making it thin, so that their faces were close.

"Don't be so sure that I don't think about it," she said. "Don't be so certain that I use such better restraint than you. Sometimes I wonder if I should have been a man after all."

They were still for what seemed like a very long time, counting time on one another's heartbeats, which twisted and interwove until their two rhythms were one. Then Zev's hand shot up and grabbed Hadassah by the neck. He squeezed so that the blood stayed in her face and her cheeks glowed pink and then red and the veins bulged in her temples. Her lip curled as if the excess blood had set her mood to smoldering. Their noses were inches apart.

Sharp, mechanical beats seemed to reach out to them from very far away as if some drummer in an orchestra pit had suddenly lost track of the score. The servant Tehrani was returning, and his footsteps were like knuckles rapping on the closed door of their cold violence.

He appeared at the door just as Zev released Hadassah's neck. Nothing else of them moved but his hand; their faces remained almost touching, and Hadassah breathed in hard. Tehrani believed that he'd walked in on an intimate moment.

"Your pardon, Mrs. Morfawitz," he said.

"No, don't go." She did not look away from her husband. "This bottle is empty. Bring us another. And these candlesticks need polish. Bring some with a rag."

"Yes, Mrs. Morfawitz."

He left the room, and only when he was gone did she sit back in her seat. She folded her arms across her chest and then started to laugh. Zev began to laugh, too. The liquor was working on them both.

"Of course, I understand," she said. "I always thought it was a hard thing for men. How much more they enjoyed it. It must make life very difficult. If I enjoyed it as you do, I dare say I wouldn't venture to think of much else."

"But now you are being ridiculous," said Zev. "Women enjoy it much more—they must. It's a matter of evolution. For a man, there is nothing to balance the pleasure against, and so the pleasure is shallow and brief. Like a jump in cold water in July . . ."

Tehrani came in again with another bottle of brandy and clean glasses. Zev continued to talk; the presence of another made no difference to him.

"For a woman, the pleasure must overcome nine months of burden and then the havoc of childbirth. That is not an easy weight to counterbalance."

Tehrani had set a rag down before Hadassah and had given her a little cup of silver polish. While Zev spoke, she put her hand out and nodded toward the candlestick and Tehrani handed it to her. Hadassah drew security from the nearness of silver polish the same way many a shooting man feels with a firearm at his hip. She rubbed little circles on the gleaming surface.

"But you are being short-sighted," she said. "Consider for a moment how much greater the reward is for a man. Nature is incentivized to give a man more pleasure, for a man who finds great pleasure in it has endless potential for procreation. A woman is limited. Whether she gets an ounce of pleasure or a gallon, she can only cash in on it every nine months. It would be a waste to make her want it much more frequently than that."

She poured her empty glass full of amber brandy, and she topped off her husband's as well. They hadn't drunk together in a very long time.

"By that logic then," Zev said, "a man ought to be quick about it. He ought to finish as soon as he enters, so as to be exceedingly efficient. Then he can go on to the next, as you suggested. But a woman's pleasure comes with time, so then the pieces wouldn't fit. Nature would not shape two pieces that do not fit together."

"You're ignoring the fact that for men, the pleasure is as much psychological as it is physical. Perhaps the physical pleasure was once similar to that of a woman, but that is why evolution shaped a psychological pleasure as well, a need to dominate. And, in this regard, once that domineering attribute was carved into men's brains, then the question of women's pleasure went out of the picture entirely. Your whole argument is precedented on the act's being consensual. I tell you that for the vast majority of humanity's time on earth, this was far from being the case. My female ancestors were raped on the fields of Ukraine. I imagine yours were, too. I can assure you that their taking pleasure had nothing whatever to do with it."

Hadassah was now pointing the wet rag at her husband, and her reflection in the clean silver stick caught the cruel victory in her eyes. She was drunk on the argument and brandy both and still, she was not done:

"Tehrani," she said, "bring yourself a glass and sit down."

As the servant went into the kitchen to fetch himself a glass, Zev looked at his wife but said nothing. He did not distinguish between men based on their profession; humanity was simply divided into Zev and not Zev. Tehrani was definitely in the latter camp and Zev could not understand why he'd been invited to sit at Zev's table.

Tehrani came back from the kitchen and sat down on the other side of Hadassah so that she was at the head with Zev on her left and the servant on her right. She nodded to the brandy and Tehrani filled all three glasses. Zev watched the amber liquid fill his glass and then surveyed Tehrani's face. There was something deformed about it as if the angles and lines had been imperfectly transferred from a mold.

"Now, Tehrani," said Hadassah. She was not slurring her words exactly, but they were long and languid, drawn out and soft around the edges. "Did you find our conversation interesting?"

"Oh, yes, Mrs. Morfawitz. Very interesting." He took a little sip of brandy, looking as if he'd never before tried the stuff in his life. His eyes grew wide and then he smiled. "Very interesting, indeed."

"I didn't think you people could drink," said Zev.

"What people?"

"Muslims."

Tehrani smiled.

"What's funny," said Zev.

"Nothing, Mr. Morfawitz. Only, I am experiencing two things that I am unused to at once. The first is to sit at this table. The second is to converse with somebody who says just what they mean."

"You're welcome to stand if you prefer," said Zev. He took a sip of brandy.

Tehrani smiled. "Do you know, sir, that *Tehrani* means 'of Tehran'?"

"I figured."

"Very good, sir. Very good. My family was there for many generations. They were not servants, you know."

"Whatever does that have to do with you?" said Zev.

"Oh," said Tehrani, laughing a strange, high-pitched laugh, "clearly not very much."

"Clearly."

Hadassah noticed the man's nervousness and regretted inviting him to sit. The unfamiliar liquor was swimming in her brain and turning her thoughts in on themselves. She'd invited the servant out of some strange notion that his history would allow him to bolster her argument and she'd expected him to do so quickly and then leave, only now she saw him for what he was: a sniveling, half-formed thing, who was better suited to carrying luggage and stirring cocktails than he was to offering opinions of his own. If there was any consolation in his fouling her table with his presence, it was that she could already see Zev's patience wearing thin. It would be rewarding to see his reaction after being contradicted by so lowly a creature, a creature whose reconstructed face gave him reptilian features—not the features of a dangerous reptile, like a snake, but something comical and patched together, like a turtle's shell stitched onto a human face. There was something else, too, something that she could not put her finger on.

"But I myself was not a servant either," Tehrani was saying, "during my time in Tehran. I grew up rather rich, you see. Not like the Shahs or their families, but my grandfather owned some land where they later found petrol. They were late to come to his land, so he avoided the mistakes made by earlier sellers, who knew nothing of the value of petrol. He knew, and he made them pay. So from the time that I was a child, we were men of the city, established in Tehran. We lived a double life—that of the nomad family from the desert and that of well-to-do city dwellers. We had an iron gate around our home with two marble Safavid lions standing guard, but also, my grandmother still told fortunes, the way she used to in their little village to the south, in the fields around Ahvaz. City people came on Saturdays to have their palms read. We had servants of our own, and drivers, but every year during Dhu'l-Hijjah we would sacrifice a lamb in our backyard. Blood would spill into the street where bankers walked in Italian leather shoes. My grandfather died quite young, but my grandmother lived right up until the night of the revolution. When I was very young, I wanted to be like her, and it was my only ambition in life that people would come from all around to hear me prophesy their futures."

"It's not too late," said Hadassah. She could not bring herself to look at him. "You might move to the Village and do palm-reading yet. Perhaps you'll be quite popular."

"But do not think, Mrs. Morfawitz," said Tehrani with a smile, "that we were not popular. People wanted to be our friends. My older brother was the target of many well-to-do young girls. Even I was thought to be something of a catch."

Tehrani took another sip of his brandy and again there was the surprise on his face, as if he did not expect the taste of it. He looked down into the glass and then at Zev and then at Hadassah. Finally, he looked back to the glass, and then he giggled. It was not natural for him to laugh, and Hadassah had the impression that a sort of steam had built up in the little man and he was releasing it by mirthlessly laughing every few minutes.

Also, she had noticed what it was about him, besides the patchwork features of his face, that made him so reptilian: it was his eyes. They were large, somewhat beautiful eyes, so green that they appeared almost yellow; and yet the color was only a tinted lens that would drag behind the natural eye's motion so that the lens was always moving slowly to catch up. Also, he never moved his eyes from one thing to another while the lids were open. Instead, he would be staring at one place and then blink—a long, protracted blink—and then be staring at another, and the green halo would slowly come to settle on his dark, natural iris. Hadassah despised him for it.

But as Hadassah's rage began to simmer, it seemed to draw the heat away from Zev's own annoyance. Perhaps, she thought, he was farther along in the brandy than she was. Or perhaps it was because Tehrani had now begun to speak about women, Persian women, with their exotic, sand-colored skin and their ruby-beaded, golden strings and their brown eyes. Hadassah hated the women for running through her husband's head while he sat at her table and she hated Tehrani for compelling them to run.

"Oh, yes," he was saying, "their fathers would lay out great banquets and the dancers would roll golden coins down the line of their brown bellies, and—"

"Why don't you get to the part where you don't like women," snapped Hadassah. Tehrani's eyes yawned to a close, but before they could open upon her, Hadassah turned to watch her husband. She saw the shock in his face, the abrupt ending to his daydream of belly dancers and brown-skinned love. *Good*, she thought.

"Mrs. Morfawitz is correct," said Tehrani. "Of course, that was the problem. You see, I never did like women so much. Before the revolution, this hardly mattered in Tehran. We were not out in the open, but if you were looking you could find us, and we were not treated as anything like criminals."

"So why did you leave?"

"Ah, I didn't leave. That is exactly the problem—that I didn't leave. And I was one who could have! Most of Iran was poor, penniless, and so they knew no better. My parents knew better. My brother did, too. He took his pretty wife and he left."

Zev pushed his empty glass forward and Tehrani refilled it.

"And then came 1979. Then came a dark cloud over the sun in the shape of a hijab, but it was not only women that it covered so completely. Now, they came searching for us. Now they knocked down midnight doors and hauled us away by the vanload. They took me and my—well, you understand that it was nothing like a husband, that was out of the question—but they took us away together. They hung him before they had even taken the black pillowcase from his head. They took it from mine so that I could watch. His neck did not break, and a terrible sound came out of this black pillow head. It was like no sound that a human should make. And then it was done. A friend of my father from the old days—which were not so very old, but already they seemed ancient!—was the one who had brought me to watch. 'You see what will happen,' he said. 'It is inevitable. A man cannot be with another man. Such a thing is a crime against God.' I asked him why, if it was so inevitable, why should he waste time to show me. Why should the cloth come away from my own eyes while the others would die? 'A man cannot be with another man,' he said again. 'That is a crime against God. It is inevitable that a crime against God will be punished. But there are certain changes one can make.' I told him that I was not interested in such changes. I asked him to consider a world in which it was against the law of God for him to love women. Would he then stop to love them? What does the law of God have to do with love? Affection is not a thing that one can change by willing it so. I told him that God had either nothing to do with it or everything to do with it. In any case, I was powerless to change either my heart or my mind. And he said to me: 'So change your body.'"

Tehrani released his glass and spread his fingers wide. He examined his hands as if he were a spirit who had just possessed this strange and alien body. Then he blinked and when his eyes opened he was looking at Hadassah, lenses moving as in parallax. Her lip curled in disgust.

"Yes," he continued. "This was the Ayatollah's great solution: do not try to change the love's target, but its origin. It is easier, after all, to change the body than the mind, and there exists no such law prohibiting such transformation."

Hadassah made no attempt to hide the contempt in her voice. "So you let them change your body. Go on."

Zev said nothing.

"Yes," said Tehrani. "Perhaps you consider this to be weak. Perhaps you think I should have said, 'No, I am not a woman who loves men, but a man who loves men. It is different.' Well, perhaps that is correct. Perhaps I should have been noble and insisted on being 'true to myself,' as Americans are so fond of saying. At the time, though, my only concern was the sound the black pillows had made when they were hung up by their necks, the shaking of their legs as the air was squeezed from their blood, dark stains on their trousers. I was aware that if I'd been given a gun or a razor, I would have used them in an instant to avoid that miserable fate. And so when presented with an option for life—a real option—I took it. I did not even think of saying no."

Tehrani took another sip of brandy but now there was no surprise in his face. It was as if emotion had been carved out of his skin.

"I lived for several months that way before making . . . use of my new self. Just because one lives within the code of law does not mean that he complies with the code of morality. I had never really expected to be taken at face value—after all, my face had changed. Much about me had changed. But this I could have lived with if only there were others to share it with, too. But everybody else who had the procedure, well . . . now we could not love one another anymore. The homosexual's great advantage is that his beauty is self-appreciated; he is capable of loving his own reflection in a way that no one else can. In changing our bodies, the Islamic Republic of Iran was not helping us to fall in line with the law of god; they were ensuring that anybody who we might have loved was now changed into a form that we ourselves found unattractive. And anybody that might have loved us for what we had become would be put off by what we had once been. There was an unspeakable truth: we were no longer ourselves. Most importantly, we could never again look in a mirror with any modicum of pride."

Zev yawned and his eyelids fluttered. He buried his nose in his brandy and Hadassah had the impression that he was trying to block out sound by engaging his other senses. She smiled inwardly now as she looked forward to the trophy of her husband's rage. Hadassah was not usually given over to daydreaming; she had compartments in her brain like built-in cabinets that separated the senses from fantasy. The liquor had bored holes in the walls and now she saw the world unfolding in many ways, its surface reality flipping like an origami fortune-teller. She envisioned tearing Tehrani methodically apart by picking at the seams where his skin was sewn together, by unstitching what those doctors had done. By removing his stop-motion eyes. Violent reverie floated in her brain and shut out the sound of talking. Tehrani kept on speaking.

"So when I came to America, I had the surgery reversed. And here I stayed, once again a man. So you see, Mr. Morfawitz, I believe this is why your wife asked that I should weigh in on the question at hand: for whom does the greater pleasure exist?"

Hadassah leaned forward in her chair, her eyes flat and exclusively focused on Zev. She wanted to see the rage boil in him, but now she saw only laughter.

"But that is idiotic," said Zev. "You are not a man who was a woman who is now a man again. A man who is made to surgically resemble a woman is not a woman, he is a man who is made to surgically resemble a woman."

"But the soul . . ." began Tehrani.

"Do not speak to me of souls," Zev bellowed. His voice filled the house. "What is meant by the word *soul* but the brain and the electricity and chemicals that move around inside of it. There is nothing of me that can be separated from the flesh. There is nothing of you either. There is nothing about a chopped-up man that turns him into a woman. There is nothing in his fake new organ that gives him an understanding of a woman's pleasure."

"The physical, maybe . . . but the psychological pleasure—"

"There is nothing about a chopped-up man that gives him a woman's brain. Whatever psychological pleasure you derived, it was that of a chopped-up man."

Hadassah reached for the bottle of brandy and then withdrew her hand. Her drunkenness unnerved her, and her patience was wearing thin. She was beginning to doubt very much whether Zev would care at all that this creature disagreed with him. She thought not and was willing to pour no more time into the subtle victory. Her eyes were growing tired.

"That's enough," she said. "Answer the question and then clean up these glasses."

Tehrani drank the last of his drink and then blinked his eyes and was looking at Hadassah. His irises enraged her and she swallowed a Yiddish curse.

"But of course, Mrs. Morfawitz, the woman derives more pleasure. Whether it is psychological or physical hardly matters, I should think. A man must work to give of himself while a woman is begged to receive. You see . . ."

Tehrani continued to speak but now his voice competed with Zev's vicious laughter, and it did not put up much of a fight. In Hadassah's mind the room went curiously silent and still. There were Tehrani's blinking eyelids, opening and shutting like a metronome with the pendulum of his eyes shifting between husband and wife but spending no time on the space between them. Hadassah felt that time had stopped and been replaced by this grotesque sequence, set into an even more grotesque and reptilian face. All of it was a gross parody of time.

Sound returned, and Tehrani stopped his babbling and now Zev's laughter was all that filled the room. Tehrani was laughing, too, in his nervous way. It was laughter in submission to Zev's will. Everything submitted to Zev's will. Hadassah felt the blood rise in her face.

"Oh, Hadassah," said Zev. "Good thing you brought your big guns. Here was your great champion that you brought to wrestle with me and now he has proven you wrong. He mocks you with his eyes!"

She grabbed her glass, realized that it was empty, and then took hold of the silver polish in her hand. Her eyes whipped around to stare her husband in the face. He stopped laughing at once and raised his hands in rare acquiescence, pushing slightly away from the table. Tehrani, unsure of what was happening, kept on with his joyless laughter.

Hadassah took the glass full of silver polish and threw it in Tehrani's face. He kept on laughing for a moment as if the alkali needed time to have an effect. Then his hands went slowly to his eyes as the corrosive began to work. He moaned at first—a heartless, animal moan. It came not from his mouth but his throat. He gasped for breath and then kicked his chair away from the table and fell to the floor.

"My eyes!" he screamed. "My eyes!"

Hadassah stood up and the angle of her body was severe. She looked down at the writhing body and there was not a trace of apology in her.

"It's my eyes you should be sorry for," she spat. "Every second that I watch you I grow ill to the very core of me. You," she said, turning on her husband. In the liquor haze of Zev's mind, there was the sound of crushing stone to accompany her turning as if the foundation of some medieval tower had needed demolition to allow the great woman to spin. He was frightened of his wife. "Clean him up and get him out. You ought to be something of an expert when it comes to that."

VII
NICO

Tehrani was left permanently blind in both eyes. With his right he could discern changes in light and shadow, but this never did him any good. In the lawsuit that followed, he settled for the equivalent of twenty years of his meager servant's pay, discounted for the time value of money. The courts were very advanced economically, but still quite rigid socially and they assumed, based on Tehrani's ambiguous gender status, that the man was not very likely to ever support any children.

Even though he had enough money to live on, Tehrani took to begging all along Museum Mile. He knew the streets around the Morfawitz mansion like the back of his hand and needed nothing but a stick to get around. Besides, the walking was good exercise and he had nothing better to do. His real motivation, though, was born of naivety: he wanted to evoke in Hadassah Morfawitz a feeling of guilt. He thought that his presence would be a thorn in the great family's side, a reminder of the consequences of their cruelty.

Hadassah sometimes saw him from her office window, and the most generous thing to say of her behavior was that she never laughed out loud. She once asked her husband, "How do you walk by that sad heap every day? Doesn't he smell like the sewer where he sleeps?"

Zev hadn't considered that he might alter his route to avoid the lonesome figure sitting cross-legged on his cardboard bed.

"It's the fastest way to work," he said.

"It would take all of fifteen seconds to go down Madison instead."

He shrugged. "It's the fastest way to work."

But as he walked out that day, he paid special attention to Tehrani. Not enough to stop or add to the coffee cup of change, but enough to give some sound advice in passing: "If you're going to sit there, you might as well do something useful. Draw pictures. Tell fortunes like that grandmother of yours."

When he came back in the evening, Tehrani had fashioned himself a cardboard sign that said Palms Read, Fortunes Told.

"Very good," said Zev. He even cracked a smile and thrust a hand into his pocket. Had there been any loose change there, he might have put it in Tehrani's cup, for he liked to see his will borne out. Alas, there was nothing in his pocket. "Very good," he said again.

But this would hardly be a story worth relating if the Morfawitz mansion gaining a clairvoyant gargoyle was the extent of what occurred; no, although the stately matriarch never gave the would-be seer another glance, Tehrani's sad fate intertwined once more with that infamous wrath of Hadassah's. Here is how it happened:

It was a Sunday afternoon in late November, and a certain well-to-do woman was walking in front of the mansion. She visited some exhibit or other every Sunday and had become a repeat customer of Tehrani's curbside services. She was good for one fortune a week. The most remarkable thing about her was her fur, and she wore a different coat every Sunday. She liked to impress people with her fur, and—knowing that Tehrani could not appreciate her wardrobe—she told him each week what sort of animal she was wearing. On the Sunday afternoon in question, it was the white coat of an arctic fox. Tehrani nodded sagely as if he'd guessed her garb before she'd even put it on. He thought her a little insane. She, on the other hand, was sympathetic to Tehrani's blindness because, as she said, her own son suffered the same affliction.

"Well," she told him, "he isn't really blind, you understand."

"Yes," said Tehrani, although really he had no idea what she was talking about. He drew out each syllable he spoke so that there was no guess as to his confidence; uncertainty was a bad thing for a clairvoyant. "There are many ways to be blind," he said, though he only knew of one.

"Don't get me wrong," she said. "I appreciate art as much as the next woman. Probably more. But my son—he's so ridiculous! He's had some success as a critic, that's true, but how can he carry on being so ridiculous! Perhaps it's the effect of growing up with an artistic mother."

"Yes," said Tehrani, "we give to our children more of ourselves than we sometimes know."

"So true. But *I* certainly never went prancing around like he does. That ridiculous purple coat and a cane to pretend that he is blind. What is worse, he makes himself really blind! Wearing nearly opaque sunglasses at all hours of the day, ones with leather blinders on the side that block out any light whatsoever. You know, the fashionable type. 'But what are you doing with those ridiculous things?' I say to him. 'How can you see where you're going?' And do you know what he answers me? Do you? He says, 'Mother, I choose to see only what is beautiful.' They love him for it in the magazines, of course. They say that he is 'saving his vision for the things that really matter.' He tells me that his greatest fear is triteness, but really it is rats. He is positively terrified of them—won't walk outside on trash night! And if he absolutely must, then he stomps off the sidewalk and into the street instead. He refuses to be trapped between a wall and a pile of garbage for fear that a rat might ambush him there. We never lived in a place with rats, so I don't understand what turned him out like this. If you ask me, I think that's what those ridiculous glasses really have to do with; he doesn't want to see the rats because they make him jump, and yet he knows that they aren't really dangerous. And so his answer to overcoming this fear of rats is to simply stop himself from seeing them! Not to avoid them or to confront this ridiculous phobia, but only to blind himself to their existence! What do you think about that?"

After a moment, Tehrani said, "We do what we must to overcome our little fears. There is a certain logic to his way."

"Oh, I suppose there is," she said in distress. She lit a cigarette. "But what a ridiculous way to go through life! And for such a beautiful, smart boy! Oh, do you think he'll be alright?"

Tehrani had somewhat lost the narrative and was not certain as to what was being asked of him. To cover his ignorance, he put a mystical inflection in his voice so that the advice would sound sage-like and true.

"If he does not discover himself," is what he said.

"That's just what I think." She took a drag from her cigarette and shook her head side to side as she exhaled so that the smoke was cast wide before her face. "Just what I think," she said. "One day, he is going to wake up and realize that he is all empty inside, just filled with other people's ideals and ideas. I hope to god that I'm dead before that day comes, before he realizes that he is flesh and blood like the rest of us."

"We are all the same," said Tehrani. "On the elemental level."

"So true. I wish somebody could talk some sense into him. Would you mind terribly if I brought him around? I think he'd be embarrassed to be forcing blindness on himself in front of you, if embarrassment is even a thing he can feel anymore."

"There are feelings which none of us can forget."

"That's so," she said. "Very well. I'll bring him around next Sunday. Thank you as always."

"No thanks are necessary," said Tehrani, but he rattled his cup all the same.

"Here's a twenty," she said. Tehrani smiled and heard her footsteps as she began to walk away. Then she came back. "And it's arctic fox today," she said. "I can't remember if I told you."

* * *

The next Sunday, Tehrani's best client came around with her son. Nico was his name. Tehrani heard the pair coming from down the street. The mother had a distinctively quick patter as if each step only moved her forward three inches; the son tapped a walking stick back and forth in such a ridiculous and abrasive manner that one did not even need eyes to see that the boy was ostentatious.

". . . but the retrospective on Manet is closing today," he was saying to his mother. "And you expect me to waste my time speaking with a beggar."

"He's a seer and a wise man."

"He's a beggar."

Their footsteps approached him and stopped.

"Here he is," the mother said, and Tehrani was not sure if she was speaking to Nico or himself. "Mr. Tehrani, this is my son, Nico. I've told you all about him. Nico, this is Mr. Tehrani."

"How do you do, Mr. Tehrani," said Nico.

Tehrani smiled without showing any teeth.

"Why are you smiling, Mr. Tehrani?"

"Back in the old country," Tehrani said, "the boys would go off to London for an education and come back with half an accent. That is how you sound. You remind me of my childhood."

"I'll leave you two to talk," said Nico's mother. "And I'll save you a place in line. By the way, Mr. Tehrani, it's mink today."

"I thought as much."

"Well," she said, impressed, and her footsteps went away.

"Well," said Nico. "So you're blind."

"So I'm blind."

"How enviable!"

"Do you really think so?"

"Oh, yes," said Nico. Though the boy spoke with lazy disinterest, Tehrani could tell that he was quite interested. He had a very difficult time imagining what Nico looked like or envisioning him existing anywhere but New York City. His voice was affected by a small lisp on certain syllables. "It's like . . . It's like if I were trying to diet, and suddenly I was transported to a little African country without any food. How splendid."

The smile was gone now from Tehrani's face. "But what is it that you do not want to see?"

"My dear little man, what is it that I *do* want to see? The world is so . . . so unintentional! How can we maintain integrity and intrinsic criteria for beauty if we are, at all times, bombarded by the ugly mistakes of the world? Are we so without agency that we shouldn't choose what we see? We choose what we eat, don't we? What would you think of a man who ate everything that was put before him? You'd be disgusted, naturally."

"Naturally. But should we aspire to perfection?"

"Perfection? Who said anything about perfection? Only intention. We should strive to see only what is intentional, and only in places where that intentionality is protected from the natural forces of the world. Intentional can be Stewart's beautiful graffiti; the natural force is his being beaten to death by police."

"Just because something is ugly," said Tehrani, "does not mean that it is unintentional. Take off those glasses and look upon my face. You'll see nothing unintentional there. Nothing unintentional in my body either. But you would be hard-pressed to find any beauty in either. Go on, go on. Really look at me, why don't you."

Tehrani heard nothing but he felt the boy's eyes on him. "Oh, dear," said Nico.

"What I would give to be able to remove my own blindness and look upon your face! Even your method of blindness as a focus of intention only functions if the blindness is one of choosing! I live the ultimate lack of intention—no matter what I wish to see, I cannot see it! What I would give to look upon your face!"

"Don't be loud," said Nico. "There are people around going to the exhibit and I absolutely won't have a scene. I'm recognizable from far off, you know. But alright. Here, put your hands against my face."

Nico knelt and took Tehrani's hands and pressed them to his face. He had removed his glasses completely to give the blind seer a feel for the shape of his eyes.

"You are a very beautiful boy," he said. "But I suppose you know that already."

"Know it? My dear, delightful little man, how would I possibly know it? If there's one thing that it should be absolutely illegal to look upon, it is one's own face. There is the greatest unintention of them all, for the face is meant to say so much about a man, and yet he has exactly nothing to do with it. For everybody else to make assumptions about you based on the shape of your face is one thing, but for you to take ideas about yourself from an irrelevant reflection and then incorporate them into your person! Well—it would be the ultimate submission to the cruel accident of nature! No, if there is one thing that a man must never be poisoned by, it is certainly his own image."

Tehrani's hands slid down from Nico's brow, lingered on his jaw, and then left his face completely. Nico raised his glasses back to his face, but before doing so, he looked up at Tehrani once more, and then behind Tehrani at the beautiful mansion behind him.

"Well," he said, "for a blind man, you haven't picked half-bad a spot. This is a beautiful house to be a part of."

"Am I a part of this house?"

"Oh, certainly. The man across the street cannot see this marble facade without seeing you here before it. Yours is an enviable position."

"If the house is a badge of good taste to me," said Tehrani with excitement, "then is it true to say that I am a stain upon it?"

Nico thought for a moment and stood up fully. "No," he said. "No, I don't think that's right. A stain implies a certain lack of intention, the mark of an error. As you said, just because something is ugly, does not mean that it is unintentional. So, no—you may not be a stain at all, but more like the slash of a red pen."

"But how to tell?"

"Well, there is only one question: do you know this house?"

At that, Tehrani laughed.

"What is it?"

"Yes," said Tehrani. "I know this house."

"I thought you did. You are ugly, yes—but far from unintentional. If it is true that you want to mar this facade with your presence, then you are just like a slash of the red pen."

"Do you believe that to be so much better?"

"But isn't that the wrong question? Don't you really mean—isn't that so much worse?"

"Yes," said Tehrani. "Worse." A faint smile played around the corners of his lips. "If we cannot destroy what is inside the house, we must do what small damage we can to the walls."

"Listen," said Nico. "I must go but first I'll tell you about my fantasy because I think you might enjoy it. I have a dream where I go around this city's museums stripping the walls of art. Only, I don't want to sell the art or anything, only keep it for myself and my trusted friends, so that it is not only the artists that achieve a measure of intentionality, but also the consumers of the art. That is called a fair relationship. A fair relationship between wall-hangings and eyes. But listen. In this dream I have a blank gallery all arranged with hooks and open walls, and then I break into each museum, one by one, with a pair of magical dice. Every roll I make, some original gets zapped back to my gallery but instead of leaving a blank space on the esteemed wall from the museum whence it came, it is replaced immediately by a replica. Only, none of the replicas are perfect; each bears some subtle disagreement. So maybe if I roll a three while standing before Leutze in the Met, then the coxswain in the back is wearing a yarmulke instead of a feathered hat. Wouldn't that be funny, on Christmas night and all? Or maybe if I get one in the MoMA and suddenly it's Rousseau's gypsy who has open eyes and the lion is sleepwalking through the Sahara. Wouldn't that be good? And do you know what happens after all the art is changed? Do you? The little people come and swarm in as they do every day and they look at the gypsy's open eyes and say, 'My, my, how brilliant he was.' Or they see the Jew rowing Washington through the ice and say, 'You see, this country really was founded on religious freedom.' It doesn't make a lick of difference to them."

Nico had worked himself into a rare but subtle frenzy. Now it was Tehrani's turn to be excited, for in his mind a plan was working.

"It sounds like your fantasy has stumbled on the ultimate 'free lunch,'" he said. "A better allocation of resources, where the exchange is not zero-sum, but only positive; for you obtain a thing you love, and the common person understands nothing to be different."

"My dear man," cried Nico, "if only they were capable of understanding the difference! I would love to do them the cruelty of depriving their eyes of authentic artistic expression, but they are too ignorant to feel such pain! You cannot punch a person on a limb they've never grown."

Each man was breathing hard: Nico in exasperated fantasy, Tehrani in anticipation of the vengeance yet to come.

"Of course," said Nico, putting one hand to his chest, "it's utter silliness. These museums are veritable fortresses. They have made the great masters slaves to the common eye."

"But if it was truly possible to save some art from the most unworthy eyes," said Tehrani, "you would do such a thing?"

"Yes," said Nico, his voice little more than breath. He stood up tall as if taken aback by his own words. The November air seemed to swarm him now. He felt a chill all through his body and pulled his purple jacket closed. He opened his mouth to speak, but Tehrani, as if he were watching, raised a finger, and all that escaped from Nico's lips was breath changed into fog.

"What if I told you," said Tehrani, "that this house behind me is home to twelve of the most expensive masterpieces currently in private collections?"

Nico's head looked up at the mansion behind him, but he did not remove his glasses.

"How would you know?" he said. "You couldn't see them, could you?"

So Tehrani told Nico the recent story of the catastrophe that had befallen him while in the employ of the Morfawitz family. He told him of Zev and Hadassah and of their magnificent cruelties and general unworthiness as beholders of beauty. Cruelty did not seem as if it would be such a serious transgression insofar as Nico was concerned, so Tehrani focused instead on the dumb, brutish figure of the grown Morfawitz son Adam, who still lived at home and who had once drawn a red crayon smile across a Modigliani face. He talked about how the family would sometimes mortgage a piece of art and receive a benefit of 1 to 2 percent on the simple contingency that the bank keep possession; the banks were generally used to clients' opposition on this matter, as most people derived their artwork's value from displaying it for company, but the Morfawitzes were happy to let their collection rot away in unlit vaults.

While Tehrani spoke, Nico paced, his walking stick tapping the concrete sidewalk before him like an erratic metronome, speeding and slowing in some vague mimicry of its holder's heart.

"So," he said finally, "what pieces *are* still on the walls?"

Tehrani listed them and Nico's tapping quickened with each name.

"And they are unprotected?"

"Unprotected?" said Tehrani. "What thing of value on this earth is unprotected? No, everything in that castle is protected in all the usual ways."

Nico stopped moving and Tehrani could hear the grind of his hard-soled shoes as they turned on the sidewalk to face him.

"Then what are we talking about, old man? Why are you wasting my time when Manet is only open until six and then gone from this city forever?"

"Ah," said Tehrani, the stitches that crisscrossed his face stretching with his smile, "because you and I are not the big bad wolves. You have your blindness and I have mine. The blindness of gods, though, is that they only have eyes for titans and the grand entry doors that a titan must use; the little mouse who wants access to the divine inner chambers needs only to find a hole small enough to escape the great gods' notice."

Nico looked up at the mansion through the nearly opaque tint of his glasses, saw only the dim outline of shadow against the gray November sky.

"Are we to be little mice then?"

"Yes," said Tehrani. "Why not?"

* * *

Tehrani and Nico were timely conspirators, if not the most natural pair ever assembled for a heist, especially one aimed against such a powerful clan as the Morfawitzes. With the twin engines of Tehrani's vengeance and Nico's pompous greed disguised as moral rectitude, the two were quick to make a plan. Also, the weather was turning cold and Tehrani was eager for an excuse to quit his outdoor post and sit inside Nico's apartment. Besides, there was a deadline that became apparent with the front page of the *Post* on November 23, 1983:

KISLEV? MORE LIKE KISS-ZEV: MOGUL Z. MORFAWITZ AND FAMILY TO OCCUPY CPS TOWER BY END OF JEWISH MONTH

It's going to be a very happy Hannukah in the Morfawitz household. Despite early setbacks, including a groundbreaking ceremony interrupted by an assassination attempt on the life of illegitimate son Asher Morfawitz, and a subcontractor's body being found in a tub of concrete, construction on the Morfawitz Tower at Central Park South has continued apace, and the mogul's family is reportedly getting ready to move in . . .

"You see?" said Nico one morning, shoving the paper before Tehrani's unseeing eyes. "They're moving, going, gone!"

"I cannot read," said Tehrani. "And I wonder: how can you?"

Nico snatched the paper back from Tehrani's outstretched hands. "For your information," he said, "printed word is as intentional as one gets. I'm given the paper every morning with my coffee. The month ends in a week! One week!"

"November ends in a week," said Tehrani. "But the Jewish month of Kislev ends the following Monday. But it's no matter; I knew of this long before we began. They have been planning the move since early this year."

"Since early this . . . you knew that they were moving, and you said nothing?"

"What was I to say? This move is irrelevant to our plan. Wednesday next we will act."

"Wednesday!"

"It is the first night of Hanukkah. The festival of lights."

"I know what Hanukkah is!"

"Good," said Tehrani. "Well, the Morfawitz family spends only one night a year out of the house, and it is always the first night of Hanukkah. Naphtali Morfawitz has a great gathering on his private beach in Sagaponack. They use bonfires instead of a menorah. It is, for the help, a most exhausting event. I myself have worked it the last thirteen years and I have spent thirteen nights running food and drink out from the house onto the sand. Naphtali's own servants run the firewood, which is grueling in its own way, but at least they do not have faces to remember and orders to get correct.

"Anyway, a torchbearer runs the candle from the shamash at the center and lights however many bonfires are due. One on the first night, two on the second night, three on the third, and so on, until a line of eight bonfires is lit with an elevated shamash, which is represented by a bonfire set on a little man-made dune at the center so that from the middle of the sound or from the southern shore of Connecticut, it must really look like a menorah.

"Sagaponack town ordinance has, in recent years, mandated a greater distance between any two adjacent bonfires, and the job of lighting the things has become considerably more strenuous. It has also had the effect of separating the bonfires from one another so that on any given night there are really that many distinct parties, each centered around one flame. There is plenty of social migration, it is true, and yet not a single attendee leaves without a sure sense of which candle they belonged to. The final night is something like a bacchanalia, with nine different parties going on at once. Anybody who is anybody is invited to join, and there is no real restriction on significant others or guests of guests. But this inclusive atmosphere is a late-Hanukkah phenomenon, and the early nights are more sparsely populated. And the first night—well, the first night is reserved only for those with the last name Morfawitz. They eat latkes and drink good wine around a single bonfire."

The details of the party seemed to calm Nico's nerves, and he seemed more curious now than afraid. "This sounds like an entertaining evening," he said to Tehrani. "But what's the point of all this?"

"The point is that this first night of Hanukkah is the one night a year when we can really plan that the house will be empty for a long period of time. Not just empty of one or two of the family, but of each and every one of them. The timing is most fortunate."

"The first night of Hanukkah," said Nico. "But that's . . ."

"One week from tonight."

"One week!"

Nico sat back in his chair and began to fan himself with the folded-up *Post*. The thing moved now from fantasy to fact, took shape in all its dangers and rewards. Cold reality settled over him and excited his nerves. Now he began to think in terms of true problems. He'd studied the blueprints and knew the entrances and exits that he was to use. He knew the codes and had the keys. He knew which paintings were where, and how they were secured in their places. It was a well-devised plan and there was a great gaping flaw in it.

"The replicas," he said finally. "We'll never be able to get the replicas in time."

Tehrani smiled and removed from his pocket a piece of paper and slid it across the table. On it was an address.

"But, my friend," he said, "they are done. She is waiting."

"She?"

"Yes, you will be pleased. This I promise. Now, go."

VIII
ELIZABETH CHO

Elizabeth Cho, the painter of replicas that Tehrani had commissioned, had been the premiere young impressionist at the New York Metropolitan Painters High School and then went to The New School on a full scholarship. By the time of her graduation, she'd had a long line of West SoHo galleries vying to represent her work. Mostly the galleries were either owned, financed, or patronized exclusively by wealthy, older men, who did not care so much for the art or the artists but were very much interested in the sort of events that their patronage earned them access to, invariably attended by young models or dancers from this or that ballet.

Zev Morfawitz had been one such would-be patron.

He, at least, had always avoided the pretentiousness of his compatriots and never pretended to care anything at all for the art. He wasted no time with one eye on a painting; both his eyes were clear in their purpose, which was to survey and make contact with the young ballerinas.

Elizabeth's art was for sale, but so was her integrity, and Zev, recognizing this weakness in her, purchased both. For him, she would hold private showings at the school's gallery, and she would always arrange for the prettiest ballerinas to be present. Also, she made certain there would be a comfortable room somewhere that had, at a bare minimum, several cushions and a bolt on the door. She took to booking out the "Lay Pose Room," which was conveniently attached to the gallery and fitted with various cushioned surfaces upon which painters could have their lounging models pose.

They had a nice little arrangement, which became so regular that Elizabeth Cho made a fair bit of money, the galleries were eager to obtain such a popular young artist, and also Hadassah Morfawitz eventually caught on. Zev hadn't been discreet. He brought home one of Elizabeth's paintings each month and they had no place to go but the trash. Hadassah had been made wise to the scheme by none other than servile Tehrani, who wondered aloud to her one day why they were discarding such good art when there was so much room on the walls.

"Art?" she asked. "What art?"

"A painting every month," said Tehrani. "I only ask because I follow such things quite closely, and these pieces will be valuable one day. By the up-and-coming Ms. Cho who is graduating next month."

As you can imagine, once Hadassah knew that a young woman was involved, it was only a matter of time before she connected the trashed art to her husband and then attacked the problem in her typical way: by making a sufficient donation to the Juilliard Art Fund so that they renamed a small part of the school (there is still a Morfawitz Wing on the third floor) and then made Zev and Hadassah honorees at the year-end gala.

Well, Zev and Hadassah's donation and attendance had made quite the stir, and the event became something of a who's who of the New York art scene. After the reception, the guests were ushered into vast galleries where the graduates were displaying their works. It was during this transition that Hadassah lost Zev, and while she tried to note the beautiful women who had been at the reception but hadn't followed to the gallery, the sheer length of the guest list (and general attractiveness of the attendees) made this daunting task impossible. So instead, she walked herself through the various displays until she came upon Elizabeth Cho's section.

She did not need to read the nameplate to recognize these as the works that had wound up in her dumpster; they were quite distinct and even—though she was loath to admit it—rather good. Young beauty was a thing Hadassah could understand, but artistic talent was a new thing altogether for her jealous rage to find.

"Where's the artist?" she asked a small, rather plain girl who was standing beside the plaque. "Elizabeth Cho, where is she?"

"You're looking at her," said the girl.

"Where," said Hadassah. "I don't see her."

"I'm Elizabeth," said Elizabeth. She put out her hand.

Hadassah looked at the outstretched hand, at the artist's fingernails caked with green along their edges, at the wrist that years of painting had made thick, at the plainness of the face that owned it.

"You?" she said, so caught off guard that she was startled into politeness and she placed her hand in the girl's. She looked up now at the art behind Elizabeth and wondered if her husband could have been patronizing this young artist because he actually liked her work. But then why was it ending up in the trash? She was so confounded that she spoke the words aloud: "But then why is it ending up in the trash?"

"What's ending up in the trash?"

"Your paintings," said Hadassah. She had let go of the girl's hand and was now perusing the wall, scrutinizing each piece, attempting to see what could have swayed her husband.

"I hardly think that my paintings are ending up in the trash," said Elizabeth.

"Oh, but they are. My husband buys them, you see, and then Tehrani finds them in the dumpster." She turned back to Elizabeth and looked her up and down, shaking her head all the while so that her silver hair rippled. "I can't make sense of it."

"Well," said Elizabeth, "I don't know who the hell your husband is, Mrs. . . ."

"Morfawitz."

"Mrs. Morfawitz, but—" Elizabeth stopped short, having digested the name. "Oh," she said finally. "Mrs. Morfawitz."

"So you *do* know who the hell my husband is?"

"Oh, yes . . . I mean, of course, I know who Mr. Morfawitz—"

"Smart girl," said Hadassah, rounding on the poor thing. "And do you know *where* Mr. Morfawitz is?"

Elizabeth looked nervously about as if expecting somebody to save her. In her survey of the room, she could not keep her eyes from straying toward the Lay Pose Room, where she knew for a fact that Zev had disappeared in hot pursuit of this Christmas season's Sugar Plum Fairy.

Hadassah followed Elizabeth's eyes and made straight for the door, but Elizabeth was quick to rectify her mistake.

"Everybody!" she called to a little horde of ballerinas and artists and patrons. "Come say thank you to Mrs. Morfawitz. This is Mrs. Morfawitz right here. Hasn't she done wonderfully to advance the cause of art? Shouldn't we give her a round of applause? Come around and shake her hand! Tell her what you personally are going to be able to do in Juilliard's new Morfawitz Wing!"

Hadassah turned violently toward Elizabeth, but it was too late; the damage was done. The crowd pressed in around her and one hundred hands reached out to thank their patroness. By the time things had finally settled and Hadassah was left to her own devices, Zev was right behind her.

"Whatever did you do," he said, "to deserve such obnoxious applause."

"Your shirt's untucked," she spat at him. "We're going."

* * *

That was the end of Morfawitz involvement in amateur art, and Elizabeth Cho was left without representation. Over the preceding year, Zev had, as per their arrangement, outbid everybody else on every painting, and the galleries were dismayed to see such a lack of diversity in patronage, especially when Hadassah made it known that her sister, who "suffered from early-onset Alzheimer's," had been hoodwinked into taking the pieces by the advantage-taking Elizabeth, as proven by the paintings being found in the trash.

With no other avenue on which to establish herself, Elizabeth eventually showed up on the Morfawitz stoop. She was led by Tehrani up to Hadassah's office. Hadassah had been expecting her but neither looked up nor offered her visitor a seat.

"Yes," she said. "What is it?"

Elizabeth tried fruitlessly to thaw Hadassah's coldness, first with warmth and then with tears. When she saw that neither was working, she succumbed to desperate truth. "They've all backed out," she said. "Every last one of them backed out. Won't you please undo what you've done? I would undo my own actions if I could. I swear that to you. I'm so sorry."

"But my sweet girl," said Hadassah, still not looking at her guest. "Whatever do you have to be sorry for? You simply wanted the gala to thank me, isn't that right?"

Hadassah finally looked up and under the coldness of her gaze, Elizabeth collapsed. Tehrani carried her down the stairs and gave her some hot tea before seeing her out.

"For what it's worth," he told her then, "I thought your paintings were wonderful. I kept several for myself. I can't afford them just yet, not at their true value, but one day I hope to be able to repay you."

At this first glimmer of kindness amid months of wintry indifference, Elizabeth began to cry and hugged Tehrani tight.

"Oh, it's over," she cried. "My life is over!"

"It is not," Tehrani said. "But now, really, you must go."

*　*　*

That is how New York Metropolitan Painters High School's best-ever graduate became nothing more than a street merchant peddling replicas outside the Guggenheim. She could barely afford the studio space she rented in Harlem. The space had no heat and in the winter months it was necessary to stir the paint often to keep it from freezing. It is also how she became reacquainted with the former servant Tehrani and how she became his clear and only choice for an accomplice in the Morfawitz heist.

Nico had never been north of Central Park—had never even really approached it—but he was well above it now. It had always seemed to him that the North Meadow sort of meandered into Canada. When he first read that Elizabeth's address was on 158th Street, he thought there had been some mistake. Certainly, the streets did not go up so high. Certainly, the landmass of the island could not extend so far north. Was it even truly an island? He'd seen the maps, sure, but the only river he'd ever walked along was the Hudson, the only one he'd ever crossed on foot was the East.

Nico was in such unfamiliar territory that he was forced to remove his blinding glasses. He asked the taxi to wait for him because he assumed they did not come so far north by chance, then read the address once more and buzzed the top-floor apartment. He was greeted almost immediately by a welcome buzz in response. The sound was jarring, violent, the sound made in movies before the prison door slides open. Nico jumped and then was too late to push open the door and had to buzz again. There was no elevator and he climbed four flights of groaning stairs covered in brown carpet and then one flight of bare wooden steps with a steepness more common in ladders. The treads were no more than four inches deep. He held on to the rough rails for dear life and by the time he reached the top had earned a splinter in each hand.

The door was wire-brushed steel and slightly open, but Nico knocked anyway. A series of bangs greeted him from the interior of the apartment, but nobody came to the door. He pushed it open with the back of his fist, as the idea of touching anything here with his open hand seemed grossly unhygienic.

"Hello?" he called, stepping cautiously inside, unsure whether it could be termed an apartment.

"Hello," called a voice from somewhere deep in the place's recesses. Nico tried to follow it. The entry was stacked high with cans of paint and rolls of canvas, which had to be stepped either around or over. It was like a fortification. Something that felt like a spiderweb brushed across Nico's face but wound up being a long chain leading up to an empty light bulb socket. There were no electric lights to speak of, but a series of skylights flooded the room beyond the entry in pale winter light. Nico's breath came out in wisps of white smoke.

The room was a large rectangle. The ceiling by the entry was perhaps fourteen feet high, but the severe slope of the roof brought it down to no more than two feet at the room's end, and so the final stretch of the room was only suitable for storage. Tens, if not hundreds, of paintings were stacked there, some framed and some not. Along the side walls were paintings standing upright, most turned toward the wall, but some of them facing the center of the room. There was *Café Terrace at Night*, two copies of *Guernica*, *Wanderer above the Sea of Fog*, *Saturn Devouring His Son*, and several Botticellis.

"But these are flawless," Nico marveled. He knelt beside a Dali whose name he could not remember, but whose subject seemed to be in vaguely the same kneeling pose that Nico was in now. He caressed the cold wooden frame and then stood up and looked around the room. He wanted to see the other paintings, too, to see all of them, even the ones facing the wall. He turned one of these around and then another, and then stood back and crossed his arms over his chest to inspect what he had uncovered.

The paintings all depicted a room very similar to the one he was in now: an attic with bare and rustic floors, exposed ceiling beams, pale winter light pouring in through overhead windows. The paintings had a temperature, conveying the coldness he now felt. The only subject to speak of was a woman, or rather, the reflection of a woman in a full-length mirror standing where the slant of the room allowed it to be wedged exactly perpendicular to the floor. Beyond the mirror, the low segment of the room was heavily shadowed, with stacks of paintings melting into darkness. Inside the mirror was the painter in the nude, an easel set to her side so as not to come between woman and reflection. At the very most, the easel obscured a little corner of her thigh.

Each painting was almost exactly the same, and the only changes were the quality of light and the shape of the woman. Sometimes she was tall and dark, sometimes squat and pale, sometimes obese, sometimes sickly. The only constant was that she never had a face, only a blank oval that matched skin color but had neither eyes nor mouth nor hair.

"Hello?" he called again.

Another voice returned his greeting once more from out of sight, and he noticed a door he hadn't seen before, the same unpainted wood as the walls so that it blended in completely.

"Where are you?" he said, looking back at the paintings. "Is anyone in here?"

His eyes settled on one with a tall, dark painter, beautiful despite her facelessness.

"In here," called the voice from the other room.

Nico turned away from the painting and walked toward the door. He pushed it open slightly and peeked inside. Here was the room from the paintings. In its center sat a great full-length mirror with dark spots where the reflective coating had been peeled away. Nico fingered the glasses that hung from his collar, his sole protector against the witness of what was unintentional. The mirror stood at an angle so that he could not possibly see his own reflection, and yet he touched his face with one hand, a gesture of defense, and with the other pushed the door fully open.

All that he could see of Elizabeth was her feet, but he could tell she was unclothed. The rest of her was hidden behind the easel, and he heard the whisper of a wet brush against canvas and then the clatter of wood as she set down her palette and brush. She stepped around the easel.

"Please," he said, "I'm sorry—I didn't know if it was alright for me to come in. Only, I came up the stairs and the door was wide open and . . ."

"Please," said Elizabeth. "Come in. It's alright to stare."

Nico looked her body up and down and felt as if there was a stone inside his throat. She was far from beautiful, and the paintings had been kind to her figure. How had she seen such different shapes, such different colors—was there a lie inside the glass? He looked between the mirror—which, at his angle, only showed the far wall of the room—and the woman, who was short and far too thin, with wide-set shoulders but no breasts or hips at all. She looked like a young boy save for the mess of black hair between her legs.

"I'm sorry," he said, trying to avert his eyes but unable to look fully away. He dug in his pocket for the scrap of paper with her address and held it out before him as if it were proof of his invitation. "Tehrani sent me to come see you. He said that the paintings are ready."

"Tehrani sent you?" she said. She said his name fondly as if it recalled a pleasant memory. Nico nodded and she smiled at him. "The paintings are ready."

"Do you want me to go and wait outside while you put some clothes on? I don't mind . . ."

"Outside?" she said. "Clothes?" Her laughter made Nico uncomfortable. "Do you mind?"

"Well," he said, "that's alright, then. Only, I should take the paintings and go. I don't mean to be rude, but I'm not alone, you know—a taxi is waiting downstairs. Your work is very beautiful, and I'd like nothing more than to stay and admire it, but really there is so much setup still to do if we're going to be ready. It's going to happen in a week. You do know what our plan is, I presume?"

Nico's voice trailed off. He had the impression she was no longer listening. She had moved toward him at a slow but steady pace while he spoke, and now she stood just before him, so close he could feel the heat of her body. She raised one paint-stained hand and touched his face with the clean part of her finger, closing her eyes as if to better commit the sensation to memory. Then a nymphlike grin spread across her face, and her body hunched at the shoulders as she looked up at him with glittering eyes.

"I don't mean to attack you," she said. "Only, you're very beautiful and I'm very weak. I'd like very much to paint you."

"To paint me?" Nico cried. "How terrible. I've never heard anything so terrible in my life. To celebrate such an accident as a face! It isn't just!" He looked around at Elizabeth's hoard of faceless self-portraits and lowered his voice. "Though, I assume you must be very much alone . . . But even if you do it faceless, like these, it couldn't be now. I told you that we haven't any time. Haven't a moment to rest. I must get back to Tehrani. He sends his regards. By the way, has he paid you? He said to make sure you check your mail."

"Just a loan," she said. "To hold me over. It's alright—I get by.

Tehrani will get me the rest in due time." She leaned her shoulder against the door and sighed. "Tehrani. How is Tehrani?"

"He's come to grief and sits alone before that house. That woman Hadassah's house. He said you'd know who she is. But to sit there at least seems to lessen his pain."

"I've had a lesson in that woman," said Elizabeth. She shook her head. "Hadassah. What's your grievance?"

"Me? Well, only that . . . you know. They've got . . . they've all that art in their house, locked up there like prisoners. It deserves to be seen by somebody who can appreciate it!"

"Somebody like you?"

"Honestly, yes. Somebody like me. Isn't that best? Tehrani is blind, after all, and while my mother may be one of his sad patients, may think of him as some sort of prophet, he's unlikely to enjoy anything visual, isn't that so?"

Elizabeth smiled, and in her smile was knowledge of Nico's wickedness, and acceptance of it, too.

"That's so," she said. "And I have patience, but best save it. Why not be honest: you're in it for profit. I certainly am."

Nico's lip curled at having his greed reflected so directly in his face. Now he thought of Elizabeth as being truly ugly.

"Alright, then," he said. "I'm in it for profit. Do you like that better?"

Elizabeth nodded. "I like that better."

She drew a robe around her body and then led Nico toward the dark side of the room, where the ceiling was low, and pointed to a group of cardboard cylinders.

"This is all of them?" said Nico.

"This is all of them."

Elizabeth popped the cap off one of the cylinders and showed Nico that there were multiple paintings in each. She began to say something now about the paintings, about how she'd changed each one ever so slightly to conform to Nico's fantasy and dream, but just then a mouse ran out from beneath a stack of paintings they had jostled and ran across Nico's foot. He felt his heart triple its furious beating so that his body and his muscles knew of his phobia before his brain was even aware it was a mouse. He fought the urge to vomit and then took two steps backward, nearly dropping the rolled paintings, hugged them tightly in his arms, and then ran from the place. Elizabeth ran after Nico to the door with outstretched arms, but then followed him no further.

Outside the building once more, Nico saw that his taxi hadn't waited. He had to walk two whole blocks before he found another and swore to himself that he would never go north of Central Park again.

* * *

Elizabeth called Nico once, on the night before the heist was to occur. She wanted to explain to him what she'd meant to explain that day, to give him one chance to right the wrong he'd done to her. Would Nico notice the small changes on his own? She somehow did not think so and figured that so rarely on this earth were people able to play out their elaborate fantasies of revenge, that it would be a tragic waste for one to do so without knowing how true to form it really was. From a pay phone on the street, she rang him at his mother's, and her heart leapt when she heard Nico answer the phone.

"Hello?" he said. "This is Nico."

"Hello, Nico," she said.

"Yes?" he said. "Who is this?" Her pulse quickened at his voice, at the subtle disdain in his tone. She wanted to answer but she was unable to say her name out of fear his vague contempt might latch on to his perception of her person, if he perceived her as a person at all. But she'd so long been invisible that something in the silence lent itself to identifying her, and Nico said, "Elizabeth?"

"Yes," she said and cleared her throat. "This is Elizabeth." She opened her mouth to say more, but before a word could leave her lips, she heard a click and the line went dead. She replaced the phone and stared at her distorted reflection in the chrome-plated surface on which the phone was hung. She poked her finger into the change slot to see if her quarter might be returned after so quick a call, but there was only the slight rattle of metal on metal, and then it was silent in the booth. Elizabeth opened the door and stepped out into the night, her heavy breath trailing along in sad white clouds and a tear on her cheek threatening to freeze in the late November air.

Now something boiled over in Elizabeth at Nico's crude dismissal. He saw her only as everybody else had seen her since Hadassah's rage had laid her low; which is to say, he didn't see her at all. He saw the work she produced—that was true—just as museumgoers leaving the Guggenheim saw the value of her replicas. But she was limited to a little rectangle of copied color, hardly four square feet in area. It is a privilege of the celebrated artist that their celebrators will look beyond the work and see the person who produced it. It was a privilege Elizabeth had once felt, and felt intensely, and overlooked as a mere way of the world. Now she felt the vacuum left behind like a vast emptiness inside her chest.

Elizabeth did not care that this was how Nico chose to see all the people of the world: in their intentional products rather than their accidental selves. Tehrani had spoken to her about the boy's blinding glasses, his aversion to reflections and reality, and yet she saw this as a pretentious choice and could not relate such an absurd and stylized behavioral gimmick with the flesh-and-blood human who had been standing in her studio. It was not an excuse for his blindness toward her. The replicas, for her, had been labors of love, of vengeance; she'd brooded over how and where to change the originals so that if the folly were exposed to Hadassah some years down the line, Hadassah might be forced to recognize her own imperfection; that at the very least she might look inwardly upon herself and think, *Woman, you're a fool.* But to Nico, there had been a transaction—nothing more. He might as well have purchased the pieces from her wire-frame stand on Museum Mile and seen her only in the canvas, not the flesh.

Elizabeth did not own heels, and her shoes made no sound on the sidewalk. If they had, though, someone else on the street would have heard her steps slowing as she approached the stoop of her walk-up until they came to a stop just before the first stair.

She stood there silently, looking at the door that led up to her work, and she thought of how the paintings Nico had carried away would enjoy a better life than their creator. They, at least, would hang in an opulent hallway; they would be admired by wealthy partygoers who neither cared about nor knew anything of art; they would be curiosities, perhaps treated with Hadassah's indifference, but wasn't that better than being served up the woman's wrath?

Elizabeth pictured her own portraits hanging in the Morfawitz gallery, and she suddenly felt grateful for the home comforts they might enjoy. Perhaps, she thought, the Morfawitz family was not the enemy. After all, hadn't Hadassah's anger been justified? Hadn't Elizabeth helped Zev to escape the bonds of fidelity? At least there was a certain honest nature to Zev's passion, to Hadassah's cruelty. They had no pretensions about who they were. They were opaque, definite, and real. They were the sort of subjects that artists love to paint or sculpt—perhaps in dark colors, perhaps in obsidian stone—because they were so concrete that even a likeness would be formidable, deserving of space. And what, compared to people such as them, was Nico? Transparency. A critic so afraid of the world that he preferred art, not because he loved it, but because it was reality that had already been chewed up and spat out by another. He was like a baby bird that needed his world predigested.

Now Elizabeth turned away from her stoop and looked back down the street toward the phone booth, which seemed to glow red hot in the cold autumn air. At first, she looked only with her eyes, and then she turned her head, and then she swiveled on her soles and walked silently back in the dark.

* * *

Anybody who reads a newspaper will not need much more of the story than that. The rest was covered extensively across all of New York's major media outlets, and most of the minor ones as well.

Elizabeth tipped Hadassah off to the heist in exchange for a sponsored gallery on Wooster Street, and Hadassah went about ruining the plotting pair in her calling-card torturous way. Knowing Tehrani's aversion to the ugly drop cloths she used to cover the paintings in their gallery, and having learned from Elizabeth of Nico's aversion to his own reflection, on the night of Naphtali's Hanukkah party, Hadassah had the paintings in her gallery swapped out for mirrors and then covered them with the canvas spreads.

An hour after both family limousines left the house on the first night of Hanukkah, bearing the Morfawitzes off to the Hamptons, Tehrani and Nico unlocked the servants' entrance to the mansion with Tehrani's old key. Tehrani stayed outside the door with the framed replicas while Nico took them one by one into the house.

Now that all the paintings were in the gallery, all that was left to do was replace each original with its appropriate replica, but the hanging originals were all covered in drop cloths and it was impossible to say which one was which. So Nico removed the first drop cloth, standing on his tiptoes to do so, stretching up with both hands to free the cloth from the top corners of the painting. His nose was right up against the thing behind the veil, so that when the drop cloth fell, he found himself face-to-face, not with eight Elvises, but with one single Nico.

His features stunned him. Here was an accident, yes, but also beautiful. What marble could compare to the soft sharpness of a cheek? What oil on canvas to the life etched in a wrinkle? What chiaroscuro to shadow cast by a troubled brow? Nico reached out to touch his face inside the glass, but his fingers could only reach themselves and then were repulsed by their own cold and unyielding reflections. He thought now of the artists he'd overlooked for their art, he thought of jungle paths that he'd overlooked for smooth pavement. He thought of Elizabeth Cho, and he could not put a face to the name.

He thought for too long. Finally, his reverie was broken by the sound of police sirens. Flashing red-and-blue lights poured in through the high gallery windows and colored his face in the mirror. Still, he could not look away.

"Nico!" called Tehrani. He stumbled into the room, one hand sliding along the banister and the other fumbling with his walking stick.

"I need to feel them once more! How I loved these paintings—how I loved them!"

"They're not . . ." said Nico. His voice was drowned out by the wailing sirens. Tehrani had reached him now and Nico took the old man's hand and laid it flat against the glass. "This is what you've done!" he said. "You old fool!"

Nico went around the room, ripping the drop cloth from each hanging square, revealing one mirror after the next, each a red-blue disco of light. With all the covering cloths now in linen pools on the ground, Nico stood at the center of the great gallery, surrounded by himself, and felt that he was drowning in his own red-blue reflections. Beside him, Tehrani lay on the floor and moaned. There were the footsteps of police on the stairs, and the would-be thieves were handcuffed and taken away.

IX
THE COMPLETION OF
TOWER MORFAWITZ

Later that night, and one hundred miles to the east, Hadassah set down the phone in Naphtali's home in Sagaponack and then went outside to join her family on the beach. They sat around the raging bonfire, its light dancing on their faces so that their eyes flashed red-yellow in the darkness. Together, she thought, they looked like a pack of lions.

"It's done?" said Zev as she took her seat beside him. Hadassah nodded and watched the embers smolder at the base of the flames.

"That boy won't make out well at Rikers," said Zev. He did not say it cruelly, only plainly. It was not a hope, not a threat, only a fact. Zev cared nothing for the young man's fate.

"He won't stay so delicate for long," said Hadassah.

On the far side of the fire, Deborah dug her bare feet in the sand.

"'My sweet rose,'" she recited, standing to better address her audience, "'my delicate flower, my lily of lilies, it is perhaps in prison that I am going to test the power of love . . .'"

A ripple of cold laughter went through the party. It was cautious, it was prodding. The fire cast light on Hadassah's face, and all the family watched it. She offered a slight smile, and it was as if the curling of her lips had broken the dark night free. Now their laughter turned louder until the group was howling, flushed with wine and fire, in the company of only themselves, of the moon, of distant suns.

The only ones who remained silent were Hadassah and Zev. They looked at one another in the eyes and saw the firelight dancing with little shadows cut out where some child or sibling was reflected. Their faces were stern and content.

Hadassah slipped her hand into her husband's.

"Come," she said. "It's time for us to be getting home."

Hadassah and Zev stood, and though their hands came apart, for a moment it was as if they were a single person. Together they turned their backs toward the fire and began walking up the beach toward the house. No word was spoken to the rest of the party, but they understood. One by one they finished their wine, filed off the beach, and were gone.

* * *

It might seem now that all was finally well in the Morfawitz household, or at least as far as Hadassah was concerned. The time to act was coming to an end and the time to record was beginning. After all, she'd dealt with threats from both within and without. Her husband's children by others had been handled or contained: Hersh was exiled, Asher broken, Marilyn and Abby had both committed to virgin lives without procreation. What momentous wealth and power the Morfawitz household had gathered was for hers and hers alone. There were two cars in Naphtali's driveway that would take them back to the city, and there was no discussion about who would be getting into each. In one of them went Marilyn, Asher, Abby, Penny, and Deb. In the other were Hadassah and the people who made up the inner planets of her universe.

I sat beside the driver in the front seat for the long drive home. The odd shape of my shoulders and hips made sitting in the back of any car unbearable; at least, that was the excuse that Hadassah pushed on me. "Firstborn, front seat," she said with a hand on my sagging shoulder, "and besides, you'll be more comfortable . . ." But it was less a hand of congratulations or even of sympathy than it was simply a hand pushing things into their place. The whole world seemed to roll out along the narrow axis of her eyes, reflected cold and silver in the slanted rearview mirror.

A simple glimpse of her cold eyes revealed that Hadassah understood that I simply wanted to avoid witnessing the sad scene playing out in the rear; Adam, who had drunk far too much wine, was now pretending to be passed out on the back seat of the limousine, and his head was resting—as if by accident—in my wife's open lap; Ahava idly twisted locks of Adam's hair as if nobody were watching, as if her fingers were acting of their own accord. The streetlights outside brightened and darkened her face as we went past, one and then the next, illuminating her great beauty and then rendering her invisible. This great beauty was a thing that Hadassah had purchased for her sons—for both of them—and she'd gotten a good deal on it at that. Hadassah watched the mounds of Adam's irises move beneath his closed eyelids, and knew that he was awake, that he felt his old lover's touch, and perhaps that it was better for him than any wine-soaked dream could be; I wouldn't know.

Yet, despite all, despite her, we had stayed put and we would go on staying. The earth might know that it is doomed to burn up in some future supernova that will swallow it whole, and yet it keeps on turning along its path around the sun; what else can it do? It was for this orbit precisely that the earth was made.

In a world without chains, what is left to coerce with but desire? Adam was free to walk away, but where would his violence land him outside the great shield of his mother? Ahava was free to leave, but her obedience had been paid for by lavish comforts, silk clothing, and winter coats of tawny mink. Me, I was unfettered then as I am now, yet the few grains of affection offered to me were scraps that I was unlikely to find elsewhere, and the fine needle of love that Mother sometimes poked through my ugly shell was attached to a thread whose purpose was to keep me tethered to the house.

"Hezekial," my mother leaned forward and said into my ear. Again there was her hand against my shoulder. "Now, I wanted you up front so that you'd be the first to see it."

"See what?"

"You'll see," she said. "I had them light it up."

Hadassah leaned back in her seat, into the shadows, and I found her eyes again in the silver strip of mirror, working hard around the edges all the time, all the time, never ceasing in her mission to reform the boundaries of the world. She knew the price that she had paid and what she'd gotten in return. Zev sat beside her, and she leaned her head against his shoulder; if he felt the weight of his wife, he did not move, he did not mind. His eyes were looking out the window, or maybe in the past; what could age do to a man such as that? What was the tick of a clock against such a force of nature as her husband? Parts of him were untamable—that was true—but even those parts were consistent; his untamable nature was knowable, dependable, and so he was dependable, too. In her eyes was the conviction that it was better to have reached the height where the air is thin and the breathing is difficult than to have reached the top of a hill only to see a great mountain behind it instead. Yes, she understood the price she had paid, and she had climbed the mountain anyway.

Now the highway came away from the earth, and as we continued along the overpass, Manhattan came into view, its north-south axis spread out in the windshield before us. In the upper bay, a great rolling storm cloud had stacked vertically and condensed above the water like a siege engine preparing to lay waste to the island. Its dark surface glowed white with the reflection of lights from the office towers that spread like barbicans to fortify the southern tip of New York.

I sat forward in my seat to see how high the storm clouds rose, and when I leaned back, I was surprised to find Hadassah there again with a whisper in my left ear.

"I remember the feeling of seeing that wall of buildings when we first sailed into New York Harbor," she said. "I remember seeing the Statue of Liberty for the first time."

"And what did you think of it?" I said. Despite the stiffness in my neck, I half-turned in my seat to face her. My mother had never spoken to me about her past, but I suddenly had the sense that she was going to begin.

"Of the statue?"

I nodded and she brought her head a little closer.

"I thought she looked bigger in pictures," she said. And suddenly there was a smell I'd never smelled on her before; it was age and death and human rot; it came from inside her mouth. *My mother is growing old*, I thought for the first time, while she said, "On this island there are bigger, more important things to see than a little copper lady. Now, pay attention to it, will you? The feeling, I mean."

"The feeling of what?"

It took me a moment to understand her, for she answered then in Yiddish, which I do not really speak and yet I knew the saying well: "*Fun zen aundz aofshteyn fun gornisht fun der nakht.*"

Of seeing us rise up from the nothing of the night . . .

Hadassah's eyes trained north, and mine followed them now in the windshield; they had trained away from Lady Liberty and the black storm cloud above her, trained over the low buildings of downtown, over the villages, squares, and parks, over midtown, until the glass-and-steel figure of Morfawitz Tower came fully into view, and then it was as if the monolith were all alone. The construction scaffolding had come down, and now it was only a dark silhouette that rose above the crowd of squat brick walk-ups, rose like a new colossus from the nothing of the night. The whole height of the thing was dark as if it were some great behemoth sleeping, save for a single light left on at the very top floor. It shone out like a torch or a beacon, reached across the river and through the winter air alive with the promise of storm.

As if the knowledge of the tower were lulling her to sleep, Hadassah leaned back now once more into the shadows. Perhaps she did not want to see that light of hers obscured by concrete or steel, by river or stone, by anything except her own will. So as the gaping mouth of the Queens Midtown Tunnel swallowed us whole and our dark limousine slipped through the yellow-lit artery and into the heart of the city, Hadassah rested her head against Zev's shoulder, closed her eyes, and fell asleep.

EPILOGUE:
A DIFFERENT VIEW OF
TOWER MORFAWITZ

THE GREAT BELOW

. . . At least, that is how Hadassah sees the family's apotheosis. And make no mistake, to her it is exactly that. It has taken me some time to accomplish the task she set out for me that night: to record the spectacular ascent of the family and our tower as we rose "from the nothing of the night." My quest of coalescing history into a solid, risen structure has taken me to curious places, to curious people—to others who also came into the shadow of Lady Liberty with nothing to their names but who were impressed enough by the statue's torch that they felt no need to erect some greater competition. To them I give the final view of Tower Morfawitz, for the impregnability of a fortress can offer no protection from the rot that begins at its core, just as an unsterilized wound—no matter how perfectly stitched—is liable to fester.

And so it was that some years later, once the family was comfortably situated in their high palace, the noted residence became the scene of the latest scandal to enthrall Manhattan.

"Gossiping little ants" is how Hadassah Morfawitz described the people far below. In her old age and new anger, she reverted to Yiddish wisdom: "What will become of the sheep if the wolf is the judge?" She failed to see how dangerous the trial could be if the mammals involved traded roles. With her shoulder leaned up against the floor-to-ceiling window of her bedroom, with her eyes on the world far below, she held the phone to her ear and spoke—through six thousand miles of copper wire—to a most unlikely confidant.

"So what?" she heard Hersh say. His time abroad had affected his speech and he spoke with some of the harshness of a native Israeli. Hadassah had the distinct impression that he was constantly faking an accent. "Ahava had an affair with the man she thought she crossed a sea to marry. Even you can't think so badly of that. What gives?"

"It was shown," said Hadassah through clenched teeth, "at some little girl's Bat Mitzvah."

"What was shown?"

"The video."

A long silence, and then: "There was a video?"

"Oh, yes, there was a video. Your brother Hezekial made sure of that. And he made sure to broadcast it where he knew it would do the most damage to this family. Your own brother! Think of it . . ."

"That poor girl," said Hersh. "Have you ever stopped to think how all this makes Ahava feel? She makes love to the man she's really in love with and because of your cruel tricks and Hezekial's jealous ones, she's made to feel ashamed."

"Hersh . . ."

"Now, now. Don't think it isn't lost on me that you called Hezekial my brother and not half brother. Whether you do it to distance him from you or to draw me closer, either way. It's understood. Now, as it turns out, I might have heard a little something about this video."

"My god," she said. "The news has spread to Haifa? How embarrassing for us. How embarrassing for Adam."

"Yeah, yeah—how embarrassing for Adam. *Emetser zol mikh azoy shemen* . . . And how'd you know I was in Haifa?"

"You're not the only one with eyes and ears, are you, Hersh?"

"Apparently not," he said. His accent had been quick to recover. "Is that all?"

"Not exactly. We've had some trouble . . . with the elevators. I'll explain it when you get here."

"When I get there? But you know Zev has my passport."

"That's right. How long will it take for you to get a new one and get yourself on a plane?"

"Well," said Hersh. "If you count the fifteen steps to my gate . . ."

He removed the pay phone from his ear, and Hadassah could hear the boarding announcements at Ben Gurion coming over the airport speakers. Raising her eyes from the streets below, swarming now with miniature traffic, she found her reflection in the glass and was surprised to find herself smiling.

"I'll be at Newark at eight a.m.," said Hersh. "You can tell me how much you missed me when you pick me up."

"From New Jersey?" It was Hadassah's turn to laugh. "Take a cab."

* * *

Trouble with the elevators, indeed.

Seen from far away, the top ten floors of Tower Morfawitz—sixty-seven to seventy-six—looked like a white limestone cube perched above the otherwise gray steel of the building. Each floor was home to a single, full-story apartment belonging to a different member of the clan. But there were other differences, too. For one, it had its own entrance on Central Park South and was known as Tower Morfawitz, while the other residents entered from Sixth Avenue and had an address of 1414 Sixth Avenue; for another, this upper echelon of the building was its own cooperative tax entity, distinct from the remainder of the tower; also, the family floors were serviced by their very own elevator, which went nowhere else.

The mechanic and operator for this private elevator was named Sol Alazec, who, after being hired for the job, promptly repaid the family by unionizing the building under the Local 88 for Hired Elevator Lift Interior Operators and Servicemen. As the only Morfawitz who did not seem to consider this as justification for murder, I was the sole passenger who greeted Sol as I rode, who tipped him at Christmas, who showed him any semblance of kindness; at least, those were the reasons he gave when he tipped me off to Ahava's frequent descents to Adam's red and lonely floor. He showed me the elevator footage to prove it and, ultimately, allowed me access to Adam's apartment so that I could wire the bedroom for capture . . .

But while Sol was able to report soberly on Ahava's misdeeds to her husband, there had been a certain camaraderie to their shared and scandalous elevator rides, something that inspired the mechanic to divulge to Ahava his own illicit passions.

"Let me get this straight," said Hersh to Hadassah. "Sol quit because he'd admitted to Ahava that he was in love with a girl from Below? I don't quite understand."

"Below" was the byword for floors one through sixty-six in the tower, floors that did not belong to the family. Hadassah was glad to see Hersh adopt the term so quickly. They were standing in the living room of Hersh's apartment, which had remained unoccupied during his exile; he had never stepped foot in it before, but now he rolled his luggage into the bedroom and began putting away his clothes as if he'd lived there all his life and had only returned from a short stint away.

"Well," said Hadassah loudly from just outside the bedroom, "for whatever else is the matter with her, that girl has a talent for getting secrets out of men."

"Some people," said Hersh, sticking his head out from behind the closet door, "just can't keep their mouths shut. But I still don't get what happened."

"What happened," said Hadassah, "is that your sister-in-law took her own little revenge on Sol for his help in getting her caught. She told the Below elevator operator about Sol's little visits. Probably bribed him with something, god knows what, but the point is that they caught him. Red-handed. It seemed it wasn't so much of an affair as it was an obsession, and they found him . . . sniffing around her apartment. You understand."

"My god," said Hersh, beside himself.

"In her . . ."

"Holy of holies," said Hersh. "Drawer of drawers."

"That's right," said Hadassah. "Well, the girl's father went berserk. Naturally, we had to fire him."

"Naturally."

"Well, you'd think so, but under the union contract, you're not allowed to fire somebody for what they do off premises."

"Ah," said Hersh. "Separate tax lots."

"Separate tax lots, indeed."

"And the strike . . . hence the climb."

"Hence," said Hadassah, "the climb."

For with the private Morfawitz elevator, sans operator, the only option for reaching Above was to take the elevator for Below to its very acme: the sixty-sixth floor. And from there the family had to access their apartments by the emergency stairs.

"Lucky for me," said Hersh, "that you only put me on the second floor. Save my legs the hike."

"It's the sixty-eighth floor," said Hadassah, but her voice was soft and unconvincing. Really, to them, the second floor is what it was.

Hersh sat down on his bed and bounced twice to test the mattress. "So that's what I'm doing here. Break the union strike, save Hadassah from a ten-story climb up to her seventy-sixth-floor throne."

"That's right," she said. "To save Hadassah her climb. To save Zev the climb, too."

"Zev," said Hersh. "I almost forgot about him."

"No," said Hadassah. "You didn't."

"And did he . . ."

"Forget about you? It's hard to say. He forgets some things these days. He doesn't know you're here, if that's what you're asking. Better to announce yourself with some good news, don't you think?"

"A union for a reunion?"

Hadassah couldn't help but smile. "Think of it any way you like," she said. "Only get it done."

* * *

Hersh did get it done, and quickly, too. His old connections had not gone dead and it was quickly decided that on the twenty-second of December the strike would end and the elevator to Above would be running once again, without Sol. In the meantime, however, the family was forced to continue their partial ascents up to the sixty-sixth floor, and sometimes even in the company of others.

And so it was that one week before the strike was to end, Ingmar Sellers, who had just moved into the building, called to an already crowded elevator to hold the door. Inside it was Hadassah.

"Don't you dare," said Hadassah to the serviceman, and she pressed the Close Door button with the tip of her folded umbrella. But it was too late, and Ingmar threw her arm to stop the bronze door's progress, then got in and squeezed between Hadassah and one other passenger.

"Sixty-six, Jack," she said to the operator, who was undoubtedly aware that Mrs. Sellers lived on sixty-six; but Ingmar liked giving out her floor. Out of the corner of her mouth as if sharing a secret, she said to Hadassah, "It's the highest floor that one can get to without being a Morfawitz."

Hadassah thought that they really ought to get faster elevators; this one seemed to be taking forever. She had, since the scandal with Sol, shared many elevator rides with Ingmar Sellers. The woman was constantly coming or going, and she always had something to say. She had an affinity for drama somewhat typical of the rich New York socialite, and her favorite topics were the men in her life: her husband's charitable donations and her having to care for her brilliant but ludicrous father.

"I'm not saying he's a burden," she was saying now to the other passenger, or to the operator, or to the gleaming walls themselves. "And he's made god's own amount of money on this dot-com business. Goes on and on about unbridled access to an interweb of things, to the dark side of humanity. Naturally, investors love it. But, my god, it was easier when my sister was around. She died, you know—grisly business, foul play suspected—but I can't say she wasn't asking for it, the way she lived. Anyway, very, very like her to just up and leave me to care for the old man. Very like her. But I don't mean to say he's a burden."

The elevator slowed and then stopped on the forty-fifth floor, and the third passenger got out, leaving Hadassah alone with Ingmar and the operator.

Ingmar looked at the tree of floors, with the circle for sixty-six alone lit up.

"Oh," she said without looking at Hadassah, "are you visiting with the Skylars then? We looked at their half of the floor, too, you know. The western-facing half. But sunrises over the bay . . . well, you just can't beat that, can you? It's a magnificent view, you know. The highest floor that one can get to without being a Morfawitz."

She said it out of the corner of her mouth, the way she had said it before. With his nose inching closer to the buttons for the floors, the elevator operator looked as if he wanted to sink through the wall. Instead, he coughed, and finally Ingmar turned to face Hadassah.

"Oh, my," she said. "But you're—"

"Yes," said Hadassah, "I'm."

"But . . . but isn't there a private elevator? I could swear they said there was a private entrance and a private elevator, didn't they?"

"Oh, yes," said Hadassah. "I just wanted to see the bay view from sixty-six." She checked her watch. "Pity about the time—sun's already up."

"But surely you've got . . . oh, but I see. It's a joke."

"That's right," said Hadassah. "Like to laugh at."

The elevator opened onto sixty-six with a ding to punctuate the silence. Ingmar Sellers turned left to her door, while Hadassah went straight ahead into the emergency stairwell.

"Oh, Mrs. Morfawitz?" said Ingmar, just as Hadassah turned the steel handle. "We're having a Christmas party tomorrow. Well, we'd love it if you and Mr. Morfawitz could join. Everybody who's anybody is coming. Even everybody who isn't anybody is coming. And don't think it's religious, my own father is Jewish, he's coming, too . . ."

* * *

During the entirety of the strike, Zev had not left the penthouse apartment. Climbing stairs had become physically difficult for him, and physical difficulty made him feel old. Zev did not like to feel old.

Perhaps, then, to prove to himself that he was not aging and that it had been his desire—and not a fear of exertion—that had kept him confined to the penthouse during the entirety of the union strike, on the day before it was to end, he insisted on going out for a walk around the block.

"Can't you wait one day?" said Hadassah. "You don't know what it's like, sharing an elevator with those . . . people. And this, of all days—that bitch on sixty-six is having her party."

But even as she said it, she slipped into the sleeves of her fur-lined coat; arguments with Zev—particularly arguments that somehow suggested a limitation on his movements—had long ago become inane. Had he known nothing of the strike, he might have been content to sit there on his throne, lording over the ants far below, gazing down at the tops of lesser men's homes, and considering only clouds as his equals. Age, age, cancerous age, had turned Zev's demons inward; such terrific heights had been attained! Such magnificent milestones surpassed and supplanted! Only, now the air in which Zev sat was so rare, so thin, that there was nobody, nothing, upon which to turn his wrath. And just as a wick is mostly safe until the wax that feeds it is exhausted, so had Zev depleted his plane of extant rivals, and now sat alone in his penthouse; only, not alone, for Hadassah was there, too.

And so, of late, his fury had been saved for small pieces of himself. He was coming apart, and in more ways than one; his knees hurt, his neck was stiff, his memory was not what it had been in his youth. Even this, the desire to go walk outside, was a reaction to its exact opposite, to a sort of insidious contentment that whispered on the morning light—fuzzy now when filtered through the early stage of cataracts—that what he would have really liked was to sit still and do nothing at all.

But each of these discomforts was like an invasion of his body, of his mind. It was not that his knees were weak, only that pain had come to haunt them; it was not that his memory was slipping, only that forgetfulness was swarming his mind. Hadassah had brought back Hersh not, as she told him, to bust a union strike that she could have handled on her own, but because she hoped that her husband's bastard son's debonair swagger, his unruly antics, even, perhaps, the memory he stirred of the things Zev once could do, would blow a sort of second wind into her husband's worn-out sails.

So now there would be a walk around the block. *Well,* she thought, *a walk is something.* She had erected a small wall of resistance just to give Zev the carrot of a hurdle to defeat so that his steam would not run out before he'd even laced his shoes. And now, they were walking! In the cool air of a gray December morning! Through the Christmas lights that wrapped the leafless trees! Into the park, past the carriages and their stench suppressed by cold, past the pond and the children feeding ducks that had not yet flown off south, past a bench where an elderly couple sat with their steaming black coffee, tearing apart a soft croissant with trembling, liver-spotted hands . . .

Zev turned away from the bridled horses, for they reminded him of the shackles of his age, and the steaming puddles of urine on the pavement made him think of his incontinence; he turned away from the children, for they reminded him of youth, of how distant it now seemed; he turned away from the old couple, who had managed to find happiness despite their trembling hands, despite the shabbiness of their wool coats, despite, perhaps, their utter powerlessness to shape the world, ultimately despite their gross contentment with a bench.

Zev and Hadassah finally arrived to where she knew they would go all along: the Umpire Rock, rising from the gray plane of frost-covered grass without so much distinction. Only here was Zev satisfied. He turned back toward the south, toward the towers of Manhattan, which rose from the dense line of gray grass and dark trees like a row of knives plunged down into the broad warm back of Eden. Their tower was there before them—its presence gargantuan, its height insane—so that if the sun had been behind the tower, its shadow might have engulfed them. Only now it cast no shadow, and neither did they.

"I'm cold," she said. The lie was white fog on the air, there and then gone. "Let's go."

They went. They walked back slowly; black ice made the pavement shine, and she badly feared a slip. The mild comfort now of making it out of the uneven terrain of the park! Of making it across the street! Of making it into the shared entrance of their building, where the elevator operator held the door so that they could walk slowly across the unfamiliar common lobby, her heels against the granite floor like a raven pecking wood, the elevator doors closing upon them like an eyelid winking shut . . .

"I know you," someone said.

Hadassah had not even bothered to see who was sharing the elevator, but now she saw. Here was an old man (*old like my husband!*—the thought exploded in her mind) and on the near side of him was a woman, and on the far side a man, both middle-aged but seeming to her incalculably youthful. Perhaps, she thought, they were his children. Half-hidden by the older man's profile, the middle-aged one even looked familiar, and yet, it had not been him who spoke . . .

"I know you," said the old man again and he was looking straight at Zev.

"I'm sorry," said the woman, perhaps his daughter. "His vision isn't quite what it used to be . . ."

Hadassah said nothing and looked resolutely ahead.

"I know you," said the old man again. He was wagging his finger at Zev's vague reflection in the semi-gleam of the bronze elevator door. This time it was the younger man, perhaps his son, who now leaned forward to apologize.

But before Caleb Cohn could speak, he saw Hadassah, and Hadassah saw Caleb Cohn. She recalled his face looking up at their old mansion, and it was like being dragged backward in time. Caleb looked beyond Hadassah to Zev, whom he had crossed the sea to chase but had never actually stood so close to before.

"Oh," they said together.

Silence reigned in the rising elevator car as if the tension in the steel cables that lifted them through the vacant shaft of the tower had wound tight time itself; their ascent to the sixty-sixth floor dragged endlessly on. Hadassah counted seconds on the slow pulse in Zev's hand, held firmly in her own . . . and now she began to smile, for somewhere in the depths of her husband's mind or heart, something quickened, something stirred. Time beating in his blood began at once to pick up pace.

"I've never seen you before in my life," Zev said to Barnabas Cohn, just as the light above the elevator door flicked on at "66" and a sound like a toaster going off announced the car's arrival. The bronze double doors slid open, dispensing with the passengers' shadowy reflections on its surface and replacing them with Ingmar Sellers, née Cohn.

"You made it," said Ingmar, looking first at her father. Her gaze darkened as she looked at Caleb and Harmonia, but quickly brightened again as it fell upon Hadassah and Zev. "And *you* made it! I'm so glad you decided to come."

She waved them in from the elevator and wedged her way into the group so that Caleb and Harmonia were left staring at her back while Hadassah, Zev, and Barnabas were ushered toward the door.

"So, you've met old Dad already, have you?" said Ingmar. "Come in, come in."

"Actually," said Hadassah, staring thinly at Barnabas Cohn, still elated at the rise of pulse in her husband's wrist, "I've left our little gift upstairs."

"A gift? But so unnecessary, Mrs. Morfawitz . . ."

"Nonsense, dear. Just a bit of spare silver. We haven't any use for it and have been meaning to give it away. Just needs a quick tune-up. Why don't you get my husband a drink and I'll be back in just a minute . . ."

The corner of Zev's lip curled up in a cruel little smirk, darkening a deep fissure of wrinkles around his mouth; they could not exactly be called smile lines on Zev. He nodded curtly to his wife and then followed Ingmar inside; Ingmar closed the door behind them just as Hadassah disappeared into the stairwell, and suddenly Caleb and Harmonia were left alone on the little square landing.

To one side of them were the exit stairs that led to Tower Morfawitz, with the door left slightly ajar by Hadassah, and they could hear the quiet metronome of her footsteps as they climbed on up the tower; to another was the brass elevator door, closed now and quiet, too matte to reflect anything but the darkest, vaguest forms; to a third side were the two residential doors, one of which— Ingmar's—was propped slightly open by a bolt, with a din coming from inside like a soft and cheerful menace; and finally, the fourth wall was a floor-to-ceiling window.

"Well," said Caleb. "Should we go in?"

"Yes," said Harmonia. She took one step toward the door but then stopped, took one step back toward the glass window. "Or," she said. "Or perhaps no."

"No?" asked Caleb, turning toward his wife.

"No."

Harmonia put her hand to the smooth surface of the glass; it was too well insulated to be cold, although outside were flurries of snow. She tapped her fingers against the pane, one after the other, as she looked up at the ten floors of Tower Morfawitz—monstrous and daunting, its white limestone walls almost one with the gray winter sky. And then she put her hands to her side and looked down, far below her.

"Did I ever tell you," she said finally to her husband, "you're the first Jew that I ever met? It's true. And there was only one real story that I had about Jews while growing up. On a class field trip to Barcelona, we learned about the famous Disputation. Two Jewish scholars—I can't remember their names—only one of them had converted to Catholicism and so the king had them debate which was the true religion and whether the Messiah had really come. And even though the king was Catholic, and even though everybody allowed to carry a sword or even ride a horse in Barcelona was Catholic—for Jews were only allowed to ride sidesaddle on mules—the king agreed that the Jewish side had won!"

"Nachmanides was his name," said Caleb. "The victor."

"Ah, so you do know this story."

"I know this story."

"Then you know how it ends?"

"The king awarded Nachmanides three hundred pieces of gold and even visited the synagogue in Barcelona."

"No," said Harmonia. "No. That is what happened next. But that is not what I asked. I asked if you know how it ends? No? I'll tell you so that you understand. Your victor understood. He fled to Palestine and never returned. Because how it ends is one hundred years later with the

Inquisition. With Jews burned at the stake or—best case—robbed of their possessions and expelled from all Castile."

"I hardly think it would've made a difference if Nachmanides had not won."

"That's probably true," she said. She pulled him close to the window. "But let me ask you then: why bother winning?"

Caleb leaned his forehead against the glass, looked up at the limestone facade.

"I know what you are thinking," she said. "You are thinking that he is old, perhaps, and harmless. But that is exactly when they are most dangerous. Your scholar would have been alright, for he was facing a strong and confident king, one who knew it was a matter of a hand wave to dispense with the old beard, and so he never had to do it. It is the injured animal that fights most viciously, for what other option is there left to him?"

She put her head beside her husband's so that they looked up at Tower Morfawitz together, and then she looked straight down at the street far below them.

"The people down there are not so much smaller from ten more flights up," she said. "It is the people here, at this height, that one means to make small by continuing to climb. But there are two ways of winning. You can continue to climb, hope that the pace at which you take the stairs is faster than the one at which your enemy does; and then . . . there is the other way."

"What way is that?" said Caleb.

Harmonia lifted her hand to his cheek and then directed his gaze away from the sky and off toward the distant horizon.

"You can go off to where nobody here can see you, from this height or even higher. One can escape the up-and-down and move in a different direction entirely."

Caleb looked away from the window and directly at his wife. In her eyes was reflected the view straight down the avenue; the unbroken rows of buildings on either side of the low-lying street were like twin walls of water, a split sea, an ephemeral road. Moving only her eyes, she looked now at him, and the vision was replaced by the deep brown of her iris. It reminded him of the wood inside their barn, the chestnut hides of their horses, the umber of their floors.

"These people are like caricatures," she said, "like flat cartoons. They think it is a curse to be in our fields, in our old country home, with our snakes in the garden and our bats in the barn. Your victorious scholar went away from the place where he could only ride mules and sought out one where he could ride horses." She kissed her husband and then whispered, "I know a place like that."

Caleb looked down; the height here was severe; it gave him vertigo; how much worse might it be from several stories up! He suddenly wanted to be as close to the earth as possible. His legs, even, seemed vertiginous; he wanted to crawl on his belly, to slither if possible. He breathed in, he breathed out; he crossed the landing in two strides and pressed the button to go down, and above the great bronze doors the light began slowly now to rise.

3 . . . 4 . . .

From inside the emergency stairwell, through the door left slightly ajar, Hadassah's footsteps had now entirely disappeared, and it was difficult to say whether they had ever truly been there.

9 . . . 10 . . . 11 . . .

"Should we just . . ." began Caleb, for the rise of the elevator seemed now unbearably slow.

17 . . . 18 . . .

And suddenly it was as though the reins on space had been released, like a blade had sliced clean through a rigid Gordian knot, and Caleb took his wife by the hand and flung open wide the door. Down, down they went, taking the stairs by twos, by threes; it was an easier direction in which to travel fast; they paid no mind to the stiffness in their joints, but let gravity do its work, and the echoes of their feet against the concrete seemed to rise like smoke or frightened birds.

They were breathing hard as they broke through the final door into the lobby, but it was an ecstatic sort of breath as if relishing in the relative thickness of the air so close to earth. They waved to the doorman, who stood still and stoic as the Queen's Guard, daring not to smile. Out they went into the cold December day, the air white like sunlight that has yet to be refracted.

They did not stop running until they found their little car, wedged tightly between two bigger ones with just enough room to get out. Get out they did, and they drove north. North, north, to the headwaters of the Hudson, to a place they could ride horses, where one could slither close to earth and enjoy the humble cover offered even by short grass.

With the rumble of their shoddy engine, the whole country seemed to hum. They watched in the rearview mirror as the tops of the towers behind them shrank down until they were no bigger than teeth. Last to go was the great white cube of Tower Morfawitz; it dipped out of sight behind a cloud and then reappeared to make one spectacular final bow, flashing in the rearview mirror like the white sparkle when a cartoon hero smiles.

ACKNOWLEDGMENTS

This book is dedicated to my late grandfather, Harry Spiera, to whom I am indebted for nearly all the jokes in these pages. Thanks also are due to the entire clans of Forman, Spiera, and Turtel for a wealth of historical material provided.

Thank you to my agent, Michelle Tessler, whom I am very fortunate to have championing my work in the world. All my gratitude to the wonderful team at Blackstone, including Samantha Benson, Megan Bixler, Daniel Ehrenraft, Katrina Tan, Lysa Williams, and Josie Woodbridge. Alex Cruz, who created the cover art for this book, has my eternal awe and thanks. And I am especially grateful to this book's editors, Michael Signorelli and Caitlin Vander Meulen, who were supportive of my occasional disagreements with English grammar and word definitions, and who made this book what it is today.